For __,

God bless you both!

POSEIDON'S
GAMBIT

Keith Braun

Love,
Keith

 **FriesenPress**

Suite 300 – 852 Fort Street
Victoria, BC, Canada V8W 1H8
www.friesenpress.com

Copyright © 2014 by Keith Braun
First Edition — 2014

All rights reserved.

No part of this publication may be reproduced in any form, or by any means, electronic or mechanical, including photocopying, recording, or any information browsing, storage, or retrieval system, without permission in writing from the publisher.

ISBN
978-1-4602-5185-0 (Hardcover)
978-1-4602-5186-7 (Paperback)
978-1-4602-5187-4 (eBook)

1. Fiction, Historical

Distributed to the trade by The Ingram Book Company

ACKNOWLEDGEMENTS

It is often said that no good deed goes unpunished, and I must admit here that it probably has more than a grain of truth for those who have so generously supported my writing.

Among those who so graciously and cordially devoted great amounts of effort and devotion to seeing this humble piece come to fruition I must acquaint you with several. First among them must be Marsha McMullin, who again surpassed all expectations in not only designing the cover for the book, as she did for Napoleon's Gold, but worked tirelessly in spite of the hurdles I created for her, to simultaneously set up my author's web site.

My editor, Sylvia Baker, who gave freely of her time to work her miracles in untangling the ragged prose, egregious spelling, and questionable syntax I bestowed her with. That she is still my friend speaks volumes about her patience and forbearance. Thank you Sylvia for all your hard work and encouragement.

There were many friends who encouraged me after Napoleon's Gold was published, asking if I would write a sequel. Thank you all for your kindness; it was much appreciated. There are a couple of individuals I must acknowledge for their particular support. The first must be my business partner and son, Adam, who never imagined his father might suppose himself a writer, yet read the manuscript, and encouraged its publication. My long-time friend John Schroeder, who not only waded through Napoleon's Gold, offering valuable encouragement, but who, together with his dear wife Leona, gave up valuable hours of vacation time to patiently listen to me read excerpts of both books. I owe you both, but that is what friends are! Dave Lehman, my son-in-law, has acted as a reader and editor for me from the very start of my writing, and has been another constant encouragement along this winding path.

Lastly, of course, Carol. My best friend, and mother of my children, she is, as always, the final and consummate mediator between me and my work, prodding me to do my best, and encouraging me when it eludes my grasp, enduring my demands for solitude, and yet cheerfully being there whenever I crawled from my lair.

Thank you all, and God bless you!

Poseidon's Gambit is a work of fiction, and while there are actual historical characters present in the novel, neither their actions nor their dialogue should be in any way construed as to reflect those of the historical characters.

CHAPTER ONE
London, July 1802

"It just is not fair! Natalie put me through hell for weeks and you refused to rescue me, even for a minute! Now you tell me Katherine is pleased with most anything you suggest, even to being married in the chapel at the manor. There is no huge guest list, no demands for outrageous costumes and exotic foodstuffs; you have undergone virtually no stress at all! The woman should be put up for veneration at the very least, if not outright sainthood. That Katherine is a fine woman I understand. But whatever have you done to get off scot-free! You deserve to suffer, at least some!" James Peters was laughing good-naturedly, but there was a hint of self-pity to his banter.

"I warned you about my sister but you were so besotted that you would not hear a word I said!" Phillip responded with a broad smile. "Now you are stuck with her, and I am delighted! It could not happen to a better fellow! I, on the other hand, have made a perfect match, and Katherine will prove to be the perfect and devoted wife." Behind all the bluster and mock confidence lay Phillip's deep insecurity about all things feminine. For years it had kept him well clear of his mother's most carefully laid plans to introduce him to suitable female companions. Now, with Katherine Chapley's sudden intrusion into his life, he devoutly hoped things would work out half as well as he postured.

"Just remember, Phillip, if you do cross the lovely Katherine, that she has killed one man already that she thought threatened her happiness! The fact that the gentleman in question was about to end your sorry life should not be considered a definite safeguard to your security. It might well be you next, if you vex her too badly." At this James laughed and pretended to point an imaginary rifle at Phillip's head.

At this fortuitous moment, Andy Barg poked his head in the study door. "Excuse me sir, but Mr. Wilkes says there is a messenger from the Admiralty. The courier insists for some misbegotten reason that he must hand the message to you personally. Also sir, it seems a message from Mr. Cobb has just arrived as well."

"Thank you Andy, one thing at a time. I will be right out to see the Admiralty fellow; we will deal with Cobb's troubles right after. How is our packing going, by the way?"

"Just fine, sir! Carter is doing most of it. If you like, I will go round before lunch and fetch the wine you ordered. I am off to pick up some shirts at any rate, and I believe my new boots might be done, sir." Andy smiled mischievously.

"Yes Andy, that would be fine, and while you are about you might stop at my tailors as well, and pick up the shirts I ordered. They are just over on Cork Street." Phillip talked as he walked from the study toward the front door, where an admiralty messenger was waiting with a packet. "Good morning, I am Phillip Hollis; I believe you have a letter for me?"

"Yes, Sir! There you are, My Lord, thank you. I apologize for the inconvenience, but I was instructed to place it in your hands, sir. I meant no disrespect, my Lord."

"None taken, I assure you. Give my regards to Mr. Nepean."

Phillip returned to the study, where James lounged, coffee in hand. "Ah, and what do our former masters have to say this lovely day?" Both James and Phillip were officers in the Royal Navy, James a mere lieutenant, and Phillip a post captain. Both had been allowed to temporarily resign their commissions to embark on a covert raid against the French, which had ended in a windfall of wealth to all concerned, at the expense of Napoleon Bonaparte. Now they were supposedly private citizens, at least for the time being, while England and France were ostensibly at peace.

"I have not yet opened the packet, as you may see, but I can only hope it contains orders to have you sent back to sea at once so that I may achieve a small measure of peace as I prepare for my up-coming wedding. Since you have had nearly a month of wedded bliss, I have a feeling that you should be sent away for a time to recover your strength!" Phillip laughed again at his now discomforted, and sometime slightly prudish brother-in-law. Seating himself at the desk he took a knife and slit open the packet to remove a thin folded paper. As he scanned the document, he could not restrain his annoyance. "He simply will not accept my refusal to even contemplate this foolishness. It is from my dear friend and mentor. He once more is importuning me to consider this voyage to the Far East. I have told him that my only interest at present is in finalizing my marriage and having some respite to enjoy it. He is now suggesting a departure in September. That will give me perhaps ten weeks after the wedding! I can only imagine what Katherine will have to say. I might have to lock up the Ferguson rifle after all!"

James watched Phillip's face and smiled inwardly. For all his bluster there was little doubt in James' mind that Phillip would, in the end, do exactly as Sir John wished. He only wished he would have the chance to be included, but the arrangements for Hollis & Company Shipping did not include him. He supposed that Phillip had just assumed he would be happy to settle down with Phillip's sister Natalie after the wedding, but that was not going to be enough to satisfy James. Increasingly, he also wondered if it was going to satisfy Natalie. Her idea of marriage seemed to be primarily focused on shopping for new clothes and going out to tea.

"Are you considering this voyage, then?" James asked, staring out over his coffee cup, "Who will you take with you if you go? If this is to be another private matter, will you take Onyx alone, or will you include one of the brigs? I am sure that either George or Patrick would be delighted to make a run past India. It could be very good for trade, you know. You might even contemplate taking Ross with Celeste." In their last adventure, Phillip had captured four French vessels; one of them a forty gun frigate, plus a large merchantman, and two sloops. Both of the sloops were being re-configured as hermaphrodite brigantines with extra cabin space to carry passengers, as well as cargo. Three former navy lieutenants, George Fielding, Patrick Morrissey, and Ross Day, all of whom had accompanied them on their mission, had bought shares in Hollis & Company Shipping, to go into a commercial partnership with Phillip.

"The Emerald is finished her modifications already and Ruby should be done in a matter of weeks. I believe that George and Patrick have already planned a voyage for Emerald and Celeste to the Cape, but do not wish to leave before the wedding. We might be able to postpone that trip so that we could travel the Atlantic portion together, but I am as yet far from committed to this venture. I must discuss it with Katherine and perhaps even with Sir Walter. He has some considerable experience in eastern trade and has travelled as far as Prince of Wales Island himself. Katherine will insist on accompanying me, but I am loath to take her on such a long and potentially perilous voyage, although I am equally reluctant to leave her behind."

"So what will you tell Sir John? He will be looking for an answer, and he is not overly fond of no! Of course, with your title and wealth, he really cannot touch you. I wonder about the rest of us, though, if it comes down to it."

"He accepted your resignations with no reservations to allow us to complete our mission for him. I do not believe he would go back on them now, especially as the peace is likely to hold for some time yet. No, I do not think you will need to fear for any conscription, especially you, once you are ensconced safely in your home on the estate. As to what I will tell Sir John, well, I have until dinner tonight to contemplate that; we are to dine at the club at six." Phillip looked up smiling, "When do you and your darling bride leave for Devon?"

"Natalie believes we may be ready in two days' time! How can it take four days to pack for a brief trip to the country? If we were moving there permanently, as I would like, I could understand it!" James grimaced. "After all, Phillip, that is where our house is; the house you gave us! Who does not live in their own home? Why should we continue to occupy rooms in your house here in London, which is supposed to be your mother and Aunt Anne's residence?" James Peters was a simple country boy at heart, and although Natalie had grown up on the estate down in Devon, she had become greatly enamoured with the fashion and social life of London.

"Perhaps, when you get her to her own home and get settled in, she may accept it. Right now, Natalie is still coming to terms with marriage, and the change in her social status! She has come to love living in London, but she grew up in Devon and I believe that once we are all down there and settled, she will again be happy to call it home, at least for part of the year. Your problem, James, is that with your share of the treasure you are now well off, and can no longer claim that you cannot afford to live in either place! Who knew that wealth was such a burden?" Phillip again laughed at his friend; comfortably enjoying James' raised eyebrows.

"When will Katherine and her family arrive in Devon?" James asked, changing the subject deftly away from his own domestic affairs.

"I believe they intend to arrive Wednesday or Thursday afternoon. With the wedding on Sunday, that should give everyone time to settle in nicely. Which reminds me, Andy said there was a message from Sam Cobb! I completely forgot in all this bother about the Admiralty and my delightful sister!" Phillip jumped to his feet and strode out of the study to the front hall. Picking up the letter from Mr. Cobb, the manager of the Hollis estate in Devon, he walked into the front drawing room to greet his mother, who was seated at the front window engaged in needlework. Caroline Hollis was a petite woman in her late forties, still full of vigour and enthusiasm. Born Caroline des Plans in Normandy, she had been carried off across the channel by Philip's father after a whirlwind romance many years before. "Good morning, mother. I hope the day finds you well!"

"Good morning Phillip. Yes, I am quite well. Your Aunt Anne has gone to the dress makers again, but I decided to rest this morning. There is only so much bustling about in the city that I can muster at one time, and I find that I am still quite worn from your dear sister's wedding! I thought a nice quiet morning with my embroidery was just the thing. Are you packing for the trip to Teignmouth?"

"Yes, that is, Andy Barg and Carter are packing for me. Why Andy insists I cannot fathom. He has no need to work at all. With the money from our good fortune in the spring, he will never need to work again, but he insists he is happier just staying with me, and feels I am not qualified to look after myself. I believe we will leave tomorrow. Being Sunday, the road will be busier around London, but it will get us down to Devon by Tuesday at the latest, and Katherine and her family will arrive by Thursday. When are you and Aunt Anne coming down?"

"I expect we will travel with James and Natalie. So far, the plan seems to be that we will depart on Tuesday morning, but I suspect that between Natalie and your Aunt Anne's dressmaker something will yet be changed before we get away!" Caroline Hollis smiled at her son. "Never fear though, James and I will get them to the estate in time for the blessed event!" Caroline laughed.

"Yes, I am sure that you will. James certainly seems happy in his new estate; I hope his wife is equally pleased! I must admit, I have not seen very much of either of them since their wedding, but then again I have not been here over much."

"No, you have not! Between trips to Colchester to visit Katherine, and back down to Devon to check up on Samuel Cobb and William, we have hardly seen you these past several weeks. You are off to Devon again tomorrow and by next week you will be a married man! Phillip, I must admit things have been moving too rapidly for my comfort! Oh, do not be concerned; I think Katherine is a perfectly lovely girl and will make you a wonderful wife. I just sincerely hope that somehow things will all settle down, but I have a feeling that I will be denied even a brief respite! Knowing you, I am sure you will not become less restless any time soon. Are you planning to go back into the Navy?"

"No, mother, at least not for the present. Why do you ask?"

"I saw the admiralty messenger at the door. I suspect it was a message from Lord St. Vincent, was it not?"

"Well, yes it was, but it was no command to resume my career, it was an invitation to dinner!" Phillip responded with as good a smile as he could muster to sooth his mother's anxiety.

"Phillip, I remember what the last dinner with Sir John resulted in! Do not begin to believe that you can smile vaguely at me and relieve my worries! I can feel that something is afoot, and I will not be treated like some… some foolish woman!" Caroline frowned and rose from her chair to cross over to her son. "I know it is not my affair, and you are a grown man, my boy. I also know that your soon-to-be wife will take great care of you, but I am, and will always be, your mother, and you had just better accept it!" Then she took his arm and walked to the settee, where they sat together.

"Mother, at this point there is no firm plan for anything. There may be a chance for another voyage in the fall, but I have not even spoken with Katherine about it as yet. I will not commit to anything before the wedding, and I will tell you if anything more comes of it. For now, enjoy this time as best you can. Who knows, before you realise it, Natalie will have you busy with little babies to fuss over! Then you will long for this relative peace!"

"So, will you take Katherine with you?" Caroline looked up at her son quizzically.

"I just told you, mother, I have not planned anything as yet, and I am not going to until after the wedding."

"She will not be left behind, I think. You may as well prepare yourself. I would not have you dwelling under any illusions about that young lady's strength of character and determination. You are simply no match for her in that regard!" Caroline smiled. "I have often wished I had been more forceful with your father when he went to India. It might not have changed anything, in the end, but, at least, I would have had that last year with him! You might do well to remember that. I shall certainly tell Katherine how I feel about it."

"Mother, I would really rather appreciate it if you did not. She will need no encouragement as it is. Besides, I have not decided to do anything or go anywhere!"

"Oh Phillip, we both know that is just your way of putting off the inevitable! Of course you will go. Lord St. Vincent would not have already begun the process of convincing you at Natalie and James's wedding if you were not going to go!"

"Mother, how did you know of that? I have spoken to no one but James, and that only recently."

"Oh, Sir John spoke to me then about how proud he was of you, of what great damage you had done to Bonaparte, and how invaluable you were to the nation in your present role, not unlike your father. I knew immediately that he had further designs on you. And you, like your father, will just accept it as your responsibility, and you will trot off at Sir John's behest to serve your country! Oh Phillip, I know that you accept this duty as a trust, and you will feel obligated to fulfill it, just as he did, going off to India on a fool's errand! Yes, a fool's! Just do not get yourself killed! I will never forgive you if you do that to me now!" Caroline again looked up at her son, and tried to smile, although it faded.

"Well, mother, I will endeavour to be more circumspect. I will go now to gather some few things and give Andy what help I may. Will you join me for lunch?"

"Lunch, is it that time already? Oh my, no. Phillip, I am sorry but I am bespoke! I am to join Mrs. Holt and my good friend Amanda

Smyth-Bigelow for lunch in our garden. Oh dear me, I do believe I had better be off to the kitchens to check with Marguerite and Hanna to be sure that we will at least eat well!"

Finally, Phillip was left to himself. He placed his hand into his pocket to retrieve the letter from Sam Cobb. What could dear Sam want now? Phillip had only left the manor some six days before and everything had been in order, with plans for the wedding well in hand. As Phillip read the missive, a smile grew upon his face. The letter was not from Sam at all, but from Andre des Plans, his cousin in Normandy. Only the covering note was from Sam, and it echoed Phillip's immediate reaction to a tee. It seemed there was another opportunity across the channel that could not be overlooked. Phillip settled back into his seat and began to scheme, but after only a few minutes he rose and, pausing only to find his hat and walking stick in the front hall, he was out the door and hailing a passing cab to take him into the City.

As usual the City was clogged with traffic and Phillip dismissed his cab some distance from his bank, deciding that walking would be faster. As he was passing an alleyway, he was bumped from behind and then quickly pushed into the alley entrance before he could collect his balance. Three thoroughly disreputable looking men were immediately upon him and he only managed to get his walking stick up in time to thwart the first goon's swipe with a knife, striking the man across the knuckles, causing him to drop the blade and sending him back a pace. It gave Phillip a brief moment's respite, but as the other two closed in, Phillip knew he was in trouble, for both carried knives and one also had a cudgel. Just then, there was a noise from the alley entrance and one of the two nearest assailants went to his knees, clutching at his neck. Before the second could strike, there was a blur as Andy Barg flew across the intervening space and tackled the man bodily.

The first man was just preparing to rejoin the fray when Phillip's walking stick landed with a sickening crunch into the side of the man's head. He crumpled to the ground as the last of the three attackers went limp under Andy's pummeling fists. The entire episode had taken only a few short minutes, but already there were cries from the street and two burly porters entered the alley, inquiring of Phillip and Andy if they were in need of assistance. A watchman pushed past the two porters only moments later, blowing valiantly on his whistle.

Of the three assailants, one was lying in a pool of blood, Andy's stiletto throwing knife sticking out of his neck, and another was crumpled unconscious from the blow Phillip had landed with his walking stick. The third man was now moaning on the ground and holding both hands to his bloody face.

"I seen all sir." The first of the porters bellowed. "This 'un here is that what pushed you first, and these others was a'waitin' in the alley! Good fing this 'ere fellow was so quick wif 'is knife. Them free meant no good to ya at all, sir!"

By now, a small crowd had gathered at the mouth of the alley, and voices called for the three men on the ground to be strung up immediately. The watchman inquired of Phillip as to the circumstances of the attack, and when Phillip responded that he had never set eyes on any of the three before, he called on the two porters to help him haul off the attackers. Before he could, Andy calmly reached down and retrieved his knife, wiping it on the dead man's shirt. Phillip gave the watchman his name and address and taking Andy's arm in his shaking hand, left the alley.

"How did you come to be here, my friend? Did some angel direct you?"

"I had just finished collecting our shirts and was passing in a cab when I saw you, sir. I was about to call out when I saw you being pushed into the alleyway. My cab is right over here. Shall I give you a lift home? Are you hurt at all?"

"No, thanks to you Andy, I am just fine, only somewhat shaken perhaps. I suppose they were after my purse."

"Sir, I will send our things on ahead, and wait here with the watchman. I want to find out more about these ruffians, if I am able. I suspect there is only the one who will be able to enlighten us, but let me see what I can learn. Would you like to take the cab home, sir?"

"No, I am quite all right. I was on the way to my bank. I have some things to discuss with Lord Bromley if he is in. I will see you back at the house this evening. I am to dine with Lord St Vincent at White's but I shall not be late."

Andy turned back to the alley after giving the cab driver directions to deliver his goods. Phillip, somewhat cautiously, continued up the street to the bank.

CHAPTER TWO
Setting the Hook

Rounding the corner, Phillip found himself on Lombard Street, just across from his bank. Walking in, he sent a note up to Lord Bromley, requesting a short visit. As luck would have it, the chairman was in and readily available. In no time, Phillip was ushered into the board room where, over tea and biscuits, the two men reviewed Phillip's near disaster. Lord Bromley took the attack very seriously and suggested to Phillip that he should keep a body-guard near him whenever he went about the City.

"You know Phillip, that you have enemies across the channel who would like nothing better than to see you destroyed for what you accomplished last spring in the Atlantic. They have long arms and are not above hiring some thugs to execute their wishes! Now, I will not interfere further, my friend, for you surely do not require my advice, but tell me, how can we be of service to you today?"

Phillip explained his ideas about Normandy and the letter from Cousin Andre. "I suppose there is some risk here, but I believe there is also an excellent opportunity, not only for myself, but to help my mother's family."

"Of course there is some risk, Sir Phillip, but without risk there is little reward, and risk is something that you understand much more clearly than most of our clients, this afternoon being an adequate example! I believe that if your family in Normandy are responsive, as you have indicated, this could turn out very well for you indeed." Sir Henry leaned back in his chair. "If I may intrude Phillip, into your personal affairs, as friends are wont to do, I will take this minute to congratulate you on your upcoming marriage, and to thank you for bringing in some welcome business to the bank from your future father-in-law. Not only is his personal business welcome, but his connections directly with the East India Company and his trading partners in Calcutta will be of some great help with our banking offices there. Sir Walter is a fine man, and I am sure his daughter will be a wonderful addition to your family! May we share a toast?"

"Well, thank you Sir Henry, of course. I am delighted that Sir Walter has shown his confidence in the bank, but really I had very little to do with it!"

"Not so, Phillip, not so at all! You see, just knowing you were a partner in the bank was enough for Sir Walter, and I believe that news is quietly making the rounds, you know! There have been several important inquiries of late. This brings me to another matter, one we must discuss most privately indeed. My very good friend, Sir Francis Baring, of Barings Bank, had a very private chat with me not three days past! Phillip, they are preparing, together with Hopes in Amsterdam, to put forward a finance package for the United States of America. It will be very large indeed, and must be kept absolutely quiet. I cannot even tell you what it is at this point, but there may be an opportunity for a very limited number of individuals or banks to be included at the very highest level of participation. This would take a considerable investment, and not without risk."

"Ah, Sir Henry, I assume you are referring to the American's plan to purchase Louisiana from France? I was made privy to the possibility only recently, in relation to the success of our recent mission."

"Very good, Sir Philip, you relieve me of the obligation to keep that matter unsaid! I tell you this, Phillip, because should you choose to participate, you will have to give me some latitude to deal with this matter should you be away for some time. I do not believe this will conclude for perhaps another year, possibly even more, but one does not know for certain, and were we to participate, we would need to give Barings our unequivocal support early on."

"Sir Henry, I must assume that you have been visiting with our friends again! I am to dine with Sir John this very evening, and he is again requesting my assistance in some matter involving Prince of Wales Island and the region beyond. I have not yet made any decision on this matter! Therefore, I may well be in England for quite some time."

"Of course, I understand, Sir Phillip, and I meant no offense. It is just that should you choose to make this voyage, we would have to make a decision on the American opportunity before you sail."

"What portion of my wealth would you advise placing in this consortium, and what advantage would it bring to me and to the bank?"

"As to the latter, I doubt very much that we would be involved at all without your interest. It would not be prudent for us should you not agree to participate, we are after all, a relatively small private bank. As to the former, I would suggest that should you offer three hundred thousand pounds, we could probably raise another two hundred among the other partners. I believe such an amount would place us at the very head of the table, under Barings' umbrella of course. Still, it is a very large sum and the terms will necessarily be quite long, although it will provide you with a very nice return and a good income! Also, we can raise your portion by selling off some of the jewels that still sit in the vaults, so it would not even infringe on your gold in the bank."

"If you think it is a good risk, let us go forward. It will certainly not hurt us to be linked with the Baring family, even if it is quietly. I may also be able to persuade some of the others from our little venture of last spring to take a small interest if that would be helpful. I am sure that George Fielding and James Peters might take a small amount each."

"There is a slight problem with that, Phillip. I am sworn to absolute secrecy with Sir Francis and may not discuss anything at all outside of the bank's partners and only in very broad terms even there, in much less detail than we have discussed here I assure you!"

"Very well, Sir Henry. May I ask you for a slight favour in return?"

The banker nodded his head, "Of course, anything at all Phillip."

"Well Henry, here is the thing. Should we decide to take this voyage, it would be most beneficial to have a covering letter from Sir Francis's friends on Leadenhall Street. Uncle Desmond had some connections I believe, but with the Celeste we could make a nice business venture of the trip to George Town."

"Phillip, I can assure you this will not be a problem. Certainly Sir Francis has weight, but he is not alone, and one of our partners is on the board of governors of the Company. They are most interested in this voyage as well, for the East India ships have suffered the greatest loss. I will see to it at once."

"Now this other matter we were discussing; should we set a preliminary amount of say, ten thousand pounds?"

"I should think that would do most handsomely! If the plan is successful, you might follow it up in the future with another offer to increase the total holding. I understand that at this time your interest is particularly for your family, but one must assume that this present trouble will not go on indefinitely, and should you be able to acquire holdings in Normandy while these prices are distressed, you might find it most advantageous some years from now. Again, we can arrange that with a letter of direction from you that Samuel Cobb could activate on your behalf. Speaking of Samuel, he is doing very well with the improvements in your mining and quarrying ventures in Devon. Should you wish to enlarge your interests, Phillip, I am certain I could find possible investors."

"Ha! Now you want to become my partner, Henry? If that is so, I know for certain that Cobb is doing the right thing and I do not need you at all!" Phillip laughed.

Sir Henry Bromley laughed right along with him, "You can't blame a banker for recognising a good thing! By the way, we have what I believe is a very good offer for approximately twenty percent of your pearls and some of the gems as well. It is above our initial estimate for these pieces by at least fifteen to twenty percent. Should we act on it?"

"Yes, I believe we should. I have taken out another group of diamonds and a rather large ruby to make ear rings and a bracelet for Katherine for the wedding, and I will want to keep some of the other gems for future gifts, but there is certainly a great deal we can dispose of. The very large yellow diamond that I identified earlier is not a part of this lot is it?"

"Oh no, of course not; none of the stones you have identified as being of interest to you personally are listed. By the way, I was able to see the ruby you chose for Katherine's ring, and if I may say so, even Queen Charlotte would be delighted with such a gem! It must be three hundred carats!"

"Well she might, but she will have to find her own, or plunder her son's chest!" Phillip and the banker both laughed.

After the visit with his banker, Phillip took advantage of the warm July afternoon to stroll down to his club, Whites, to await Lord St. Vincent and ponder his future. The voyage did appeal to him, if only to satisfy his desire to see the Far East and travel beyond Cape Town, which was the furthest point he had been. Most of Phillip's naval career had been spent either in the Caribbean or in the Mediterranean. He vastly preferred the eastern Mediterranean, with the Italian coast and the Aegean bringing his fondest memories. His first real command after the Nile had been mostly spent in the eastern Mediterranean, capturing so many prizes that he had been the envy of post captains and even a few admirals. In one fantastic period of three weeks, they had brought in seventeen captured merchantmen and one Spanish brig. It had been a heady time and he and Andy Barg had thought it might last forever! That was it, Phillip thought. He really missed the adventure and the thrill of the chase. A cruise to the Far East would give him some of that, although there were not likely to be any prizes involved in this voyage. What would Katherine have to say?

"Saunders, could you get me a glass of sherry in the reading room?" Phillip asked as he strode in from the sun into the cool darkness of the club. "And Saunders, please inform me when Lord St. Vincent arrives."

"Yes Sir, of course, Lord St. Vincent. Can I get you anything else, My Lord? We have some very nice cold grey partridge and some quite good Stilton cheese if you would like a plate made up, Sir."

"Oh, perhaps just a small plate, Saunders! The partridge sounds very nice indeed."

Entering the lounge, Phillip noticed three older members sitting in a group around the cold fireplace involved in an animated discussion. One of the gentlemen looked up and frowned at him, then looked back to his companions and made some remark that had both the others suddenly look up as well. The largest, with the red face and bluster of an ex-army officer, cleared his throat and called out, "This room is reserved for members, young man. We would desire you would find a spot elsewhere!"

"I assure you sir, I am a member here, and I do not believe that my presence will cause you any inconvenience. I believe the room is open. Please carry on!" Phillip tried to smile and remain in a good humour in spite of the querulous attitude from across the room.

In a raised voice, obviously meant to be heard, one of the others at the table commented, "I say colonel, cheeky young devil; probably the son of some Tory backbencher. Not enough manners to recognise his betters. Would have settled his hash in the eleventh foot, eh?"

"I say, and had him calling for his mother!" this from the man who had first looked up and frowned at Phillip's entrance.

"The Eleventh Foot, isn't that a Devonshire regiment?" asked Phillip as he rose and walked across to the three men.

"What is that to you, sir?" asked the colonel as he rose to his feet, somewhat shakily.

"I am a Devon man myself, and as I recall my family have been patrons of the eleventh for many years. Your men were stationed as marines on our ships in '97! I remember them well, and was proud to have them with us. I am Captain Phillip Hollis and served with Sir John Jervis at the Battle of St. Vincent. I understood the regiment was now in the West Indies, stationed in Jamaica!"

"Hollis? Related to the Earl of Brixton are you?"

"In a manner of speaking sir, as I am the current Earl of Brixton. Whom, may I ask, do I have the pleasure of addressing?"

The colonel bowed, all the bluster gone in an instant, "I beg your pardon, My Lord, I am William Connor, Sir Phillip, ex-colonel of the Eleventh Foot. I was still active at the time of your Battle at St. Vincent, Sir. A bloody good show it was, if I may say sir. Please, I beg you excuse some old men caught up in their cups. I assure you my lord, that your family is held in the highest respect in the regiment. It is a great honor to meet you sir. I assure you we meant you no disrespect!"

"Not at all, just a misunderstanding, I am certain. Please allow me to get you all a glass. Ah Saunders, there you are. Do me a great favour would you, and find these fellows a glass of what they prefer and put it to my account. Thank you Saunders." With that Phillip returned to his seat across the room to enjoy his sherry and cold partridge. No sooner was he seated however, than the three men politely called across to invite him to join them, which he did. As it happened, two of the men had been in the regiment, while the third was a country gentleman, a friend of Mr. Connor, mostly occupied with fox hunting and fishing for trout in Scotland. Still, it rather pleasantly wasted away some time, and Phillip learned much more about the regiment than he ever really wanted to know. The three men were now as effusive in their good opinions of most anything Phillip spoke to, as they had been disagreeable earlier. Just when he was looking for a way to extricate himself, Saunders walked in to announce that Lord St Vincent had arrived at last and would he like to join him for dinner? Having now duly impressed his acquaintances with his credentials and his dinner partner, he excused himself to find Sir John.

"Ah, there you are Phillip; I do hope I did not keep you waiting too long?"

"No, of course not, Sir John; I was just visiting with some gentlemen, ex of the 11th Devonshire Foot." Phillip responded with a smile.

"Ah, Mr. Connor and company, then I really do owe you an apology! Tedious lot indeed, I am sorry Phillip!" Sir John chuckled as they were seated.

"Shall we order first, Sir John, or are you content to importune me over this voyage to the east and then attempt to eat in peace after I tell you that I am not overly interested?" Phillip asked with a smile.

Sir John only smiled and looked vaguely pleased with himself. A moment later Saunders appeared with a bottle of hock and two glasses. "Your dinner is ordered Sir John, and will be out shortly. I have instructed the kitchen to prepare the eel and the grey partridge as you suggested, My Lord."

"Now, Sir Phillip what was it you were asking?"

"What exactly is it you need done at Prince of Wales Island that cannot be done by His Majesty's Navy?"

"At Prince of Wales Island itself, probably nothing, specifically. Near there however, ah, there may be some small service you might render, should you find yourself in the vicinity." Lord St. Vincent smiled as Saunders poured two glasses of wine. "You see, there are reports of pirates in the Straits of Malacca, leading extensive raids against our shipping and that of our friends, and we have reason to believe that they have the active support of both the French and Dutch navies. Not so very different than the fellows you had occasion to deal with in your last little cruise, Phillip. They are almost certainly there with the support of the French government. With this damnable peace in place we have to tread softly, but if you were threatened or attacked, as a private vessel or vessels, you would certainly have the right to defend yourself. Also, there is another situation that we would be desirous of having you look into." Sir John frowned. "The Sultan of Kedah has been having ongoing difficulties with the Burmese, and some little intervention would go a long way to improving our status with him. It was to have been an understanding that the Company would provide some military assistance but that has been replaced by a monetary fee. Unfortunately that fee will be of little use if the Sultan is deposed. Yet, we are treating with the Burmese as well, and cannot very well intervene with our navy for fear of driving them into the arms of the French."

"So, let me be certain that I apprehend your agenda. All you really want is for us to get rid of a batch of pirates, take on possible French and Dutch sponsored privateers, chase off the Burmese Army, and perform a small diplomatic mission in our spare time! Is there anything I have missed?" Phillip looked faintly amused, but unconvinced.

"Well, putting it in that light Phillip, I can understand a certain lack of enthusiasm! Nevertheless, this is of some considerable importance to us, and there is a potential opportunity for financial gain. Not that you should ever again require any! The pirates, should you chase them to ground, have been more successful than we would like, and there's every likelihood that you may liberate opium and spices, not to mention gold. Also, the Sultan may be quite grateful for any aid you may be able to offer in his ongoing difficulty with the Burmese. Of course, there is always the chance that you may capture either Dutch or French prizes as well."

"Of course, there is also the chance that I will be hung from a French yardarm! Should I go, I would probably consider taking one of the brigs with me as an escort. Perhaps we could carry some passengers or freight, at least as far as India, to offset some of the cost of the mission. Then, there is Celeste. She was to go to the Caribbean after Cape Town, but that could be altered. I did speak briefly with

Bromley about that and he believes the Company might look upon us favourably. What do we know of the location of these pirates, and what sort of ships they utilize?"

"I understand that it is mostly large sea-going proas, those double hulled galleys, some lateen rigged, although there are reports of Chinese or Siamese style junks as well. The twin hulled proas are really quite weatherly and with slaves at the oars they can, of course, go directly into the wind. I believe you had some experience against a couple of similar vessels in the eastern Mediterranean after the Nile. They will not have anything even approaching your firepower, but it would be the very devil to be caught against them with no wind. They typically travel in large groups of up to several dozen vessels, each carrying up to fifty fighting men and might well simply overwhelm you. They have been reported all along the Strait of Malacca and into the Java Sea. There was a report received recently from a Chinese vessel that seemed to place the greatest activity at the south end of the Strait, where there are a great many islands, and that, of course, is the closest point to the Dutch base at Batavia. One of our great problems is a lack of good charts. There are very few and many of them are contradictory."

"I would need to find a good Sailing Master, as I fear old Dick Marsden will be delighted to remain on shore with his grandchildren, spending his prize money! I could use some help with that perhaps, but I would ask Dick for advice first. It is a tight knit community and he will know of anyone reliable with experience in those waters. Could you get me copies of whatever charts the admiralty might possess?"

"I can do better than that. I will get you a fair copy of the charts the East India Company uses, and, as usual, they are a fair sight better than ours! Oh, and I can also help to offset your expenses, at least somewhat. We have a garrison in George Town that requires supplies and pay. Normally that would travel by Company ships, but they have graciously offered to have you carry it for us, so long as you offer to deal with the pirates that have been mauling their ships. Really, of course, it is not the pirates we wish you to engage, unless the opportunity presents itself, but the Europeans who are supplying and encouraging them. The French and Dutch are the real reason we want you to make an appearance, and the reason we choose not to send naval frigates. It will put them on notice that two can play this game of pretending to keep the peace in daylight, while stabbing viciously in the dark. As you know, half the fleet is laid up, so you should have no difficulty in finding men to crew your ships, especially as it is no great secret that your last crew all went home rich and happy!"

"Sir John, I must discuss this with Katherine. We are to be married in one week, and it simply will not do to surprise her with this on her wedding night! I remember that you asked if I would take her on a wedding cruise, but this is more than a cruise and fighting pirates or the Burmese Army is no sight-seeing adventure! I will send you an answer by messenger from Devon within ten days, if that is satisfactory."

"Quite satisfactory, I assure you my boy; although we both know that you are not cut out to settle in as a country squire just yet! By the way, Nepean and I have convinced the board that your name remains on the post list, albeit with a caveat. This way your seniority will not be lost if and when you return to active duty, should this war resume. I understand that the Emerald has completed her modifications, and that Ruby will be completed in perhaps three or four weeks. You might consider sending Emerald ahead on that voyage to Cape Town as planned, escorting your big new merchantman, your great French lass, the Celeste. Really, Phillip, if you keep this up you will have more French ships at sea than Bonaparte! In point of fact, at this rate, Phillip, you will have your own navy soon enough! At any rate, you could then pick her up when you sail south. If George left right after your wedding, he could probably even make a trip all the way to India, and have Emerald back to Cape Town in time to meet you and Mr. Morrissey. That way, you might have all four of your vessels together. It would allow you to bring back a sizable load of spice and pepper from the Malay ports. After all, George Town is an open port and you will still retain both your letters from the Crown and from the Admiralty! I cannot imagine that funds to purchase goods in the east will be any problem for you! If they are, I would be delighted to offer you a loan at very reasonable rates! Shall we say six percent?"

"Now where have I heard that figure just recently? No, Sir John, I believe I have the means to finance the trip, should we go." Both men sat back and laughed quietly.

"By the way, Phillip, that information you sent us from your cousin Pierre about the building going on in Le Havre has been confirmed. Barges are beginning to appear along the banks of the river there and at Calais and Boulogne-Sur-Mer as well. Only one possible use for that many small vessels and that means our friends are planning to pay us a visit as soon as this peace ends. You might find it safer in the Orient than in Devon!"

Leaving the club, Phillip was surprised to see Andy Barg lounging just down the street. As Phillip walked toward his old friend, he noticed the glint of a pistol in Andy's belt and the barrel of a second protruding from his left sleeve.

"Andy, has something happened? Why are you here?"

"Have you already put that attack this afternoon from your mind?" Andy answered with a sharp frown. "Well, if so I am here to remind you, and to tell you those men were not just after your purse. It was as I suspected. When we got to talk with the only one capable, we discovered they had been hired specifically to attack you and no one else. Of course, he didn't know who hired them, but I suspect we can both guess at that. At any rate, his loosened tongue will get him on a ship to New South Wales instead of a rope. I have the carriage just 'round the next corner, sir, if you'd care to join me."

"So, our friends across the Channel have not forgotten us yet, is that your guess?"

"I reckon it is more than a guess, Sir Phillip. You must believe that your actions have made you a marked man. I think it is time you accepted the truth. You are not safe on your own, not here at any rate. So I intend making sure you are not on your own." Andy smiled and led Phillip around the corner to the waiting coach.

As they rode back to the house in Mayfair, Andy thought about his best friend and employer. Sir Phillip was a good man, but he needed looking after, and Andy was committed to making that his life's work. Phillip had saved his life on more than one occasion, but much more than that, he had saved him from himself and Andy would never forget it, nor could he walk away from his fierce loyalty to the only man in his life who had cared enough to stand up to him and make him face himself honestly. Thanks to Sir Phillip, he was now a wealthy man, but that did not amount to much, for it was thanks to Phillip that he had become a man, and not just a brawling, snarling, and very adept thief.

CHAPTER THREE
Painting a Future

Early the next morning, Phillip was busily going over details with James as Andy Barg supervised the loading of the coach that would carry them home to Devon. "Just remind your wife that the wedding will proceed with her or without her, and, should she keep mother and Aunt Anne from arriving on time, I will not vouch for her safety!" James laughed but shook his head.

"I have decided, Phillip, that immediately after the wedding I am taking Natalie home to West House, burning all her clothes, and giving her a shift and a hoe and sending her out to the garden!" James exclaimed, "She will be allowed in only to take meals and perhaps to conceive a child!"

Phillip imagined the scene and burst into laughter! "I will pay you ten pounds per day, but only on the condition that they must be consecutive days!"

"Let me see, ten days would give me one hundred pounds. Enough to purchase a new light carriage and a nice pair of greys to pull it! That just may be the best bargain I have had since we captured the Isle de France!"

"I will see you in four days, brother. We will have much to discuss. My meeting with Sir John last evening was interesting, and we may have a voyage to plan for. If so, I could use your help in the preparation. We would have to find crew and get the Onyx ready, look for a Sailing Master, and find officers to man her. I believe George and Patrick, with Ross's help, have already crewed both the Celeste and the brigs."

"Until then, Phillip, and I will certainly give the voyage some thought. Perhaps I will call on Dick Forest, as he is living only some ten miles out of the city. It will give me something better to do than waiting for my wife to choose, for the fifth time, which clothes to take to Devon. Ten pounds per day you said…"

The horses were blowing as they climbed yet another rise coming out of Salisbury. In the coach, Andy Barg and Phillip were engaged in a debate that had little chance of being resolved. "Andy, you are a wealthy man! You have a greater income than two admirals combined. You could purchase a fine home, start some commercial enterprise to keep you busy, find a good wife, perhaps Angeline, and raise some brats! There must be something you would like to do!"

"As for Angeline, she is a fine lass, but she is for settling down, and that is not my game. I have now repeatedly told you sir, what I wish to do is to remain with you! I do not trust you on your own, and that is God's truth, sir! After all, that attack in the City yesterday just proved my point. You go off and get yourself killed, and what would Miss Katherine have to say? She would, like as not, shoot me! I cannot say as I might blame her either, sir. No, I reckon you need some looking after." Andy smiled, "Look, Sir Phillip, we have been together for near six years. I reckon we make a fair good team, you on the quarterdeck and me on the main deck! I would not last long on shore, and we both know it. No adventure and I would be forced to create some, if you catch my drift, sir. Odds are Lombard Street to a China orange I would end up back on the dock for some mischief! No, I reckon you are just stuck with me sir, and it is for both our good. "

"So you too, think that I will make this trip to the east. It seems everyone is convinced except me! What do you think I should do with Katherine, just marry the poor girl and run off?"

"Well sir, two things; if you marry her she will hardly be a poor girl, will she? She will be a rich woman and make no mistake! Other thing, sir, is if you think for one minute she is going to let you run off without her you had better hide that Ferguson rifle before you tell her! No, I reckon we all go together and that is no lie! We might have to make a few changes to the Onyx to suit your new estate, but that is neither here nor there. You just leave that up to me, sir! Tell me what we need to do and I will fix her up. The bigger question is whether James and Natalie are to join us. I cannot figure James being pleased to see you go off without him, and if Miss Natalie finds out that Lady Katherine is going..."

"Oh no! I will not have my sister on the Onyx! No! Not for all the spice in Penang! You must be mad, Andy. Can you just picture it? I swear I will sink the Onyx first! A trip of this magnitude could easily last two years. Could you imagine two years of Natalie begging for clothes, fresh water, whatever! There would be mutiny." Both men sat back and laughed at Phillip's heated protest.

Arriving at the Manor was always a pleasant experience for Phillip. He just loved to turn up the drive and climb through the rows of trees to the new gravelled turning circle at the front door. It just seemed so right and he knew Uncle Des would be so proud! As usual, Sam Cobb was waiting on the front steps to greet him.

"Good afternoon sir, and welcome home! May I offer you a glass of chilled hock or a brandy, sir? Good afternoon Mr. Barg, it is good to see you again."

"Good afternoon Sam! My, it is good to be home! Just tell me everything is ready for the guests and I shall be delighted! Are the rooms prepared? Is the food in hand?"

"Relax, Sir Phillip; everything is as ready as can be!" Sam Cobb ticked off items on his fingers, "Andre des Plans and his lovely wife Agnes arrived just last week, and they are staying with Pierre and Giselle. The Chapleys are not expected until late tomorrow or Thursday, and your mother and Lady Anne will not be here before Thursday or Friday. Of course well wishes have been coming in already, and have been deposited in your study, for the most part. The required food is crammed into the pantry and the ice house. The portrait of Sir Desmond arrived this week, sir, and I placed it in your Aunt Anne's room as you requested. It will be transferred to the great hall in time for the wedding."

"Thank you, Sam! I only hope that she likes it. So what do we have to do in the interim? There must be some tasks to keep us occupied for a day or two."

"Well sir, I assume you received the letter that I forwarded to London? We could begin to create a plan to explore the options that Andre has proposed." Sam Cobb looked at Phillip thoughtfully, and then beckoned him toward the study door. "Unless, of course you would prefer to rest and conserve your strength for the rigors of the wedding!"

Andy laughed and waved as he wandered off toward the kitchens.

"That was a remark worthy of James perhaps, but not of you, Sam! I thought you at least would be on my side!" Phillip laughed, "Let us indeed take a few minutes in the study so you may acquaint me with your views and where you believe our greatest opportunities lie. I must say, this is all rather new to me! I never fancied I would be making such investments as you propose, although Sir Henry Bromley at the bank seemed to think the idea had possibilities."

"Certainly there are possibilities, but you will have to proceed with utmost caution!" The two men continued to converse as they walked to Phillip's study. "Should the authorities stumble upon the truth of who the real owner is, there would be grave consequences, not only for yourself sir, but for your family as well. Still, if your objective is to provide a certain degree of security and wellbeing for your mother's family, for a start, while at the same time enlarging your own interests, I believe this may serve. There are two parcels of land that Andre believes may be available now, or in the near future. One of them contains what he believes is a viable apple orchard of approximately thirty hectares. It also has a rather good house, some out buildings, and some hay land. With the conditions in France being as bad as they now are, he believes that more property may soon be for sale. People in general are very pessimistic and some of the lands that were held by the nobility of the ancient regime are lying in waste."

"We can easily afford to make some investment, even if there is no return for many years. For now, I am more concerned that the family in France has some chance at a future beyond fishing. I am prepared to spend up to ten thousand pounds now and more in the future if we believe it is warranted."

"Sir, I doubt you will be able to spend anywhere near that amount! With where prices are now, you could purchase half of Carentan! The first property, which consists of some thirty hectares and the house I spoke of, the land of which nearly half is orchard and the balance pasture, would not cost much over fifteen or twenty thousand francs. Phillip, at the current rate, that is four hundred twenty-five pounds. With ten thousand pounds, you could purchase twenty such properties. We will have to go much slower than that to avoid serious scrutiny. Your cousins would have no way to account for such wealth and it could place them in jeopardy of the widow maker."

"Sam, I believe we need to call on Andre and Pierre. We need to create some plan of action, but if we are only speaking of such a limited investment, perhaps we should be looking at greater opportunities either in Normandy or here in Devon. I had been thinking in terms of reacquiring all of my maternal grandfather's lands in Normandy between the town of Carentan and Isigny-sur-Mer, and perhaps the Doucette land near Sainte-mer-Eglise. I am not sure, but I believe that would have been six hundred hectares near Carentan, and another two or three hundred at Sainte-mer-Eglise, perhaps more. Even so, if the prices are now only one hundred fifty or two hundred Francs per hectare, it is no great amount."

"For such a large purchase the prices would certainly be substantially higher, but I do not believe that it could be done at this time! Were your cousins to attempt a purchase of such a tract of land it would draw too much attention, especially with Pierre being here and an openly hunted man in France! No, I believe you will have to be content with moving slowly. Understand that the ongoing venture centred on Carentan House is providing the entire family in France with a livable income. They are already much better off than any of their neighbours, though certainly not well off. At least they can eat well, clothe their children, and stay warm in the winter and for France these past few years that is good indeed."

"Speaking of Pierre, how are he and Giselle doing?"

"You might be much better informed if you asked William that question, Sir. He sees them much more often than I do, as they are living in a rather nice cottage near Carentan House. I believe they have purchased it, along with a small plot of land. It is just across the North Road and quite close to the estuary. I believe it was the home of old Colonel Winters."

"Ah, yes I know it. Well, if they have purchased a house, I suppose it might mean they are settling in. Still, I am worried about them; too much guilt and too little time." Phillip paused, seemingly lost in thought for a moment. Looking up he seemed to collect himself. "Sam, how are the tin mines down in the south west holding out? Have we made any progress with the smelting?"

"Sir, for the time being, we are much better off sending the ore to Penzance! For a fraction of the price we have been spending with the locals, we can ship it there and we are getting an extra hundred shillings per ton. The north mine near Whiteworks is doing quite well, but I believe sir, that if we made up a prospectus for the lot we could make as much in selling them as we may realise through mining. The interest is very high just now, and the mines are profitable, so William and I believe we could reinvest the money in copper mining. William and I believe this would be a very good time to make a major investment in copper. The Duke is still doing quite well, and I believe that we could join forces with him with the proper investment and have a much greater return in the long run. With the peace in effect and the fleet being laid up the price of copper has fallen slightly, but we are certain this won't last. When war again resumes, as you believe it must, the prices will certainly spike. I believe that there is much more stability and because the capital investment is greater, there may be fewer competitors. We would need to invest above what we could realise from the tin mines to begin, but I believe there is an excellent opportunity to partner with your late uncle's good friend the Duke. He has considerable interests and is looking to expand. I believe, sir, that we would realise considerable capital from the sale of the tin mines; a shift of assets with a cash infusion of perhaps thirty thousand pounds should benefit you with at least a fifteen percent better return, and that would give us a minimum of ten percent or better clear return on the new funds invested. With a resumption of hostilities that might double."

"Excellent, Sam. Capital idea! Carry on, but I am still concerned that we do not abandon the Normandy prospect. Also, after the wedding I will want to get Onyx prepared for sea. She needs to be careened and have the copper inspected and I want all the spars and rigging checked as well. We just may be taking her out on another voyage. Our good friend St. Vincent has been making plans for us again! With all the ships that are laid up, we should not have any difficulty finding men to crew her, but I have not yet broached the subject with Katherine."

Sam Cobb just raised his eyebrows and remained silent, which had Phillip grimacing. "Why is it that everyone believes Katherine will be difficult about this? She has a wonderful disposition! By the way, have you heard when George and Patrick will be arriving? I need to discuss some sailing matters with them." Phillip was trying to change the subject before he could no longer believe his own judgement on the matter of Katherine's likely response. In fact, the closer the matter came, the less he liked his chances of convincing her of his plan.

"I believe that they are sailing over from Plymouth, and might arrive by Friday. Are you planning on speaking with Miss Katherine about the proposed voyage before the wedding, sir?"

"No, I do not believe there will be time." Phillip responded too quickly.

"Oh, I do believe that is very wise, sir!" Sam said with a broad smile.

Wednesday morning dawned to a clear sky and warm enough weather that there was not even a trace of dew as Phillip made his rounds of the orchard and paddock. Willie Church was already busy with Bob in the stables when Phillip stuck his head in to wish them a good day and ask for the big red hunter to be readied for a ride to Carentan House after breakfast. Phillip heard the sound of a song coming from the old stable as he passed, but Andy was at the door before he could open it, and informed Phillip that he could kindly wander elsewhere! Breakfast was one of Mrs. Wilmark's finest, with fresh biscuits, eggs, sausages, bacon, cheese, marmalade and steaming coffee. After two heaping plates, Phillip reluctantly pushed back his chair and groaned in satisfaction. Why on earth would he ever consider leaving this place?

Pierre and Andre were standing on raised planking, busily painting the window trims on Pierre and Giselle's new house when Phillip rode up in the late morning. As Phillip approached, he could not hide his amusement for the two men were wearing as much paint as the house. It seemed not to bother them in the least and there was a steady stream of French banter going on. Phillip was glad, as there had been altogether too little in the way of smiles and laughter in Pierre and Giselle's home since the return with the news of Armand's death. When Andre saw Phillip approach he immediately climbed down from the platform, grasping any excuse to stop painting. "Phillip, you are just in time! My poor arm was about to leave my body. We just arrived and were conscripted into this cruel slavery! My cousin is an evil task maker, yes?"

"I believe it is task master, but I agree whole heartedly with the sentiment!" Phillip laughed. "Pierre, if you have an extra brush I would offer to assist, but not on the same scaffold as you; I value my clothes and Katherine will not be delighted if I show up at the wedding with green hair!"

"Have no fear, Phillip, I would not believe that you know how to paint any better than this poor excuse for a fisherman! You may call Giselle. I am sure she will have some chilled wine in the house, or failing that, perhaps some lemon drink. That wine with the oranges we had from Madeira is also very good with lemons!"

"I will do exactly that! Perhaps if you can spare us a minute or two, we might discuss the matter of the orchard property and what other chance we may have to redeem your family's estate in Normandy?"

"I will be down in just several minutes. If I do not finish this first, Giselle will cat me all day!"

"Pierre, I think you mean hound you, yes?"

"Perhaps, but she does not bark, she snarls!" Pierre laughed and shook his head.

"I heard that Pierre!" A voice came out of the house, and was followed by the lithe form of Giselle Doucette, carrying a pitcher and a tray of glasses. "Welcome, Phillip! It is not a very formal greeting this morning, but we are busy using the help that your wedding has provided in the form of Andre and Agnes! We have them only for these few days and we must not miss this opportunity!"

"They will think twice before they cross the channel again! If you really need help I can send some men from the estate. It would be no problem, at least after next week when all this craziness will be done with!"

"No, no!" Andre answered "What is family good for if not to take advantage of? Besides, we are negotiating the terms of a loan at this same time!"

Pierre laughed, "If the amount of paint you spill is added to the loan, dear cousin, you will never be able to make the payments!"

"Ah, that is why I am here." Phillip interjected. "I got your message through Sam Cobb, and I am more than ready to help. Tell me what your plans are and how you believe we could proceed."

"Ah Phillip, I am sorry, but Andre did not understand that I am now in a position to help the family on my own! You have already done so very much, now it is my turn! We can make this work easily enough." Pierre spoke up as he was climbing down from the platform.

"I understand Pierre, but perhaps we can do this together. After all it is my family as well! Andre, what is available to do now? Sam told me about the property with the orchard. Is that still the best starting point?"

"Agnes would love it. It was her grandfather's farm, and many years in the family. Now that we have started to enquire seriously though the price is beginning to rise! At first, they said perhaps twelve thousand francs as a down payment, and now, they say perhaps fourteen or even sixteen thousand, so who knows when the money is in hand. Then, they want another ten thousand over ten years. Those cretins, the Bassalt family have it. They stole it during the revolution and now act as though it is a great family legacy!"

"Andre, really two thousand francs more or less is not an issue. We can work it out!" Phillip responded.

"That is what I have been telling him!" Pierre broke in. "It does not have to make any return for me, as long as they can build a life for themselves!"

"Phillip, please understand, we have been living off your family's generosity for too many years! We need to make this a working arrangement. At twelve thousand francs, we could make enough money from the orchard and the hay land to repay the loan with perhaps three or even four percent interest! At sixteen thousand, I am not sure it would generate enough so that at least two families could live there and survive."

"Andre, what if we make a different arrangement? I suggest that you offer Bassalt twenty five thousand in one payment. There is no sense in giving them payments that they can try to change over time. I need no interest on the money for the present time, and I doubt if Pierre does either. What if we rather make an arrangement where we will create a fund of money for the family to use as land becomes available. Pierre and I are not going to be very welcome in Normandy for a long time, I think, so you and Jacques with some advice from Aunt Celeste and Uncle Richarde, if you want it, should just keep your eyes and ears open. When opportunity presents itself, you can be ready to take it! I am willing to put up one quarter million Francs."

"I would match that, but Phillip I do not think they can use it, at least not yet. I would suggest we each put up fifty thousand for a start. Even that will be quite a lot. I also am interested in how you propose to do this."

"My thought is that we would become partners in this with Andre and Jacques. Whatever land or enterprise you choose is entirely up to you. You use the money as you see fit, but it must be responsibly, so that there is a return. When you begin to show a decent return above fair living cost, you begin to share that return with your partners. When the return has paid back all the initial investment plus one percent profit, I am paid out. At the same time, I would like you to look for other opportunities for me. I have decided that I want to acquire property in Normandy for myself, but whatever you decide would work for the family must come first. However, if there are opportunities that could benefit both the family and myself, such as purchasing extra land that some family members could farm, I would be most interested in it. I will not speak for Pierre as he has different circumstances, but I will tell you, eventually, I wish to have considerable holdings around where Mama grew up."

"That is more than fair to me. Phillip, I also do not have a huge estate to keep running! Giselle and I have far more than we will ever need, and with the investments that you made for us with your bank, we are very comfortable indeed. Andre, so you understand, my fifty thousand francs will not even use up one year of my income! Let us help you, and this way you have freedom to find ways to secure the future of the family in Normandy! Perhaps Phillip and I will join forces to find other investments over there that we can claim after this war is over. Just one thing, I have spoken with William and it is good if we can keep the smuggling going!"

"Of course, and Phillip we would be honoured to help you with purchasing property for yourself, but really I do not know what to say!" Andre stood with his hands on his hips and stared at his two cousins.

"Then do something different and say nothing for a change!" Agnes stepped down from the front porch of the house and approached Phillip. She smiled and wrapped her arms around him in a great hug. "Cousin Phillip, it is so good to see you again! Though we see you so seldom now, one thing at least we can count on, you are never boring! Either you come to steal ships, or you send for us to buy us a future! I will take care of Andre, never fear. What you and Pierre are doing is very good for the family, if not for you! I will just say Merci, and God bless you, Phillip and you too, Pierre! There are at least ten families, plus grown children, that will benefit from your generosity!"

They all sat on the front porch and the talk ran from farms, to shops in Carentan, to houses that were sitting empty. Eventually the talk ran back to old times and happier days before the revolution.

Giselle began to open up more as the morning progressed. "Not everything was wonderful before the revolution either! Some of what they wanted to change was good, but it just developed a life of its own and that was when it all went wrong!"

"Yes," Agnes agreed, "The church for instance, had too much power and wealth that it stole from the people. It was right to stop that, but all the senseless killing, all the terror of wondering who was going to go to the tumbrels next, there was no excuse for that. So many young people were ruined by the lies and the hatred!"

There was a moment of uncomfortable silence. "Yes, you are right." Gisele looked at Agnes, "and our son was one of them. Armand was always headstrong and he fell in love with the revolution. We became his enemies, and not just Pierre and I, but all the family. When I think that he nearly killed Phillip!" There was a look of shame and torment on Giselle's face.

"Giselle, I am so sorry. If I had known..." Phillip began, but he was cut off.

"Oh no, Phillip, you may never apologise in this house for Armand! He created his own end and while I may weep for him, it is for what he might have been, not for what he was. Understand me well, Phillip. You of all people bear no responsibility for what happened! It is bad enough that I have to see that scar on your head every time we meet. Andy Barg also has come to me to beg my forgiveness, but there is nothing to forgive! Whether Pierre should have told you earlier I do not know, but I understand why he did not, and am satisfied. I was Armand's mother, and he struck me, and cursed his father. He ended as he chose. Agnes is correct; so many were ruined, but they chose to be ruined and the lies were ones that they wanted to believe in."

Pierre took her hand, looking at Phillip. "Yes, that bloody revolution took our son Armand and the man he was named after, my dear friend Armand Le Croix. I don't know if you ever met him Phillip, but he was a man you would have been proud to know! He was my idol in the old navy, a frigate captain like yourself, a man who loved to take chances and defy orders. But he was loyal to the ancient regime and they took his head because he would not bow to the masses. So, you see, one dear Armand I lost because he was a man of honour, the other because he had none!"

It was the end of all possible conversation. Giselle was in tears and Pierre was morose. Sighing to Andre and Agnes, Phillip mounted his horse and quietly left the four friends.

On his ride back to the manor, Phillip wondered about what lies people choose to believe in. Were there some in his own life?

He hoped not, but he was far from sure. It was so easy to choose to believe what suited him best, and it was always so much easier to see the falsehood and self-deception in someone else's views.

CHAPTER FOUR
Kate

By the general commotion at the house when he got back, he surmised that the Chapley family had indeed arrived. It was not long before Sir Walter came down the front stairs, a look of total bewilderment upon his visage. Phillip was standing in the front hall talking with Samuel Cobb and, looking up, could not help but smile at the unfortunate father of his bride-to-be.

"Sir Walter, it appears that you are in need of fortification!" Phillip quipped.

"If by that sir, you are in mind of something in the restorative way, I would be most honoured to join you! My goodness, those women have worn me to the very nub! I say Phillip, I do not suppose we could get this wedding done tomorrow, could we? I am afraid I simply do not know how many days I have left in me!"

"Come with me Walter; I believe I have just the thing. Sam, I will see you before evening. Could you just check with Mrs. Wilmark about dinner? Be sure she knows how many we will be. That reminds me Walter, has your son come out as well?"

"No, unfortunately he was not able to join us. I must apologise, but after the fiasco he created while we were in India, it was decided that he would accompany another of our partners on a buying trip to Canada. It was high time the lad began to earn his keep, and this should be an excellent chance for him to do so, as my partner is a strict Methody sort of fellow, and understands full well what is required!" Walter smiled as they turned down the hallway toward Phillip's study, "I understand they will be going by canoe to purchase furs and beaver pelts!"

"Here sir, try a little of this calvados! It has considerable power to right many wrongs and rejuvenate the spirit! Have a seat Walter, and let us put the wedding on hold for a few minutes if that is possible."

"God bless you, Phillip! This is just the thing. As to the wedding, I suppose we should talk about a few matters. There is the matter of Katherine's dowry that we have never spoken of. Now, I know that your personal wealth far outstrips anything I could even dream of bestowing upon Katherine. Yet I would not have my only daughter come into her marriage penniless. I am prepared to provide her with an income of four hundred pounds per anum, for her own use, if that is acceptable to you Phillip. Of course, she also has the twenty thousand that you so generously gave her. I have invested it on her behalf and it may give her some additional six hundred a year."

"Sir Walter, whatever you choose is perfectly fine with me. I will bestow a living upon Katherine for her lifetime, of two thousand pounds per year, for her own use absolutely. It will be set apart from the general funds for the running of the estate, and will allow her to have at least certain freedom, should she choose to exercise it. It will be hers from the moment we are wed, with no conditions attached."

"Phillip, that is uncommon generous of you, sir. I hardly know how to respond, except to say that your handsome and open handed nature never ceases to impress one. I hardly need tell you that Charlotte and I are more than delighted in this marriage, and we wish you every happiness in the world! I hope you do not mind, but I have taken the liberty of purchasing a small token of our affection for this event. I have acquired a set of matched Manton pistols that I would very much like you to have. They are being engraved with your coat of arms and will be shipped down from London in a few days."

"Well, thank you indeed. That is most kind, Walter. I will look forward to trying them out, hopefully not in a duel, but Katherine and I can have a great time in target shooting! While we are here and alone, there is something I would like to ask you about on a totally different topic. You are, I believe, somewhat familiar with Prince of Wales Island and George Town. What can you tell me of them?"

"I was only out the one time you understand, most of our trade is in India and Ceylon, but the Spice Islands and the Malaysians are certainly worth trading with, oh yes. George Town was not so very bad, except for the heat. I believe there are somewhat over eight thousand souls living there, many of them Chinese and even Burmese. Good trade, and the place is well fortified with a solid garrison, I believe. Are you thinking of sending your ships out there, then? Going head on against the Company might get a bit prickly, what with their legal monopoly. You certainly would not be allowed into the tea trade, unless you wish to join."

"Actually, it is something else, somewhat akin to our recent efforts in the south Atlantic. It seems there are some pirates becoming quite a nuisance in the Straits of Malacca. The Navy could deal with them, I am sure, but we have been led to believe that the French and Dutch may be using them to hide their complicity in attacking our shipping. Our friends have asked us to consider a voyage to run them to ground and make it less profitable for them to harass our commerce. At the same time, we would be given a free hand to bring back whatever cargo we could carry. We would also be given cargo to carry out to the fort, supplies for the garrison, as well as their pay, which should help to defray our costs. While there, our friends would also like us to help the Sultan of Kedah with some problem he seems to be having with the Burmese army."

"Well, it is a bloody good thing they do not want much! The Burmese can be more than a handful all on their own, never mind the Malay Pirates. I must tell you Phillip, those are total barbarians; they will kill you just for the sport! Yes, I can certainly see why Sir

John would love for you to go and solve another prickly problem for him! The Dutch are really only the French in different uniforms. They have huge holdings south of Penang and are not happy with our presence there. Holland being a virtual French province does not help matters. When do your friends expect you to leave?"

"By September at the latest. I realise that is only ten weeks from now, and it does not give me much time to gather up a crew, get the Onyx ready for sea, and prepare Katherine!"

"Oh, good luck with that, then! Do you propose taking her with you? Charlotte will have a fit if you do, but Katherine will be worse if you do not. It is not a good place to take a white woman, although there are several at least in George Town, and I suppose you could leave her there while you go about chasing pirates. It is a given that they will be based further south at the bottom of the Strait of Malacca, or even around into the Java Sea. More islands than you can check out in five years, and they just keep moving. Best bet would be to find their Dutch or French friends and force them out, or follow them to the Malays! Tough work though, Proas and big bamboo sailed junks most likely. "

"Well, the die is not yet cast. I must talk with Katherine first, and I have told our friends in London that they will have an answer within a week of Sunday. I would be glad for any more advice you might offer; it is not a part of the world I am familiar with. I also would like some advice about how to approach Katherine, if you have any."

"That is easy. Just lock up your guns and explain it from a distance!" Sir Walter laughed uproariously, "Seriously, the last time Katherine paid any attention to anything I said was too long ago to be of any value. No, I think you are on your own, and good luck to you, Phillip. Yet, I would imagine that it could be a very profitable venture. Should you be looking for partners, I might well be interested in making an investment."

"I had not thought on it, but we can discuss it should we go ahead. Well, it is nearly dinner, so I believe I will mull over this until at least tomorrow, but I have now determined to discuss this with Katherine before the wedding, in spite of every piece of advice I have received to the contrary. Somehow, it does not seem fair to marry the dear girl and then tell her, what? Walter if there are any names or connections you might have in India or Penang I would appreciate very much..."

"Oh, of course, and certainly I will be delighted to help where I can. We have quite a few people with Percy Newcomb, our partner in Madras, and I can give you some names for George Town. Our offices in Madras can help you with goods for the Island and Butterworth in the Straits Settlement, although if you are carrying supplies from the government you may not require much in that way. I would advise you Phillip, that you have a commodity right here in Devon that will certainly be worth carrying, and that is your wool! The Indians will pay you a very good price indeed for woolen fabric or even bales. You also own several tin mines, I understand, and tin in India will fetch a fine price, for the Dutch have sewn up the great mine at Muntok, and it is effectively closed to our trade. You could double your money, especially since you already own the tin at a discounted price! In Calcutta, the main trade item will be opium for the China market, but you will have to deal with the Company to acquire it, as they have the growing all sewn up. At George Town you can find pepper and spice coming back to India or even England, and of course rice, but I doubt that would interest you. Trading opium into China requires some finesse as it is technically illegal, but you will be able to trade for silks at a very good rate and bringing back the silks and porcelain will make you a fortune in one trip. I have connections if you should decide to send Celeste all the way to Canton. In fact, Percy might even be persuaded to join, as he seems to relish those trips. I would suggest, Phillip, that once you have made a determination that you are going to make this voyage, we should talk further before Charlotte and I return home."

Phillip could not wait any longer, and excused himself to find Katherine, who came rushing down the stairs the minute she heard that he was back in the house.

"When did you arrive back? I did not know, or I would have come down at once!" She exclaimed, smiling broadly as Phillip wrapped his arms around her.

"Oh, I have been here for some time visiting with your father! I thought you were too busy with your mother for me to interrupt!"

"You Sir, are terrible! I rode all this way and you prefer the company of my father! Phillip Hollis, you simply must apologise at once!" To quiet her, Phillip simply kissed her soundly, which seemed to work nicely.

"Phillip must we wait until Sunday?" the breathless girl asked softly.

"I am afraid so, since everyone is invited. It would look quite strange should they arrive to find us already married! Tomorrow morning, though, we are going to take a picnic to the stream over by the west pasture and have some time to ourselves, and I care not what anyone thinks of it!"

Katherine smiled back, her eyes bright. "Why not leave before breakfast? That way I will not need to explain anything, not that mother will mind; she is nearly as excited about this wedding as I am! Father already has been talking about how proud he is of his son-in-law for weeks. I believe I am just a commodity after all, to link my family to you, the savior of the Chapley family! According to father you are 'the one man who could tame their ungovernable daughter.' Can you, do you think?"

"Oh Katherine, I have no desire to tame you! I love you just as you are! You and I are not like those denizens of Mayfair, who are so enamored with conformity and bound by its conventions! We will build a life for ourselves that suits us. And one where you will never be asked to be tame at all! I promise you!"

"Oh Phillip!" Katherine wrapped her arm around Phillip and kissed him with such passion that he was nearly bowled over.

Pulling back, she smiled at him. "I believe I should go up and prepare for dinner, before we consummate this marriage three days early in your front hall!" With that, she was gone. Phillip decided that a walk in the garden would be a very good idea before dinner. Perhaps it would return his heart to some semblance of a normal rhythm. On the way he would see Bob Thornton and arrange for two horses to be readied first thing in the morning. Oh, and stop by the kitchens to ask for food to be packed up as well. A bottle of Hock, of course, and some fruit, berries perhaps, and oh Mrs. Wilmark would know what to do!

As he stepped out into the garden, he nearly ran into his mother and Aunt Anne, who were just returning from a stroll of their own. Aunt Anne immediately wrapped her arms around Phillip, giving him a warm hug. "That portrait of Desmond is wonderful! I just sat and cried; it was so like him! Thank you Phillip, I hardly know what to say. How did you do it?"

"Well, I did not do it all on my own! Actually Uncle Desmond helped quite a bit. You see, he had begun sitting for the portrait last winter; it was to be a surprise for you. I just got to complete it and had this large second one made for the great hall. The slightly smaller original version will be waiting for you when you return to London!" Phillip beamed down on his aunt. This had been exactly the response he hoped for. Looking up, he saw his mother smiling up at him and slightly shaking her head, as if in disbelief at her son. That look was worth everything!

Dawn was still pink in the eastern sky when Phillip walked over to the stables to fetch the horses. Willie Church was waiting for him with Baxter, his big red hunter, and a large creamy grey mare, with black mane and tail, and with a lattice work of black lines etched across her shoulders and rump like some fancy shawl, saddled and bridled. "I haven't seen that mare before Willie. When did we get her?"

"Oh, sir I thought you might as well have her now. She is a gift from all of the estate for Lady Katherine, sir! Mr. Cobb had Bob go up to Exeter and fetch her. She is five years old and a jolly good jumper. I believe she will keep up with Baxter quite well. I do hope Miss Katherine will like her sir!"

"Willie, Katherine will love her! My, what a lovely thing she is too! Thank you Willie, thank everyone! I am sure Katherine will thank you as well." Phillip led the two horses back around to the rear door of the house, where Mrs. Wilmark was waiting with a large basket, which Phillip tied to Baxter's saddle.

Just then, Katherine stepped out and the sun cleared the horizon! It was one of those strange, serendipitous moments, when just for a second, time seemed to stand still. The dazzling rays of streaming sunshine lit Katherine's face as she looked up from under a dark red bonnet, the very bonnet the sailors on Onyx had created for her. It was matched by a red and creamy parchment dress that brought out the color of her hair and of her complexion, and Phillip was in awe! Mrs. Wilmark smiled knowingly and retreated into the house.

"What a lovely horse Phillip! I cannot remember seeing a finer." Katherine smiled as Phillip led her to her mount.

"It is your very own! I only found out this morning, but it is a gift to you from the staff of the estate! I just realised that I do not even know her name. Perhaps we can stop by the stable and ask Willie."

"This lovely thing is mine? Oh goodness, Phillip, I am amazed. She is just gorgeous, like a duchess in grey silk and fine lace! Let us go and find Willie at once; I must have her name!"

They mounted and walked the horses across the yard to the stables, where Willie Church and Bob Thornton were both waiting, smiles on their faces. "Well Sir, that looks mighty fine, if you don't mind me saying!" said Bob with a grin.

"Oh, Mr. Thornton, thank you ever so much, she is a thing of matchless beauty! Can you tell me her name?"

"Oh yes, her name is Lacy. Did Willie forget to tell you?"

The first stealthy hints of warmth were creeping in as the sun continued its stately ascent and the riders cantered over the middle meadow amiably distancing themselves from the Manor, enroute to the south pasture and the stream hidden in the willows and elders. "I cannot guarantee any flowers this late in the season, but the butterflies should still be around in some numbers, and the dragonflies are always hovering over the little pond that forms in a bend of the stream."

Katherine just smiled back at Phillip, her heart full. Could life with this man really be the dream she was living? Would he really be content to have a wife who had her own ideas and wanted to learn very practical things, and be as independent as possible? Perhaps, at least for a while, he had told her so only yesterday. The power of the big mare underneath her was palpable and, with no warning to Phillip, she released her and began to really fly! The ground became a blur beneath Lacy's flying hooves as she reached her stride. Katherine carefully tightened her grip on the reins and leaned forward, lost in the exhilaration of the beautiful horse beneath her. Looking up, she was startled to see that there was a fence approaching very rapidly, and, just momentarily, Katherine became unsure of her proper course. Before she had time to consider, the big mare was airborne, and the fence gracefully passed beneath them.

Phillip had been taken totally unaware when suddenly Katherine had leaped ahead and began a mad dash across the meadow. For a moment, he was content to watch her let the big mare run, but Baxter was having none of it, and Phillip gave the gelding his head. He was beginning to catch the fleeing mare when he saw Katherine leap the fence and then begin to bring the mare back under control. Baxter cleared the fence easily, and in a matter of minutes he was back alongside the mare. Phillip was about to make a remark about Katherine giving him some notice, and warning her about holes in the fields, when he saw a look of apprehension cross her face, and instead he just smiled.

"That was a good run; she is a fine and smooth jumper no doubt of that! My guess is she was raised as a hunter. Did she surprise you?"

"Just a little, I must admit. I am sorry if I surprised you as well Phillip. It just seemed to come over me that she wanted to run!" Katherine blushed most prettily.

"Well, as long as we don't open the wine in our lunch box too soon there will be no harm done! Right now, I believe we might be wearing it. The stream is just over beyond that copse of willow at the bottom of the pasture. I believe Matthew has some sheep in this pasture, so we may have to look out for them, but they will most likely be alongside the rail fence on the west side. Come, let's cut across to the east and find a place in the sun on that hillside up near those elm trees. We can find shade near the brook later when it gets hot."

"How far does your land go, Phillip?"

"It is our land now, darling. Well, from the manor house, which is at the very south end, nearly overlooking the Channel, to the far north corner it is now a bit over five miles, about one mile from the manor, the land drops down west to the estuary behind Teignmouth, where Carentan House sits. The estate borders on Bishopsteignton, goes around to the northwest, and on the west goes to the main road from Exeter to Kingsteignton and Newton Abbot. In all, I suppose it covers perhaps some fifteen square miles. Then, there is another tract of slightly smaller size, to the west near the border with Cornwall, where we have mostly sheep, and some tin mines. I am somewhat embarrassed, but I have never even seen the mines! My uncle opened them while I was at sea, and as he died just when I arrived home, well, there really has been no opportunity. Perhaps we could drive down some time later in the summer."

"I think I would like that. There is so much that I do not know. I want very much to be a good wife to you, Phillip, but I am afraid that I do not even know where to begin! My mother has been giving me endless instruction these past weeks, trying, I suppose, to make up for everything I refused to listen to until now! Yet, I feel as though I am back at sea, not knowing a sextant from a binnacle! How many people work on the estate?"

"On the entire estate, do you mean, or just the house? The house and garden staff, including Bob and Willie in the stable would be perhaps fifteen, and then there are the tenants on the estate, and the people at Carentan House, and those at the West house. I really do not know. I suppose maybe another hundred, plus their wives and children. We could ask Sam; he would know to the last infant, I imagine."

"What on earth will I do with such a staff to contend with, an estate that covers nearly thirty square miles, with that huge house, and gardens and, and everything?" Katherine looked bewildered and about to panic.

"Here, let's climb down and walk for awhile." Phillip put his arm around Katherine as she led Lacy. "Katherine, no one expects you to have to take charge of anything! You certainly may, if it is what you choose to do, and no one will gainsay you. Aunt Anne left the running of the house to Mrs. Wilmark, and she will be happy to help you with anything at all. The running of the estate is largely in Samuel Cobb's hands, with William to aid him, and even I do not interfere in that. You may do anything you like, or you may do nothing at all. You have only one obligation, and that is to be my wife! I do hope that does not overwhelm you."

Katherine stopped and turned to face him. "Dear Phillip, as I so brazenly said last evening, I am fully ready to be your wife! That is not the role I fear, in spite of mother's warnings about the nature of a man's appetites!" She looked Phillip fully in the eyes and smiled broadly.

"Kate, be careful or you will yet tempt me beyond endurance! Your father thinks me a gentleman, and I would not despoil his only daughter before she reaches the alter! Still, three days does seem a long time." Phillip leaned in and kissed Katherine, only to have her wrap her arms around him and fully return the embrace.

It was mid-afternoon and the remnants of their lunch lay scattered around them on a blanket in the shade of a large willow. Two pairs of bare feet cooled themselves in the brook as they sat companionably on a branch hanging over the water.

"Katherine, there is something I would discuss with you. It concerns our future and is of some importance, I think."

She looked over at him questioningly, "You are not trying to find a way to ask me about having your children are you? I have already told you. I am fully ready to be your wife. I assumed that would include giving you an heir, perhaps, if we are fortunate, several!"

"No, it is not that, although that is also of importance, especially to mother and Aunt Anne! No, what I wanted to discuss is that my friends in London have asked me to embark upon another mission for the government, rather like this last one, although of greater duration. It seems that we have some difficulty in the Far East; Prince of Wales Island, to be exact, and they would value my intervention. I have not given them an answer! I informed Sir John that I could not, before discussing it with you. You see Kate; it could be two years, perhaps more."

Katherine looked at Phillip questioningly. "I am not sure quite what you are asking me. If you are asking if I would consent to joining you on such a voyage, and leave this beautiful place behind, then my answer, dear Phillip, is that I would go with you to the end of the world. If you are asking me to give you my blessing to marry me this Sunday and then to prepare to sail out of my life in a matter of weeks, I do not know! I want to be a good wife, but how can I be that if we are apart for years? I want to spend my life with you, Phillip. I will give myself to you right here and now on that blanket with no regrets, but to have you leave, so soon?"

"Katherine, I have been struggling with this question for weeks. Please hear me out and do not despair! At first, I told our friends that I was not at all interested, but they have persisted and I must now give them an answer within ten days. I am afraid for your safety on such a mission, for there are pirates that we must confront, and they are deadly. However, in talking with your father yesterday he suggested that there is a decent town being built up at George Town, around Fort Cornwallis, and it might be possible to have you stay there while the more dangerous portion of the voyage is undertaken. That way, we could sail together and I could still hopefully keep you safe. The thing is, you know how limited we are on Onyx for accommodation; we could not take many servants. Perhaps Angeline if she is coming with you, and Carter of course, but nothing much more than that."

"What do I care for servants? I will share your cabin and your bed; that is enough for me. We will share sunsets in the foremast crosstrees, and now I will know where we are going when we are walking on the quarterdeck! Will we go alone, or will Emerald or Ruby accompany us?"

"I have not yet spoken with George or Patrick, but I believe that we would take two ships for certain. Perhaps Celeste and Emerald would go on ahead and we could meet them. I would leave Natalie and James here to help run the estate, perhaps, if it is what he wishes."

"Oh it is too sad that they would not be with us on one of your ships! Then we could visit back and forth, and who knows, in two years there could well be children born! Natalie and I could help each other!"

"Oh my! That is something I had not thought of at all! Do you not think it would be too dangerous? I mean having a child in that tropical heat and caring for it on board a ship? What if there were complications? What about a wet nurse, a midwife? We have none of those things aboard ship! No, that would not do at all."

"Phillip, the only way to ensure that I, or Natalie, does not become with child is to have us sleep in separate quarters! I do not think James would approve, even though you seem so determined to keep me pure!"

"Kate, again you are tempting me! My concern for your chastity ends resoundingly on Sunday! I will make no arrangements for us to travel together for two years in separate quarters!"

"Phillip, please believe that I am more than happy to hear that. It does raise a question, though. All those men aboard ship, well, they are in enforced abstinence. How will they feel about your having your wife on board with you? Will it not create difficulties for you?"

"Actually there are many private captains who travel with their wives and families, even some in the Royal Navy, although that is frowned upon by the Admiralty. Certainly, it is a reminder to the men of what they are missing, but if handled well, it is not impossible. The other thing is that you will be, as of Sunday, a Countess of the realm. That title, while of no great consequence to us, perhaps, will be a mark of great honor to the seamen aboard Onyx. They will hold you in their hearts like a talisman. Mark my words."

"Phillip"

"Yes, Katherine"

"Just kiss me."

Riding back to the manor, Phillip told Katherine about the wager he had made with James regarding Natalie, and they both enjoyed it again. "Do you believe he would really do that? I mean burn all her clothes except one shift?"

"I doubt that he will actually burn them, James is much too frugal. Lock them up in a chest in the barn more likely, but that he would tell her they were burned, well, he is determined to cure her of her fashion fever. I must admit that my hope is that he does go through with it! That woman needs a reminder of where she belongs!"

"Oh, and would you do that to me?" Katherine asked with eyebrows raised in mock indignation.

"Well, not exactly, no." Phillip responded.

"What do you mean, not exactly?" Katherine asked, still pretending to be offended.

"Well, for one thing, I would not leave you a shift!" Phillip laughed.

Katherine blushed and looked ahead for a moment, then turned back to Phillip. "Well sir, you confound me! You had your chance this afternoon to steal my honor and you distained my offer. Now, you would have me parade about without as much as a shift? Really sir, what sort of marriage am I entering into?"

"One, I hope, that will be endlessly enjoyable, amusing, and never boring!"

"I have no doubt in my mind concerning the boring part at any rate. How many brides are offered a wedding trip half way round the world to chase pirates? It is not exactly a tour of the continent."

CHAPTER FIVE
Adjustments

The wedding went off without a hitch. James, George, and Patrick were all dressed in Naval Officer's uniforms, and the ladies looked lovely. Lunch was served on the lawn, and half of Teignmouth came to pay their respects. Between Charlotte, Anne, and Caroline, there were enough tears shed to start another fountain, although all professed to be delighted. Phillip made one attempt to steal away with George Fielding and Patrick Morrissey, to tell them of the proposed voyage, but Katherine was having none of it. "Tomorrow dearest, you may have a little time to yourself! A little, but today you are mine alone! George and Patrick will not be gone so soon, and there will be ample time to discuss the ships and our plans. Today, you are alive to serve only one function, and that will have nothing to do with them."

It was well after noon on Monday when Phillip crept down the stairs to find George, Patrick, Ross, and James about to leave for a ride over to the estuary to examine the newly refurbished Emerald. Baxter was soon saddled and the five comrades departed in high humor, with many jibes at Phillip's rather late appearance. On the way, the subject of the voyage was avidly discussed. The pros and cons of having two or even all four ships away from England for up to two years while they were just beginning their commercial enterprise, was weighed against the potential profit of such a venture, bringing back pepper and spices, and perhaps even silks from the China market. Ruby's modifications and final outfitting would be complete in four or five weeks. Emerald, of course was ready to sail at any time, as was Celeste for whom a cargo for Cape Town was even now being finalized along with several passengers. George hoped to have them ready to sail from London in two weeks, and the close bond between the three captains ensured an efficient and harmonious start to Hollis & Company Shipping. The men enjoyed the inspection, and even more the camaraderie of being together again around a glass of brandy in the captain's cabin.

Of the five men, Patrick, as usual was the most exuberant, while George, normally the quietest, was finding his place, both as the foil to Patrick's humour, but also as the solid and pragmatic leader among the three active captains. George was planning to take the mail coach up to London from Teignmouth to visit his family before Patrick would bring the Emerald up to take on passengers and freight. The Celeste, in the meantime, under Ross Day, would be loading cargo in Plymouth. She would carry both wool and tin, as well as lumber, to Cape Town and Madras. Ultimately, she would also carry the passengers that would be picked up in London. Then, Patrick would sail back to Plymouth with George, and take over the last fitting out of Ruby. By the time the officers had returned to their horses to ride back to the manor, the decision was forming to take all four ships east in a bold stroke to fight the pirates, or their French and Dutch backers, and to hopefully deal with the Sultan of Kedah. In the meantime, the Celeste would be loaded with goods for England, or perhaps together with one of the brigs, make the journey to China with opium and tin to trade for silks, porcelain, and jade. Being the only one who was not included in the plans, James remained somewhat quiet and, Phillip thought, slightly wistful.

On the way back, Phillip asked James when he planned on taking Natalie home to West House, as everyone still called it. James just smiled but would not be drawn into that conversation at all.

Over dinner on Monday night, Aunt Anne and Caroline announced that they were going back to London the following day, in order, they insisted, to give the newly-wed couple the run of the house, and to be back in London in time for some important social event they were loath to miss. James announced that he and Natalie would be leaving in the morning as well, but for West House, which he announced they were going to rename "the Indies" because it had been while James was in the West Indies with Phillip that he had begun to write to Natalie, and she to him. This announcement clearly took Natalie by surprise, but she had the good grace to accept it calmly, at least at the table, which Phillip suspected was James' plan all along. With the ladies returning to London so quickly, it was decided that George would accompany them rather than take the public coach. The Chapleys were in no great hurry to leave, and Phillip was happy to keep them a few more days so that he might gain more information from Walter.

The happy couple were most noted by their absence in the following days, but together with Walter and Charlotte they made an afternoon carriage ride to Newton Abbot just for a view of the scenery. During the ride, the voyage was fully discussed and over Charlotte's considerable reservations it was decided finally that they would certainly go ahead. This gave Phillip the freedom to begin the work of gathering a crew and preparing the Onyx for sea. Walter offered to accompany them, but Charlotte would have none of that. In lieu of his presence, Walter offered to write letters to all his contacts and his partner, Percy Newcomb, in Madras, and Phillip offered Walter a share in the voyage for all his help.

Meanwhile, over at the Indies, things were not going quite as sublimely. The ride over from the Manor had been mostly quiet, with Natalie allowing that a few weeks in the country would not be so bad, if James insisted. James refused to respond to her supplications, saying only, "We are going home."

Upon their arrival, James asked Natalie what she proposed to do to help turn the house into their home, as he was preparing to do some work on the barn and stable, and perhaps later in the summer, he thought he might have cobbles brought in to pave the front drive. He thought she might enjoy sewing up some new curtains for the front sitting room, as the existing ones were quite dark and heavy looking, or perhaps she would like to work in the garden and help the gardener with the flowers and weeding. Her reaction was not unexpected; while she had watched her mother do all of those things, she had no desire to follow suit! She might do some needlework, she thought, and read. Perhaps she would go for rides in the carriage or on horseback to see Phillip and Katherine.

It would not do. James took her by the hand and marched her up to their bedchamber. Here he sat her down. "Natalie, I love you dearly and I am delighted that you are my wife, but I will not allow you to waste your life with frivolous behavior and your wretched addiction to fashion. This house is our home and here we will live. I will not be a tenant in your brother's house in London, and nor will you. Now, you will please change into a plain shift and come out to the garden, and help with the work that needs to be done!"

"No, I will not, James. I also love you sir, but I am not a servant, and I will not become one!"

"Natalie, you have exactly ten minutes to be changed and downstairs, or I will come back up and change you myself! This is not a negotiation, nor will it be! You are my wife and you have promised to obey me as your husband, so now we will see if your vows were meaningful!" Without another word, James strode from the room and descended the stairs. After a brief stroll around the grounds, he returned to the house to see if his wife was yet to be seen, which she was not. Retracing his steps to the bedroom, he found the door locked. He thought of his bet with Phillip and smiled in spite of his frustration with his wife.

"Natalie, either you can open this door, or you can wait while I go and fetch an axe to cut it down. If I have to cut it down, I promise that I will use a portion of the wood to paddle your backside, and I am not in jest!"

"You would not dare! You would not strike your own wife!" Natalie called from behind the door, clearly concerned now.

"Open this door and you will not have to find out," James responded evenly.

He heard the click as the lock was sprung, then listened to the sound of Natalie's feet crossing the room. James reached out and opened the door to see Natalie sitting on the bed, still dressed in the same satin dress she had worn on the ride from the manor. She had a determined look in her eyes, but was clearly uneasy.

"Take your clothes off!"

"James, I think this is hardly the time." Natalie tried her utmost to look both enticing and slightly offended.

"Natalie, take your clothes off or I will take them off of you. Now, where is there a simple shift you can wear to the garden?" James began opening wardrobes and taking out dresses only to drop them on the floor. "James, stop! You will ruin them! Please you must not drop those dresses. They are of the finest material!" James paid her no heed and continued to search for a plain frock he could put on her. Finally, in the bottom of a chest, he found just the thing; a sleeveless summer frock of cream colored cotton with buttons down the front.

"Here this will do nicely. Have you not yet started to take those clothes off? Natalie, I will help you, but you may not like it!"

"I will not wear that horrid old thing! It is from before Mother and I went to London; I used to wear it in summer when I was just a girl! It is ugly and old."

James calmly walked across the room and placed his hands in the front neckline of her satin dress. "I gave you more warnings than you deserve!" He brought both hands down in a quick jerk and the front of Natalie's dress came with them. "Now, I will sit right here on the bed while you get these clothes off and put that dress on. Then, you will go out to the garden to work until I come for you." Natalie stood still, shaking like a leaf. Slowly, she began to disrobe and then she walked over to pick up the offending cotton dress. With quiet sobs, she began to put the dress on.

"What else must I do?" she asked between sobs.

"I have already told you. This afternoon you will work in the garden, because you would not choose some other worthwhile occupation for your time. Tomorrow, I will give you other choices, or you may suggest something that you might prefer. I would also suggest you find some more practical shoes. Those fancy slippers are not likely to last long in the garden."

Natalie began to walk around the room picking up her gowns. "No, leave them! I told you to go to the garden and that is where I want you. Now go!"

As soon as she was gone, James began to gather up all the silk and satin gowns, and carry them from the room. Next, he returned and fetched all Natalie's fancy petticoats and under things. Finally, he gathered up her prettiest shoes and hats. Then, he went to the barn to begin his work of fixing some trim boards he had noticed were loose above the door. After an hour of hammering, it dawned on him that Natalie would need more than one simple dress. He saddled a horse and riding round the front yard, left for Bishopsteignton to find a bolt of plain cloth that Natalie could use to sew herself an extra work dress.

When James returned, it was already early evening, but Natalie was still out in the garden working with the flowers and weeding the beds. James walked over to invite her in for dinner. She formally assented and asked whether she would have time to bathe and change her clothes. "It will just be the two of us for dinner," he responded. "I have already dismissed the servants for the evening, and the cook has left us dinner in the kitchen, so we might as well eat as we are." Turning on his heel, James walked toward the house, fighting to keep himself from sweeping her up in his arms. He could not back down now, or this was all in vain and Natalie would be spoiled forever.

They ate silently in the dining room, neither of them wanting to begin another round of hostility. After dinner, Natalie excused herself and went up to their room. James returned to the kitchen and began to heat water on the great stove. When he had a large pail heated, he carried it up to their room and began to fill the porcelain tub in the corner. It took him three trips, but the tub was filled. All that time Natalie lay in the bed, her back to him, still in her cotton dress.

"Come and bathe, my dear. The water is hot and you are dirty." She looked at him then, with tears in her eyes.

"Where are all my lovely clothes? What have you done with them? Am I truly to be a servant here?"

"Your clothes are safe enough, my dear. You will have them all back, when you earn them. You are not a servant, but neither am I your servant, and if we wish to make this house into a good home to raise a family, we need to be about getting it ready. That means we will, both of us, be busy for a time working to create a home. While we are at it, we will work to create a marriage, not just a game of dolls and dress up teas. You are now my wife. I warned you before you married me that I wanted a wife and a home, children and a comfortable living if we could afford it. You agreed, do you remember?"

"Yes, of course I remember. But that was before. Before you and Phillip got all that prize money; we don't need to do all that now. We are well off. You said so yourself!"

"Yes, we are, Natalie, but at the rate you have been spending, and with your ideas of a lifestyle, we will not be for long. We do not have anything near the resources that your brother has, and even he does not live like you seem to feel you should. Phillip warned me, Natalie, but I would not listen, because I love you! Well, I love you too much to watch you waste your life. This ends today. Now, come and bathe. I do not want you in our bed in your present condition, and yes, it will still be our bed, and I do want you in it."

The next day went better, and by late afternoon of the third day, Natalie came around to the barn to see what James was doing with the trim boards and with repairing the door. By Thursday morning, Natalie was making suggestions over breakfast for improvements to the front porch and asked about material to change the front curtains. Shortly before lunch, Natalie found James in the stables, talking with Ferguson, the handy man and gardener, who doubled as the groom. "James may I intrude for just a moment? I believe I have come upon a possible idea for the front curtains."

"Of course my dear, what is it?" James smiled back at her, delighted that things were going as well as they had, yet wondering when the next crisis would occur.

"James, among my dresses, there are, er were two of yellow and green silk material lined with similar colored cloth. If I used the skirts of both dresses, I believe it could make a pair of curtains, and from the bodices I could make ties and trims. It would not cost anything at all, except perhaps for Mrs. Ferguson's help in sewing them up. I could do some of it, but perhaps I will need some help with the cutting and laying out. After all, I will not miss the dresses, will I?"

"The dresses are in a wardrobe in the front guest room. The key for the door is in the left top drawer of my desk in the study. Help yourself! Oh, and Natalie, you may choose one other dress to take back to our room."

Natalie just smiled, "That won't be necessary James, I have nearly completed the dress from the material you fetched me from Bishopsteignton. It will do for the time being."

Friday morning, the Chapleys left for home, and right after lunch, Phillip and Katherine had the horses saddled for a ride to visit James and Natalie. Phillip's curiosity was killing him, and he could wait no longer. When they arrived at the Indies, James was on the front porch with Ferguson, replacing a pillar that had cracked. He waved them over and called into the house to Natalie. "We have visitors, my dear!" Natalie burst out of the front door, wearing only a well-worn, off white, sleeveless cotton dress and simple sandals.

It was clear from the dress that there were no petticoats beneath it, and her head was bare, with her hair pulled back.

"Welcome here! We have been busy, as you can see, or we would have invited you sooner, but I am so glad you have come. Sit on the porch here and I will fetch us some cool lemon tea. James is busy trying to replace that pillar, but he can take a bit of a break I am sure, can't you dear?"

"Of course. Ferguson, give us a few minutes; I will call you when we are ready to continue. If I had known you were coming we would have prepared something for dinner, but as things are we have just been eating on the run as we continue to fix up the house. Natalie is well on her way with new curtains for the parlour. She is making them from two of her gowns. Is that not clever?" James smiled at Phillip.

"I concede. How much is the debt?"

"Well, this is day four, but today is all on her own, so I do not believe it would really count, as I offered her one of her gowns back yesterday as a reward, and she refused."

"I think you two are wretched!" Katherine interjected as she dismounted. Then she smiled at James. "I think you are a very wise and loving husband, who will reap a rich reward for your efforts. Now I must go in and see for myself how these gowns will make curtains!"

On the ride back to the manor Katherine filled Phillip in on all the details she had learned from a secretly delighted Natalie. "Do you know that James tore the dress right off your sister? Then he sat and watched while she had to disrobe and put on only that cotton sundress. She says they have never been happier or, well, more romantic. She is truly happy and she knows James loves her! It is just what she needed, not to be a fancy doll, but a real woman, a woman with a purpose. He has done her a far greater favour than ever he can imagine."

"Ah, are you suggesting that I should rip your dress off as well, then?" Phillip leered at his wife.

"You would not, and besides, you would have to catch me first!" With that, she kneed Lacy and was off across the fields. Phillip sat and watched her run for a moment, then laughed and gave Baxter his head.

Three days later, the idyll ended with the news that George Fielding had been killed in London; run down by a run-away carriage. It appeared he had tried to stop the carriage from hitting a woman and had been dragged beneath the wheels. His family was taking care of the burial. By the time the news reached Devon, it was too late even to go and pay their last respects to a man they had all come to love and respect. He had been the quiet one among the officers that they had assembled for the raid to steal Napoleon's gold. Beneath the quiet and reserve however, had been decisiveness, an iron resolve, and willingness to do whatever was asked of him without question. George would be sorely missed. It would also require a re-thinking of the entire plan for the shipping venture, of which he was a partner, and of the proposed voyage to the Far East.

Phillip sadly rode over to speak with James. He found his good friend sitting on the newly refurbished porch with his wife, sipping tea. Natalie was wearing a nice summery frock, but not the one he had seen last nor a fancy gown from London. The news brought James low. He and George had each captained the nearly identical brigs and had grown quite close.

"What will you do about the voyage?" James inquired after a few minutes of silence.

"I do not know. This is so sudden. I believe I will see if Patrick will take Emerald to Cape Town with Ross and Celeste. He was to take her to London in a few days at any rate, to pick up the passengers and light freight. It will mean I will have to go down to Plymouth to see to the completion of Ruby. I suppose we can readjust and make the voyage with three ships instead of four. If we do, I can use the crew from Ruby to partially crew the Onyx, and put her up for sale. I must first speak with Patrick. They were both my partners, along with Ross now, so it must be his choice as well. If I go to Plymouth, it will be a good time to begin the work of finding a crew and preparing Onyx. I have been idle too long. Unlike you, there is precious little for me to do at the Manor. You have both done remarkably well here. The new curtains are very pretty, Natalie. I am proud of you!"

"Are you really?" Natalie looked up at her brother with sparkly eyes. "Do you know how long it has been since you said that to me?"

"No, but I suspect it has been too long. I am sorry, sister dear. I must admit I was not so proud of you for a time, but that is behind us now, and you are everything a brother could ask for!"

"Thank you, Phillip. That means a great deal to me." Natalie hugged James' arm and smiled deliciously.

"Katherine has asked me to invite you to dinner tomorrow. Patrick will come as well, though Ross is in London. We will make it our very own private wake for George. Say about two bells of the first dog?"

"We will certainly be there."

CHAPTER SIX
Friends in Need...

Just as the five friends were sitting down to dinner, there was a knock at the door and the butler announced someone was asking after Lord Phillip. An elderly gentleman, the butler intoned, but he had no card. Phillip excused himself to find none other than Dick Forest standing at the door.

"My word, Dick, what brings you all this way? Do come in, please. We were about to sit down to dinner. You must join us."

"Sir Phillip, thank you, I will be more than happy to join you if it is not too inconvenient. If you have guests however, I will be happy to await your leisure in the library. I have spent many happy hours there you will recall!"

"Not at all. James is here with Natalie, his wife and my sister. Patrick is with us as well. Have you heard about George?"

"Yes, as it came about, I was with him at the time! It was dreadful Phillip, but it was so typical of George. With no thought for himself, he threw himself at those horses to rescue that poor young lady and her daughter. His last words upon this earth were for you, and that is, in part, why I am here."

"Come in, I believe the others will want to hear you out as well!"

Phillip lead Dick into the dining room to everyone's surprise. Katherine immediately rose from her chair to give the elderly sailing master a huge embrace.

"My dear Mister Forest, it is indeed good to see you. What brings you down to Devon?"

As everyone was seated, Dick Forest told of the last minutes of George Fielding's life. "We were on our way back from lunch, had a grand time. He was so excited about the Emerald being ready and about your proposed trip to the Far East, sir. Couldn't stop talking about it; had been going on for several days! Then the carriage came wheeling round the corner, clearly out of control, and that poor woman and child in the street. Well, George just flew out and grabbed the bridles, but he slipped, you see. There was nothing anyone could have done for him, and he knew it. He asked if the child was all right, then he told me sir, to thank you for the best six months of his life. Then, he was just gone!" Dick looked down at the table for a moment, clearly overcome. "I had to come myself and tell you, sir. Then, you see, I started to think about what George had said, and I realised he had the right of it! The time we spent, on the Onyx, first stealing her, and then that mad dash down to save Lady Katherine, and capturing Celeste and the gold, well it was special sir. That is why I am here to reenlist."

"What are you saying Dick? You are not a young man, and you have more than enough with your prize money to last your lifetime and then some! This is going to be a long haul, not some three month adventure like the last time. We are off to Madras and from there to Prince of Wales Island; it will be near two years if we are lucky!"

"Phillip, hear me out. I am not so old that I cannot still be of service. After all I am still only in my fifties, and I have served both captains and admirals much older, and I have sailed those waters, which is more than any of you can say! Phillip, my wife is gone and I will not remarry. The prize money is well invested as you recommended, and my children and grandchildren will benefit from it for many years, but they have their own lives. I have been at sea for most of the past thirty-five years. I am a stranger to them, even though they treat me well enough. The truth is, they do not need me, and you do! So here I am."

"Well said, Dick!" James spoke up, "While we are speaking of re-enlistment, I should like to offer my services as well! Only it will be our services. You see, Natalie and I have discussed this non-stop since you left, Phillip. If it is agreeable to Patrick, and Ross, and to you, I should like to purchase George's share of Hollis & Company Shipping, and join you, together with Natalie, on this voyage. We are of one mind in this. Natalie understands that I am not ready to sit idly at the farm, and she is not ready to remain behind."

Patrick stood and surveyed the room for a moment. "I suppose I knew George better than anyone in this room. We served together on that bloody Orion, and then came together to serve you, Sir Phillip. George was right. It was the best of times, and I am heartily sorry that he will not be with us on this voyage, but I know for certain that there is no one he would have rather handed his place to than you, James! I most heartily welcome you into the Firm and the voyage!"

Katherine beamed. Phillip looked around and smiled. "You realise Natalie, that it is you who will tell mother of this!" Natalie looked horrified for just a moment, and then she smiled back at her brother. "Yes, I will, and I will remind her that she has told me she should have been with father in India! I am first of all James' wife, and only secondly her daughter. I will go with my husband, and support him in everything he does, and, if I die by his side, it will have been enough!"

"Oh Natalie, that was marvelous! We shall have such an adventure together, and we will be able to lean on each other when we must! I am so delighted that you will join us." Katherine jumped up from her chair to walk over and embrace her sister-in-law.

"James, there are a few details of our arrangements inside Hollis that you should know. Ross has also become a minor partner, with ten percent, while Patrick and George each held one quarter. The other forty percent is mine, and we have made an arrangement whereby we will get a share of all the profits, no matter which ship has provided them. I hope that is satisfactory."

"Of course it is. I am just delighted to be back among the best seamen I have ever sailed with, although I most heartily regret the loss of George Fielding, a man I grew to be more than passing fond of. Say, I have not seen Andy Barg about the place since the day of your wedding. Where has he gone to?" James suddenly asked. "All this talk of another voyage and it just seemed he should be here with us. After all Phillip, your two have been inseparable all these years."

"Andy will be here soon enough. He is presently in London on some errands. Have no fear; he will not allow me to sail without him! He is, I believe, convinced I would not clear the Teign on my own." Phillip laughed and Dick Forest joined in heartily.

"Besides," Katherine smiled, "I rather suspect there may be another reason lurking in this house."

"So," Natalie raised her eyebrows, "Angeline still captivates Phillip's captive burglar?"

"It would seem so! Although I am sure they would both hotly deny it. Yet, Angeline, for all the terrible time she had on our last voyage, has made it very clear that, where I go, she will follow."

Just then, a servant entered carrying a large tureen of soup, which he placed on the long rosewood sideboard, and began ladling bowls. Dick looked hard at the man, who had a queue tied back with a black velvet ribbon, and wore black trousers, with a white frilled shirt and a light blue jacket. On his feet were highly polished black shoes with gold buckles. As he turned to bring the first two bowls to the table, Dick laughed and slapped the table. "Well, my stars, and I hardly recognised you Carter! You do look a proper steward now. I believe Lady Katherine has done a world of good for you. Perhaps, if I stay about for a time, she may even gentrify me!"

"Oh, I doubt that sir!" Carter tried to keep up his stonily firm demeanour, but could not quite manage, as everyone around the table had a hearty laugh at Dick's expense.

"It is at least good to see the change is only external; the same rogue resides beneath the clothes!" Dick responded.

Over a dinner consisting of leek and potato soup, roast chicken with sprigs of fresh cut thyme, asparagus drizzled with Italian olive oil, fresh peas and baby onions, curried lamb over a bed of rice with fresh buttered cabbage, and finally, a plum and orange custard, the talk was of reminiscences of George, of the shipping company, and the upcoming voyage to the east.

James asked Patrick about his crew, and who his officers were. "Well, now I am taking George's ship, I will take his crew as well. My first will be none other than Wallis Foster, whom you remember, we got off the Triton. He never quite got around to re-signing with the Navy when we got back, but did not relish life ashore, either, so when he heard of our plan, he signed on! You will also know the first on the Ruby, James, for he is our old ship-mate Terrance Bernard. Of course, you know that Ross has the Celeste!"

"Ross, yes of course, why is he not here with us? Where is he now?"

"I am not quite sure, but he is to meet me in Plymouth in two weeks' time. I believe he went up to London to visit some friends in the meantime. His two mates, Fischer and Speaks are with the ship in Plymouth getting the last of the cargo into the holds. I believe he has also found a seasoned master."

"Do you know his name at all?" asked Dick.

"I believe the name is Hutchins, Mr. Forest."

"Not Billy Hutchins, out of the old Triumph?" Dick Forest looked truly impressed. "And you thought I was old! Bill Hutchins certainly has me beat, but I will say this; if it is Billy, a better sailing master for the seas east of the Cape you will not find."

"I believe you have the right fellow, Dick, for he is not a young man certainly, and Ross thinks very highly of him." Patrick answered.

"Tell me, Sir Phillip, is Mr. Andrews, your clerk, rejoining us as again as well?" asked Dick Forest.

"No, he has moved into London and has begun to study law! The sea has lost a good clerk only to add to the ill of more solicitors!"

"I am going to be Phillip's clerk!" Katherine exclaimed. "Before you argue with me dear, let me explain. I have a good head for figures; Mr. Forest can verify that. I enjoy working with numbers, and I write more than passably well. It will give me a reason for being aboard, and you and I will get to work together! Also, as we do not have a purse man, I can check supplies, and be useful in keeping the wages and helping with purchasing goods! You can teach me!"

"Katherine, first of all, it is purser, and the responsibilities you are undertaking are huge! You do not comprehend what is all entailed in this." Phillip argued.

"I think that she has an excellent idea." interjected Patrick. "She is correct about so much of it. As Dick says, she has an excellent head for numbers, and she can certainly keep up your ledgers. The only point where I agree with you, Phillip, is that crawling around the hold checking water butts and salt beef barrels is not perhaps the proper domain for a Countess of the Realm, but as far as the rest, it is a great idea."

Dick smiled, "I think we can surely find helpers to do the actual physical checking of stocks for Katherine."

Natalie looked up at James. "Can I do that for you, do you think? I would gladly be useful and my writing is presentable. I am not so very sure about my numbers, but I would be willing to learn and try! After all, I cannot very well spend my time in the garden weeding on board ship, now can I, and our agreement is that we will both contribute what we can to our marriage. Katherine, can you perhaps help me learn before we sail?"

"Of course. You could ride over here several days a week, and we could spend time with Andy Barg or Mr. Forest getting acquainted with what is involved and practise sums and learn about what sorts of supplies to purchase."

James looked over at Phillip and shrugged. "We have to feed them anyway; they might as well save us two other mouths to feed and house!"

It was further decided that Patrick would take the Emerald to London and, in George's stead would sail her as Celeste's escort to Cape Town. If he could find a cargo there, he would continue on to India, and the four ships would meet up in Madras. With decent weather, if they could be ready to sail by early September, they could make Madras by late January. Of course, Emerald would have a six week head start, but she would have to spend at least a week or two in Cape Town, quite possibly more. Phillip had the name of a good shipyard in Madras and he intended to bring each of the ships in to have their bottoms cleaned and copper checked. Also, if Patrick and Ross arrived in time, he planned to have entire sets of light sails made up in India, where the cost was a fraction of that in England, and where sails could be made up in a very short time. Patrick would have dimensions and lists for each ship, as well as the names of two good sail makers in Madras and Calcutta, in case he found a cargo for that west coast port.

"Phillip, if Patrick is leaving for London in only a few days' time, who is going to Plymouth to supervise the completion of the Ruby? I know you told us you would go, but if she is to be my ship, I think Natalie and I should be the ones to go. It will give her a chance to see where we will live, and she can perhaps make some little changes that will make her more comfortable."

"Oh Phillip, could we not all go?" Katherine enthused, "It would give Natalie and I much more time to prepare together, and you would be able to begin recruiting a crew. Mr. Forest could come as well, and as soon as Andy returns from London, he could meet with us."

"As for me, I must return to London. There is much to do there before we leave, and I have a little recruiting to do as well." Dick smiled at Phillip. "I have already taken the liberty of speaking with Dr. Cluff. I believe he would welcome another voyage, as might Mr. Curtis! I must also see to finding charts, especially of the Strait of Malacca, which is notorious! Fortunately, I have a very good friend in the Company who will be delighted to help me for a small favour or two. I have no fear for you, Lady Katherine. The log books from our last voyage are right here in the library, and if you examine them, you will find much of what you seek in terms of the amount of various supplies required, the cost of goods in various ports, the amount of spoilage, and so on. If you share them with Mrs. Peters, I am certain you will come out right."

"Katherine, your idea of us all moving down to Plymouth for a time may have merit. Certainly I agree with your assessment James, that you and Natalie should move down and take charge of completing Ruby. Dick, as to the charts, Sir John has promised me a plain copy of the best that the East India Company has! That should save you some time and effort. You will no doubt be able to pick them up at their offices on Leadenhall Street. Do you wish to consider switching ships, Patrick? I know that George insisted he would rather sail the fast and manoeuvrable Emerald to Celeste, even though she is much larger and roomier."

"I am of the same mind. Ross can gladly have the extra space. It is rather like choosing between a frigate and a seventy-four. The two-decker has the prestige, but the frigate has the fun!" Patrick smiled waving his hand depreciatingly, and turned to James, "As you know, we own the ships together, and we agreed that Ross had the most experience on a large ship like Celeste. The fact that George was to have Emerald was done by lots between us. I actually like her raised quarterdeck; I am sure James will miss it! Although, I will admit that the flush deck on Ruby does make working the sails and guns easier. No, we will all be together again, and that is the main thing. We will endeavour to reach Madras in good time so that we have the sails in hand and have Emerald and Celeste out of the shipyard, as I do not foresee that much maintenance will be required in so short a time. We have just re-coppered all three, and all the rigging is in excellent condition. We have plenty of spare spars and even upper masts stowed in the lower hold. George insisted on spare blocks and even a spare bower."

As the evening ran on, the plans became more and more definite. Dick would stay only one day, and that would be holed up in the library helping Katherine and Natalie with the logs, and reading some volumes on the Malay peoples he had discovered on his last visit, that he thought would be useful. Patrick was directly off to Plymouth in the morning, and then to London with Emerald. The best news Patrick had for James was that the crew for Ruby was nearly all set, and included several of the men who had been on her in spring.

James and Natalie stayed for the night and, the next morning, the two couples continued to plan over breakfast. Dick would take information to London for printing handbills to be distributed on the docks and in the various taverns frequented by seamen. Phillip would do the same in Plymouth, and Andy Barg was already in Sheerness, looking up some old comrades and prospects. With the wages they were offering, Phillip had no doubts about finding enough men. The trick would be to find good ones, with no rotten apples in the barrel.

It was nigh mid-morning, with the women ensconced with the sailing master, when a pony and dog-cart came up the front drive. In it, were Pierre and Giselle Doucette, with another offer of help. Giselle begged Phillip to take Pierre with him. She was used to his being gone for long periods of time, and while Pierre had tried very hard to settle in at the house they had purchased, she knew he was not happy. It would, she said, give her the chance to return to France for a time, to visit her family and his. It would also give both of them time to heal from the death of Armand, which still lay like an open grave between them. "Have no fear, Phillip. I love Pierre and he knows it, but he needs this, and I need it as well. Take him with you, I beg you. Save him from himself, and for me!"

Phillip looked at the silent Pierre, who nodded and said softly, "It is so."

"You knew that you would always be welcome, Pierre! Giselle, is there anything we can do for you?"

"You have already done so much! I will be fine, really. I will stay with Pierre until you leave, of course, and then I will return to Normandie for the winter, I believe. If it begins to sound like war will resume, I will return here, so that I will not be trapped in France. This will be our home. When Pierre returns, I will be here waiting for him."

In the final deliberation, it was decided to sail the Onyx over to Plymouth, where they could have her prepared for the voyage while the modifications to Ruby were being completed. Phillip and Katherine rode down into Teignmouth to see about arranging a skeleton crew to sail her down the coast. It would be a short run of perhaps fifty miles, easily sailed in less than a day, and Phillip was sure that enough men could be hired from the town to sail her down. Then, the men could be ferried back on board the Mistress Anne, his late uncle's schooner.

He had not been down to the town for some time, even though it was only a little over a mile from the manor, and he was surprised by the building boom going on. There were at least seven new houses in the process of construction, and he saw a very nice new fishing boat in the harbour, with the name "Our Gold – Teignmouth" on her transom. It turned out that many of the men who had been with them on their spring voyage were using some of their prize money to build new homes and upgrade the fishing fleet. A quick stop at the pub was all the asking Phillip needed to do. The first man he saw was none other than Jeb Winston, the man who had taken James and him to France to scout out the raid on the Clorinde. When Winston learned what Phillip was after, he had only two questions. How many men, and what day?

"Sir Phillip, we will be delighted to sail her over for you. There is not a seaman in Teignmouth who will not volunteer. We can also bring your schooner back, no doubt of that! My guess is we could do it with twenty men, as we will not need to have more than one watch, but I will find thirty in the next two hours, I promise you! When do you think to be ready, sir?"

"I will require one week to load our belongings on her, and I have a few things to prepare at the manor. To be safe, let us say the first good weather day after the twenty-fifth. Is that all right, Mr. Winston?"

"We will be ready, have no fear. Perhaps sir, I might suggest that we bring Onyx into the harbour and you could load her here. It will be easier than ferrying everything out from your little dock in the estuary. Plus it is closer to the manor, as well. There would be no need to sail her. I will get men and we will tow her over. It is not much above a mile from where she sits at anchor now. As I said, sir, we will be happy to do it!"

That was that! Katherine wanted to stop by a few shops while they were in the little town, and she managed to purchase some fabric and several dozen boxes of candles. Everywhere she went, the shopkeepers were delighted to see her and to help with any little thing, even if it was only some advice. It took some time but it finally dawned on Phillip that the financial impact of the prize money on their little community had been staggering. In some way or another, nearly everyone in the village had been affected. Secret or not in the nation, in his home town everyone knew full well that Sir Phillip had brought home enough gold to transform the lives of the entire estuary. Now, there was simply not enough that the people of Teignmouth could do to thank Phillip and Katherine!

CHAPTER SEVEN
Old Foes

Plymouth was unchanged, except that there were fewer Royal Navy ships in the harbour, and many tied up in the deep anchorage, lashed together in several rows like a floating winter forest, masts bare of yards and sails, bleaching in the summer sun. Phillip counted nearly twenty 74's alone, and many more frigates and transports. While it was a sad sight, it also meant that there were a host of men on the beach, and not all of them would have been taken up by merchantmen.

James and Phillip walked over to the dockyard and found the Ruby in a dry-dock slip, and with dockyard workers covering her like ants. Having the Navy laid up was proving a huge incentive to getting the work expedited. Where six months ago they might have waited for weeks for a single bid on the mast modifications, now three separate dockyards were sharing the work. One crew was changing out the yards and rigging, while another was working on the cabin and hold renovations, and a third was finishing up the work on the hull. All the planking had been checked and some pieces replaced. New copper was being laid in place and it looked like she would be ready to float in a very short time.

When the two returned to their inn, just off the harbour, they found two ladies deep in lists and paperwork. Ledgers and sheets of loose paper were on every available surface.

"Phillip, how many men will we have on the Onyx? How long will we be at sea before we can replenish supplies?" Katherine looked up, pen in hand. "I need to know! Do you have any idea how much foodstuffs we shall require? It is mountainous!"

"Yes Kate, I know. We have done this before. As to the crew, I believe we will stay well under our usual component of three hundred and thirty, for that would include a company of marines. Perhaps two hundred twenty would suffice, but we will need more for so long a journey for we are sure to lose some. Also, because our greatest need for manpower will come at the extreme edge of our range, I believe we should plan for two hundred fifty men, and I would be happier with two hundred sixty. We can stop at Praia for supplies, and then again at Cape Town. Our longest time between ports might be forty days or so from Praia to Cape Town. But from Cape Town to Madras is over five thousand miles and we would have to allow at least fifty days, although with good weather it can be done in thirty! We could stop off at Mauritius for water, but the French have control and I would be loath to go into their harbour. To be safe though, we have to allow at least another twenty-five percent! On top of that Katherine, we may not be able to get good meat in Praia, so we will need to have enough salt meat to get to Cape Town, which will be about twelve weeks with a safety margin! Another time as much to get to Madras! The only things we can count on are water and fruit in Cape Verde. You will need to substitute sauerkraut from here, because we won't find enough lemon or lime juice."

Katherine went back to her figures for a few minutes, while the men continued to talk about the final stages of modifying Ruby.

"Well Phillip, using the notes from your last voyage, six weeks of water for Onyx will be eighteen tons, if you really believe it will stay drinkable for that long! To reach Cape Town, we will require 9,000 lbs of salt beef, an equal amount of salt pork, 20,000 lbs of bread and biscuit, plus 1 ton of rice, 4 tons of peas or beans, the same of potatoes or turnips, 1400 gallons of rum, and 3000 lbs of cheese, not to mention molasses, and butter!" Katherine looked exasperated. "Tell me, do we have room for all of this?"

"Yes, there is room. Plus room for gun powder, shot, spare timber and spars, and cloth for sails and clothing for the men! Do you see now what a task you have set for yourself?"

"Natalie and I will need to begin shopping! How long will it take to load all these supplies? When will the ships be ready to begin loading?"

"Hold up there my dear! I will give you a list of merchants who can supply us what we will require, and they will bring the goods out directly to Ruby and Onyx. We must have crew on board to receive everything before we can begin, and we will want to wait with loading, especially water, until just at the last. What you will have to add to your lists though, is the amount we will use up in port. That can be another several weeks in all!"

"I never dreamed it would be so much!" Natalie looked at James, "We will require a great deal as well, enough for seventy men plus the officers. Tell me, how will we have room for carrying the other goods for the soldiers in the fort?"

"Most of that will be in Celeste. Nevertheless, when everything is properly stowed, we can carry a great deal. The hold will be quite full leaving Plymouth, though. That is why everything must be carefully placed in the right order, both for weight and so that we may access it. Here, ladies, let me show you what I mean." James sat down beside the two agitated clerks and began to draw up a diagram of the ship, showing where various things might go, and explaining the problem of weight distribution. In the meantime, Phillip was busy writing down the names of various mercantile houses in Plymouth, and what they might purchase in each.

"Katherine, on our last voyage we had Sam and William Pierce salt down beef and pork for us and it proved vastly better than anything we could get from the usual purveyors, because they started with good fresh animals. I believe that if we gave them time and sent down barrels enough, which we can surely find here, we might be well served to do the same on this occasion. It will also save us the trouble of haggling over meat prices. I believe six tons of each would serve both vessels to Cape Town."

In the afternoon, the couples walked about Plymouth, and the women began to get a feel for what purchasing was like, as opposed to shopping for dresses. Even so, Phillip was surprised at his sister's grasp of what was needed, and she was soon deeply involved, haggling with the clerks and demanding to inspect the quality of each item, outrightly rejecting some that Phillip would have accepted. She would simply turn on her heel if she felt she was being taken advantage of, and march out. After a few hours, it became clear that, while Katherine had the much better grasp of figures and could quickly calculate amounts, it was Natalie who would drive the bargains and demand value for each shilling before she would assent to make a purchase. In one shop, the merchant, after haggling unsuccessfully with Natalie for quite some time, finally, in frustration asked her to name the price that would satisfy her. Without a moment's hesitation, Natalie rattled off a figure that even Phillip thought was very low indeed. The merchant blanched, then blustered about giving his goods away, to which Natalie responded that he could then keep them until the war resumed and he could sell them to the government, if they were not spoiled! After a further moment's remonstrance against women staying in their own world, he agreed to exactly the price she demanded. Katherine beamed!

"James, if the admiralty had your wife to purchase its goods, we could afford to keep half again as many ships at sea. I have never seen the like! Those merchants thought to take advantage of two women, and were nearly skint by the time Natalie was through with them! This may be our secret weapon for the entire shipping company. We shall make her our head purser when we return!"

"These merchants are nothing compared to a London milliner! James, you have no idea what a handful of dedicated London ladies could accomplish with this lot! Why, I have had a much harder time trying to purchase a good piece of lace in Piccadilly off some cart girl than any of these good gentlemen could muster! I believe, Katherine, that we shall do quite well at this. These fellows are so condescending of us poor women that they simply have no chance at all!" Natalie was feeling much more confident, and James and Phillip were happy to watch their master purchaser at work.

Four tired pairs of feet were resting under a table at the Inn, while their owners discussed the amazing progress they had made in one day. Phillip was beginning to realise how much having Katherine as his clerk was going to add to his work load, at least for the foreseeable future, and yet, he also was excited by the prospect.

Suddenly James jumped up from his seat, and without a word nearly ran out the front door. Moments later, he reappeared with Andy Barg and Terrance Bernard in tow. "Look what I have found," he laughed, "and it seems there are more to follow!"

Andy bowed briefly to Katherine, and then smiling at Phillip, he said, "Eighty-six sir, but only this one is with me. I thought to bring him back before he changed his mind! There are a few though, that you will remember, for when the word went out that we were again recruiting, some of our old friends showed up. Elias Grange, Simms, and Potter all came together, and Douglas Harris will come as well."

"Where are they all now? Sitting in London, waiting for wagon rides again?" James asked with a smile.

"Oh no, sir," answered Lieutenant Bernard, "we stopped in Teignmouth and Jeb Winston is taking the schooner up to Sheerness to load many of the seamen there. He also talked about a new boat they had that would accompany him. They should all be down within a week or ten days on the outside, depending on the weather off the Medway."

"I do believe Mr. Winston really does enjoy sailing that schooner." Phillip laughed. "I should probably put him in charge of her."

"I saw the Onyx at anchor when we came up, sir. She is still riding high, so I do not suppose loading has begun. Point me to your clerk and I will begin to arrange for stores to come up." Andy looked at the captain expectantly.

"Well, Mr. Barg, my clerk is right here. Katherine, would you like to tell Andy what you have done so far?" Phillip smiled at his wife, who smiled up at Andy in return.

After a hasty dinner at the inn, the group decided to take a stroll along the dock to check on the progress being made on the Ruby. Phillip paused on the way out to check on rooms for Andy and Terrance, and so he and Katherine were a few steps behind the others as they stepped into the street. They were just about to cross over the street when two disreputable looking men cut in front of them. In a flash, one of the men bumped Phillip while the other grabbed Katherine's purse and attempted to flee. They did not count on Katherine, who, instead of releasing her purse, gave it a sharp tug back, spinning the man about. In a whir, a knife appeared before her face, as the man lunged. Phillip, gaining his balance, threw his arm in front of Katherine just as the knife came down, catching the blade on his outer forearm. The second man was about to close when he suddenly sank to his knees. The first assailant pulled the knife out of Phillip's arm and was about to strike again when James Peters arm went about his neck and lifted him bodily from the pavement. As the man flailed, Terrance Bernard appeared in front of him, a short sword pointed at his chest. Phillip looked down to see blood pouring from his slashed arm onto the prone figure of the second man lying at his feet, the ivory handle of Andy Barg's stiletto throwing knife sticking rigidly from between his shoulder blades. Katherine, seeing Phillip's blood spurting from his arm, suddenly felt very faint. In a moment, Natalie was there beside her, holding her, as a bystander rushed over from the inn to wrap a towel around Phillip's arm.

Shouts sounded in the distance and, in minutes, two constables appeared to take charge of the scene. One man was led away, the other, unceremoniously dumped into a push cart. When the constable was informed who Phillip was, and that there were witnesses to the entire event, his only interest was to help find a doctor, and to escort the party back to their inn.

Sometime later, his arm stitched and bandaged, Phillip was resting with Katherine in their room. "My dear, why did you not simply let the brute have your purse! It was not worth endangering your life."

"Darling, my purse contained all our lists of purchases! Do you have any idea how long it would have taken me to re-create all those notes? Natalie and I would have spent a whole day attempting to remember what we purchased where, and for what prices! No, I could not let those beastly men have our papers. I am only sorry that you were hurt, Phillip. Do you suppose that in future I should carry a weapon?"

Phillip looked at her incredulously and then began to laugh. The more he laughed, the more indignant Katherine became. She was about to begin the argument in earnest when there was a knock at the door, and Andy Barg peaked in. With a wave from Phillip, he was followed into the room by a somewhat embarrassed Terrance, who had checked over his shoulder before closing the door behind him. "Sorry to disturb you sir, but I believe that we have some information that you ought to know of. Seems sir, that the two fellows that attacked you and Lady Katherine might not have been exactly what we first believed. The bloke the constable took in doesn't speak much English, sir. Frenchie for sure, and James now believes he has seen these two before, speaking with another chap down at dry-dock, where the Ruby is being completed. This other chap was a short sort of fellow, definitely better dressed, James says, which is why he remembered. Says this other bloke looked too polished to be with the likes of these, but says there were three scruffs, not just the two as we caught. What else was there, Terrance?"

"Oh not much, excepting that the toff was wearing a dark green jacket, and had a fancy walking stick."

"A short fellow, you say, with a green jacket and a walking stick... I suppose there could be many men who would fit that description, but I happen to have seen one in particular that I have no wish to have about our business!" Phillip looked thoughtful, "If it is who

I suspect, and he had men near the Ruby, we will need to be very careful indeed. Where is James now, do you know?"

"He and Mrs. Peters were going to visit a friend here in Plymouth who might be useful in recruitment. He advised that he would meet us back here for dinner just after second bell. If I may ask sir, whom do you suspect?"

"Andy, I believe that man may be a M. Otto. He is officially a representative of the French in matters of prisoner exchange, but, in reality, he is a very clever spy. I last met him in London before we sailed for Cape Verde. I must send a message to Lord Hawkesbury, and to Sir John. We must inspect every inch of the Ruby, and set guards around her! See if James can help you discover where this Otto fellow might be staying. He should be able to recognise him. If you can find his whereabouts, perhaps I may have a little job for you later."

Phillip began to rise from where he was propped by cushions on the bed, but Katherine restrained him. "Dearest, you are going to stay here! You need to rest, at least for this afternoon, and Andy and Terrance can organize an inspection of the Ruby. Is that not so, Andy?"

"Of course, your Ladyship! We are on our way! Come Terrance, we will gather some of the workmen and check everything that could have been tampered with. While we are at this, I will send a message to Onyx to warn the men to keep a good watch, and I think sir, that I will shift aboard Onyx. I will be more comfortable if one of us stays out there. Lady Katherine, if you do not mind, please give my greetings to Miss Angeline. Have no fear sir, I will find James and relay the message."

Dinner with James and Natalie was nearing completion when Lieutenant Bernard entered and immediately strode over to their table. "Excuse me sir, but your suspicions have been realised! We have some serious issues on the Ruby."

"Please sit down Terrance," Phillip looked around the room to see if any other diners had taken notice of Mr. Bernard's arrival, but it did not seem so. "Quietly now, what have you found?"

"Sir, three hanging knees in succession on the starboard side have been cut near through, and someone had begun on the fourth. I would not want to be responsible for what might have happened in a storm, or God forbid we had tried to fire the guns above. Also sir, at least two stanchions have been loosened and then reset, but not attached at the base. There may yet be more. The master of the working party from Fucher's Yard is still inspecting. It was very good we checked sir; you see they had completed their work on the starboard side and they had no reason to recheck it. They were quite angry at first when Andy and I insisted on another inspection; felt, I suppose, that we did not trust their work. Well, all that is changed now sir, and they have offered to work through the nights if required to keep her on schedule and get her out to sea on time. They will also post guards and no one will get on her again. Andy was most particular, sir, that no word of this should get out! The Master from Fucher's was most agreeable, but I suspect for different reasons!"

James looked grim and ready to attack someone. "Very good Terrance, where is Andy now?"

"He has gone over to the Onyx sir. He said he would not be satisfied until he had seen her for himself!"

"Please, Terrance, order some dinner and join us. They have some nice cabbage soup and an altogether edible goose pie. We will need to gather tomorrow to plan for our security until we leave port, and possibly after. I am not so worried about the ship, but the brig would be vulnerable if the French decide to take some direct action. Perhaps they intend to provoke us into firing those guns that would have put her in jeopardy."

"Phillip," James asked, clearly still agitated. "Are there not some measures we can take against this Otto fellow? Can we not track him down and corner him?"

"Well, he cannot be touched, I fear. The risk would be too great, and he is an official diplomat of the French Government, with whom we are now officially at peace. The best we can do is allow them to believe that they have been successful, and to remain vigilant at all times. Still, I have asked Andy to speak with you and try to locate Otto's lodging. We may be able to learn something from his effects, if we can study them. Patrick should be on his way south by now with the Emerald, for Celeste left harbour some days before we arrived. He had no plans to stop off here to confer with us. We must assume he is well south of us by now, and out of harm's way."

At that very moment, Patrick Morrissey was standing on the deck of the Emerald, some two hundred eighty miles south-west of the Lizard, plodding south-west through light seas with the wind broad on his starboard beam. Celeste was sailing crisply enough some three cables ahead and slightly to starboard. Twice that day he had seen sails on the horizon, but that was to be expected in the shipping lanes from both Africa and America. The crews had settled down well by the time they reached the south end of the channel and now both crewmen and officers were accustomed to their watches and the vagaries of the ships. The lookout called down from the main mast, "Deck there, sail on the horizon, just abaft the larboard beam!"

It should not bother him, but it did. There was this niggling feeling in the back of his head that would not be stilled. "Mr. Prentiss, take a glass up and tell me what you make of her." "sir." Prentiss was in the rigging in a second, glass strapped to his back. "It is a ship, sir. I make it a French frigate, about five miles, and broad on our beam, sir!" "Very well, Mr. Prentiss, you may come down. Marcello, fetch Mr. Foster, if you please. I believe he is in the gun room."

"Mr. Foster sir, yes, I get him."

In very few minutes Wallis Foster was on deck and approaching the captain. "You asked for me, sir?"

"Yes, there has been a sail, just visible on the horizon for some time. Just a few minutes ago, they got a little bit careless, and Prentiss got a good look at them. A French frigate, shadowing us for at least this past six hours. I do not like it one bit. I know there is supposed to be a peace in place, but what if someone got wind of our real mission? What do you recommend, Wallis?"

"Sir, they know we are here. If they are after us, I suspect they might try to get in position to take us at morning light. It is late afternoon now, and they would not catch us before dark, but if that captain closes, they would put us on our guard. No, if I were them, I would stay out of sight until dark, monitoring our course, and then put on more sail at dusk and race round behind us to be upwind in the morning, ready to pounce."

"I think you have the right of it, Mr. Foster! Now then, get a message to Celeste. We will maintain our course until dark, as though we had not a care in the world. As soon as the sun is down, we will alter course and increase sail. We will use the dark to our advantage, for there is no way for Celeste to out-sail that frigate. We will alter course to due west for four hours; then we will see what the winds are doing and adjust course for the remainder of the night. Please speak with Mr. Elliot and make certain he is aware of our situation. He will be on watch at sundown. I would go across and confer with Captain Day, but I do not wish to send any alarm to our friends east of us."

"Yes sir, if that is a French frigate, we will have to be lucky or very good to outrun her, sir!"

"Let us hope then, that we are lucky, for I already know that we are not yet that good! We do have some advantage, however. We know they are there, and we can use this night to hide our trail. As soon as it is well dark, we will douse all lights. Make sure Ross is kept informed of our plans. I will speak with him right after dark."

"Do you not fear sir, that if they lose us here, they will simply head south and wait for us off Funchal?"

"They might indeed, if they are that intent on us. If that is so, we will know it, for we cannot play this hide and seek game all the way to Cape Town. You do give me something to consider, though, Wallis. What if we made a change in plan, and headed directly for the Canary Islands?"

"Our passengers might object. We did state that we would spend some time in Funchal," the lieutenant remarked with raised eyebrows.

Patrick smiled back, "Yes, and they might object even more if that frigate out there starts throwing lead through our hull! Ross will deal with his passengers."

As the evening began to darken, Patrick kept a man in the tops with a glass, keeping steady watch for the frigate, which would appear just over the horizon every half hour, and then would once again sink from sight. It was now clear that they were being stalked peace or no peace, and Captain Morrissey had no intention of dueling with a frigate that could stand off out of his range and dismantle his ship, or re-take the Celeste. With her much larger crew, the frigate could also just come alongside and overwhelm them. This would have all the markings of a fox hunt, and he would have to be a very shrewd fox indeed. In the end, if he and Ross combined their guns effectively they might be able to drive the frigate off, for the Celeste had twelve and eighteen pounders, although not enough men to really fight them.

"Deck there, light is going sir, cannot make her out against the eastern sky!"

Just then, Mr. Elliot came on deck to take his watch. "Evening sir! Mr. Foster has explained our situation, sir. Has anything changed this past hour?"

"No, she is still keeping just over the horizon, and we have steadily maintained our course and speed. Light has just left us, looking east, but I suspect they will have our sails against the western sky for at least another half hour. At any rate, I plan to keep our course until full dark; then we will extinguish all lights and change course. Ross has answered our signal and we will keep position on him as long as we are able. He will give us one light on his starboard beam, which should be nearly invisible to the Frenchman. My first thought was to use the advantage for a few hours to simply offset our course, but Ross believes we ought to head up as close to the wind as Celeste will sail and hold her there, with as much sail set as she will bear."

"Yes sir, where is our wind now then? Has it altered much since the afternoon watch?"

"Just slightly, it seems to veer a bit more westerly for a short time and then return to the north-west. Strength is holding, which is a good thing, seeing as that frigate is well down wind of us. She will have a good night's work ahead trying to maneuver upwind of us, only to find an empty sea, if we are lucky! Call me when you are ready to change course and have the signal from Ross." Patrick left the deck and went to his cabin to brood. What the devil did that frigate want with him? What had he done to warrant its attention? Oh my, what if... his whole life seemed to be made up of what ifs! George Fielding had been so much more definitive. No second guessing, and that was what had given him the lead role between them in every circumstance. George would not be here today to give him that assurance and confidence, but he could almost hear him repeating Sir Phillip's advice about not second guessing your decisions. Well, this just might be his answer, for if the French were after him to avenge what Phillip had done in the spring... and if it was, that frigate was going to be more than a passing problem. Alright, let's make an assumption, and then we will live or die by it! Either way, that frigate was going to have to work to catch him. Ross had insisted that Patrick take the role of senior captain, not that their experience left much to choose between. Now that insistence made Patrick somewhat less comfortable than he would have liked. They had been sailing close hauled for nearly four hours, and it was approaching eight bells of the first watch. Patrick left his cabin to check yet again on the winds, which had been slowly shifting over the past hour, moving ever more from the west. As he reached the quarterdeck, Lieutenants Foster and Elliot were just changing watch, so he joined them at the binnacle and patiently listened as they went through the recitation of sails, wind, heading, standing orders, and the location of Celeste, only a little over two cables off their beam. That was dangerously close for night sailing, but Patrick was determined not to lose her in the night. They had four extra lookouts tasked with keeping her in sight at all cost. The wind was indeed continuing to shift, and was now at just under three hundred degrees. The best westing they could now make was two hundred fifty degrees, and that was going to become steadily more south west as the wind shift continued. The good thing was that the strength of the wind was not increasing, which helped them more than the frigate. The large fore and aft sail on the brig was an advantage in light winds, while the frigate would swallow them up in strong winds, because she could pile on much more sail, and had a longer keel.

"Gentlemen, I would like to have your opinions on our current state. What speed are we making?"

"Sir, at the last cast of the log we were making just six knots, which has dropped off just a bit in the last two hours. We have also shifted course as the wind has continued to shift into the west north-west. Really though, Celeste is doing very well. For a big merchantman, she sails better than any a two-decker in His Majesty's Navy."

"Very good Mr. Elliot, what do you believe the frigate is getting, Mr. Foster?"

"Sir, I would guess she is lucky to be making six, but her course cannot be higher than two hundred thirty, if she is even steering that high. I would bet on about two hundred twenty, sir."

"Exactly what I have just been charting! Now, if you were her captain, you would have no reason to worry, because, as you said, we made no secret in London that we were heading for Funchal. He knows therefore, that all he has to do is remain on his course and we have to come back to him within a day or two! Let us hope, my friends that he is just that confident! We will hold our course through the night, Mr. Foster, and by morning we should, with luck, be some twenty-five miles upwind of that frigate. We are not going to turn back at all, and we will pray that the wind does not back further into the west. We are, if my calculations are correct, approximately eleven hundred miles from Ponta Delgada. That is our new destination. We will allow that French frigate to search for us first at Funchal and, when he does not find us, perhaps he will move on to Tenerife. We will use the Azores as our watering port and I plan to sail from there directly to Cape Verde, giving both those ports a wide berth! We may yet have to deal with her, but we will buy ourselves valuable time and distance. If we are fortunate, she may have limited cruising grounds. Ross is in agreement, and if we lose him this night we will meet there."

CHAPTER EIGHT
Remedies

The next morning at Plymouth was occupied with evaluating the damage to Ruby. It was extensive and would take many weeks to repair. As Phillip and Andy sat over a last cup of coffee, Terrance and James walked in all smiles.

"I have found our French friend, Phillip!" James whispered as he sat down, "He is residing in a house not three hundred yards from where we sit. It is down an alley behind the hospital on Stone House Creek. There is a small wall around it, but nothing that cannot be scaled. We left Prentiss and Miller watching the back, and Forbes has the alley with Billy Curtis as a runner. If he leaves either way, they will send one man to us and the other will follow him at a distance."

"Andy, I think we ought to be prepared to inspect M. Otto's rooms. It just might give us a clue as to what he plans, although, if he is as good as the Foreign Office suggests, we may find very little."

"If it is there, we will find it sir." Andy replied with a small smile.

"Have some coffee Terrance, James. We might as well settle down to wait. If Otto does go out, I want to know where he goes. There is still one man missing from the group James saw him with, and I would love to find him."

It was only twenty minutes later that Billy Curtis strolled in, nodded his head in their general direction, and walked back out of the Inn. The four men rose as one and followed him out. "He has gone out, sir. Forbes went after him, heading toward the docks, but we left Prentiss and Miller watching the place."

"Very well done, Mr. Curtis. You may return to the docks and take up your watch on the boats." Terrance said with a nod.

"Andy, we are off. James, see if you can pick up the trail of Forbes and Otto. Terrance, I would have you come with us and set up as a lookout down the street in case our friend returns too quickly." With that, the three men turned and strolled up the street, while James and Billy Curtis walked off the other way.

They readily found Miller pretending to be sleeping off a drunk in the alley, and were directed to the house in question. It was a two storey affair, set back off the street some twenty feet, behind a four foot stone wall. The main floor windows were shuttered and those on the upper floor were heavily curtained. Andy took one look around, vaulted the wall, then scurried to the side of the house, and out of sight. What seemed like only moments later, the front door opened slightly, and an arm protruded for a brief second. Phillip leapt the wall and made for the door, which opened as he reached it.

"Welcome sir," Andy smiled, "Looks like we got the place to ourselves for the moment. Give me a minute to check out the parlour and we can head upstairs. My money says if there is anything here, that is where we find it." The parlour revealed nothing, and Phillip was already on the stairs when Andy came back out. "Take the front room sir. I'll take the back."

Phillip had given the room what he thought a decent inspection, but found nothing, except a small trunk of clothes. He was about to leave when Andy came in. "Anything, sir?"

"No, just this small trunk in the corner, and that has nothing but clothes."

"Mind if I have a peek, sir?" Andy asked as he crossed the room. He did not bother with the clothes, but checked the lid of the trunk with his fingers, both outside and in. Finally he shrugged and stood. "Nothing there."

"I do not suppose we should have expected it would be that easy. He was not likely to have just left us a clue lying on the table."

"The table, sir? What an interesting notion! Now why did I not recognise that? Andy Barg, old sod, you are getting careless in your old age." Andy was across the room and down the stairs in a flash, with a confused Phillip following in his steps.

Into the parlour, Phillip followed Andy directly to a side table standing near the shuttered window and beside a large armchair. "See here sir, the table, it does not belong here. The floor has marks where it was pulled across from that nook by the fireplace." Andy reached under the table and chuckled. Next, he lay on the floor and looked under. Reaching up with both arms, he came away with a thin blue book. "This might be what you are looking for, sir."

Phillip took the book and opened it. There were many pages of notes and he quickly turned to the back. "Series of names and numbers; could be a code of some sort. Wait, this is interesting, ednirolc. Andy that is Clorinde simply spelled backwards. Here are others: etrebil, apsiva, etselec. Numbers beside the last two, 6.10 and 6.13. Here is something else, more letters: eneris, nodiesop, rednut. Numbers again 5.15. I am not sure, but I believe these are all ships, but what the numbers mean I have no idea. We must not take this book, or Otto will know we are on to him. Yet, I would love to show this to our friend from the Foreign Office."

Andy scoured the other drawers in the parlour and came up with several blank pages of paper. "Here sir! You write what you think is most important while I look about for a few minutes."

Phillip madly copied several of the last pages while Andy checked books for loose pages or hidden compartments. He was on the last shelf when they heard a shrill whistle from the street.

"Time to go, sir. Oh but what is this?" Andy showed Phillip a large book with the centre cut out. Nestled inside were two vials of clear liquid. "I am willing to wager that is not water, sir. I am guessing poison of some type."

"Well, as much as I would like to take it, we cannot. We had best be on our way, and quickly."

"One moment, sir." Andy ran to the back of the house and returned with two small glass jars, one filled and one empty. He quickly poured the contents of the two vials into the empty glass, and then refilled them with the water from the other. "We are off, sir." he smiled.

The two men went out the back and climbed across into the next yard, still carefully holding the glass of unidentified liquid, and from there, out onto Stone House Creek Road. They were back in their lodgings in minutes, where Andy poured the liquid into a small blue bottle he had procured from an apothecary down the street.

After a hasty conference, Phillip decided to leave for London immediately to meet with Sir John and Evan Nepean at the admiralty. In the meantime, James remained occupied with the two wives as they continued with their progress purchasing stores. Terrance, meanwhile, was sending barrels to Teignmouth for the salted meat that Sam and Williams were preparing, and most importantly with finding crewmen for the Onyx. In that regard, good news arrived from Dick Forest, who had not only conscripted the good Doctor Cluff and Mr. Curtis for good measure, but had passed the word of the upcoming voyage about in the new Crab & Anchor. Jason Marbles had posted bills on all the tables, and Dick had already interviewed nearly sixty men, all of them rated former navy seamen, and all having heard from the old crew about the possibilities of sailing with Lord Phillip Hollis. Among the men were no less than five warrant officers, including a gunner, two bosuns, a master carpenter, and a sail maker. The gunner, whose name he withheld, happened to have a fine French pattern rifle, with newly repaired sights! Katherine was ecstatic! So many of the old crew were coming back to join in this voyage, although none of them needed to.

Phillip reached London in two and one-half days of feverish riding and rode directly to the admiralty office. Fortunately, Lord St. Vincent was in, and would see him directly.

"Sir Phillip, you look as though the devil was on your heels! To what do we owe the honour of your visit? I understood you were down in Plymouth outfitting for your voyage. What has brought you back to London?"

"M. Otto has brought me back, sir. He has been very busy down in Portsmouth." Phillip went on to explain the attack upon him and Katherine and the damage done to Ruby, and the discoveries they had made in Otto's lodgings. "I have the mysterious vial with me, sir; I thought perhaps Mr. Percy at the Foreign Office might be able to tell us what it is. Sir, I haven't many options, nor do I wish to take up your valuable time. We have come to believe that the list we found in Otto's possession may be a list of French ships sent out to hunt us down. You see, the names of all our ships, at least their original French names were on that paper, along with Emerald and Celeste's sailing dates. The other list names three ships and at least two of them are large French frigates, the Sirene and the Poseidon. The Tunder I am not familiar with, but I assume she is another. Here is the thing; Ruby will take weeks to repair, perhaps even months, as we have found damage even near her keel. She simply cannot sail in time to make the trip. I am loath to take Onyx out alone against three frigates. I have a proposal for you, Sir John. I will sell you the brig for a very good price if you would like to have her, in full repair of course, and in return the Royal Navy can sell me the Aquilon at whatever price you choose."

"Phillip, that is not a decision that I can make on my own! We would need to convene the entire board, or at least whoever is available, but at what price? How do we outfit her fast enough? She is laid up in ordinary, it would take weeks! No, it will not suffice! We must think of another way." Sir John looked down at a list on his desk, and slowly a smile began to cross his face. "Mr. Nepean!"

The secretary of the Navy Board came through a side door almost at once.

"My Lord?"

"Evan, is Triton not down at Plymouth?"

"Sir, she is out of the dock just last week. She is to go up to Portsmouth in a few days and be laid up there."

"So, she still has her sails, guns, rigging and all! She just got her bottom cleaned and re-coppered. Mr. Nepean, how many of the board can we gather for a very quick meeting? I wish to dispose of the Triton and we will require a quorum. It must be today!"

"Sir John, if I may be so bold, we do not require a meeting. It was decided in the last general meeting that we should break up three old frigates, three fifth rates, and six of the old 74's if you remember, sir. I realise that Triton was not actually listed, but the ships to be chosen were at our discretion. The Triton is at perhaps half her useful life, since she was launched in' 91. As I recall sir, she cost the Government just over fifteen thousand to build, including fitting and yard costs. Was Sir Phillip to offer the Government a reasonable amount, say perhaps five thousands plus the brig in Plymouth? Another option sir, which might serve, would be for Sir Phillip to lease Triton for a specific period."

"Evan, you are the only reason anything gets done here! It is a much better plan. Phillip, you get a frigate that has just been sorted out, and she is in Plymouth. I can have word sent down to the port admiral immediately! Should you rather lease her for this voyage, Phillip? Let us say six hundred pounds per annum."

"And what is my liability if I should lose her?"

"I accept the lease cost for two years, plus the Ruby as collateral. Do you agree?"

"Done Sir John, and thank you Mr Nepean! I will not keep you. Please send the paperwork over to our solicitors, and I will inform the bank to send a draft. I must be off!"

Phillip made a whirlwind stop at his bank, at the house in Mayfair, and in only three hours was back on a horse on his way to Plymouth, with a brief stop in Teignmouth! The two clerks were going to have a heart attack when they realised how much extra would have to be purchased and stored for all the extra men this would take!

Supplies were being loaded, while Katherine and Natalie panicked on the afternoon that the Mistress Anne sailed into port, followed by Our Gold. Both boats were filled with men, and standing in the bows of the schooner were Paul Marsden and Dick Forest. The holds and decks of both boats were full of barrels of salt pork and beef, which were transferred into the Onyx and Triton, both lying at anchor together now that Triton had been snatched from the Navy, and quickly inspected by a jubilant James and Natalie! Most of the extra men needed for the larger crew had been found right on the ship, as they were to sail her to Portsmouth and then be dismissed. A ten pound per head signing bonus had attracted more than sixty takers! Phillip offered to hand over a dozen or two from the Onyx if they were still short on sailing day, but that did not appear to be very likely.

The last few days were a haze of feverish activity; with workmen still climbing all over the Triton making last minute changes to the cabins and holds, to accommodate both Natalie and the last goods destined for the East. The last nail was hammered on the first day of September; they were ready to weigh anchor. The recruiting had gone even better than Phillip had dared hope, and in the last three days they almost had to turn men away. Officers and men on the Onyx totalled two hundred sixty-five, while the Triton carried two hundred and forty-eight. Nearly all were experienced ex-Royal Navy, except for six men from Teignmouth who had arrived with the Mistress Anne, and a group of seven men who had approached Phillip on the docks. They were all East India veterans, and were eager to join. At first Phillip was unsure, but the leader, Bradford Sykes, spoke out assuring Phillip that the men were not shy, and that they had all sailed the Straits and through to the Java Sea and China. Twice they had encountered pirates and had fought them off. That was enough for Phillip and Andy Barg, and on they came. In the final tally, twenty-seven of the hands were back from the spring raid, not including officers.

Phillip addressed the men before leaving Plymouth, reminding them that while Onyx was a private ship, she would sail mostly under admiralty rules, with his usual exception of no flogging, and no purser. The men were delighted, also with the fact that the pay Phillip promised them was better than anything they would find elsewhere! The holds were crammed with supplies for the garrison of Prince of Wales Island, plus, taking Sir Walter's advice, tin bars from Phillip's own mines, and bales of wool, both from the estate and from neighbouring farms. The tin and wool would be sold in Madras. It felt strange to Phillip to be involved in trade, but the extra cargo would more than pay for the entire voyage, and the men were delighted because Phillip promised them a share of the profits above their already generous wages.

The plan was to make their best way directly to Cape Verde, only stopping at Funchal or Tenerife if the winds were contrary and the weather forced them in. Katherine and Natalie were both in high spirits and waving to one another as the two frigates made ready. Soon the call came from the bow, "Anchor's a'peak."

Pierre, who had the watch looked over at Phillip who simply nodded. "Weigh anchor; sheet the fore course!" Sails were dropped and anchors fetched. For better or worse, they were away!

Patrick and Ross's ruse in the North Atlantic seemed to have worked perfectly. They had made the Azores by the third day of August without sighting the frigate again. The stop for water, fruit, wood, and fresh bread had taken only three days, and even the passengers, two men from the Foreign Office and a missionary teacher and his wife, all bound for Cape Town, had been quite cheered by their good progress and mostly favourable winds. Just before sailing, a British packet schooner, the Nymph, entered harbour. She was enroute from Jamaica to England, and as luck would have it, she was bound for Plymouth. In a hastily scribbled letter to Phillip, Patrick relayed the information about the French Frigate, and his impression that they were perhaps being hunted. He also gave Phillip the revised route he was following. From Ponta Delgada to Praia the winds had remained remarkably constant, and while they had sighted sails twice passing nearly three hundred miles to the west of Tenerife, none had been the French frigate, and none had seemed to take much notice of them.

Arriving in Praia, on the fifteenth of August, Patrick and Ross had visited with Don Esteban de Pina Abrantes, the Governor of the Islands, and a man of Sir Phillip's acquaintance from their visit in April. The good governor was pleased to see the Emerald back in his harbour, and asked after James Peters, who had been her captain on the last voyage. Upon learning that not only James, but also Sir Phillip would be returning in a matter of perhaps five weeks, Senior Abrantes was all too eager to give whatever assistance he could. No, he had not seen any French warships in the past days, nor had he heard of any, but they would know they were not over welcome in Praia, in any case. Perhaps, Patrick thought, he had truly escaped!

Ross's first voyage as captain of his own ship was becoming somewhat of a sobering and challenging experience. Having come up from before the mast, unlike most officers in the Royal Navy, he had always maintained a deep rooted scepticism of authority and a deep love for the common seaman. It had only been with his acquaintance of James Peters, and his service under Phillip Hollis that he had begun to believe that there were other officers who truly cared for their men and did not abuse their power. Now that final authority rested in his own hands. He was finding out just how difficult it was to maintain a balance between controlling the ship and her men and avoiding the pitfalls of tyranny. Although he hated to admit it, he realised that he had possibly misjudged some of the former officers he had served with. Phillip, knowing Ross's nature, had warned him of the morass of trying to be friends with the crew. He found the isolation of command a harsh and trying price.

Fortunately, Ross had two excellent mates and a sailing master old enough to be his father, who had unending patience for the new captain. Bill Hotchkins was proving to be a blessing in many ways, not the least of which was that Bill, as a master seaman had also come up from among the common seamen and understood Ross's struggle, which the two former Royal Navy lieutenants, as good as they were, did not.

Ross was sitting and enjoying a late afternoon glass of wine with the sailing master in the huge main cabin of the Celeste, trading stories of learning the ropes, when there came a knock at the cabin door.

"Enter," Ross called out casually.

"Sir," Bart Fischer poked his head into the cabin, "sorry to bother you sir, but we've a slight problem. Seems two seamen have got at loggerheads over their ration o' grog and one of them, Billy Sykes his name is, took a belaying pin to his mate. Second man, name of Willis, main top, is down in the orlop with a broken arm. Question is, do we put Sykes in irons? No one seems to have actually seen anything and Willis claims he fell."

"I do not comprehend how a man who is nimble enough to be a top man can be so clumsy, but I must have seen it a hundred times in my days." Bill Hotchkins laughed.

"You may laugh, Bill, but without we can find a witness, we will be hard pressed to force Willis to talk, and barring that Sykes walks scot free. Still, I will not tolerate fighting on this ship."

"Begging your pardon sir, but if Sykes or anyone else knows that they can get away with it, won't we be inviting more?" asked Fischer, with a grimace. "Not my call, sir, but I believe we ought to make an example of Billy Sykes to let the others know this sort of thing cannot be tolerated."

"What would you suggest, Mr. Fischer, that we put Sykes in chains in the cable tier? With no witness and no proof? How do you even know he did this?" Ross asked irritably.

"Sir, well, Sykes sort of told Connacher, the surgeon, when he helped Willis into the orlop, but then Willis denied it and Sykes went back on deck to his duties. Still sir, the two were heard arguing about a tot Willis supposedly owed Sykes for some favour."

"Very well, leave it with me for the moment Bart. I will consider it but I will not act on impulse. Does Torey have the watch?"

"Yes, sir, I will go on watch at the next bell, sir."

"Please have Mr. Speaks come down to the cabin when he goes off watch. I will consider this until that time."

"Yes, sir. Thank you, sir."

As Fischer left the cabin, Ross looked over at the sailing master, "He is a very good watch commander, and for the most part he treats the men reasonably well, but he is apt to see everything in white and black."

"It is how he was trained, Captain. You must not expect more from him unless you are willing to teach him, and that means overcoming years of prejudice. The same sort of prejudice you are now having to unlearn, if I may be so insubordinate for a moment. He is not all wrong, you know. You are concerned that Sykes must be given the benefit of the doubt, but Mr. Fischer is concerned for the order of this entire ship. It is not only officers who take advantage of their positions. If I recall, Sykes is captain of the main top, and Willis serves under his leadership." Bill smiled at his captain's discomfort.

CHAPTER NINE
Anchors Aweigh

As the anchor came up off the harbour floor and the graceful Onyx began to turn towards the sea, Phillip noticed a schooner entering the harbour and proceeding directly in his path. "Pierre, better take note of that schooner coming in. She seems in a god-awful hurry and she is coming right across our course. She will have us in irons if she doesn't get over; either that or she will get run down, and I don't think we need the damage on our first day out."

The schooner kept on her course directly for the Onyx, and only at the last minute did she veer to starboard and drop her sails at the same time. "Is that the Onyx?" came a cry from her bows.

"Yes, this is Onyx. Were you trying to run us down then?" Pierre shouted back through the megaphone.

"I am most sorry, sir. However, I have mail for you, and could see you were getting underway. The captain of the brig Emerald gave it to me with instructions to see you had it before you weighed anchor. Give us a minute and we will have a boat over."

As Triton continued toward open water, Pierre gave orders to back the sails to keep the Onyx stationary as the Nymph's boat was lowered and manned. In a matter of minutes, the packet was hoisted aboard, and Onyx was again underway. Phillip took the letter and retreated to the aft railing. Patrick's message was brief but succinct; without knowing it, he confirmed their fears from Otto's notebook.

Phillip uttered a short prayer that Patrick and the Emerald had been successful with their change of route, had escaped the frigate, and were safely on their way to Cape Town.

"Pierre, news from the Emerald. Patrick has taken her and Celeste to Ponta Delgada. It seems he was being shadowed by a French frigate on his way to Funchal so he changed course at night and ran for the Azores! We will need to confer with James as soon as it is convenient. This means that perhaps our suspicions about the sabotage are more serious than we had hoped, and our guess about Otto's notes may be correct."

"Perhaps once we are well clear of the harbour we can have him rowed over, or would you rather wait until dinner?"

"There is no urgency yet. According to Patrick's letter he was some two hundred fifty miles south west of the Lizard when they spotted their shadow. I doubt they would attack us openly in the channel; too much chance of being discovered, and maybe being taken as well. Send up a hoist that he is to come over at the start of the first dog watch." Phillip looked out over the break in the quarterdeck, seeing Mr. Simms down below on the main deck helping sort out some of the new men and getting the ship cleared from leaving anchorage. "Mr. Simms, how are you? How is that shoulder of yours?"

"Sir. Just fine, thank you sir; the shoulder is near as good as new. The doctor did a fine job of sewing it back up. Happy I am to be back on board, captain! Congratulations on your marriage, sir! The crew is delighted to have Her Ladyship on board. It will make for a happy ship sir, not that we wouldn't be, you understand!" Simms beamed in genuine pleasure at being singled out and that the captain had remembered the bullet he had taken on their last voyage.

One of the new men looked over at Simms, "You a friend of the captain's then?"

"Naw, mate, but I sailed with him on his last cruise, didn't I? I took a musket ball in me shoulder, right up there on the quarterdeck, an' he was just sayin' howdy and seeing me fixed up like."

A few others began to gather round. "Say then, is it true you were rolling in prize money? I heard you got hundreds o' pounds, that true? How'd you go through that much in just a few months then?"

"We all got a lot more than that! I got near nine hundred invested in funds, I have. Captain set it all up for all of us. I get near on eight pound six sent to me missus every three month! She wants for nothing, I'll tell you. An' me kids got good clothes and are goin' to school."

"You havin' us on?" One of the men listening asked incredulously. "If you got all that flash coming in, what you doin' out here with us? I tell you, I'd be holed up in some pub with a doxy on each arm!"

"Ya, and pretty soon you'd be back here with nothin' just like most of us has been afore! I come back 'cause I wanted to sail with Sir Phillip one more time. I will tell you now. He is the best you will ever get, but do not take his no flogging rules and all for his being a soft touch. He is a personal friend of Horatio Nelson! That should tell you where he stands. Just do your duty and keep your nose clean and this here will be the best voyage you ever get. He takes care of everybody, but he expects you to do the same, see!"

"Did more of your old mates come back then? Even with all that prize money in the bank?"

"Ya, there is better than twenty 'fore the mast, and another half a dozen in the ward room. Believe me, mate, none of them had to come back. You see, when we got back from our last run, the captain made everyone o' us sign a paper to put at least half our prize money into funds, so as we wouldn't just do what this here fool just said! Every one of me mates is set for life! I earn more than twice what the navy paid me as able seaman just in the interest on what the captain set up for me, and that was after I kept back three hundred pounds to buy my Mabel a new house and give my old Mum enough to keep her well!"

"So what you hear then, Simms? We out after some rich prizes again? That is why you came back, right?" Some of the men gathered around were actually licking their lips in anticipation.

"Can't say as I know, but I'll tell ye this; no matter what, Sir Phillip will do right by ye. You all can count on that! Now I reckon we better get to work here or you maybe get to see another side of the captain!"

By mid-afternoon, they were bowling along at a comfortable eight knots, the English coast on the starboard beam, not ten miles off. The wind was coming from the north east, and as long as it lasted, Phillip was determined to take every advantage to keep close as they rounded the south tip of Cornwall at Landewednack, and made for the open sea to clear the Bay of Biscay. If this wind would last for a day or two, they would be in very good shape indeed! He was almost loathe to clew up his sails to let James ferry over from the Triton. It seemed like it was wasting this gift, even if only for a few minutes. Katherine was down in the cabin, conferring with Dick Forest about their proposed route and examining charts. As if she did not have enough work to do with her duties as clerk! Phillip still was unsure of just how that had happened either; he had been fine with the idea of bringing Katherine along without putting her to work. He knew, though, that his wife would never have been happy with that arrangement, and he had promised her that he would not try to tame her or keep her from doing the things she desired.

"Andy, what say we give Triton a hoist and clew up sails so James and Natalie can come over? No sense waiting much longer and the seas are calm enough now. I will go below and tell Katherine. Just send them down when they get aboard."

"Aye captain. Mr. Sykes, is that hoist ready for Triton?"

"Aye sir, been ready this past half-hour sir, just as you asked."

"Hoist away then, Mr. Sykes! Mr. Harris, clew up the main sail if you please. Get the way off of her. We got a boat coming over from the Triton in ten minutes, and break out the bosun's chair, for Mrs. Peters 'ill be coming with Captain James."

As Phillip left the quarterdeck, he wondered if everything would just happen if he forgot to give the orders. Between Andy and Carter, he seemed to be always one step behind. Entering the main cabin, he saw Katherine and Dick Forest pouring over a chart spread out on his desk. "What is nothing sacred on this ship anymore? We have a chart room I am obliged to share with my sailing master, and a bed I am obliged to share with my clerk. Now not even my own desk is safe from predation!" Phillip laughed as he came around to see what it was they were studying.

"If you do not wish to share your desk with me, sir, you may not have to share your bed either! It could be your choice." Katherine beamed back, and Dick Forest chuckled as he held his hands up signalling he wished no part in this discussion.

In response, Phillip wrapped his arm around his wife and gently kissed the side of her head. "Have no fear; you are welcome to the use of both! So what has your interest here? Is that Funchal?"

"Yes, Mr. Forest was just showing me our proposed route, and we were estimating the time to various landfalls. If we stay to the east of Funchal and sail directly through the Canarys, we should have a clear run down to Cape Verde, if the winds hold. Mr. Forest was just showing me the set of currents along this stretch off Portugal, and how they might affect our course."

"Well, I do not mean to alarm you, but there may be something else that could affect our course. We received a letter from Patrick just as we sailed. It seems he was shadowed by a French frigate just some three hundred miles south of here. He lost the Frenchman in the night by altering course for the Azores, but he is convinced they were in wait for him. It fits rather well with our experience in Plymouth, and I am inviting James to come over in just a few minutes for a conference. I imagine he will bring Natalie, so Katherine, please have Carter inform the cook that we will have guests for dinner. Of course, by now he probably already knows!"

"Allow me to clear off these charts, sir; I am taking a watch in just a few minutes, so I need to be along at any rate." Dick gathered up his charts as he was speaking and lumbered off to the chart room.

As soon as Dick had left the cabin, Katherine wrapped her arms around her husband. "Do you realise, that tonight will be our first experiment in that hanging bed of yours? Remind me not to drink too much wine at dinner; I would not want to be seasick!" As Phillip reached for her, she spun out of his arms and smiled, "I have to go and find Carter, my love. He seems to be somewhat afraid of being in the cabin with me. I am sure he will get over it with time!"

James, indeed, brought his wife across with him, along with Lieutenant Bernard, and as soon as everyone was seated around the table, including Pierre Doucette, Phillip read Patrick's letter aloud. "I am pleased that Patrick and Ross took evasive measures under the circumstances. They could hardly have opened fire on the frigate, and if they waited for the Frenchman to come along side it would have been too late! Hopefully, Patrick will have made his next leg to Praia safely. If that frigate is still north of Funchal, we must assume she will have an interest in us as well. Together we are more than a match, I believe, for any frigate the French can throw at us, so long as she is alone, and not the lookout for a larger force as mentioned in Otto's list. What are the questions we need to ask?"

"As I see it, the first question must be," James prompted, "do we evade and change our route early, perhaps to keep away from their cruising ground, or do we carry on, eyes open, and prepare for possible hostilities? The other thing is that they will hardly be looking for a pair of frigates! Really, unless they have a seventy-four out there, we are probably not in great danger!"

"Well, evasion might be possible if we begin it very soon. We would, I suspect follow in Patrick's trail but swing outward toward the Azores early, and if we do stop there, make a course for Recife in Brazil. It would be somewhat longer, perhaps one thousand miles, but the trades would take us back to Cape Town well enough," responded Pierre.

"If we are still at peace with France, do you think this will prove a privateer once more?" asked Katherine. "It is perhaps a bad question, but if so, she is more likely to be alone. If this ship is French

Navy, then I would guess that peace or not, we are being hunted for what you accomplished in the spring, and there could be any number of vessels sent out to find and destroy us…"

"Dearest, I think that is an excellent question, and gets to the nub of our situation, but we have no way of knowing the answer unless we commit to meeting them head on."

Terrance looked across at Phillip, "Sir, what we do not know is if this ship, whatever she is, has any intentions other than to monitor our progress and perhaps shadow us. If they do not attack, our only course is to evade them or accept their observations, which I expect we would find wearying. If we are being tempted to make a move that could provoke an overwhelming response, like having us declared pirates, would we not then be wiser to evade or ignore this ship?"

James' head jerked up. "You may well have something there, Terrance! I remember George saying that when you captured Le Liberte, the remaining officer was most concerned that they would be adjudged pirates. What if the French are looking for an excuse to have us branded, so that if we do reach the Malay Straits, they can set their French and Dutch capital ships on us?"

"Right, that is a plausible argument," Phillip looked around the table. "I still do not relish being shadowed by a French frigate, privateer or not, all the way to Cape Town or even India. We are heavy, and will be much of the journey. Though we have clean bottoms we probably won't outrun them. I would rather not fight them either. We are at the beginning of a long voyage, and damage now will prove costly in time. We could be laid up for weeks at Funchal or Tenerife."

"Is that perhaps what these people are after?" Natalie asked quietly, "What would be the result if we were delayed? Perhaps I am wasting your time, and I apologise, I realise that I am here only as James' wife, not an officer, but what if they just need to slow us down for some reason? Is there something we might miss?"

"Natalie, you just keep asking questions! There may be volumes to what you just asked us! It was imperative that we be on our way by early September, but exactly why we were never told. It certainly was not for the monsoons, for we will in all likelihood be too late for them. Typical admiralty practise of giving their captains half the information they need! Why I am not sure, but I believe my sister may have just hit on something. If we either delay by sailing around via the Azores and Recife, or face these privateers and risk damage, we will lose time. Do they want to keep us back? Why? Perhaps it is so that they may find Patrick alone in the Indian Ocean, or to keep us away from Penang for a time. Remember, there were three ships on that list we liberated from M. Otto. Patrick and Ross seem to have found one, but where are the others?"

Natalie smiled cautiously at her husband, reassured by her brother's acceptance. James raised his eyebrows, but smiled back.

"There is simply too much we do not know." Pierre scanned the table. "Every course at this point could be wrong. I suggest, sir, that we simply keep to our plans with our eyes open, and remain prepared for the possibility of an attack. It at least gives us good reason to begin gunnery practise and work the men up for action, and as James said, we now have two frigates, not just a sloop as consort! That really does change everything in our favour."

"One more thing just occurred to me. Let us make an assumption; they find us and begin to shadow our progress. At some point, they will cease to be alarming. It is the nature of things. I would hate very much to wake some morning with a pair or three frigates upwind of us, or, even worse having gotten between Onyx and Triton. If we see this ship or ships, we assume from the first moment that we are at war! James, I want Triton in sight of me at all times. Onyx, with her twenty-four pounders, still has much greater firepower if it comes down to it. Furthermore, we will wish to remain in constant contact. Only if the seas get up badly will you sail astern of Onyx. I do not want them to be able to use you to force us into an action we cannot control. One more thing; we begin great gun practise tomorrow and we exercise the guns every day until you get three broadsides inside of two minutes!"

This brought general nods of approval all around the table. The two women just looked at each other somewhat apprehensively.

CHAPTER TEN
Face Off

It was the morning of the tenth of September; the wind was a fresh breeze from the northwest finding the two frigates on a broad reach heading south south-west, with the mains, topsails, and royals set. The men had been at the guns for two hours steady. Phillip was still not satisfied, but things were getting better. They had three broadsides down in under three minutes, but the men were tired and eight bells was about to ring. Phillip strode to the break in the quarterdeck and looked down on the sweating sailors, some of them leaning on spikes, rammers, or even each other.

"I know you are all tired. You are sick of gun drills and wondering if you accidentally signed onto a Royal Navy frigate by mistake!" This brought a few murmurs, but more laughs. "God willing, we are going to be sailing into the Malay Straits, and we have been told, that among other things, there is a fifty gun Dutch light two-decker out there, that has been causing havoc. If we meet her, and have to engage her, we will have to fire faster and more accurately than she can, and the Minheers are not going to ask if you are tired, so you can stop for tea and biscuits!" This carried more cheers and laughter back to the captain. "We also know that there are potential threats here in the Atlantic, and the better you are with the guns, the better our chances of coming out victorious and with fewer casualties! I am working you all hard, because I wish to keep you all alive! We are near the end of the fore-noon watch; you are all dismissed to your noon meal." This brought cheers from the men below. "However, at four bells of the afternoon watch we will engage in one hour of small arms practise." The cheers changed to groans, but they were mostly good-natured. Phillip waved to the men and turned to climb down to his cabin to fetch his sextant for the noon sighting, but Katherine was already on her way up carrying both hers and Phillip's.

They joined with Dick Forest and Pierre and after noon was declared and sightings taken, the agreed position put them some one hundred miles east of Funchal and nearly three hundred north of Tenerife. They had been making very good time with mostly favourable winds and only one day of stormy weather. As the group dispersed to their various duties, Phillip and Katherine started for their cabin for the noon meal, looking forward to some time alone. Just then, the lookout on the foremast called down. "Deck there, signal from Triton, sir; sail on the southern horizon." The signal from Triton found Andy Barg turning over the helm to Pierre, and Phillip was back on the quarterdeck in moments. Signals flew between the two ships and both changed course to the south west immediately in order to reach for the weather gage and ascertain what the other vessel would do in response. In any case, with their ships now on a beam reach, if the other ship was approaching them, it would not be able to cut across their route, for she would be close hauled. If the other ship was also southbound, they could either overhaul her or steer further into the west and wait for further developments. In only a few minutes, it became clear that the other vessel was indeed a ship and heading north. Phillip decided to leave Triton in the lead, with Onyx following some three cables back and slightly downwind. Signals from the Triton, shortly after the new course was established, confirmed that they were indeed approaching a French frigate, and that the frigate was holding her course, which would put her well within two miles on a closing course, but downwind of Triton and Onyx. As signal flags continued to fly between Phillip's two ships, the men were called back on deck to clear for action and the great guns were again manned but not run out.

As the French frigate approached, every glass on Onyx and Triton was raised to observe the stranger. She was a forty gun heavy frigate, nearly identical to the Onyx, and she looked well manned, for there was much activity on her deck. As she passed along the larboard beam, some one and one-half miles off, she began to turn up into the wind, as though to come around and follow the two frigates or to work her way to windward and capture the weather gage. Phillip called a meeting on the quarterdeck, with Pierre, Dick Forest, and Andy.

"As I see it, she has been out here longer than we, and could be slowed down by weed. I believe we have two choices; we pile on as much sail as she will bear, and try to outrun her, or we reduce sail and see what reaction we get." Phillip looked around the little circle expectantly.

"If you want an answer to her intentions," Pierre proffered, "reducing speed and forcing her to make a move will give it to you the quickest. However, if she turns upwind to take the weather gage, we must be prepared for her to have the choice of actions."

Dick was busy looking over his shoulder at the now distant frigate as she continued her slow turn seemingly to come in behind the Onyx at perhaps three miles. "I think she plans to shadow us, so I might agree with Pierre that we reduce sail and place ourselves and Triton across her path. If she keeps on, which I doubt, we would have to make a decision as to how close we are willing to let her get."

"Let her come! Let us get on with it! If she comes within hail, we give her a warning and after that, with two frigates to one, even though Triton only has twelve pounders, we simply sink her!" Andy spoke with vehemence. "I cannot see why we want to let them play their little games any longer. We know what they did in Plymouth and I say we owe them no quarter!"

"Assuming, as Dick does, that if we reduce sail the Frenchman does the same thing, we either increase sail again, waiting for him to follow suit, or we turn upwind and make him turn away, or face us." Pierre spoke with his eye to a glass, watching the Frenchman behind them. "I say, sir, that we make him run or fight, so long as we do not fire the first shot."

"Yes, and who is going to believe who fired first?" Phillip questioned, "They certainly won't admit it if they are trying to provoke us into an action that they can condemn." He looked back at the French ship, now completing her turn and clearly following in Onyx's wake. "No, I am not going to take their bait. Let us see how good they are. Signal to Triton to increase sail! We will give them everything we can carry, and come tonight, we will wait for dark and then reduce sail and see if she overtakes us in the night. Have the men stand down from quarters. I will be in my cabin. You have the watch, Pierre; call me if things change."

Katherine was waiting in the cabin, clearly anxious about the French ship that was plainly visible through the transom windows. "Are they going to attack us, Phillip?"

"No, it does not seem so, at least not for the time being, but as we discussed in the early hours off Plymouth, we will not know for certain until they make some move against us, which I believe they must do sooner or later. Perhaps they will wait to see if we stop off at Tenerife. I do not plan to give them an easy time, but we will not attack them. Right now, we are going to see if they will stay with us, so we are setting all the sail Onyx will carry, and James will do the same on Triton. Still, it will be some time before we can really be sure of anything, so why don't we work on our reports and logs!"

"I just knew you would be full of fun!" Katherine laughed as she sat at the desk and began to pull out the daily log books and records. "I already checked with Dr. Cluff and there are two men in sick bay, one with a hernia and the other with grip. I have entered them into the log."

It was six bells of the afternoon watch when Phillip returned to the deck, all paperwork in order once again. Katherine was turning out to be a stickler for paperwork! How the Admiralty would have loved her devotion to minutia, coupled with Natalie's skill at driving bargains. One glance aft told Phillip everything he needed to know. The French frigate was just visible on the horizon, directly in Onyx's wake. "How long has she been there?" he asked Pierre.

"She slowly gave way until she was sitting about four miles back; that was maybe two hours ago. Now she just sits there on the horizon. We are making just less than eleven knots, sir, which is all Triton can manage. How long do we keep this up?"

"We will run until the end of the first dog if this wind holds." Phillip glanced up ahead at the Triton, not two cables off the starboard bow. "Pierre, I am going below to check the charts, but by our noon sighting we should still be well over two hundred fifty miles to Tenerife. I am thinking we should change course now and sail further west. It will increase our distance to Praia somewhat, but we may just pick up some better north westerlies out there. It will also keep our friend back there from being able to make a dash into Tenerife for assistance or to relay a message. If he does, we lose him! Send a message to James to alter course two points to starboard."

Back in the cabin, Phillip went over his plan with Dick Forest. "If we steer southwest for the next day and the wind holds, it should put us approximately one hundred miles east of Santa Cruz de la Palma. That means, if the Frenchman needs to send for help at Tenerife he has nearly two hundred miles to go. Too far out for them to send a pinnace. It will still leave us slightly over eleven hundred miles to Cape Verde, but not so much further than if we cut the corner through the Canary Islands."

"It may cost us no more time at all, if these north westerlies continue. It is the right season for certain," Answered Dick with a grimace. "Then again, we could hit a period of calm out further into the mid-Atlantic."

"I think we have to chance it! The benefit of keeping the Frenchman on his own outweighs the risk of lighter winds, a risk we do not know exists." Phillip responded, "The risk behind us is real, and we have to find a way to mitigate it. I do not want this

Frenchman shadowing us all the way to Cape Town or beyond. If the wind holds, I intend to keep as much sail on as she will bear all night! We will signal to Triton to keep only mid-ship deck lights on, with nothing on the mast at all, and we will station ourselves off of her quarter. We will run in the dark and see where the Frenchman is in the morning."

With that the conversation ended and Phillip went back on deck to inform Pierre to send the appropriate signals to Triton. The wind predictably died some overnight, and the frigate's speed fell off to seven knots. In the morning, the French frigate was still behind them, albeit much closer and was clearly beginning to fall back to take up her position some three miles astern.

Phillip decided it was time for a general conference, and called for James to row over to Onyx for a meeting with him and Pierre. Sails were backed and James came aboard shortly after the guns were stowed, and in time for breakfast. "So, what do you make of our shadow, James?"

"I have to think he is waiting for something. It makes no sense for him to follow us endlessly. I take it you altered course last evening to put us further from Tenerife, if that is where his help may come from," James responded. "If the French have sent out only one frigate, what is their purpose? To shadow us to where they must already know we are going? No, it does not help them at all. I believe Otto's notes, which means there are other ships involved. Either they intend to stop us here, which means they expect to rendezvous with that help, or they are prepared to follow us into the Indian Ocean and look for more help out of Isle de France."

"It would be more sensible for them to try here, do you not think?" asked Pierre. "After all, they are closer to home, and if they miss us near Mauritius, we have the advantage from Madras to George Town, assuming Emerald and Celeste will be in Madras."

"Phillip, what do you think?" asked James after a moment's silence.

"I believe that Pierre is probably correct. The more I think on it, the more sense it makes for them to make a move sooner than later. Perhaps they are rethinking now that we have two frigates rather than the Ruby, which would not have posed much of a threat. Still, they would be foolish to attack with just the one. I am afraid we will find her sister ships near Tenerife or between it and Cape Verde."

"Assuming that you are correct, what is our course of action?" James asked with a pointed looked at Pierre.

"If another warship approaches, we need to be ready to take charge of the situation before that frigate behind us can come up. I would not give them the chance to combine against us. I know we are supposed to be at peace, but we have already seen what that peace means to them in Plymouth. We cannot afford to be casual in our approach. If they come within range, I say we run out our guns and challenge them."

"If the opportunity presents itself, I agree with Pierre that we ought to double up on whichever of their ships is closest, if we can, and then take on whatever remains!" James was still angry at the loss of the Ruby and the attack on Phillip in Plymouth. "I know you do not wish to play into their hands, Phillip, and you are always loathe to start an action in which your men may be needlessly put in danger, but doing nothing may also be just what they want, so they can set the stage in their favour. I would not give them the choice! In the final moment the peace treaty is neither here nor there. If we feel we are being threatened on the high seas, we have the right of self-protection, and how we define that as private ships is really not the government's issue."

"Phillip, with all due respect, I must agree with James." Pierre nodded. "Neither of us is accusing you of being shy, please understand. We have stood by you in action. However, it is in your nature to avoid bloodshed if you can, which is admirable, sir, but in this case I have to agree that we should take action if we believe it is warranted, peace or no peace."

There was an uncomfortable silence in the room. The question that had hung over the issue of the French frigate from the moment of their meeting off Plymouth was now firmly on the table, and the officers waited while Phillip dealt with it. Everyone in the room knew that Phillip's personal issue with violence was what fueled his no-lash policy and, because of his obvious concern for his men, it had largely served him well, although, on occasion, he had placed himself in a position where his crew had certainly taken advantage of him. It was a risk he had been willing to take. When a fight was unavoidable, Phillip had proven himself a great strategist and fearless adversary, but he was always happier if it could be avoided. Now, he was being asked by his senior staff to take the offensive and perhaps provoke the fight that might be avoidable.

"All right, I will not turn and attack this single frigate, because I do not believe that she alone poses a significant threat, but if another French warship should attempt to join her, we will act in whatever manner we believe secures our safety and our mission." Phillip had crossed his Rubicon. "Let us take a few minutes to discuss possibilities. Let us say this other ship is another frigate and not a ship of the line..."

It was early Sunday morning, September twelfth, when the second French frigate appeared on the southern horizon. Not waiting until the first frigate, still shadowing them from about four miles back, would see the new arrival and close, Phillip called for the immediate implementation of their plan, and both his ships quickly increased sail. The wind was nearly abeam, coming from the west north-west at twelve to fifteen knots, allowing Phillip to set top gallants. As their plan was set, all that remained was to see how the French would react. Both English frigates immediately altered course to the south south-west and Triton took a slight lead. By altering course early, it would guarantee them the weather gage, and keep the initial French ship to leeward or well behind them.

"I make initial sighting at forty minutes after eight. Make it so in the log, Andy. The men are at breakfast so we will let them be for the moment. Call Pierre and Dick to the quarterdeck, if you please. The next few minutes should tell us what the French will do."

Only a few minutes later, a signal came from Triton and Harris called out, "French ship is 36 gun frigate, heading north, Sir."

"Acknowledge, Mr. Harris." Andy Barg called out.

"Now, let us see which way she turns, for I do not believe she will come straight on. Either she turns to the northeast to evade us, or she will have to turn west to try to head us off."

"Signal from Triton sir, French ship is altering course to the west!"

"Very well, Mr. Harris, signal to Triton 'alter course due south.' Andy, we stay on our course and we will see which way she jumps. In the meantime, keep an eye on the frigate behind us; I want to know the minute she changes course or begins to close." Phillip checked the binnacle chronometer; it was five minutes before nine o'clock. It had only been fifteen minutes since the sighting, but already the French ship was clearly visible from the deck. "Call the men to quarters, Mr. Barg." Turning, the captain addressed his First Lieutenant and Sailing Master. "I intend bracketing that French frigate. Triton will endeavour to cross behind her while we run up on her starboard quarter. If she alters course to range alongside of Triton, James will open his gun ports immediately and he will take her across the bows; we will turn to take her larboard side. In either case, I wish the issue decided before this other fellow behind us can get close enough to give assistance. Pierre, load the front six twenty-four pounders with bar shot and tell the men to aim high. I am going to use their tactics and take out her rigging if I can. We will be out of range of the carronades on the first few rounds, but Andy I want them loaded with grapeshot. We have to neutralize this frigate completely before the second can come up."

Phillip approached the quarterdeck rail and looked down at the seamen on the main deck. "This is the first test! There are two French frigates out there and they mean us no good. We must disable this first one quickly so that they may not join against us. We must shoot better than ever we have! Have a good eye, gunners, and make every shot count. The lads in Triton are counting on your support this day, for they are likely to have the first taste of that Frenchman's guns. We must hit her fast and hit her hard. Do your best! I know I can count on you. We will let her feel the sharp edge of a polished Onyx!" There was a massive cheer in response.

Triton and Onyx were drawing apart as Triton turned to the south and Onyx continued to the south south-west. They were now nearly a quarter mile apart and the French frigate was clearly visible some two miles ahead, still heading west. As the distance continued to close, Triton began to change course to nearly parallel Phillip's Onyx, keeping the Frenchman directly ahead. Phillip continued to make minor course corrections to keep his position upwind of the French frigate, denying her the weather gage.

At just under one mile, the Frenchman finally committed and began to turn through the wind to get upwind of Triton. That French Captain was impatient. It was a massive error in tactics, for it guaranteed Phillip a chance for a two-ship-to-one contest. It was another sign of the inexperience of the French Naval Officers since the revolution. James immediately turned back to his course of due south, which would put him slightly across the Frenchman's bow, and at the same time opened his gun ports. Phillip gave the order to alter course two points to larboard and to open his own gun ports. All the guns were loaded and ready to fire the minute the guns were run out.

James clewed up his fore course, preparatory to beginning the engagement and the French frigate's gun ports opened and the barrels of his twelve and eighteen pounders rolled out. Phillip stood on his quarterdeck, his glass wavering between the two frigates ahead of him. "Don't wait James! Fire while you still have a bit of advantage!" Those twelves of James' were no match for the Frenchman's eighteens. Even while he stood transfixed, the first bow chaser on the French frigate fired. As though it signalled the start of a race, Triton's entire starboard side lit up! The battle was on. Phillip would be in range of the French frigate in perhaps two more minutes, but it would be much more effective if he waited until the range was closer and he could engage his entire larboard battery. To do so was going to cost James at least one full broadside, perhaps two if the Frenchman was quick about it. As he stood watching, the Triton began to turn to the south west, to come directly alongside of the Frenchman, who was holding his course of roughly northeast. The move forced the French captain into a decision and he began a rolling fire from his starboard guns. Phillip reacted by altering course yet again and opening fire with his two bow chasers as he did. Turning back to the south south-west, he now had the French frigate steering slightly away from him and giving him an excellent view of the Frenchman's larboard quarter and stern. "As they bear!" He shouted.

"Fire as you bear!" He heard Andy repeat from the foremast station.

On Triton meanwhile things were very hot indeed. As the bigger French frigate finally made her move to come round from his westerly heading, James was ready.

"Alter course due south. Open the gun ports and prepare to fire. Terrance, hold your fire until his guns come out!" James looked over his deck; his boats were already in the water behind him, so that was ready. What had he forgotten? Well, no time now! Just then, the two bow chasers on the French frigate opened up. One shot went clear through the rigging, miraculously not hitting a thing, but the other struck high in the foremast rigging, and struck the top mast. Fortunately, James had clewed up his fore course and the mast held. "Fire as you bear, Terrance!" The whole starboard side opened up with one great roar, as smoke instantly billowed back over the deck. Smoke or not, the men were at their guns and reloading in seconds. "Now, everybody on the main deck, get down!" The men flattened as the French frigate opened fire all along her starboard side. "Alter course three points to starboard! We must come alongside him to give Phillip the chance to get around. Fire when ready!" Instantly, the forecastle carronades barked out their gravelly greeting, spewing grape across the Frenchman's deck and followed a moment later as the second full salvo from the Triton hammered into the Frenchman only a few hundred feet away. Only one of Triton's guns failed to fire. It had been put out of action by the first French broadside, but many of the men had simply moved over to other guns to help out. Clearly they were winning the battle on firing rate, for James was getting nearly two broadsides off to the Frenchman's one. Then came the second French broadside and everything changed. Three guns were overturned, and the third gun exploded! The deck was a shambles of screaming men and blood. Fortunately, no fire ensued, or they would have been put out of action. Men from the wrecked guns were lying everywhere, and James saw Terrance Bernard lying among them. "Collins, get down there! Terrance is down. Get those remaining guns firing. We must support Phillip. I just heard his broadside from the frigate's larboard!" Even before he had finished speaking, he saw Vandegraffe, the bosun, ordering the remaining men back to their guns! First one and then another fired, and as others began to carry the wounded down to the orlop, order began to be restored on the Triton. Looking up, James saw that they were nearly around the frigate. "Bring her round! We need three points to starboard and we can get behind her!"

The guns began to roar out their challenge, just as Phillip saw James's second salvo light up the side of the Triton. It seemed all his guns were still firing, so he must have survived that first broadside. The bar shot in the front guns found their mark and Phillip watched amazed as the mizzen on the French frigate seemed to come apart just above the main gaff. Then, the Frenchman fired again and although Phillip could no longer see the Triton, he knew she was taking a terrible pounding. The Frenchman began to swing round to the north, trying perhaps to come around parallel to Onyx, but he had left it too late by far, and Phillip's second broadside opened up, this time close enough for the carronades to engage the French quarterdeck with one hundred fifty pounds of grapeshot.

The sixteen twenty-four pounders on Phillip's larboard side then spewed out round shot at under three hundred yards and moments later the main mast on the French Frigate began to topple, while on her deck, there was a huge hole in the bulwark where her last three cannons had been.

"Fire again! Keep at her now, and we have her!" Andy cried to his gunners. Finally six of the Frenchman's larboard cannon fired. The Onyx staggered as two shots struck home, and one man at the number eight gun was cut nearly in half by a large flying wooden splinter. Another fell clutching his thigh as blood poured onto the deck. Seconds later, Onyx's entire battery opened fire again, and the French Frigate seemed to shudder as shot after shot pummeled her. One of the great guns had found her quarterdeck and the wheel and binnacle disappeared in a cloud of red spray. Her upper main mast was hanging over the starboard side and her mizzen was almost entirely shot away. Just at that moment, the Triton appeared, coming round the Frenchman's stern, still firing from at least six of her guns. Her upper foremast was hanging crookedly, and several of her guns were overturned, but she would survive, and the Frenchman might not. As Phillip tried to take in the scene and prepare to give further orders, his own guns began another terrible rumbling crescendo as from fore to aft they mercilessly hammered the French frigate one more time. "Cease fire!" he called out. That ship had no fight left in her, and with her wheel shot off she was drifting and falling off the wind. Already, his last salvo had ripped through her stern and she looked a derelict.

Just at that moment, Pierre called out, "Second French frigate is turning away, sir! She is abandoning the fight!" Phillip spun around to see the larger Frenchman veering away from his starboard quarter.

"Pierre, give me three points to starboard. Man the braces! I believe he is really going to abandon his consort. Turn after him! Range, Mr. Forest?"

"He has to be near a mile off and gaining. I simply do not understand it! He is leaving his brothers to their fate."

At that moment on the Triton, James was observing the final onslaught on what he could now see was the Tunder. As he began rounding her stern, he saw her quarterdeck seemingly dissolve as the wheel and binnacle were utterly destroyed. "Fire!" he shouted and his last six twelve pounders still in action launched their deadly gifts through the Tunder's stern. "Keep coming 'round, Ross. Pull through behind Onyx and you will have a clear shot at that other..." James felt the wetness on his leg, but still felt no pain. Then, as hands reached out, he felt himself sliding into some dark grey place.

"Let him go!" Phillip called out. He walked to the aft rail and observed the Triton as she sailed in the opposite direction. She had taken some damage, and no doubt casualties, too, but the French ship was finished. Her captain had acted in haste and foolishly, and it had cost him dearly. He hated to think of their butcher's bill, but it would be huge. "Put us about Pierre, and bring us alongside of Triton. Then get a boat over to reach the Frenchman. You take a launch out to that wreck off to starboard and fetch me her captain and all her papers, if they are not already on their way to the bottom."

"Very well! Signal for James to send a report of what aid he requires. He can send Terrance and gather what material he needs. Again, I want to see the captain or whoever is the standing senior officer back on Onyx." Phillip walked over to the binnacle and checked the chronometer again. For a moment, he thought it must have stopped in all the gunfire, for it read ten minutes after ten. From the first sighting, it had taken only ninety minutes to totally destroy a fine ship. The other Frenchman was heading for the horizon with all sail set. He would never catch her now, and James might require assistance. It took another twenty minutes to come alongside and grapple to the Triton. The first thing Phillip noticed was Bill Collins on the quarterdeck with no sign of James. With his heart in his mouth, Philip jumped across.

"Mr. Collins, where is your captain, sir?" he asked fearing to hear the response.

"He took a splinter in his leg, sir. Not serious I think, but as soon as the fighting stopped, Mr. Curtis ordered him to his cabin. I believe sir, that we have nine killed and some twenty wounded. We took a bit of a beating in that second broadside, but we gave them as good as we got! Our guns never stopped firing, at least the ones we had left, sir." Bill looked fiercely proud of their action and Phillip was glad to see it.

"You did very well, Collins! We were sorry not to be able to come to grips with her sooner and give you more help, but we needed to get into position to really hit her! I believe together we have had a splendid morning so far. Too bad the other Frenchman declined to join in the festivities! I am sorry about your men. I will have Dr. Cluff come over as soon as he is done with the Onyx's injuries. We were much more fortunate than you. It should not take him very long at all. I will just go and check on James. By the way, has Terrance gone over to the French frigate yet?"

"No Sir Phillip, Terrance was hit, and is in the orlop. I believe he is in a bad way, sir. I have sent word back to Pierre and Mr. Vandegraffe has joined him, sir. He is our senior bosun and has excellent French and Dutch as well! He served on a Dutch East Indiaman for four years sir, but he didn't take to the French giving all the orders, so he joined a British merchantman three years ago and we got him off of her in London, sir. He is a good man, could make a watch commander if Terrance is down for any length of time, sir."

"Very well, Mr. Collins. I will speak with you further on my way back." Phillip was down the stairs in a moment and knocked, then walked into the great cabin. Natalie was standing at the bedchamber door, her face ashen, but composed. When she saw Phillip, she crossed over and took his hand.

"Mr. Curtis says the wound is not too bad, but there is a splinter he is trying to retrieve! It must come out or James will surely lose his leg. He seems to have lost rather a lot of blood!"

"Mr. Curtis, do you require Dr. Cluff at all?" Phillip called to the bedroom, not wishing to leave Natalie alone.

"Thank you, sir, but no. I believe I have got it all. Mr. Phelps, just hold your hand right there for a moment. I must find better light." The surgeon came into the main cabin holding pieces of wood in his bloody hands. He laid them on the desk and carefully fitted them together. Finally he stood up and smiled across at Natalie. "I believe we have all of the pieces, Mrs. Peters! The last bit of cloth came out some minutes ago!" Then, looking at Phillip, he nodded. "I must sew him up now, and then I am urgently needed in the orlop!"

"Dr. Cluff will be over in just a few minutes to offer his assistance. I believe he is nearly done on the Onyx."

"I am happy sir, that you were so fortunate. We have several hours of work ahead of us, and too many for whom there was no help, sir."

"I am all too aware of your sacrifice, Mr. Curtis. These are my men too!"

"Sir, I meant no disrespect. It has just been a hot time, and we will have a bill to pay. I do not mean to question your decision nor that of Captain Peters, sir!"

"Natalie, I must return to the deck. I will send Katherine over as soon as possible; she and Angeline were helping Dr. Cluff in our orlop."

Phillip returned to the quarterdeck, and after a brief discussion with Collins, he returned to the Onyx to take charge of the scene. The French ship they had engaged was the Tunder, and while she was adrift with her steering gone, she was still floating reasonably well. Her consort however, the ship that had shadowed them for two days, the Poseidon was no longer in sight. Triton had three guns destroyed; her top foremast shattered, much of her standing rigging a mess, and twelve feet of her starboard bulwarks and railing were missing. The final tally was ten dead on the Triton, with nineteen wounded, two seriously, including Lieutenant Bernard, and two dead with six wounded on the Onyx. On the French ship it had been much worse, with the Tunder having lost ninety-four men. The Captain of the Tunder had not been fortunate, as he had been among those killed when the last broadside had destroyed the quarterdeck entirely. The orders found in his cabin made for interesting reading, and Phillip was delighted to have them. They would certainly prove that his self defense was warranted, and came from the government in Paris, and not even from the French Admiralty, but from the Chief Directorate of the Paris Council, which in effect meant Napoleon and Talleyrand. The orders specified that not only were Phillip's ships to be attacked and destroyed, but also that Phillip Hollis himself was to be killed by any means possible.

It was well into the afternoon by the time all the French prisoners had been treated on the Tunder, and she had been taken in tow behind the Onyx. She would be taken into the harbour at Los Llanos on the western side of La Palma, the nearest of the Canary Islands. It was a small out of the way harbour that would serve well to leave the French to their own devices. It would take them many weeks or even months to repair their frigate, and by that time, Onyx and Triton would be in the Indian Ocean. Before taking her in tow, Phillip had removed much of her gun powder, some barrels of supplies, and several dozen cases of good French wine. What gunpowder was left aboard the Tunder that Phillip or James could not use was thrown overboard, and three of her twelve pound cannon were hoisted across to replace those lost on the Triton. With both carpenters aboard the Triton, repairs were underway by the time they began the slow trip east to find La Palma. While it was only ninety miles, it took nearly two days to make the voyage, towing the crippled Tunder. On the morning of the fourteenth, La Palma was clearly in sight to the east as the sun rose behind her, and by noon the tow was released in Los Llanos harbour, freeing the two English frigates to resume their journey.

Lieutenant Bernard, who had been struck down when one of the twelve pounders had exploded, killing six of her crew instantly, was beginning to come around. The left side of his face and his left hand and arm were badly burned, and he would bear the scars for the rest of his life, but the doctor now believed he would live. Dr. Cluff had transferred him to the Onyx, and was caring for him hourly, and giving him laudanum to help with his terrible pain. The doctor thought that his eye might be saved, but only time would tell. Katherine spent hours at poor Terrance's side, reading to him when he was lucid and sitting and bathing his burns when he was not. James was up and about in only a few days, but in the meantime, Phillip had loaned him Andy Barg and agreed with Pierre to raise Mr. Vandegraffe to a watch commander, making him an acting lieutenant. The mast on Triton had been repaired and her bulwarks and railing restored to something approaching her former state. Only two more of the badly injured had succumbed to their wounds and for the most part, the rest were recovering. It was time to begin an earnest run for Cape Verde, which lay over one thousand miles to the south.

CHAPTER ELEVEN
The Cape and Praia

His passengers jubilant after their timely passage, Ross's Celeste dropped her anchor in Cape Town harbour on the seventeenth of September, in a slight drizzle. The sea was calm with light winds, and the boats had an easy time transferring their guests and baggage ashore. Patrick and Ross had been given an address to visit, where, by mentioning Phillip's name, they might find information and possible passengers or cargo for Madras or Calcutta. Entering the building, which sported no name or indication of its reason for existence, Ross was at first taken aback by the smell and dark and dingy character of the place, but as his eyes adjusted, he noticed small groupings of men sitting at tables back in alcoves. A young woman approached them, smiling and asked their business. "My name Madam is Morrissey, but I represent Hollis & Company Shipping. I was asked to stop in here on their behalf."

"Ah, Mr. Morrissey, of course, come with me please." Turning, she led the two men to a corner table in a quiet alcove of its own. "Someone will be with you in just a few moments, sir! May I bring you anything while you wait?"

Not knowing the etiquette, Patrick lowered his voice and asked, "What, madam is the normal practise?"

The girl turned and smiled, "I will take care of it, sir."

Ross covered his mouth with his hand as he smiled at Patrick's obvious discomfort. Captaining a ship was something the two were at least familiar with, but this kind of arrangement was something totally new and it was the sort of thing again that George Fielding would have taken in hand himself.

In just a few minutes the girl returned with a bottle of Irish whiskey, a pitcher of sparkling water and several glasses. "I may suggest sirs, as you are new here, use much more of the sparkling water and very little of the whiskey, although it is quite good!" The young lady had just left when a rather large and florid man got up from another table and ambled over, sitting down without waiting for an invitation. "My good fellows, word has it you are east-bound. Any particular destination or are you open to some options?"

"Some, perhaps, on the sub-continent. We are not interested in island hopping, preferably Madras, but we could make a run to Calcutta if the price was right."

"Yes, well, nearly everyone will do that, you know. That is the preferred route. I might have something else in mind, but it would pay well. You would need to make two stops, one at Dar es Salaam and the second just north of there on the island of Zanzibar. You would load there and could deliver your load either to Madras or Calcutta, as I have connections in either port. The man slipped a paper over the table to Patrick; this is the price per ton. You could have as much as you can carry. I will be back here tomorrow for your answer."

Patrick glanced at the paper. "Just one thing, sir. I will not carry slaves; my ship is no blackbirder."

"No, of course not! I would not think of it. The cargo is mostly ivory and some skins. There will be three passengers as well. They will not trouble you as they have no English." With that, the large man rose, finishing a drink Patrick had not even notice him pour, and left.

Patrick slid the paper over to Ross, who looked, then raised his eyebrows as he calculated their available tonnage. Patrick was intrigued. While the Celeste was still nearly fully laden for Madras, Emerald was not. If he loaded fifty tons in each ship, which would be a safe bet, it would be quite a profitable haul. The number on the paper was thirty-eight. Wages to the men, food and water, ships' supplies and allowance for sail wear altogether would not total much over one thousand pounds for the voyage. It was another thing that Patrick owed to the late George Fielding. When they began to plan for the shipping company, George worked out the average cost per day to keep a brig like Emerald or Ruby afloat, and it came to just about eight pounds! While the Celeste was much larger, bigger than a heavy frigate, she actually had a smaller crew, and cost less per day. He had to allow at least fifty days reaching Madras and unloading his cargo. With an extra hundred ton cargo at thirty-eight pounds per ton, he could realise enough profit to return empty if need be! The two captains debated the offer for several minutes. Ross was much more hesitant. The offer, for just regular freight, was too good and Ross trusted no man's generosity. He suggested leaving and returning to the ships when another man approached. He was slight of build, although not short, and his hair, such as he had, was a dirty yellow color. He nodded and indicated he would like to sit. Patrick half-rose and offered the gentleman a chair. "You half maked the deal with meester Portis?"

"If you mean the rather large fellow that was with us some minutes ago, the answer is no." Ross answered.

"He made a very fine offer, although we have not yet accepted it." Patrick added, hopeful of finding out more information, but secretly already counting his share of the profits from the trip outward to the horn of Africa.

The man slowly took a seat, as if expecting it to be uncomfortably hot. As he did he kept his eyes on Patrick, as though worried he might make some sudden move. Once settled, he took a moment to peer around the dark room, focused on Ross for a moment, and then he leaned forward conspiratorially. "I half a message for Phillip

Hollits from someone he knows as Grey Man. You will take it, yes?" Patrick nodded in agreement.

"You do not take dis deal with Portis. He is meaning to steal your ships. He hafes bad friends in Zanzibar, Arabs take your ships, kill all you men! You wait here one hour, dark man come in, red shirt. He have for you hides and skins for Madras. Price not so good, but you can trust. He is also knowing Grey Man. You load here in tree day," the man said holding up three fingers. With that, and a quick glass of the diminishing whiskey, the fellow rose and walked quickly from the room.

As good as his word, one hour later Patrick and Ross had a cargo for Madras. At eighteen dollars per ton they would not get rich on it, but it would still bring in a decent profit and would be loaded in Cape Town within four days. The load, mostly hides, would not endear him to his men, as the smell would be considerable, but getting a fast turn around and a direct load to Madras was too good to pass up. Ross was also much relieved for he had feared Patrick's greed might overcome his good sense. They decided to give all the men rotational shore leave to soften the reaction to hauling the hides to India.

Back aboard the Emerald, Wallis Foster and Simon Elliot were busy loading supplies when a boat came along side. "Is Captain Morrissey aboard?" came a voice from the boat's stern. Wallis looked over the side to see a rather large, red faced gentleman sitting in the stern.

"Who may I ask is calling, sir?"

"I am a friend of your captain. I wish to come aboard."

"The captain is not presently aboard sir, and I have no orders to admit anyone. If you would leave your name..."

"Is this how you entertain visitors, then, by calling out from your deck like Thames dowagers?" The man seemed surlier than was called for, and Patrick had given instructions that no one was to be allowed on ship.

"I am sorry sir, but we have our orders. If you would give me your name, I will relay it and perhaps arrangements can be made."

The face in the boat got several shades redder. "You will be made to pay for this insult! I will certainly remember you, do you hear?" Then he said something quietly to the men on the oars and they began to row back to shore.

Not two hours later, the two captains returned from a pleasant visit with the Port Admiral, who had also warned them to stay clear of the nefarious Mr. Portis, who it seemed, was just enough of a legitimate trader to keep him from being thrown out of the colony entirely. It was well known that Portis had connections with the Arab slavers on the east coast, and possibly with the French in the Indian Ocean, as well. The Admiral had also offered to pass along a packet from Patrick to Sir Phillip when he arrived. Learning from Wallis that the man had tried to bully his way on the ship did nothing at all for Patrick's nerves, but it did get the watch doubled!

It was the afternoon of the twenty-third of September when Onyx dropped anchor in the harbour of Praia, Cape Verde. Both Natalie and Katherine were eager to get ashore and begin shopping for the extensive list of goods needed to replenish the two frigates, but were forced to wait while diplomatic pleasantries were exchanged. Don Esteban was delighted to see his old friends back once again! Dinner would be arranged and, of course, the wives of the gallant captains would be included. Katherine shuddered, remembering the last dinner with the two 'dressed up sailors' as she termed Governor Abrantes' daughters. Yet, they needed the Governor's good will to purchase goods at favourable prices and to water both ships as well. It would be worth the tedium.

As it happened, she was pleasantly surprised, for both daughters were now in Portugal for the summer, it being deemed by the governor's wife to be too hot and sickly on the Island for the girls' health. With only his young wife as escort, the dinner was a much livelier affair, and really quite enjoyable, except for the squid dish that Katherine had to force to stay down. Looking across the table, she smiled as she watched a desperate Natalie quietly push some of her squid onto a side plate. The ride back out to the ship put her in mind of the last time, when her father, slightly drunk, had provided such a lovely opportunity for Phillip and her to be alone for a short time. Looking across at her husband, she wondered if he remembered. When the bosun's chair deposited her on deck, her husband was waiting.

"Well, tonight we do not require the services of your dear father to allow us some time alone on deck! Shall we take a walk to the bows, do you think?" Katherine's answer was to grab Phillip's arm and turn forward, before he changed his mind.

"Darling, so much has happened in such a short time. It is only just over five months since we were here, before we captured the French treasure ships, before you asked me to marry you, and before I learned how wonderful it is to be your wife." Katherine looked up at Phillip, her eyes sparkling in the night stars. "I believe, Phillip, that I am the happiest woman in the whole world!" Then, laughing she added, "And the only clerk who gets to sleep with the captain!"

Phillip joined in her laughter. "I certainly hope so! Tonight we do not have to worry about the French or about the seas. The men will get just enough shore leave to lighten their wallets and their tensions! I propose we do the same on board!"

"What on earth have you in mind?" Katherine playfully pouted, pretending to be alarmed.

"Well, as for lightening our wallets, we could make a wager. I would be willing to place a bet, that were we adventurous, we could make love at the break of the foremast!"

"Phillip Hollis! Who collects on this wager?" Katherine blushed, "It seems to me that should I consider such a thing, and allow it, you would have already won! If I refuse your peculiar advances, I have won nothing! It seems a most foolish gamble indeed."

"Only if I raised the stake with you!" Phillip smiled down at her.

"And who else would you make it with? Will you have the entire crew watching while you have your way with me up at the mast-top?"

"No, that would be churlish of me, and it would not be becoming of a countess! I only thought to make the wager with James and Natalie."

Katherine choked, "You what?"

"It is not that they will join us! They both agreed that your word at breakfast tomorrow would be sufficient. They trust you implicitly!"

"Your sister is correct. You sir are a rogue! And what, pray tell, is this wager to cost us?"

"Only twenty pounds, my dear. It is a trifling sum really!"

"Twenty pounds! We can purchase several barrels of salt beef for twenty pounds! We can purchase enough coffee to last to India for twenty pounds. Phillip Hollis, the things you force upon your longsuffering wife are disgraceful!" Katherine stood her ground for a moment, and then a smile slowly spread across her face. "How do you propose to accomplish this thing, husband? I can hardly climb the rigging in a full frock, but if I put on my climbing trousers..."

"You just go and change. I will work out all the details and meet you at the starboard foremast chains in ten minutes." Of course, it had to be the starboard chains, because the Triton was anchored to starboard of the Onyx, and how else would James and Natalie be able to see them begin to climb by the light of the lantern Phillip had promised to place at the fore-chains.

The next morning, when James and Natalie arrived for breakfast, the first thing James did was drop a bag of sovereigns into Katherine's lap. There was a moment of silence as Katherine blushed furiously, and then they all laughed. "Oh, Katherine that was so very brave of you!" Natalie enthused. "I could never have done it! Up there, ninety feet above the deck, and well... Oh my!"

"Well sister, perhaps you would like an opportunity to win your money back tonight?" Phillip grinned at her.

"What, and have you watch me climbing those ropes in my under things? Not for fifty pounds!"

"What do you mean, watch you?" Katherine looked slightly horrified.

"Have no fear, Katherine," James responded, "We could only watch the beginning of your climb, from where Phillip placed a lantern on the deck. By the time you were half way up, you were nearly invisible!"

"Nearly invisible! To whom, may I ask?" Katherine was now looking at her husband with a certain degree of venom.

"Why, only to James and myself, dear. We were the only ones allowed on the larboard forecastle after we returned from dinner. I dare say, Katherine you do climb awfully well. And I will admit, if it is a consolation, that we found your daring, well... invigorating."

"I think that is enough of this!" James was now the one blushing. "What say we call Carter for breakfast? I, for one, am famished this morning!" That brought a last laugh and the entrance of Carter caused a definite change in subject matter.

Soon the discussion was all about re-supplying the ships and what could be gotten for what prices, if at all. It was decided that the two women would go ashore after breakfast, with Andy Barg and a dozen of his best to guard them as they made the rounds of merchants. Lists were drawn up and revised several times until it was time to depart. James would stay and confer with Phillip about the route to take and time for departure, all to be done over a bottle of Port received from the good governor.

In Cape Town, meanwhile, Ross was nearly loaded with supplies and cargo. Mr. Portis had not returned, much to everyone's relief, and it was reported that he had departed overland for Port Elizabeth. While that concerned Patrick somewhat, because it would give him access into the Indian Ocean, the blond man, whose name it turned out was De Groote, assured him that it would take many days to make the trip across by cart, and that with luck, Emerald and Celeste would be past the port before Portis even arrived there.

Just as Patrick was preparing to weigh anchor, a boat came alongside. In it, was an Englishman who desperately wanted to book passage to Madras. It seemed he was a functionary of the East India Company, and had been sent to Cape Town with an Indiaman, but now was needed back in the Madras Office. His name was Thomas Burke, and Patrick was delighted to have him for company, not to mention his fare!

Just after noon on the twenty-fourth of September, the last water was aboard and the Emerald set sail for India in Celeste's wake. While the winds off the coast of Africa proved light and unstable for the first few days, once they had sailed clear of the Agulhas Current off the Cape by slipping south to the forties, things began to improve, and by the eighth day out they were bounding along eastward into the Indian Ocean proper. Mr. Burke proved a very agreeable passenger with a host of information to share with Patrick and Wallis Foster. He had been born in India, in 1778, of English missionary parents, but had joined the East India Company as a junior clerk at the age of 14 rather than follow in his parent's footsteps. Now, at twenty-four he was senior enough to be sent to various posts as an emissary. He had travelled extensively throughout the east, including several trips to George Town, on Prince of Wales Island, and to Canton. A man of some wit, he often had Patrick and Wallis in gales of laughter at the antics of the Malay and Chinese inhabitants and their desperate attempts at learning the English language, and their sometimes confused conceptions of what English customs should be. "In fact," he said, "the Chinese especially have become much more English than we are! Their innate devotion to ceremony lends itself to a thoroughly aristocratic behavior." Behind all the humorous stories, there was a wealth of knowledge that Patrick carefully recorded in his logbook to share with Phillip and James whenever they should meet.

But the most important information the ebullient Mr. Burke shared with them was the presence, in the western Indian Ocean, of a small flotilla of French warships, anchored by a large frigate based out of Isle de France. With the memory of the French frigate shadowing them in the Atlantic still vivid in Patrick's mind, a hurried conference was called to discuss their alternatives. Mr. Burke was invited to join, as Patrick, Ross Day, Wallis Foster, and Bart Fischer, Ross's first mate, spread out their charts, to plot the safest course around the possible threat. While at first incredulous, Thomas Burke was soon a keen contributor to the discussions. The initial plan had been to sail northward, taking the Mozambique Channel, but with the concern over the nefarious Mr. Portis and his ties to the Arabs situated at the north end of the channel, they had planned to steer east of Mozambique, between it and Isle de France, which would be the most direct route to Ceylon and the strait to Madras. Now, with the potential of French warships in the region, the question was which risk was greater. Thomas Burke had seen two French brigs between Isle de France and Madagascar on his way south to Cape Town, but his ship had not been harassed. The final decision was Patrick's to make, and, in consultation with Ross, he chose to avoid both routes by continuing to sail east along the mid-thirties until they reached sixty degrees east. From that point, they would begin to angle north, hoping to find the last of the south east trades. If the monsoons were late, as Thomas Burke believed, they might catch the tail end of them north of the equator and use them to reach Ceylon. It was possibly going to add several weeks to the voyage, but it should enable them to stay well to the east of the French.

James was recovering well from the splinter wound he had received, now only using a walking stick when he began to tire. Terrance was not so lucky, and would not be back at his post for some time to come. Fortunately, when the gun exploded, he had instinctively raised his hand to his face, and Dr. Cluff was now quite sure his eye would be saved. The hand, however, was another matter. Two fingers had been amputated and the remaining fingers and his thumb would never be totally straight again. The hand resembled a claw more than a human hand, and the lower arm, as well as the left side of Terrance's face were still a maze of angry red welts and blackened scars. The heat of the exploding gun powder had left his arm desiccated and nearly one inch shorter than his right. He also walked with a pronounced limp, although that was slowly improving, and the doctor had hopes for some added recovery over time.

While the two women found the merchants on Praia to be more difficult than those at Plymouth, mostly because there were fewer merchants and they all knew the two ships needed supplies, they were successful in getting their lists completed. In the afternoon the governor arranged for the two women to be driven out to a river mouth just west of Prainha Beach where they were delighted to find a large flock of migratory Greater Flamingos. They returned with an armful of the lovely white and pink feathers, which James and Phillip would have to find room for in the cabins!

The cook, Mr. Pilcher, was able to stock up with a variety of fresh fish, chickens, and several spotted hogs. The doctor and Mr. Curtis surprisingly found a good quantity of medicines at an apothecary the Governor suggested, and Dr. Cluff came back aboard with a rather large lined box, containing some strange leaves from the mountains of Peru in South America. They were said to have great restorative powers. Called coca, he had read of them in journals and was excited to be able to actually try their effect. It was his hope that they might help Terrance in his recovery, and wean him off the laudanum that he was afraid Terrance was becoming too dependent on. With fresh livestock hauled aboard, water butts refilled, and the last man dragged back from shore leave, the two ships were ready to resume their voyage after only three short days.

It would be a long haul, the furthest they had yet gone, with well over four thousand miles of open sailing to reach the southern tip of Africa. If the trade winds held until they reached thirty degrees south, they might make the Cape in thirty-five days.

The first ten days south from Praia went smoothly, averaging over 140 miles per day, and Phillip and James were beginning to think they would have a very good run indeed. Then, five degrees south of the equator, and nearly one thousand miles off the mouth of the Congo River, the winds began to fail. They had found the doldrums, and it was anyone's guess how bad they might be. It was not that there was no wind, just no steady wind, and nothing of any great consequence. There was only one day when they were nearly becalmed, and the men had great sport, though all the women were asked to remain in their cabins. Off both ships, large sails were lowered into the bathtub warm water, buoyed up around the edges with spars and cables. The men were then allowed to swim or splash about without danger of either a shark attack or drowning. Everyone, except Natalie, Katherine, and the two maids, thought it was great sport! Fortunately, the next day saw just enough wind to give the two ships leeway as they struggled south west to find the beginning of the trades.

The following morning, light winds were sporadic and Phillip was contemplating getting the boats out and beginning to tow the ships, when the lookout called out that the sea to the south west was beginning to ripple. By noon they had a downpour, which got everyone busy with sailcloth and buckets to catch fresh water. Katherine ran out on deck and blissfully got soaked, having her first chance to wash out her hair completely since Praia! The next day, the winds began to pick up, albeit out of the southeast, which was where they wanted to go! The trades had returned, and any wind would give them progress, even though they would now have to sail much further west toward Brazil, until they reached the westerlies, well down below the thirtieth parallel. Still, all and all, they did well, and arrived off Cape Town early in the afternoon of the second day of November.

Phillip's first duty was to call on the Port Admiral, and then the governor of the Colony. From the Port Admiral, he discovered that indeed Celeste and Emerald had made port and were now well on their way to Madras, with an additional cargo of hides, animal skins, and ostrich feathers. He also learned of Mr. Portis, who had not returned to Cape Town since Emerald's departure. The message from Patrick and Ross indicated that they planned to take a route East of Madagascar due to the warnings of Arab pirates operating in the Mozambique Channel. This route would take them just to the west of Isle de France, which Phillip thought dangerous, but of course, Patrick could not know of their fight with the two Frenchmen in the North Atlantic.

For Katherine and Natalie, the first order of business was shopping, and not just to replenish their ships, but to find things for themselves, including new undergarments that had not been washed in salt water! They were accompanied by James, who found various excuses to avoid entering the shops he was too embarrassed to be seen in. Nevertheless, he was soon festooned with packages and parcels, yet gamely offered to take the women to a decent eating establishment while they waited on Phillip, who arrived to see three extra chairs pulled up to their table and all buried under packages! "Ah James, you have been shopping again I see!" he quipped.

James just shook his head in disbelief, laughing "I thought I had made such good progress before we left home Phillip, but now Katherine has poured oil on the fire and they are both unstoppable! We may require an extra ship, just to carry their wardrobes! Really Phillip, how many undergarments can one woman possibly require?"

"How many miles did you say it was to Madras?" his wife asked, her eyebrows raised for emphasis.

"Do not forget, James Peters, that I am the only one of us who has made that trip before! I know how many days I will be washing my clothes in sea water, or what fresh water I can steal from the cook!" Katherine laughed back at him.

"Perhaps, since you are the ship's clerk and acting purser you could just requisition some extra water to wash your necessary garments?" James suggested innocently.

"Oh, and please tell my husband, while you are at it, that I require another twenty gallons per week to bathe in!"

"Dear, that is unfair! I gave you water to bathe in between Praia and here!" Phillip argued.

"Yes, dear, you did, every time it rained, so long as I was willing to go and stand on deck to get soaked in the downpour, and have the men staring at my clothes sticking to me!" Katherine retorted.

Phillip just laughed, for it was more than a slight exaggeration, and everyone knew it. "Well, as long as we are in port, you may bathe every day! You may wash your clothes in fresh water, and spill what you may."

CHAPTER TWELVE
A leopard and a Lion

That very day the Emerald, leading Celeste, was nearly fourteen hundred miles south of the Island of Ceylon; still making some progress, though the winds were not what Patrick might have liked. Just after four bells of the forenoon watch the lookout in the maintop called out. "Deck there, sail on the starboard quarter." It had an instant effect on the entire brig; Patrick was called from his cabin, men off duty found excuses to come on deck, and an extra lookout was sent aloft with a glass. Any ship on their starboard side would certainly have the weather gage, and with the light winds, there was nowhere to run. As the officers gathered on the quarterdeck, a shout came from above. "Deck there, it is ship of the line, sir! She is heading north west, sir."

Patrick knew that with the light winds, and with the Celeste downwind, he had very little chance of outrunning whoever it was. With his position, he could perhaps sail closer to the wind, but that would put him right across her bows, something he certainly did not relish. His only alternative would be to haul both ships right round, and make a run to the south, giving up all the distance they had laboriously gained in the past three days. Only a few minutes later his worries were dispelled. "Deck there, signal from Celeste, she says the sail is the Leopard sir!"

The horrible old Leopard, but what a relief! She was an old fifth rate, a fifty gun two-decker that tended to gripe badly. As she was no longer considered stout enough to stand as a line of battle ship, she had been reduced to escort duty and now was returning to India from the penal colony in New South Wales. As signals flew between the ship and the brig, they drew closer, and Patrick was happy to place both Celeste and Emerald in the old girl's lee for the balance of the trip northward. As for the Captain of the Leopard, he was delighted for the company, and the gifts of wine and brandy that accompanied the visits by Captains Morrissey and Day, as well as Mr. Burke, hardly went amiss.

It would take them at least another ten days to make the slow trip northward to the coast of Ceylon with the aging Leopard, and from there at least another week to reach Madras, but they would have the security of not having to watch for the French along the way. Arriving in Madras in late November would still give Patrick plenty of time to refit the Emerald and unload and sell much of the cargo in Celeste. He and Ross could get all the sails ordered for Ruby and Onyx, and then find a cargo to take east, for the Onyx would surely not arrive before January.

North of Cape Town meanwhile, the two couples were riding across the veldt, in the company of Mr. De Groote and several of his men. While the relationship between the Boer settlers of Dutch decent and the English was not usually very good, De Groote seemed an exception, and was more than willing to take Phillip's money and had offered to create an excursion inland for several days to see the African wildlife and scenery. They had left Cape Town by a good road leading generally north and slightly east, and had crossed some fairly rugged mountains. The riding the first day had been a challenge as all four of the English group were much more accustomed to walking on deck than sitting in a saddle. But now, they had left the Cape Town Colony behind and were crossing beautiful rolling country to the north nestled between mountains both steep and forbidding. The days were filled with truly beautiful vistas, a mixture of steep and rocky mountains interspersed by lush and verdant valleys, and the sounds were as intriguing as the views. In the valleys, there was a mix of farms with their ubiquitous kraals, and open land still rich in all sorts of game. They saw giraffes, with their long necks and strange hair covered horns, the striped zebras in groups of up to hundreds, warthogs with strange bumps on their faces and huge curved tusks, and many strange and beautiful varieties of antelope, including the Kudu with its spiralled horns, one of which De Groote's men shot for their dinner.

Each evening as night fell, De Groote's men would pitch tents and one of them would ride off to the nearest farm or settlement and return with supplies. They mostly ate what they shot, but each day they would be treated to fresh bread and butter, soft cheeses and often some homemade jams as well. While there was no coffee, there was good strong tea, and local wine that was really quite excellent.

North of Paarl and just into the domed mountains for which it had been named, they came across a pride of lions. De Groote asked if either Phillip or James would care to stalk a lion, and was somewhat shocked when Katherine answered instead. With Natalie and James staying with the horses, they began a stalk, Katherine carrying only Phillip's trusty Ferguson rifle. Phillip was at Katherine's side with a double barreled shotgun loaded with slugs should Katherine miss. There were two large males as well as three or four females, plus another female further back with four or five young waiting their turn at dinner. The lions were upwind, but the sun was behind them, so De Groote led the hunters around a group of thorn trees to get a better view. When they came out, the lions were in the open in front of them at perhaps eighty yards. The grass was long enough to nearly hide the young lions and Katherine wanted a sure shot. She stepped out in front of De Groote and calmly stalked to within forty yards, while the lions, guarding a downed zebra, became more and more agitated and low throaty complaints issued from the big cats. By this time, even the usually unflappable De Groote was becoming nervous, and began to raise his gun as well. At last, one large male with a black mane stood and roared at Katherine, turning his back on the kill and, lowering his head threateningly, began to approach. De Groote whispered, "Be careful now! Be ready; he will run!" It was enough for Katherine and she calmly raised the rifle, sighted on the approaching beast and fired just as the lion began to leap forward. The already dead cat continued for several yards, then dropped not twenty feet in front of Phillip, who had jumped in front of his wife. The Boer hunters cheered, as the remaining lions roared and threatened, but stayed back. The bravery and the good shot instantly combined to raise Katherine's status among De Groote's men, and soon they were all busily trying to outdo one another finding more game for her to shoot.

Two days later they came upon three farmers, out hunting as well, for a large bull elephant had torn up a kraal and they were trying to round up their scattered cattle. The elephant, they said was not far away, and De Groote's men spread out to seek it. Within an hour, it was located and James had the honor of bringing it down with a pair of shots from within thirty yards. The ivory was removed and slung on a pack horse, but Natalie felt sad for the enormous beast. De Groote explained that there were really too many elephants in the region and that they did much damage to the farms. The reasons were lost on Natalie.

For six wonderful days, they travelled inland. They rode through countryside that was as beautiful as it was strange. All the while, they laughed well and ate well, drank the surprisingly good, home-made South African wines, shot some fantastic game, and enjoyed the peace and tranquility of having no responsibility except for themselves. Even Natalie was convinced to take up a shotgun and enjoyed some bird shooting in the lush valleys. When they arrived back at the harbour, they found their ships loaded and the men mostly sober and nearly ready to depart. Terrance Bernard had at last returned to the Triton, and pronounced himself ready to resume duty. His eye was still giving him some trouble, but his gait had improved and he was learning to use his left hand very effectively. On Triton, his scars and injury were a mark of distinction, for the men all respected him and knew the price he had paid alongside them at the guns. James, with Phillip's blessing, decided to leave Mr. Vandegraffe as a lieutenant, which relieved him of the chore of taking a watch. Natalie was delighted, for she would have her husband in her bed every night!

Phillip decided he would follow Patrick's route and, ignoring the Mozambique Channel, would sail to the east of Madagascar, but to the west of Isle de France. Dick Forest agreed that it was the most direct route, although it would mean a short period of sailing against the Cape Agulhas current. As they began to reach further north, the predominant winds would by now be from the west, so they would have to keep their heading as westward as possible during their initial southern voyage. Early, on the morning of the tenth of November, both frigates weighed anchor and began what would be their longest run, over 5700 nautical miles. With good weather and favourable winds, which were unlikely at this time of year, it would be a trip of forty days. They had to assume more, perhaps as much as sixty, if they hit adverse winds north of the thirtieth parallel.

For the first week, Phillip was sure his worst fears were being fulfilled, for although they had wind, it was weak and variable and the current was against them. In one period of twenty-four hours, they managed only twelve miles made good. At this rate they would have to alter course and run up to Durban, on the east coast of South Africa, to refill water before attempting the Indian Ocean crossing. After a hurried conference with the Sailing Master and James aboard Triton, it was decided to turn further south to try to get out of the effects of the Agulhas current and reach for possibly stronger winds. The gambit was a success and two days later they were clipping along at a steady eight to nine knots. They held course, slightly north of east, for five days until they had cleared the African continent and began their climb to the north east. It had taken twelve days to sail what Phillip had hoped to accomplish in one week, but at last they were now making the headway they needed.

For the next twelve days things went much better, and the pair of frigates logged fifteen hundred miles made good, putting them just one hundred fifty miles due east of the south eastern tip of the island of Madagascar. It also placed them just five hundred miles south west of Reunion and Isle de France, the two main French possessions in the Indian Ocean, and nearing the cruising zone for French warships patrolling the western half of the Ocean. It was time to renew gunnery practise which had grown somewhat slack, and to keep sharp lookouts in the tops, checking for sails on the horizon.

The extra vigilance paid off two days later. They had been making good progress and were now some two hundred fifty miles south west of Reunion, when a lookout on Onyx, which was leading Triton, called out. The sail was only visible for a short time, and appeared to be a large sloop of some sort, but was sailing east, and disappeared over the horizon. Phillip was convinced the sloop belonged to the French and was scouting. He sent a message to James to be prepared for action the following day, for they had no real option but to continue to the north east, which would put them within one hundred miles of Reunion when they passed the island, hopefully the next day.

At dawn, as Phillip had suspected, there was again a sail to the east. As the sun rose and the visibility improved, the lookouts spotted another vessel seemingly coming up on the first, now clearly a brig. The French, for so they were, would have the weather gage and all Phillip could do was wait, and be prepared for whatever they chose to do. By six bells of the forenoon watch, the two strangers, a brig and a frigate, had closed to within three miles and were sailing a parallel course. Phillip, knowing he had the stronger force, signalled to James and began to alter course two points to the east to close the gap and force the issue. The French allowed Onyx somewhat within two miles, then fired one gun and turned away, declining engagement. Phillip called down to Andy at the main battery, "Andy, one gun if you please!" The returned salute was noted as the French flag dipped and then rose again; there would be no conflict.

In the following weeks, Katherine was more than glad for the extra clothes she had purchased in Cape Town, for the skies remained obstinately clear and the water supply continued to diminish, resulting in no fresh water to be spared for washing a woman's delicates. The sextant, however told them they were still making progress, and Dick Forest insisted that they should be well into the chain of atolls called the Maldives' Islands. The islands, scattered over more than thirty thousand miles of sea, were however not only small, but of very little elevation. The highest of them, North Male' Atoll, was at its highest, not ten feet above sea level. It was quite possible to pass many of the atolls at no great distance and never realise they were there. With over eleven hundred of them, however, some were sure to fall across their path. It also meant careful sailing with two lookouts in the tops looking for shoaling water by day and very slow and cautious creeping along by night. When they finally sited three larger atolls one morning, they knew they were within five hundred miles of Ceylon, and only four hundred from the tip of India, which meant only eight hundred miles from their destination at Madras! After all the countless miles from Cape Town, it seemed a trifling sum, but it would still be six or seven long days.

CHAPTER THIRTEEN

Madras

It was late afternoon on the sixth of January, 1803 that the two frigates made their anchorage at Madras, but the peculiar smells of the sub-continent had been with them for days as they sailed up the east coast of India. It was a smell of spice and dung, of countless fires and masses of humanity, of perfume and decay. The Emerald, newly refitted with fresh paint and rigging, was waiting for them in the harbour.

Celeste was not to be seen, for she was docked upriver, where her cargo had been delivered to Sir Walter's warehouse for safekeeping. While there, she had been hauled up to have her hull thoroughly inspected. She was even now nearing completion, and would be back in harbour in another week. Ross, however, was on board Emerald, conferring with Patrick when the frigates arrived. It was a splendid reunion, for they had not seen Patrick and his crews for nearly five months. Patrick and Ross were astonished to see the Triton, having expected James to arrive with Ruby. When they learned of the sabotage in Plymouth, and the engagement in the Atlantic with the two French frigates, the two new captains were even more relieved that Patrick had chosen to alter course for the Azores, for they would have stood little chance of surviving such an encounter. Phillip, meanwhile, was equally surprised that Patrick had altered his plans after leaving Cape Town and, sailing much further east, had avoided Isle de France because of Mr. Burke's advice. It was decided that Triton would be the first into dry dock, to be careened and re-coppered while awaiting new sails, as the ones ordered for Ruby would be of little value. In the meantime, the Onyx was refitted with her new light sails and work on painting and bright work began at dockside. The two clerks were busy, learning from Ross how to deal with the Indian merchants, and running up lists of supplies that would be required for the next leg of the voyage.

Sir Walter's partner in Madras, Percy Newcombe, now proved a great asset in disposing of Phillip's cargo, both from the Celeste and the extra tonnage secreted in the holds of the frigates. Percy went abroad with samples of the wool and the tin from the warehouse and, in three days, had four offers for the wool, and two for the tin. In both cases, Phillip was more than willing to leave the decisions in his capable hands, and as a result, realised a significant profit from both, enough, in fact, to more than cover the cost of the expedition in its entirety, even without the goods still in the holds for George Town and Kedah.

One afternoon, the two women returned to the docks with a dozen porters following, all nearly invisible under mountains of cloth. As the piles of material began to accumulate on deck, Phillip came up to check on the commotion. "Mr. Doucette, could you please have the men all come on deck?" Katherine asked.

"Yes, My lady. If you wish." Pierre seemed somewhat uncertain, but was not going to argue with the captain's wife, for she had never made any strange demands before.

"Mr. Harris, please call all hands on deck!"

Phillip just stood back to see what would develop. In no time, the men were streaming on deck, but with no further orders they just began to mill about. Katherine climbed to the quarterdeck, and with an uncertain glance at Phillip, walked to the rail. The men began to form up at the break in the deck, looking up expectantly at Katherine and Pierre, who was at her side.

"If I might have your attention," Katherine began, suddenly realising that she had no idea how to address the two hundred and fifty men before her. "I regret disturbing your afternoon here in harbour after your many days of diligent labour bringing us half way round the world. I understand, however, that liberty ashore will begin quite soon, and I have reason to remember what excellent tailors seamen are." At this there were shouts of approval from the men who had sailed on that first voyage of the Onyx, men who had helped to create a wardrobe for Katherine and her maid. Katherine smiled down at the men. "Yes, well, I have brought aboard enough good light cotton material for each seaman aboard to sew two sets of clothes. I think it would be very smart indeed if all the Onyx's were dressed alike in clothes more suited to this climate. The cost of the cloth will not be deducted from anyone's pay or share of our voyage profits, I assure you, for I have purchased them personally on your behalf as a mark of my thanks for your diligence and willing service to Sir Phillip, myself, and the ship. Thank you. Please see that the cloth is fairly distributed." Katherine stepped back, unsure of what response she would get.

For a moment there was total silence on board, for everyone was dumbfounded. It just was not done! Then pandemonium broke loose with men laughing and cheering, until one voice overcame all. It was Elias Grange, a man universally respected among the crew, but not one ever considered loud or forward. Now, he shouted for silence, and the demand was carried forward by twenty more voices. "Lady Katherine, if I may be so bold, some of the men were right concerned when they first heard you were to be the Onyx's clerk, and be in charge of provisions, ma'am, as they did not count a Lady as yourself would know what was required. By now ma'am there is not a man on this here ship as doesn't know we have been the best fed and provisioned ship afloat this five month. But what you have done this day, My Ladyship, goes beyond what any here could expect. We will be honoured to wear your colours, and have no fear, ma'am, there will be a fair distribution an,' should the Captain see fit to grant a make-and-mend day, we will have these here togs ready afore one man sets foot on shore." With that, there was another great cheer and thumping of feet on the deck.

Phillip just nodded to Pierre, who informed the men that all duties not required for the safety of the ship would be suspended forthwith to allow for the sewing of new uniforms. In minutes, the situation was brought to order as the sail maker and Doug Harris, the chief bosun, lined the men up and began to sort through the bolts of cloth, measuring and dividing up the various colors and fabrics. Soon, teams were formed and some men began cutting out pieces while others laid out fabric and still more began to pull out needles and thread to start sewing. The entire ship was humming with activity and clearly the seamen were favorably impressed with the material, which was a mix of black, white and burgundy, just like the paint on the Onyx. Shirts would be made of burgundy and white striped, light cotton material, with enough heavier cloth to make sets of white and black pants. There was also burgundy cloth to make neckerchiefs. The men were capering about the deck like children at Christmas, and Katherine was delighted.

"So, just what has this little extravagance cost me then?" Phillip asked his wife, smiling.

"Not one farthing! I used my own money and you told me yourself I did not owe you any explanation of how I spent it! This will not cost the voyage or Hollis & Company anything other than the time the men may use to sew their new clothes. That, I believe, will be more than recovered by the pride it may give them, and the ability on shore for them to find one another quickly should the need arise."

"Katherine, you are a marvel! You never cease to amaze me. I am so very proud of you. Do you have any idea of what you have just accomplished with these men? They will do anything and go anywhere for you! This simple act of generosity will not go amiss, I promise you. It is not because it is so costly, but because it is so unexpected and because it comes from your good heart."

"Well, Natalie has also purchased cloth for the men of Triton, and we could also find some green and gold for the Emerald, and blue and silver for the men of Celeste. That has yet to be delivered, but it will be ready later in the day. Perhaps you and Patrick could take care of that. The markets here are simply amazing, if they do not have it, they create it overnight! It was also very reasonable."

Phillip just laughed and put his arm around Katherine's shoulder.

Within days, all the ships crews were outfitted in similar but slightly unique uniforms, including identical hats that Phillip and Katherine had made up on shore. As they went ashore in lots of fifty men per ship, and twenty from the brig, they made quite an impression.

They had been in Madras for nearly two weeks when Phillip noticed that Katherine did not seem herself. She was remaining in bed later in the mornings and appeared somewhat pale. Her appetite seemed affected as well, and he began to worry that she might have picked up some sickness in the teaming city with all her dashing about the markets. When he suggested she call for Dr. Cluff, she only smiled and declined, saying she would see the doctor when she needed to. It was nearly a week after that, over breakfast one morning near the beginning of February, she suddenly rose and ran for the necessary closet. When she returned to a clearly worried husband, she smiled thinly and calmly announced that her illness would probably pass in about seven months! At first Phillip was alarmed, and then when he comprehended what his wife was telling him, he was truly alarmed! He was also ecstatic! He jumped up and wrapped Katherine in his arms and was about to twirl her around when he saw her face begin to go grey! He immediately set her down and knelt at her feet.

"I know, dearest, that I said, back at home, how this should not happen, but please believe me when I tell you I am worried for you, but delighted in this prospect!" To his considerable chagrin, Katherine immediately burst into tears. "What is wrong, Kate? Have I said something wrong?"

"Oh no!" Katherine blubbered, "I was so worried that you would be so very cross! I did not plan this, Phillip. It just happened, and I ..." it was as far as she got before the tears took over entirely.

"Dearest Kate, I am not at all cross! I am so very happy! You are wonderful and we will get through this together and it will be the start of our family! We will hire an extra maid to assist Angeline, or a midwife, or whatever you require!"

When Carter came in a few moments later, he found the captain and the countess sitting on the floor beside the table wrapped in each others arms. He quickly and quietly retreated to the pantry muttering under his breath about how people of quality displayed their emotions!

While Phillip was prepared to move heaven and earth to accommodate his wife's condition, she was repeatedly informing him that she was not ill, only carrying his child. After much negotiation and assurances from Dr. Cluff, it was decided that a second maid would be employed who could also assist with the delivery and care for the child, which would almost certainly come while they were in George Town.

It was over dinner two days later with James and Natalie that Natalie smiled and remarked, "Oh, I see my brother has gotten the news! How are you doing, Phillip?"

Phillip turned to Katherine, "You mean she already knows?"

"Dearest, there are some things you cannot hide from another woman, especially one as close as a sister!"

"Will someone please tell me what we are talking about?" James asked, somewhat befuddled.

"Yes, of course James, it seems we are going to have a child!" Phillip responded grinning from ear to ear. "Seeing how you have been married a whole five weeks longer than us, you had better check your powder!" Phillip laughed as Natalie turned bright red and James laughed aloud.

"Well, seeing that I was keeping watch every third night until recently, while you had every night with Katherine, I would say you have probably had the greater opportunity, but if you think taking Natalie up to the mast head some evening might help, I would be most willing!"

"James Peters! I am not climbing to any mast head, and do not imply you have not had opportunity!" Suddenly Natalie realised what she had said and covered her mouth with her hand as Katherine and Phillip howled with laughter!

Mr Newcomb, clearly a man of many talents, now offered to assist in finding a woman, who was not only an experienced maid, but who had helped with the delivery of all her mistress's children. Her name was Anusha, which, she told Katherine, meant beautiful morning star. Angeline at first seemed slightly put out by the newcomer, but after a quiet visit with Katherine, who assured her that her role was not being usurped, things settled down nicely, and soon Angeline was all too happy to divide the chores. She found it gave her extra time to spend with her favorite burglar.

Mr. Newcombe, meanwhile, informed Phillip that there was not much in the way of goods to take out to George Town, but they still had the goods for the garrison, and Phillip wanted to load extra shot and powder for the forays against the pirates or the French, not to mention five hundred muskets, shot and ball, for the Sultan of Kedah in his ongoing skirmish with the Burmese. This, of course, could all be carried in the two frigates and, if necessary, in the brig as well. That left the roomy Celeste with no real chore to undertake. Percy had a suggestion. He had a warehouse filled with teak that had a very good market in Calcutta. If Phillip would like, he would hire the Celeste to carry the teak to Calcutta, with himself as a passenger, and in return, he would find a very profitable load for Ross to transport back through Penang to China. In fact, Newcomb suggested, the load for China might be a joint venture for Hollis Shipping, Percy Newcombe, and Katherine's father. After some negotiations, Phillip sealed the deal by purchasing one-half of the teak in the warehouse and agreeing to make the entire round trip a joint venture. Percy had the means to get the Celeste into Canton, for he was well connected and could insinuate them under the umbrella of the East India Company monopoly. He vowed they would make their fortunes on one run into the forbidden land, as long as Phillip had no qualms about the cargo they would carry. Phillip agreed after Percy promised it would not be connected to slavery, and then told the incredulous Mr. Newcombe that he carried a letter of charter from John Company.

By chance, Phillip discovered that Sir George Leith, the Lt. Governor of Prince of Wales Island as well as the new lands on the mainland called Province Wellesley, was presently in Madras conferring with the Governor of Bengal and other East India Company residents. A luncheon meeting was arranged ashore and Phillip and Sir George shared ideas on how best to lure out the French and Dutch privateers who were supplying and inciting the pirates in the southern straits. At first, Sir George seemed somewhat uncomfortable with Phillip's presence, until he learned that Phillip had no interest in interfering in any way with the settlement. Once that was established, along with Phillip's letters from the King and the Admiralty, there was no more hint of animosity, even though Sir George was an army man and Phillip was navy. The Lt. Governor had some pointed ideas though, about not getting too involved with the current problem of the Sultan of Kedah. He did not believe that the Sultan would ultimately survive, and he was loath to see the British be identified too closely, for fear of what it would do to relations with the Siamese, who, he thought, would soon rule much of Kedah. As for the Burmese, whom Phillip was to discourage, Sir George was not as concerned. They were not as strong, nor as well situated, and if Phillip could drive them back, mostly from the islands fifty miles north of George Town, it would not upset the Siamese, and it would help the Sultan and probably bring some good will. If Phillip could just limit his involvement to the Burmese, everyone might be quite satisfied.

Not long after the successful luncheon, Patrick sent word that his friend Thomas Burke had returned from his journey inland,

and proposed they meet to learn more of what Mr. Burke could tell them of the Malay situation. All four captains, Dick Forest, as well as Mr. Burke and his companion, a Mr. Thomas Raffles, convened together in the Celeste's sumptuous cabin to share knowledge and brandy over as good a dinner as Ross could orchestrate in short notice. Both men proved most interesting, with Mr. Burke having first-hand knowledge of the settlement, and Mr. Raffles considerable insight into the culture and disposition of the people on the mainland. When Mr. Burke learned that Phillip was considering leaving the two women at George Town while the ships moved south into the strait near Rang Sang and Bulan Islands, he had some extra advice. "If you wish to be free of worry for the welfare of your women, please contact Koh Lay Huan. He is the elder of the Chinese on the island and has great influence. There are more Chinese on the island than any other group, and Huan will be able to guarantee your wives' safety better than the garrison in the fort!"

Mr. Raffles and Dick Forest were soon deeply involved in a side discussion on the wild life of the region, which seemed to interest the young man enormously. He hoped, he said, to be posted to the region in the near future, for he had definite ideas of how to curtail Dutch interference and to gain Malay support. The British, he asserted, should be moving further south to solidify their still weak position at George Town.

By the time both frigates were out of the dockyard and the new sails were bent on the Triton's yards, it was mid-February. Celeste, loaded down with teak and the last of Phillip's wool, was already enroute to Calcutta with Ross and the enterprising Mr. Newcombe. The two men seemed to get along famously, and Ross was looking forward to the trip around the sub-continent. It had been arranged that they would sail directly back from Calcutta to George Town and meet up with Phillip and others there before continuing south and east to Canton. The winds would remain steadily from the west until summer, helping Ross, but making the voyage to Prince of Wales Island a slow and difficult passage. Philip was not willing to remain in Madras for three months however, to await the possible beginning of the monsoons. It was only six hundred miles across the Bay of Bengal, and then hopefully crossing between Little Andaman Island and Car Nicobar, they would turn south into the Andaman Sea and make their way the final 400 miles to George Town.

While they were in all respects ready to leave by February 16th, strong east winds kept them bottled up in the Madras harbour until early afternoon of the 19th. The men were all getting anxious to be underway, as the daytime temperature was never below 95 degrees with high humidity, and even at night, many of the men slept on deck as the heat and humidity below decks was nearly unbearable. The winds were still eight knots from the south-east as they departed, forcing the little fleet to head further north into the Bay of Bengal than they would have liked, but Phillip and James were not willing to keep the men idle in harbour for one more day, as tempers were beginning to flare and morale was, nearly for the first time in the entire voyage, showing signs of severe stress. When the orders to weigh were given, there was an almost palpable sense of relief on all three vessels. Heading east north-east, which was as close as the winds would allow, would add some time to the voyage, but staying at anchor with the overpowering smells and humidity of port was also adding time and it was idle time, much harder on everyone.

CHAPTER FOURTEEN
Natalie's Challenge

They had barely sunk the land when the attitude seemed to improve, but then, on Triton there was a setback, as two sailors, both seemingly believing a neck-scarf belonged to them, began a scuffle that almost immediately escalated and, before the bosun could intervene, one man lay dying with a knife in his chest. Instantly, sides were taken, and James, with no marines on board to restore order, was concerned lest mutiny break out. Men were gathered in bunches on the gun deck, and while no weapons were visible, everyone knew they were there. James and Terrance stood at the break of the quarterdeck, looking down as Mr. Vandegraffe and the bosun, Bill Collins, tried to restore order. It was not going well, and then, before they knew it, Natalie was on the gun deck. James nearly jumped over the railing in alarm, but Terrance grabbed his arm.

"Is this how you really wish this voyage to end?" she asked aloud, and instantly the deck became so silent the only sound was the wind in the rigging. "I have thought so much better of you than this! I still wish to. Who among you will come and stand with me, who will come and be Triton's first and foremost! You must all know that we are, all of us, beastly tired of the heat and smells of India, but we must not allow it to make animals of us! We are a proud and loyal crew, and we owe everything to one another. Please, I beg you, join me here on this deck and allow the captain to see that justice is done!"

As she spoke Vandegraffe had silently moved over to stand beside her, and now Terrance Bernard stepped quietly to her other side, a cut down sword in his hand and a pistol in his waist. Natalie looked over at him, and calmly took the sword and dropped it onto the deck. There was a moment, seemingly frozen, when nothing happened, and then men began to disentangle themselves and move toward the main mast where Natalie had placed herself. At first only a few, and then in increasing numbers, the men took up Natalie's challenge until James could no longer see his wife for the press of men around her. Just as James was about to go down to the deck, Natalie appeared from among the men, walking softly, with a bloody knife in her hand. "Here, darling, the man who did this thing is standing with Terrance. He has surrendered the knife to me, and I have promised him a fair hearing. Please forgive my interference! I did not mean to disrupt the authority on the ship, but I could not help myself!"

"Natalie, I would very much like it if you might now climb up to the quarterdeck and stand with Mr. Curtis. What you did, my dear, was very brave, but also very dangerous, and perhaps somewhat naive!" James was visibly shaking with relief. "You have frightened me near to death, and if you will allow, I will again take over the ship." James waited as Natalie climbed to the quarterdeck, and then stood clearly visible beside a thoroughly astounded surgeon, who had to fight the temptation to put a protective arm around her.

James turned and walked into the knot of men, who moved aside to give him passage. At the base of the main mast he found Terrance and Vandegraffe standing with their backs to the mast, a crewman named Josiah Turner standing between them. James turned to address the men who were gathered all around the mast, as thick as flies on jam. "Anyone who was not in the vicinity of the struggle, please clear the deck! We will get to the bottom of this, I promise you, and as my dear wife has told you, there will be a fair and honest hearing. Now though, we need to keep this ship sailing and we need to have space to work. Any man who has evidence to give, please gather at the lee rail abaft the foremast and Mr. Bernard will be with you momentarily. Mr. Vandegraffe, please take the prisoner to my cabin." James turned on his heel, as though his orders were already complied with, and headed for his cabin. The men, with glances up at Natalie on the quarterdeck, began to file to their duty stations or go below. A handful of seamen headed for the lee rail where Terrance was already standing with Bill Collins at his side, should tensions suddenly erupt again as those who saw one thing clashed with those who saw another.

In the captain's cabin, James, seated at his desk, had Seaman Turner standing before him with Lieutenant Vandegraffe at his side. "Josiah, you have never been a trouble maker, and you are, by your officer's reports, a good man. You know this could end very badly! You could hang for what you have done. I will keep my wife's promise to you, Turner, but I will tell you now, I will not countenance violence on this ship, and I will not excuse murder." James face was as tight as a drumhead. "Mr. Vandegraffe, who was the dead man?"

"He was Andrew Harper, in Tommy Fischer's mess sir. A bit of a scrapper, sir, and if I may say so, we had a bit of trouble from him in Madras. Missed his return from shore leave and we had to get him out of a fight over a woman who seemed pleased to see him leave, sir."

"Still, no cause for a knife in the chest! That woman have anything to do with you, Turner?" James looked the seaman in the eye, and waited to see if he would lie.

"No, sor! I was on board; we did not have liberty at the same time, sor. I had no grudge against Harper, sor. He stole my scarf, sor, and then dared me to do something about it. When I reached fo' it, he grabbed my arm and drew a knife, sor. I just was quicker 'an him and turned it round, and he sort of stepped into it, captain. I did not meant to kill him; in fact I did not mean nothin' sir. I had an extra scarf; if he would have asked polite like, I would have given it to 'im." Turner looked beseechingly at the Captain.

At that moment, Terrance stepped into the cabin, with a quick nod to the captain, and then stepped back out. "Mr. Vandegraffe, please stay with the prisoner." James rose and headed for the door. Just outside, Terrance waited. "Sir, it appears we may have some confusion. The knife that Turner gave to Natalie is not his, sir. It isn't Harper's either. I believe that it belongs to Fred Howell. He is a member of Turner's mess, sir."

"Howell, little fellow with the missing front teeth? Works the carronades with Potts and Turner. Of course! So, how does Howell's knife end up in a fight between Harper and Turner that was supposedly about a damned scarf?"

"James, from what I gather, apart from two men in Harper's mess who are still sticking up for him, the general consensus is that Harper may have stolen Howell's knife, and then grabbed Turner's scarf when Turner came to Howell's defence! I just spoke with Tommy Fischer, sir. He is a good man and though he is trying to remain loyal as he can to a mess mate, I don't see him missing Harper much. He as much as said it would be a pity for Turner to hang for the likes of Harper, sir."

"This just gets worse. I want you to find out more if you can. Talk to Howell and bring Potts back to see me." James turned and re-entered the cabin.

"So, how about we start over and you just begin by telling me the truth, eh, Turner?" James asked as he sat back down at his desk.

"I told you the truth, sor. I swear I did." Josiah was sweating in the stuffy hot cabin, but he looked James right in the eye as he spoke.

"Yes, Josiah, perhaps you did, but maybe not all of it. What should I ask Fred Howell, do you think?" James looked back at the seaman, waiting for a reaction.

Turner grimaced at the mention of Howell, but remained silent.

"Josiah, whose knife was it?" James asked quietly.

"Sor, I didn't have a knife. I told you, Harper pulled the knife. Fred had nothin' to do with this; it was between me and Harper, sor!"

"Yet, it was Fred Howell's knife you stuck in Harper's chest, Turner. Fred Howell, who is in your mess, and who works with you and Potts on the carronades, is that not correct?"

"Yes sor, Freddie works the carronades, and he is in my mess. Freddie was no match for a man like Harper, Captain. Harper knew it and took advantage, but Fred was not involved in this thing. I was."

"So, you are going to take the blame for this alone, even should it cost you your life?" James stood and looked Turner square in the face. "My wife risked her life to offer you justice and a fair hearing! You are going to stand here in my cabin and toss that aside? Well, I am not going to let you, Turner! I will have all of the truth, whether from you or in spite of you. But I will warn you Turner, that if I catch you lying to me I will have your hide for it, no matter what Lord Phillip says on the Onyx, do you hear me?"

"Sor, I hear you. I have not lied to you, Captain."

"No, perhaps not, but you have not told me all of the truth either! Turner, did Harper steal that knife from Fred Howell, and did you know it?"

Turner's countenance sank, "Yes sor, he did. He even bragged 'bout it. Everyone in his mess knew it. Fred was not going to do anything, because he was afraid of Harper and Conrad. I went to ask for the knife back, sor. That was when he grabbed my scarf, sor. So it was as much about my scarf as the knife. I did not lie about that!"

James sat back in his chair. He knew that no seaman was going to report the theft to the officers, because it went against the whole culture of those before the mast sticking together and no one ratted out a ship-mate. Still, it was exactly that culture that prompted this sort of situation, where things were dealt with in a rough version of justice that left James with a nearly irresolvable mess.

Before he could react, there was a knock at the door, and Terrance entered with both Potts and Fischer. "Beg your pardon, captain, but you said you wanted to see Mr. Potts, and Mr. Fischer wished to come down as well, sir."

"Enter please, Mr. Barnard. What would you like to tell me, Mr. Fischer?"

"Captain Peters, sir; I don't know what you heard sir, but Harper did start things. He took that knife, more as a lark than really to steal it. I believe he meant to give it back, but he just enjoyed taunting poor Howell, sir. Then when Turner here challenged him, he just could not find room to back down in front of his friends. I was on deck sir. Bob Conrad was at Harper's side, and Conrad sort of looked up to Harper. I am sorry sir, but I think Harper felt trapped, so he grabbed Turner's scarf to kind of change the focus. Turner saw things one way, and he probably had the right to, but I believe Harper would have gladly given the scarf back, but things got serious real quick, and then he took that knife out, and Turner thought he was going to attack. I do not really believe Harper would have attacked him; more likely, he would have made some remark and handed it over. Harper wasn't a fighter sir, just not too bright sometimes!"

This was getting worse and worse! James was beginning to see just how this all came about, and he was liking it less and less. "Mr. Potts, do you have anything to add?"

"Sir, I understand what Tommy here is saying, and he may be right, but Harper had more than enough chance to give Howell's knife back, and he did not do it. It was dividing the crew, sir, for he took the knife several days ago, and everyone in both messes knew about it! Josiah here went to get the knife for Fred, and Andrew was the only one started that fight! If you want to punish someone, the man you need is dead, but I will stand with Josiah sir, 'cause I grabbed Bob Conrad to keep him back, and Tommy saw me!"

"Captain, William did nothing wrong, and he did not attack Bob, just kept him from doing something stupid!" Tom Fischer responded.

"Something stupid indeed! We have a dead seaman aboard, another accused of murder, and all because you men, who are both mess captains, did not do your duty and report a theft to the officers! I do not care a whit whether it was a lark, as you say, Mr. Fischer, or whether it was done in malice! I will not have this sort of behavior on my ship, and I hold you both responsible! I thank you both however, for coming forward and keeping a mostly innocent man from hanging for another man's stupidity. Fischer, can you vouch for Conrad? I do not want to hear of retaliation!"

Fischer placed his knuckles to his forehead, "Sir, my apologies. I did not go to the bosun about the knife, and I knew about it. I will vouch for Conrad. He is a follower, not a leader, and I will put him with someone who can lead him in a better direction sir."

"A better direction indeed! You are both dismissed. Mr. Vandegraffe, please escort Mr. Turner to the wardroom, and remain there with him for the time being. I will call the men on deck presently to announce my verdict." James sat tight lipped as the men began to fall out. "Mr. Vandegraffe, please ask my wife to come down to the cabin."

Natalie came into the cabin even more hesitantly than the two mess captains had left it. She knew her husband well enough to know he was not going to be pleased with her, and she had been on the quarterdeck, where she could overhear some of what was happening below her through the skylight. She had been thinking of that day when James had been so angry with her that he had torn her dress off, and she was sure that what she had done this day had been much worse.

"Natalie, I am sorry to have left you so long, but this has been a trying afternoon! I needed this cabin to get to the bottom of things, and that meant you were left on deck for some time."

"Yes, I know James, and it was time I could use to examine my actions and try to see them from your perspective. I remember Katherine telling me of how she nearly got Phillip killed once because she lost perspective in her fear for him. I have no such excuse, because I really was not afraid for you, but for the men! I was afraid that they would form sides and the harmony of the ship would be forever altered. I know that what I did was rash and I understand that I frightened you. I am sorry! I should have gone below and locked the cabin door I suppose, but that seemed an act of cowardice, and I thought that if I, a woman, would show them that we could come together, perhaps it might calm the tensions! Yet, in retrospect, I took action to which I was not entitled, and I do apologise!"

"Natalie! I was quite prepared to be very angry and stern with you. Now you come down here, admitting you were in the wrong, and apologising to me before I can yell at you and relieve my fear and frustration. That, I think is not totally fair! I accept your apology, darling, but have you ever thought of what a mutiny looks like? The men could have attacked you, and down there I could not have even reached you! They could have used you as a hostage, and we would have been powerless!"

"James, I know, and if I had thought for a moment that the men were angry with the officers I never would have dreamed of intervening, but I knew it was between them. Yet, I was wrong, and I am not trying to make excuses! I will accept whatever punishment you choose!"

"Now you are tempting me! Perhaps, I should again take all your clothes away so that you could not go on deck at all! I think, though, I should regret that, for Willis would certainly not serve me my supper if you were here undressed! No, Natalie things have turned out all right, and you are forgiven. I have to decide however, what to do with Turner, and I have not much time to do it, for the men will be waiting for a verdict."

"Thank you, James! What can you do with Turner? He was, it seems to me, acting in defence of another, and ultimately in self-defence when Harper pulled out the knife. Clearly, he cannot be hung for murder, and as you have to follow Phillip's no flogging rule, what else can you do? Have him in chains for the remainder of the voyage, or stop his infernal grog?"

"Natalie, I believe you have hit upon a capital idea!"

"Putting poor Turner in chains?" she looked horrified.

"No stopping their grog! Not just Turner, but all the men in both messes! We have to teach a lesson that their solidarity must have limits when it threatens the peace of the entire ship. As acting ship's clerk and purser, you will accompany me on deck so that the men will know whose idea this was!"

"Oh James, perhaps I have interfered enough. I would be happy to stay down here while you conclude this matter."

"No you won't! Come, we are going to the quarterdeck and will call the crew to hear our verdict. I will announce that Mr. Turner is found not guilty of the death of Mr. Harper, due to Harper's theft and by reason of self-defence. You are going to announce that because both messes withheld evidence of crime, they are equally guilty in the resulting death of seaman Harper and they will all have their daily ration cut by one half for ...how long, do you think?"

"This is serious! I would cut it completely, but what if we say for the remainder of this voyage? That should be about ten days, if I heard you and Phillip correctly. But James, why just the two messes? Surely there were others who knew?"

"Of course there were, but we will never prove it, and we must appear to be fair. We know from the two mess captains that they all knew."

"Would it be better James, to break up these messes? Could we just have the men assigned elsewhere?"

"No, I think we leave them together. There is unity there that will help them in the days to come, especially for Fred Howell, who may yet be blamed more than anyone."

James and Natalie went on deck and announced the verdict to a very quiet crew. When James announced that Turner was found not guilty, there was an audible sigh of relief on the deck. When Natalie announced the two messes would have their grog reduced, there were some groans, but as it only affected fifteen men, with Harper dead, the crew in general were quite pleased. Then, Natalie took it upon herself to speak to the men of what had just happened.

"I suppose many of you were as surprised as the captain, when I challenged you on deck here just over two hours ago! Please understand that what I did was only out of my concern for you, and that the tension we were all under did not escalate. I was wrong in that action, and I have apologised to your captain, but I would ask you, if you bear me any good will, to let us all learn from this terrible incident and remember that we are all one crew, and we have, all of us, a debt to each other that must go beyond our particular mess or friendship. This horrible incident could have been avoided, and I know that there are others among you, not of these two messes, who knew of the theft and, believing they were being good shipmates, kept quiet. Well, because of this silence a man is dead, and another might have died this day. We are all Tritons here, and we must all, not just the officers, look out for all of us. God bless you!"

As soon as she stepped back there was a thunder of "Tritons" from the crew and a "cheer for Mrs. Peters!"

When they got back to the cabin, James laughed as he hugged his wife. "You have a funny way of handing me back my ship, Natalie! I believe the crew would elect you captain if we gave them half the chance!"

"Oh, no! You are my captain, and always will be! I am just you clerk and bed-partner, by the way, are you tired at all?"

CHAPTER FIFTEEN
Burma & Kedah

The winds continued from the south-east for three days, while the three ships tacked across the Bay of Bengal, but found it nearly impossible to turn south-east to the entrance into the Andaman Sea near Nicobar. Finally, they agreed to carry on further to the north of North Andaman Island, and then run south along the coast of Burma. It would only add perhaps two hundred miles to their route, and they could use the south-east wind to get there. Nearing North Andaman, they found increasing traffic of mostly coastal vessels. There were small proas and some fishing boats as well, from whom they were able to purchase sea bass and a variety of halibut that were very good indeed. As they neared the Burmese shore, well into the Andaman Sea, Phillip kept a good lookout for signs of the Burmese army or any military vessels at sea, but was not successful in identifying either.

It was their second day working south along the coast, and they were well into the Mergui Archipelago just off Hangapru, when they were challenged by four large sea going proas, possibly of the Burmese Navy. Phillip watched with some fascination as two of the boats, long low twin hulled galleys with single masts, desperately paddled in order to get directly upwind of his ships. In the bow of each proa was a small four pounder, but even a four pounder could do considerable damage, although they would have to get close to have any real effect, and even though he could not sail at them into the wind, his bow chasers and even his larboard carronades could easily outreach them. As he watched, the remaining two galleys were manoeuvring around to his rear, but that put them off James' leeward quarter, and his carronades came out immediately. Phillip was loath to fire on the galleys, knowing that the rowers, of whom there were perhaps forty in each vessel, were all slaves chained to their seats, and that they would all perish with their boats. He had the men at their stations and the guns run out to warn off the Burmese, but all he could do was wait and hope they understood their odds against three warships. In the meantime, Patrick, in the Emerald with her fore and aft rig, had moved out of her position astern of James, and was now coming up to leeward of Triton and piling on more sail to get abreast of Onyx. In doing so she would avoid being in the peripheral range of either of the frigates, and she would be to seaward of the four proas, should any of them be caught downwind of the frigates.

Fortunately, as Phillip's little fleet had come into Burmese waters, the winds had shifted more from the east south-east, and they were now sailing nearly straight south. It would place the two forward boats alongside on his larboard quarter in only another half mile, and then his entire battery would be able to fire on them, if they continued. At a range of just over one-half mile, the drums began to pound in earnest and the many oars flashed in the sun as the two forward boats seemed to jump in the water.

Dick Forest was standing alongside Phillip and Pierre on deck. "That is no false alarm! They will close as quickly as they can and fire that cannon of theirs; then dart back to re-load, or they will try to board, sir."

"What do you suggest, Dick? Would you have me sink them before they even fire on us?"

"No captain, but I would have you fire a warning shot, and I would do it quickly!" Dick retorted.

The two boats were closing the distance very quickly indeed. Finally, Phillip nodded to Pierre and the order was given without hesitation. Andy sighted the gun himself and, when he pulled the lanyard, the thunder of a twenty-four pounder momentarily drowned out the sound of the drums. The ball's arc took it directly between the two proas, where it landed with a splash and a bounce, sinking just before it reached the further of the two galleys. Both boats rocked as they passed through the waves, but they did not falter and kept their advance.

Phillip grimaced, for while he was prepared to help the Sultan of Kedah, he had no wish to engage these galleys. Yet he could not turn away, for there was little enough sea room in the channel he found himself in, and the galleys could then position themselves upwind on his flank and continue to harass him or wait for reinforcements and perhaps board him after dark.

"Give them one more gun," Phillip ordered, but just then James's larboard bow chaser fired at the two rear proas, which Phillip had momentarily forgotten about. Turning, he saw that one was now closing on his stern, perhaps only three cables off, while the other was angling across to get a shot at his quarterdeck. The ball from James's forward twelve pounder landed directly ahead of the nearest proa as she began to turn, and then, just as it seemed she would turn back, her cannon fired. As the gun went off, the galley began to turn again and James' second bow chaser barked out its greeting, landing in the middle of the proa and splitting it in half. That settled things, and Pierre gave Andy the order to fire on the front two galleys that were already turning to line up for a shot at Onyx. In seconds, sixteen of Phillip's windward cannons fired in a long and electrifying volley. The first of the two proas simply vanished in a cloud of flying debris. The second turned on its axis and began a frantic run back behind the small island they had emerged from. Behind him, Phillip noticed that the last remaining proa was now angling itself to get a shot off at James, but things were not going well for the Burmese captain, for he was sailing directly through the wreckage of the first galley and men in the water were desperately trying to climb aboard and were pulling on the oars from the water, making his progress more and more difficult by the second. If he did not get underway very quickly, James was going to run him down, and the huge frigate would simply slice through the galley like butter.

Patrick, on Emerald watched the whole drama unfold around him, and began shouting orders to alter course and reduce sail. While he knew it would be dangerous to try to pick up survivors, he could not just sail on. For just a moment it looked like the last galley would be fortunate and that James would miss it, but just the very stern, with the drummer and the captain, caught the knife-edge of James' bow and with a loud crunch, disappeared. It was more than enough to flip the boat and suck it under. Emerald turned and ducked around Triton's stern. There were precious few swimmers left in the water, but Patrick managed to rescue half a dozen. All were slave rowers from the last boat that Triton had hit. To their great surprise, one of the wet and bruised slaves began to thank them in broken English!

Timmon Brunner had been captured off a Dutch merchantman just six months previous, and had been in the galley nearly the whole time. While he claimed to be thirty-two years old, he looked more like fifty-two, and was skin and bones. For the first half hour on board the Emerald the man simply sat and wept! The Emerald's men gave him water and some soft biscuit to eat, as his teeth were mostly missing and he was in no condition to chew any solid food. His body was covered in open sores and his hands were raw from rowing. The Emerald's surgeon bandaged the worst, and recommended that he be transferred to the Onyx, where Dr. Cluff might be more adept at bringing about a speedier recovery.

As Mr. Brunner began to recover, he proved a fountain of information, and it was information he was all too happy to share with his rescuers, even though they were English and he was Dutch. It seemed that his erstwhile employers, the Dutch East India Company, had been offered his release for a small ransom fee, but had refused to pay. Now, he was prepared to help Phillip in any way possible, in return for being allowed to remain with Phillip's fleet and hopefully being returned to Holland at the end of the cruise if that was possible

The three ships continued southward through the maze of islands that went on for two hundred miles, and ended near where the Burmese and Siamese borders reached the sea, marking the south extremity of Burma. From that point it was only another two hundred odd miles to George Town, but, before reaching it, the ships would stop at Alor Setar, the capital of Kedah, and treat with the Sultan, who was at his palace of Anak Bukit just five miles north of the capital.

Phillip remained on Onyx in the harbour at the mouth of the Kedah River, six miles downstream of the capital for two days, while arrangements were made for him to be received by the Sultan. Only forty miles from George Town, it was infuriating to be so close to their destination and to be at a standstill. James just laughed, as the two couples lunched together. "Ah the life of a diplomat! Sail half way round the world to wait at the convenience of some jumped up petty king!"

"Jumped up, indeed!" Dick Forest quipped back, "His lineage is three times as long as our present monarch! Kedah may not be very large, I will admit, but it is ancient, and we must allow the Sultan his pride."

Katherine and Natalie were in their own world, paying precious little attention to the men in the room. Katherine's morning sickness was not getting better and she was happy to be at the end of their voyage, at least for a time. Natalie avidly listened to all the news of how Katherine was feeling, of bodily changes that were beginning to evidence themselves, and of mood swings that were driving Phillip to exhaustion in his attempt to understand and humour his wife. Natalie tried to control her laughter as Katherine told her how one day she would feel most amorous, while the next she could hardly stand to see Phillip even look at her! What was her poor husband to think! Her one constant was Angeline, her maid, who was also her friend and confidant of many years. Now as well, there was Anusha, the extra maid and midwife from Madras, who had become a teacher of all things Bengali, including the language, which the three women studied together every day.

The Sultan's vizier informed them the next morning that they were welcome ashore and could have an audience with the Sultan within just a very few days. While the news was received with delight by the ladies, Phillip was sure it would signal the beginning of long and drawn out delays, for which the Muslim Sultanates were famous. The decision was made to leave Patrick in charge of the flotilla, while Phillip, James, Dick Forest, and the two wives, along with their three women servants, the two stewards, plus nine personal bodyguards went ashore. The vizier allowed that it was a manageable number, although he clearly had hoped for less. Dick insisted that it was the smallest possible number if Phillip wanted to be taken seriously. Dick also seemed to feel that there was significance in the fact that, at nineteen, it was a prime number, which he said would be seen as very desirable to the Sultanate. Phillip thought it all nonsense, but wisely kept silent.

They were shown to quite fine apartments and the women were delighted for there were large heated baths, as well as ones with cool water! The food was too spicy for Katherine's already touchy stomach, but Phillip and Dick were pleasantly reminded of the West Indies by the peppers and lush fruit. The vizier, who it turned out, was the Sultan's uncle, was as good as his word, and the Englishmen were informed that they would have an audience the very next day. Dick insisted this was because of the auspiciousness of the nineteen people they had come with, while James insisted it was due to the fact that the Sultan did not want to keep feeding so many guests.

Sir George Leith had explained the customs of the court to Phillip, and he hoped he had remembered. George had informed him that the women would not be welcomed at court, and would be expected to be left behind for all formal visits, although they might be included in a dinner, if the Sultan wished to see them. Phillip was surprised, therefore, when the message came that both captains, their wives and advisor, which was how Phillip had styled Dick Forest, would be welcomed to enjoy lunch with the Sultan. It was a fairly informal affair, and there were not above thirty or so people present. The Sultan seemed in a great hurry to get the meal over and they had barely had a dish set before them before it was whisked away to be replaced by another. The vizier looked quite unsettled, and Phillip was already beginning to become worried that things were not going well when the Sultan clasped his hands together and made some announcement that Phillip could not even begin to fathom. People all around them rose and began to file out of the room, bowing repeatedly as they went. The vizier, who had surprisingly good English, informed Phillip that the women should now return to their rooms, for the Sultan had questions for his guests. With a glance at Phillip, Katherine rose and led Natalie toward the doors, inadvertently turning her back on the Sultan. James jumped to his feet, bowed deeply, and escorted the women out properly, then saw to it that men from the ship were there to safely return them to their rooms. In the meantime, Phillip made apologies to the vizier, who in turn mollified the Sultan that no offense had been meant.

The business of the afternoon now droned on. First order of things was a lengthy diatribe from the Sultan on the shortcomings of English help, initially promised to his kingdom for the right to Prince of Wales Island. After listening to this for nearly an hour, Phillip had enough and held up his hand, palm outward, asking for a pause. He then reminded the vizier, and, hopefully through him, the Sultan, that the English had in fact re-negotiated the terms and were paying him in Spanish gold, which he could use to purchase weapons or manpower to aid in his defense. Thus, he insisted, the English were not avoiding their promises at all! This simply began another harangue of the same invective, which Phillip allowed to proceed for several minutes before again requesting a hiatus. Now, he informed the vizier that not only had he brought five hundred muskets to aid the Sultan in his current dispute with the Burmese military, but he had also sunk three of their galleys on his trip down the coast.

Somewhat mollified, the Sultan now told Phillip that he needed at least two thousand muskets and that there were seemingly hundreds of such galleys just waiting to descend upon his kingdom!

Phillip was sure that his credentials as a diplomat were going down the sewer, but he had been abused enough for one day, and told the vizier that he was now leaving and continuing his voyage to George Town and would be taking the muskets with him if the Sultan felt they were of so little use! Furthermore, he reminded the vizier that he, too, had a title and was considered a person of nobility in his own land, where he was a personal friend of the Crown Prince. He wished the Sultan well, but was no longer prepared to be treated as some pawn of Malaysian politics.

At this, there was a furious dialogue between the Sultan and his uncle, with much gesturing and many passionate outbursts that sounded to Phillip like imprecations of a particularly vile sort. After several minutes, the vizier turned back to Phillip, his face ashen, and begged him to remain, if only for a short time, as the vizier's own head might be forfeit should Phillip leave now. It was plain, the Sultan had proclaimed, that the vizier had misrepresented him and should Phillip now attempt to leave with the coveted muskets, there would be no one to blame but Phillip and the vizier! Furthermore, the vizier continued, the Sultan might attempt to forestall their departure by seizing Phillip's women!

"Should he make such an attempt, many would die, including some in this room, and you make sure His Highness understands that! We came here in good faith, to offer His Highness our assistance, in return for his assistance with our mission. I owe him nothing at all, and my government understands my mission and my views intimately! I have three warships in your harbour, and perhaps you should remind your nephew what happened when he tried to reclaim Prince of Wales Island! Now, you will tell His Highness that any further threats against my wife or my sister will bring about an instant alliance between my ships and the King of Siam!"

Phillip was not even sure there was a King of Siam, but it sounded good at the moment! Evidently, the vizier thought so as well, for he turned and spoke at length to the Sultan, who looked at first furious, but, as the lecture went on, became increasingly uneasy. At long last, the vizier halted and the Sultan made a few remarks, and then bowed ever so hesitantly in Phillip's direction.

"His Highness wishes to assure you that there has been an unfortunate misunderstanding, and I have sadly and deficiently misrepresented what he intended, Sir Phillip. It is no doubt due to the appallingly dreadful lack of my English, sir. His Highness wishes you to be assured that your wife and sister are not only in no danger, but that His Highness will protect them with his very life! His Highness also wishes to show his appreciation for the Burmese ships you sank, and would like to present you with a fine sapphire for each of the ships."

Phillip smiled back at the vizier, who had just artfully shown Phillip his excellent grasp of the English language! "Please inform His Highness that I fully understand the difficulty in communicating in a language and manner that are unfamiliar! If I might ask you, sir, would you think it prudent to move our wives and servants back aboard our ships?"

"I do not think that would be either necessary or advisable, Sir Phillip. You have made your point and I assure you, it has been received! The Sultan certainly does not wish the enmity of the British Empire, and he does wish for your aid. Your women folk and servants were never in any danger. My master was posturing and he has now come to realise that you are a man of action, but not, shall we say, a diplomat."

"I suppose that is unfortunately so, and I will admit that most of my life has been spent at sea, not at court! There is an art, I believe, to this sort of negotiation that I will readily admit to being in want of. I am a rather direct person, and I am very protective of my family! Let us leave that be. If I may ask, sir, where are the Burmese proving the most threatening at this time?"

"The Islands of Kedah which lie only perhaps twenty miles northwest along the coast, and specifically the town of Kuah on Langkawi's south shore, in the channel between Langkawi, Dayang, and Tuba are currently invested! The town will certainly hold out for some time yet, I believe, but it is rumoured that the Burmese may be bringing up reinforcements. The Sultan fears that if the Islands should fall, the resulting chaos might embolden our other neighbours, especially the Siamese, who lust for our land. Your ships could make a great impact in discouraging the Burmese, and should the Siamese note your involvement, it might also discourage their adventurism. As to that other matter, Sir Phillip, I will be frank with you, which is also not possible in court diplomacy. Your reaction to His Majesty's threat to your wife and sister were somewhat transparent, and had I translated what you said, His Majesty would have had a great advantage. What I told him was a slightly altered version, more in keeping with your dignity being endangered. Let me add one thing more, if you will, so that we fully understand each other. I am totally devoted to His Highness, and my loyalty must not be in question here. I am, however, sometimes discerning in the exercise of that loyalty, if you will, for my nephew is also more of a man of action than one of diplomacy!"

Phillip smiled back at the vizier, "I believe that we may be able to be of some service to one another. I would be prepared to unload the muskets and ammunition that we have with us. Then, however, we must first make a passage to George Town to make arrangements for the garrison, for whom we are also carrying supplies, and to have our women remain there while we are involved to the north. Our main goal, however, is to the south, where we understand there has been considerable difficulty with both Malay and Javanese pirates who are operating with the help of French and Dutch privateers."

"Of course, we will be very thankful for these muskets, and should you have people to train our soldiers as well, that would be better yet! As for your wife and sister, Sir Phillip, they would be most welcome to remain here as well! As you have seen, we can provide accommodations for them and I assure you they would be well protected and given every courtesy! In the interim, I shall make enquiries, and if we can discover any useful information about these Dutch or French ships or bases, we will be pleased to be of service."

"Thank you, sir. You have been most kind and I will give that my full consideration. Please express to His Highness that we are pleased to continue this discussion at his leisure, but for the moment I would like to retire for a brief respite."

The vizier engaged in a quick exchange with the Sultan, who had grown increasingly restive during their lengthy dialogue. Now, the Sultan smiled and nodded to the three Englishmen, then rose, and with another brief nod of his head, exited the room. Phillip rose as well, and led the others from the room and back to their quarters, where both Phillip and James were delighted to see their wives sipping tea and eating bits of sugared fruit.

"I do not trust these rascals one inch!" James exclaimed, pacing about the room. "One minute Natalie and Katherine would be honoured guests, but should we decide we were through with helping Kedah against her neighbours, they might be hostages the next. That vizier fellow seemed all right, I grant you, but as for the Sultan, I would as soon keel haul him!"

"Really, James," Dick Forest responded, "the whole thing was a set piece from start to finish, and I do not think there was ever the least bit of danger to anyone. They wanted to know where we stood and whether they had any leverage. They now know that they really don't, and, as the vizier said, they do not dare risk the enmity of Britain, for they have trouble enough with the Burmese just now, and the Siamese are waiting for the opportunity to strike if they show any weakness. No, I believe we are all safe enough, and Phillip you must admit this is a fairly decent place, better by far than anything we are likely to find in George Town!"

"Well, we will all go down to George Town first, at any rate. I am not going to leave Katherine or Natalie behind now, for we will be in George Town for at least a week getting all the supplies out of the ships and making arrangements with the garrison. After that we will have plenty of time to weigh our options, before we return here and perhaps head north to smoke out these Burmese fellows on Kedah Island. Dick, by the way, do you have any good charts of this Island and whatever that town is called?"

"The town is Kuah, Sir. Not much more than a big fishing village, I believe, but as the vizier said, it could have real significance in terms both of territorial gain for the Burmese and of the politics involved with the Siamese. I will check the charts!"

James was sitting with the two women and enjoying the sugared fruit while listening to the exchange between Phillip and the sailing master. "You may be as comfortable as you like with these people, Dick, as it is not your wife, but mine! I will not rest until we are free of this place. I do not trust any of them, the vizier included."

Katherine looked up at Phillip. "What is all this discussion about Phillip? I am beginning to believe we have missed something vital."

"I will tell you what it is about," James interjected. "The Sultan threatened to take you and Natalie hostage if Phillip did not do his bidding!"

"I tell you it was all an empty threat!" Dick was beginning to get angry, "No different than when Phillip threatened Captain Marten that the Onyx was about to blow Triton out of the water! He wanted to know what we would do, and when Phillip offered to ally himself with the Siamese, which has to be the Sultan's worst fear, the bluff was called and the Sultan folded!"

"As I said, Dick, it is not your wife!" James retorted, now also clearly upset.

"Enough!" Phillip stood between the two men. "James, you well know that Dick would never endanger one hair on Natalie or

Katherine's head! Furthermore, we cannot be heard to be arguing here, for you may rest assured, there will be people listening to everything we say."

"What makes you say that?" Natalie asked her brother.

"Because it is what I would do, and these people are much better at this sort of thing than I am! James, can you fetch one of the men and get a message to Patrick and Pierre that we will begin unloading the muskets and shot first thing tomorrow? I would like us to be on our way by tomorrow evening or early morning of the next day at the latest. I believe that before we leave, I will ask for a private audience with the Sultan. There are a few loose ends that require stitching."

Supper that evening was a delight. The Sultan was indisposed, so they ate outdoors with the vizier, in a fabulous enclosed garden of tropical flowers, waterfalls, curving pathways, and paper lanterns. The food consisted of rice, three kinds of fish, scallops, and fruits of all kinds, many of them new to everyone except Dick Forest, who ran a commentary throughout the meal. He was especially helpful in identifying the various curries and warning of the ones that had some real pungent power. The vizier sat with Phillip and Katherine and was most congenial, offering inland sight-seeing trips, chaperons to take the women to the market, and the personal use of his own masseuse, a young woman who, he assured Katherine, would make her feel total alignment of her body and the universe! While it did not appear that there would be time to take up most of his offers, Katherine was pleased to arrange for the masseuse for the following morning. The vizier seemed delighted and told her the experience would not take above three hours, and that he indulged at least once a week, together with his wife, and that it greatly increased the harmony of their humble home.

Just before they left to return to their quarters, the vizier leaned in and informed Phillip that the Sultan would be pleased to meet with him at mid-morning, and that they would indeed be alone. Then, smiling slightly in recognition that he had proved Phillip's suspicion of being observed and listened to, correct, he whispered, "All the Sultan's people will be gone by now. No one will bother you during the night, nor hear what you may do or say!" Straightening, and speaking more loudly, he wished them all a good night and promised to send a breakfast for them in the morning.

Back in their suite of rooms, there was a polite debate as to whether they were now free to talk or whether it was just what the vizier wanted them to think. Consensus was, believe what you will, and watch what you say!

CHAPTER SIXTEEN
Candles & Muskets

Phillip and Katherine at last retreated back to their private rooms, which included a small enclosed garden of their very own that featured a soaking pool in one corner, lit deliciously with floating candles, and where they now found two fine folded robes, lying across a small stone bench.

"It would be simply too rude not to take advantage of such a thoughtful gesture, Phillip! Come join me, and let us forget, for a little while, about the intrigue and violence around us and just be lovers!" She did not have to ask twice, and Phillip was disrobing before she had even finished.

Later, lying on the surprisingly comfortable mats on the floor that were the Kedah version of beds, under covers so light Phillip thought aloud that they might float off during the night, they talked of the options before them. Phillip had come to trust Katherine's judgement on so many things, and in a short time they had developed into a good working team, as well as a very happily married couple.

"So, first we must get down to George Town, is that not so?" Katherine asked, as she turned on her side to face her husband in the dark.

"Yes, I believe so. We need to deliver our goods, which the garrison is awaiting, and also the strongbox that will keep everyone paid.

Furthermore, I believe it would be in our interest to find out more of how the local situation is unfolding from a source other than the Sultan!"

"Will you return here before you begin your forays into the south?"

"With some force, yes, I believe so, but I cannot yet say what with any assurance. It has crossed my mind to send one ship south on a scouting expedition, but we will know more after we have been in George Town for a few days. I also want to meet with that Chinese fellow, Koh. It is nearly always more useful to get a local opinion than that of the occupiers! In this case, the soldiers at Fort Cornwallis will have one opinion, probably the one they have been given, and it may or may not serve us. That is something I learned in the West Indies; the truth was easier to find in the alleys of the towns than in the offices of the forts!"

"Should you come back north, I would be closer to you here than at Fort Cornwallis. I am not afraid of being here, no matter what James thinks. The vizier seems a decent sort, and, as you said, with three of the most powerful warships in the region, I do not think the Sultan really wants you angry with him. I have not seen George Town, of course, but by father's description, I am not looking forward to being left there." Katherine stroked Phillip's arm as she spoke.

"If you are trying to disarm me with that little gesture, don't bother!" Phillip laughed softly. "But I do take your point; this little campaign up here will not be of any lengthy duration. I would imagine a few weeks, a month at most, should be enough. If not, it will take a much larger force than we have to make a difference. No, the way I envision it, we will blockade the channel around the south end of the island, perhaps sink a few more of Burma's galleys, and if necessary, bombard their forces on shore it they are near enough to the coast. You could well stay here, for I do not believe we will be here when the child is due."

"And you would not have me give birth here?" Katherine asked.

"No, I want my son or daughter born on British soil, or failing that, on a British ship, which is about the same thing. Prince of Wales Island may be about as far as we could get from Grosvenor Square, but it is currently British Territory."

Katherine laughed into the blankets to keep anyone from hearing. "Under that cloak you spread of not being another hidebound typical upper crust aristocrat, you are a fraud Phillip Hollis! What a conventional thing to say. What if the facilities and birthing help here are much better than at some outpost village fifty miles away? Would you really risk my life, or the life of our child, just so you could say it was born on British soil?"

"No, of course not, Kate; you know full well that I would do nothing to put you in harm! It is just that there is a hospital on the island and..."

"A hospital, and full of soldiers with fevers, no doubt! I will not deliver you of this child in any army hospital; it is a sure way to have us both perish! I would sooner deliver in the middle of the street. No, I have Angeline, Anusha, and Natalie, and hopefully, if need be, Dr. Cluff. That will be more than enough. Quite frankly, darling I would rather deliver our child right here or on our ship than in some army hospital."

"Now Kate, we have been through all this! You came along on this voyage with the understanding that before we undertook ferreting out the French, or going after Javanese pirates, you would be safely ensconced in George Town! If we substitute Alor Setar, that is fine, but the fundamental decision remains the same!"

"Yes, well that was before we knew what we know now, wasn't it? It was before we had already defeated one French warship, chased off two more, and sunk three of those galleys. It was before I was with child, and ..."

"No! Kate, just please let us not argue about this tonight. It has been such a lovely evening, I do not wish it to end with an argument that we will not resolve tonight without harsh words." Phillip reached over and stroked Katherine's hair lovingly. The argument could wait another day.

Early the following morning, Phillip and James were pacing the docks, waiting for the Sultan's men to become organized enough to begin the unloading of the cases of muskets and shot. It was not that the manpower was not there, but there appeared to be some problem and people were milling about, seemingly aimlessly, while nothing was done. Finally, a rather stout fellow in a bright yellow jacket strode down the dock, scattering porters before him as dried leaves before a spring wind. All this while, the Onyx lay at anchor some two hundred yards out in the harbour, with the cases piled on her decks, looking for all the world like a stack of coffins, while seamen stood about waiting helplessly.

The fellow in the yellow jacket planted himself in front of James, stuck his hand out, along with his jaw, and in a guttural approximation of English, growled, "Wang! Membayar."

James laughed, which was probably not the correct response, because the man drew himself up, his face reddening, and repeated, "Wang!"

Phillip stepped forward, "We are delivering arms for the Sultan. Why on earth would we pay you? Do you understand me?"

The man in the yellow jacket looked dumbly at Phillip, clearly not comprehending a thing he said. "Wang. Membayar!" He repeated. Phillip reached down into his purse and pulled out several silver coins, and held them out to the man, whose face lit up in a broad grin. He picked one of the coins from Phillip's palm and pointed to a boat sitting along the dock. Then, he picked up another coin and pointed to a second boat. Phillip, looking at the size of the boats, thought it might take at least four or five to carry all the guns and ammunition ashore, so he reached into his purse and took out more coins, but the man shook his head and held up his hand palm outward. Then he made a small bow and, turning began to give orders to the men on the docks. At once, ten men jumped down into each of the two boats and began to paddle out to the Onyx.

Meanwhile on the dock, the man in yellow was seemingly busy giving a constant flow of instruction to the men remaining. Very quickly, a line of large two wheeled carts began to form along the street at the end of the dock. Two of the porters ran down the dock to begin jabbering at the cart men, while others were busy laying out ropes with flat cloth loops on the ends. As James watched all the commotion, he realised that the first boat was already on its way back to the dock heavily loaded, with piles of crates hanging over the gunwales. As it approached the dock, the loud jabbering increased as men on the boat and those on the dock gestured and shouted back and forth.

With the crates of guns hanging out over the sides, the boat could not, at first, tie up to the dock. Ropes were tossed out and some of the men on the boat grabbed the ropes and hung on while other began to push the crates gingerly out as men lying on their stomachs grabbed down to secure them, and slide them up onto the dock. Once on the dock they were lifted and the laid out ropes were passed around the crates several times until only a few feet were left on each side. Other men stepped forward and the cloth loops were placed about their heads, with the tail of rope going down at their sides. Once secure the men ran down the docks to the carts waiting at the street. For all the complications, it was actually relatively efficient and the boat was unloaded in good time. Like seamen, the dock workers sang a repetitive chant-like song that kept them all working at the same pace. As soon as the boat was empty, it departed for the Onyx, where the second boat was just departing for the dock.

When the second boat, also heavily laden, was nearing the dock, ropes were again thrown out, to be caught and secured on the boat, but one was missed and, as the dockworker pulled it back in to re-try his throw, he slipped just as the rope came out of the water. The rope flew through the air like a missile, the knotted end striking the yellow clad foreman squarely on the side of the head. He dropped like a limp sack, and the poor workman jumped up and ran for the shore, but before he was half way off the wharf, another man stepped out of the throng and dropped him with a savage blow to the head with a wooden mallet. The man twitched once or twice and lay still. Not one person came to his aid, and James was about to move in his direction when Phillip grabbed his arm and cautioned him to keep still. In the meantime, three men had gone over to the yellow clad foreman and were helping him to his feet. As he regained equilibrium, he shook off the dizziness and then walked over to the unconscious worker. First, he kicked the man twice in the ribs, then using his feet, he rolled him off the dock and into the water, where he landed with a resounding splash and disappeared beneath the pilings.

James was outraged and would have intervened, but Phillip warned him that it would be a disaster, and as they were alone, very dangerous. It was a vivid reminder of the code of hierarchy in the Sultanate. A lowly dock worker could not afford to make such a mistake and be allowed to be seen to get away with it. No matter that the poor man had slipped, the result was that his superior was hurt. As James fumed, Phillip reminded him that there were captains in the British Navy who were equally insensitive and brutish, men who would automatically flog a seaman if he inadvertently stumbled and brushed against an officer. The remainder of the dock workers and boatmen took no notice, or so it seemed, and continued their duties. In two more loads, everything was ashore and carted off. James left to find the women and Phillip turned toward the palace to find the Sultan and vizier for their appointed meeting. "I am truly distressed that you witnessed the unfortunate incident during the unloading of your cargo, Sir Phillip. It must have seemed cruel indeed, as I understand your friend Captain Peters felt great temptation to intervene. I believe you restrained him, and that was wise, for the outcome could not have changed. You see, Sir Phillip, these men working on the docks respect only one thing, and that is predictability. It is simply an issue of cause and effect to them, and if you tried to reason with them about justice they would not comprehend. To one such as yourself, who has great authority, this will perhaps seem unduly harsh and perhaps even iniquitous, but I assure you, if the poor man had gotten away, his own family would have cast him out or stoned him for the dishonour he brought upon them, and to save the remainder of the family from losing their positions." The vizier was sitting and drinking tea with Phillip while they waited for the Sultan to complete his morning bath.

"I believe that I understand, to a point. Every culture has its own set of norms, I suppose, and what we consider right or a mark of civilization might be frowned upon elsewhere. Yet the poor man only slipped and everything that followed seemed out of proportion to the offense."

"Yes, and yet if this man's unfortunate mistake was allowed to be overlooked, the next man might plan to slip! This would lead to chaos, for there would now be no sure security for those who must wield authority. It is not so different than on your ships, where I have seen men flogged for minor violations that we would overlook, such as falling asleep, or perhaps drunkenness. The Chinese, who are so very proud of their ancient civilization, and consider all of us barbarians, are the most brutish and insensitive to their lower classes. If a Chinese laborer is caught stealing and it is his first offense and nothing of consequence was taken, he will only have his fingers cut off! That is, to my mind, a guarantee that he will never be able to employ himself again, and so, will have to resort to crime, which will lead to his execution on the next capture! I am sure we could find corollaries in English or French society as well! Just do not judge us because our idiosyncrasies are different from yours."

"Oh, Your Excellency, I do not judge you at all! We certainly do have similar issues in our society, and I am ashamed to say I have learned to ignore them. If I might change the subject for a moment, with your permission, there is another matter I would beg to discuss before we meet with His Highness." The vizier smiled and nodded his head softly.

"Your Excellency, I have a small personal problem, concerning my wife. You see, she is with child and I am loath to have her on board ship if we are to engage in perilous activity, such as seeking out the Burmese, but I am also unsure about leaving her at George Town for I do not know what sort of care she might receive in the little colony. I know that you indicated yesterday that the women might remain here, at least while we are occupied in the north with the Burmese, but …"

"But you have reservations, especially after what His Highness did not threaten yesterday about taking your women hostage! Perhaps you even have reservations about how they would be cared for should this blessed event occur while you were away. We are not diplomats this morning, just good acquaintances sharing mutual concerns over a cup of tea, yes?" The vizier smiled and folded his hands in front of his jade green silk jacket.

"Yes, if that is possible!" Phillip responded, lifting his eyebrows.

"Among men of good will, many things are possible, but only if that good will is shared, yet kept within close reach. I will answer as best I can, Sir Phillip; the care in His Highness's palace would of course be the best he has to offer, however you must still remember that this is not London. The care in George Town could still be more than adequate, for after all, children come into the world every day, do they not? Yet, perhaps not the child of an Earl of the Realm! As to the other matter, which concerned you and your sister's husband yesterday, I would not give it one moment's thought. It was a clumsy ploy, and it received the response it deserved. Never, and I repeat, Sir Phillip, never would His Highness do anything to jeopardise the safety of your people, especially your wife, whom you are so clearly devoted to! Consider this, my friend; in all these years since your people took over the island, you are the first to actually come to our aid! Why on earth would we wish to offend you?"

"Yet, kings can be fickle, as well I know, and I cannot guarantee to bring you the results you desire." Phillip wanted to get everything on the table at this one and, perhaps only, opportunity.

"If results could be guaranteed, sir, we would have either won or lost this war long ago!" The vizier now openly laughed. "I believe you are correct to take the women with you to George Town and then decide for yourself whether to bring them back here if you return! If you do, I will vouch for their wellbeing, and should you then decide to journey to the south to engage your foes, they would certainly be welcome to remain here for whatever time you might require."

Just then, a servant opened a door, bowed, and motioned that the Sultan was available. The vizier rose and led Phillip into the same room they had met in the previous day. The Sultan was reclining on a large settee surrounded by dozens of orchids. He bowed his head minutely as Phillip entered and bowed. The vizier spoke briefly with his liege, who responded in a most animated fashion.

"His Highness wishes me to thank you for the muskets, Sir Phillip, and has asked if there is anything he might do in return. I will ask him about the French and Dutch bases in the south. If he does not have that information, he may well be able to get it from his cousin in Batu Pahat, in the Sultanate of Jahore. Is there anything else you might require of His Highness?"

"One thing does come to mind. If we are to be involved in the relief of Kuah, it would be helpful if we could regularly replenish water and some supplies here. I would like to do so with some contact upon whom we might rely on a regular basis."

The vizier smiled knowingly, "Very good suggestion, Sir Phillip, and I am sure His Highness will have just the right merchant in mind to accommodate your wishes!"

During the next brief dialogue, Phillip surmised that indeed the idea would give the Sultan the opportunity to spread his favour at Phillip's expense, but, as he would require a contact, it might as well benefit the Sultan, which in turn might prove to Phillip's ultimate good. It seemed by the Sultan's sudden smile and enthusiastic chatter, that the vizier must have told him of the discussion they had regarding Katherine and her possible return. The hand waving and the vizier's bowing and smiling seemed to be good signs, but then again, for all Phillip knew they might signify that he was to lose his head! After quite some time and several exchanges, the vizier bowed a final time and turned to Phillip.

"His Highness has most graciously offered, Sir Phillip, that if the Lady Katherine should desire to return to our humble home, His Highness will be pleased to have her carried to the Sultan's hilltop home, Ganung Keriang, where his own wives spend the summer. It is at a higher elevation where it is cooler, with refreshing baths and women of high birth to keep the countess from being lonely. Also, this is where the Sultan's wives go to give birth and it is considered most auspicious!"

"Please thank His Highness most effusively for me," Phillip smiled back. "Would there be anyone there who spoke English, do you know? It might be somewhat difficult to communicate elsewise."

"Yes, of course! I would be delighted to send my own humble daughter! I have been instructing her for quite some time, and while her English may certainly be limited, she would be delighted to be of some small service!"

"That is most kind, your excellency!" Phillip responded, "Now, as to our involvement with your present troubles on the Islands, what does His Highness request, exactly?"

That question began another long series of exchanges and explanations of what was requested and what was possible. It became quickly apparent that the Sultan would love nothing better than an immediate attack on Mergui, the Burmese most southerly main base within Burma, some four hundred miles to the north. When Phillip explained that any attack on Burmese soil was well beyond his allowable intervention, it was agreed that he would, within several weeks, return and patrol the area around the Islands of Langkawi and Dayang, searching out Burmese vessels and perhaps helping by bombarding their bases, should they prove within reach of the ship's cannons. Phillip also offered to inquire at Fort Cornwallis for any assistance in training Kedah's army with its new muskets.

Katherine was certain that there was not a single muscle in her entire body that was not demanding attention. She ached in places she had, until very recently, not even known about. The masseuse had been most thorough, and after overcoming her embarrassment in being asked to totally disrobe, she had been literally covered in aromatic oil, then kneaded and prodded and stretched in every conceivable direction. The young woman had even used her feet to work the muscles in Katherine's back and buttocks. After she was done, the masseuse had wrapped her in warm blankets and left her to sleep while she applied her various torture techniques to Natalie, who had grown more and more uncertain about the treatment as she watched Katherine and listened to her groans and grunts during the process. Now the two women were sitting together in a cool bath trying to imagine how long it would be before they would be able to walk again, much less be free of pain. To think the vizier and his wife went through this once a week!

The door to the bath chamber opened and the masseuse beckoned them to come out. Katherine shook her head, declining further torture, as Natalie just whimpered at the thought of further treatment. The masseuse disappeared but moments later another face came around the door. This girl spoke English.

"Please come. It is most desirous that you must finish the treatment. I promise you that it will not be uncomfortable at all. If you do not complete the treatment, you will be very sore."

"Dear young lady, we are sore now! I do not believe I can endure another round of this torture!"

"Oh. I am most sorry! This one did not realise you were unaccustomed to the treatment. She may have been too enthusiastic. Still, please come with me now, for the rest of the treatment will ensure you will feel much better, and there will be no pain, I promise you."

Warily, the two women rose from the bath, were again wrapped in warm towels and taken to another room where Natalie insisted they were actually in an oven. They were carefully walked down a narrow path between rows of rocks that had clearly been heated.

When the two women were lying side by side on low tables, several girls came in and began pouring water on the rocks until the steam filled the room and they could barely see one another. Meanwhile, another girl was carrying in large bowls and setting them around the tables. When the desired amount of steam had been achieved, all the girls began digging into the bowls and plopping copious amounts of warm mud onto the two women. When they were totally covered in the warm goo, they were again wrapped like mummies. Two caldrons of hot water were then introduced, and poured over several trays of flower petals. The entire room was soon infused with the fragrant aroma and, in spite of her apprehension, Katherine found herself drifting off to sleep.

The next thing she heard was Natalie giggling, and looking over she saw the girls were unwrapping her and scrapping off the mud. When the mud was mostly gone, the two women were again taken to the bath to be washed and oiled. Katherine realised, coming out of the tub, that she no longer ached, and that her body seemed more relaxed than she could remember.

"Natalie, how do you feel?"

"Like I was twelve years old? I don't ache anymore, and I think I might be an inch taller!"

"I just want to curl up and go back to sleep! I have not felt this relaxed since before we left England. Do you think we could steal that girl?"

CHAPTER SEVENTEEN
George Town

The trip south to Prince of Wales Island was a peaceful and pleasant sail of only a half day, as the winds had finally turned, and were now easterly. Fort Cornwallis was situated on a point of land closest to the mainland, on the north east corner of the Island. The channel between the fort and what was now called the village of Butterworth in the new territories was only slightly over a mile wide. There were several protected inlets just to the south of the fort and, in no time, the three ships were moored and surrounded by boats full of excited Malays, Chinese and several Englishmen as well. Two of the Englishmen were desirous of knowing if Sir George Leith might perhaps be aboard, and discovering that he was still in Madras, they returned to shore, but not before including an invitation for Phillip and his officers to visit at the Company offices in Fort Cornwallis. As water and supplies had been replenished in Alor Setar, there was nothing to keep the Captains or clerks from venturing ashore almost immediately.

The first impressions were of chaos. It was evident that the settlement was in the process of rapid growth, and construction or destruction were difficult to differentiate. Everything to the north of Chulia Street seemed at least to be laid out in some sort of order, with China Street running north toward the fort. At the foot of China Street, on Chulia, was a mosque that marked the beginning of the Muslim Quarter stretching to the south. To the north were mostly Chinese and Europeans, and the street names reflected the English origins of George Town, with names like Pitt Street, Light Street, and Beach Street. Directly to the west of Fort Cornwallis was a square housing the administration buildings and behind them, the hospital. The assistant Lt. Governor, a Mr. Dunning, who insisted on acting as their guide, informed Katherine, on whom he openly doted, that the population of the town now exceeded twelve thousand souls, if one counted the Malays and Chinese! In fourteen years, the colony had tripled in size, and was still growing, much to the displeasure of the Dutch, who believed they alone should control all commerce in the East Indies. The Dutch, who were mostly situated further south on Sumatra and Java, had distinct opinions on an English presence closer to India and at an ideal stopping off point on the closest pathway to China.

The notion of finding suitable accommodations for an extended period of time seemed to perplex the dear man. Certainly there were some places where they might stay for a short while, including an inn of a somewhat dubious nature, but Mr. Dunning's best advice seemed be to that Phillip should contract to have a house constructed. There would be no difficulty, Phillip was assured, in disposing of the house when they were ready to return home. When Phillip began to muse aloud about the size required, having at a minimum six bedrooms, three sitting rooms, a suite of offices, a separate kitchen, and grounds with some security, Mr. Dunning became quiet for a moment.

"The sort of accommodation you refer to would take a considerable time to construct, and the cost might be significant. We would need to find a suitable plot of land, and finding enough workers could prove a challenge as well. I believe, if you are seriously contemplating such a dwelling, we might be well advised to contact Huan!"

"Ah yes," Phillip answered, "Koh Lay Huan, I was told that if there was anything I wanted to accomplish here, it would be well to ask Mr. Huan."

"I would not go so far as that; no, certainly not," a clearly offended Dunning answered. "The administration will be able to give you all of the assistance you might require. In matters of local workers however, Huan can be quite helpful, that is if he chooses to be!"

By this time, the group, consisting of the two couples, Patrick, Pierre, Dick Forest, and Andy Barg, had made their way to Fort Cornwallis and across to the hospital. "So," Katherine asked conversationally, "is the hospital kept quite busy in this tropical climate?"

"I am afraid so, yes. It seems some fever or other is always breaking out among the men, mostly our troops. It does not appear to affect the locals as much, or at least we do not recognise it," Dunning answered with a thin smile. "I am afraid that while this is a beautiful land in so many ways, it is not perfect, and the heat and tropical maladies do not really make it so very suitable to westerners coming from more moderate climates. I am sure, Sir Phillip, that you have discovered the same things in the Western Indies of the Caribbean Sea."

"Certainly! We lost more men by far to Yellow Jack than we ever did to the French or Spanish. I believe it has greatly to do with the humidity, miasma you know, but our Doctor Cluff has been reading some ideas that even the flies and those interminable mosquitoes may have something to do with it. I cannot see how, but when we sailed over, he insisted that we have netting to sleep under whenever we were near shore or there was little wind, and we have made this entire trip with not one single outbreak of fever, thank God!"

Coming back round to the entrance to the fort, they were greeted by Colonel Sir Willis Strong, the acting commanding officer, and his adjutant, Major Harris. The Colonel invited the group to tea, and promised a more fitting reception, with a full dinner for the following evening. James responded by inviting the Colonel and his adjutant to dine that very night aboard the Triton, as Phillip had already indicated he wished to find and meet the illustrious Koh Lay Huan. Dunning proved most helpful and offered a guide and interpreter to aid in speaking with the Chinese leader, whose English was, it seemed, sketchy at best. Leaving James and Pierre to speak with Colonel Strong about the possibility of finding instructors for the Sultan's troops, Phillip, Katherine, Andy and Dick strolled off with the guide, whose name was apparently also Huan. This could get interesting, thought Phillip, as they strained their ears to catch at least half of what the man was telling them. Back down King Street, across Bishop, and right on China Street brought them to a small wrought iron gate leading into a passageway. Following the guide, they found themselves in a totally enclosed courtyard, where they were invited to remove their footwear and be seated on a series of low benches. In no time at all, which surprised Phillip after his waiting on the Sultan, a plainly dressed older Chinese man appeared through another doorway and joined them with much bowing and smiling.

This was the illustrious Koh, who was delighted to meet the British Earl who had come to aid his friend the Sultan of Kedah! When Phillip queried the guide how Koh Huan knew of Phillip's plans, the guide only smiled and nodded his head. Koh then spoke in rapid Mandarin to the interpreter, who reddened and informed Phillip that the Burmese were no friends of the Chinese community, either here in Penang or in China, where there were many century old feuds. Therefore, "the enemy of my enemy being my friend", Kedah was now firmly embraced by the Chinese in Penang! After their tea it was possible to begin to discuss matters of a more practical nature, and Phillip asked if Koh Huan might have advice for him in the matter of housing and also of the advisability of sending Katherine back to Kedah while he helped the Sultan with the Burmese problem.

Koh Lay Huan smiled and bowed. "Why you are asking this humble servant on matters such as this? You English are masters here; why you not ask Sir Leith or Dunning?"

Phillip bowed back and decided that he might as well be forthright, and ignore all the advice he had been given, as it had served him well with the Sultan's vizier. "Honorable Koh Huan, I am seeking guidance through truth, and I have been informed that you are one who may possess this truth. My people at Fort Cornwallis will tell me what they believe I wish to hear, or they will tell me what they wish was truth. It does not matter which, for neither will serve me well."

Huan looked up and sat for a moment staring into Phillip's face most intently; then he smiled slowly and gave a brief bow of his head. Next, to Phillip's total surprise he dismissed the interpreter, and waited while the man left the courtyard.

"Lord Hollis, you are much too forthright to last long here, I fear. I have had some practise in studying the eyes of people, which are, as you know, the windows to the soul. I believe your eyes are telling me to put our customary wariness aside, and I am willing to chance this with you. Therefore, I will try to be of what service I may, suggesting only that we keep this visit between ourselves. I accept your questions in the spirit with which I believe you have come. This house you require must be built soon, yes? Your wife is with child, and this is your chief concern. Yet, this must not be done imprudently. We can help you if you have resources, but the land must be arranged with Mr. Denning. Two alternatives to consider; one is to place this property near the water, so that you might have easy access from your ships. The second alternative is to examine Flagstaff Hill, some short distance to the west of the settlement, but a location that provides cooler weather and some degree of isolation from the noise, press, and diseases of the town. The hill rises some eight hundred meters, and provides cool clean air and good water. You might consider, if resources are indeed not a problem, to build in both locations. An office and house on the waterfront to aid in securing and storing supplies would be efficient, while a residence in the hills for your women and child would be both superior for their health and, perhaps, security."

"Thank you Koh Huan and what would be your advice as to the other matter of having Katherine accept your friend the Sultan's hospitality?" Phillip asked.

"Lord Hollis, the enemy of my enemy may be my friend, but he may not be my brother! I may make alliance with the bear while I hunt the tiger, yet not wish to keep my children in his den. He has, I believe, already threatened the safety of your women once. You must follow your own heart in this matter, but I would caution that the Sultan may be a superior ally if he is not distracted by the temptation to coerce you."

"I thank you, Koh Lay Huan, for your patience, and for your advice. May I impose upon you with but one more question? Assuming I might make the arrangements for the plot of land we require, how long would you believe would be needed to construct a good sized house, and which house would you believe we should begin with?"

"Ah, but that is two questions, Lord Hollis!" Huan smiled and looked over at Katherine. "The child is not expected for some time yet, is this correct?"

"Not until perhaps August, if all goes well." Katherine answered, smiling at the wispy grey beard.

"Then I would suggest that there is ample opportunity to accomplish everything you require, Sir Phillip. The construction of a simple facility near the shore would not take above two months' time, and perhaps less if, as you say, all goes well. In the meantime, the work on the hilltop house may also proceed, although this will be of longer duration owing to the possible difficulty in clearing the land and moving supplies up the mountain side. Still, in four or five months all may be accomplished if enough workers may be hired! The cost, however, could be considerable. Perhaps in a few days we might meet again and, if it is suitable, I might have some estimate for you, should you choose to use my people."

"Thank you, Koh Huan, for your assistance and generous offer. If I may further burden you with my lack of knowledge, could you tell me what you know of this Burmese threat to Kedah?"

"The Burmese are carrion fowl, Lord Phillip. They smell an easy meal and a way to stake a claim before the tiger arrives. Should the game they stalk prove to have sharp teeth, they will flutter back to their nest to peck their wounds and wait for a better opportunity. They also fear the Siamese, who are the real tigers in this instance! Yet, I do not believe the Siamese will attack any time in the near future, for they have their own issues at present on their eastern borders. No, Sir Phillip, your real struggles will be in the south, as you suspected. I will perhaps be able to gather some information for you by the time you return from your adventure with the Sultan. If I may ask, when do you leave for the north?"

"I suspect you already know that better than I do Koh Huan! We must first unload our supplies and make certain arrangements, but I believe we could be prepared to depart in one week's time."

"Ah so, may I humbly suggest you not depart until the 8th day from today. In my calendar it is a much more auspicious day to begin a journey. That would be the 12th day of your March and it is a good day to make departures. Also, this will give us ample opportunity to develop the plan for your desired houses. I will be away for two days; I am sorry but this is needful. When I return, I will send to your ship to arrange a time it might please you to receive my humble person."

With that, the conversation was clearly at an end, and as they walked back to the docks, Phillip realised that there was much he had neglected to ask Koh Huan, especially about the situation here at George Town. He would have to begin to make notes! James and Natalie were waiting when they returned, and Andy Barg spread a sail above the quarterdeck to provide shade, and arranged several of Phillip's dining chairs along with a small table for them to take refreshments. The news from the fort was what Phillip had expected, and no assistance would be forthcoming from the soldiers to train the Sultan's troops. Nothing could be done that might set the colony on a path that would endanger further involvement with Kedah's external threats. In fact, the Colonel had been quite displeased that Phillip had already supplied the Sultan with muskets. They were on their own.

The two couples sat together and discussed the options available to them for building and the time that might be required. At the earliest, no accomodations would be ready in time for the planned beginning of the campaign to the south, which might be as early as late April. At best, if Koh Huan was to be believed, some facility might be ready near the docks by mid-May, and any house in the hills would probably not be complete until well into July.

"Phillip, what are your thoughts on our involvement in the north with Kedah? Can we safely divide our forces and send one of the frigates to the south to explore and gather information on the French and Dutch bases?" James queried.

"It is something I have been contemplating, yes. The bigger question is, 'Where do we go?' We have precious little information at this point, and until either the Sultan or Koh Huan can give us some useful insight, I wonder if we are just presenting our enemy with a target and a warning."

"But was that not a part of our mandate, to present a warning?" Katherine asked.

"Yes, but in what manner? That is something we have never really decided. Should we simply wave a flag and hope they take notice, or do we destroy their bases if possible and disrupt their supply lines? I favour a more aggressive approach, and if we give them plenty of warning ahead of an assault it may only make them more difficult to find and weed out. What I am thinking now, is that perhaps we ought to leave one of the frigates here as a base and a safe place for Natalie and Kate to call home for the next few weeks, while the other frigate and the brig head north to rout the Burmese."

"Why not leave the brig? It is the smallest and most lightly armed, and would have the least effect in any bombardment," James suggested, clearly not wanting to be left behind.

"The advantage of the brig is that we can get her in much closer in shallow water. There is a narrow inlet on the north side of Langkawi and two rivers on the east side that the brig would have a much easier time navigating, not to mention the channel between Dayang and Tuba. With her carronades, she would still have some punch at close range and the Onyx would be there to back her up."

"If I might suggest then, why not take the Triton as well, and anchor her in the bay in front of Kuah. She would be relatively safe in a good deep anchorage and it would give us a presence on the south shore while the rest of our little fleet explores. Should any threat develop, we could simply up anchor and either sail east or west, depending on the winds. The anchorage is every bit as good as here, and we would be in nearly constant touch." James was angling to get as close to the action as possible, just in case he might have a chance to use his ship.

"Oh Phillip, that sounds like an excellent plan!" Katherine enthused. "We would be closer if you needed us, and yet quite safe in the frigate; not only that, but I would certainly see you more often, and we would not require the Sultan's hospitality."

"You would not require the Sultan's hospitality if you stayed on board here in the harbour either, Katherine. Do not think for a minute that I don't see through the little ploy you and James think you are perpetrating! I do not believe we will need all three ships to convince the Burmese that the risk outweighs the potential reward, although I had thought in terms of sending one frigate slightly further north to intercept any idea of reinforcements the Burmese might try to interject into the conflict. That, however, was before we knew of the complication of finding suitable housing here in the short term."

"This all still begs the question, dear brother, of what we now propose to do about establishing a more permanent base here. Do we really need one? If we are only concerned with this voyage, then it seems to me that by the time all this building is complete, we will be nearly ready to leave, should all go well. Can we perhaps convince one of the officials here now, to give us the use of their house for a goodly fee and save the bother of building, or do you conceive of future missions back to the east to engage in either trade or further diplomacy?"

"Good question, Natalie, but I am afraid I have not yet gotten that far. I am certainly not prepared to leave you and Kate in some inn here in the settlement that cannot be vouched for, and there is no suitable accommodation in the fort itself. As Koh Huan seems to echo James' fear of accepting the Sultan's hospitality, it does leave us with limited options."

"Phillip, suppose we estimate a time line for our mission here," James suggested. "We will be at the middle of the month by the time we are in position to begin against the Burmese, and allowing some time to evaluate their situation, it may well be April before we begin the campaign. How long do you allow for this phase of our voyage, do you think?"

"I would suppose, perhaps, a month or six weeks should see us through. It is difficult to make any estimate with so little knowledge of their strength and disposition. If we are correct, that could bring us back to Prince of Wales Island by mid-May. Time will be required then to replenish supplies and gather up what intelligence we may, before we head south. It is over five hundred miles to Singkep but there are hundreds of miles of islands and channels to explore along the way, unless we get some information beforehand. It would take weeks just to make one good sweep, never mind going further east toward Rempang and Bintang. We are literally looking for a moving needle in a very large hay stack! Once we find the privateers, we still have to smoke them out and deal with their protégés. The only clue we have is that most of the attacks have occurred in the south portion of the Strait. The pirates could also be based on the southern tip of the Sultanate of Jahore. It is full of convenient channels and the Dutch have had a presence not far from there before. I do not think they will be as far south as Java, for that would be too great a distance to be sure of finding the merchantmen heading for China. Still, even to the south coast of Sumatra is over 1000 miles. If we divide up and scour the channels, it could still take months!"

"So, in total perhaps six months from now, and then we still have to decide if we send one or more of us on to China! The biggest difficulty I see is the one Natalie has already touched on. Do we use time and considerable funds to construct a base here?" James shrugged, "It is questionable, I think, unless we do want to maintain a presence out here and rethink the plans for the shipping company. Do we begin to establish a route to New South Wales? This could be a valuable base either to go south, or north to China. We need to call in Patrick and discuss our vision for what happens after this raid is complete. I, for one, do not see how we make a considered decision about the buildings until we have done that, unless you simply want to sell them when we leave and accept the losses! If we do that, I would suggest that we only build one."

"Well, all this is great speculation, but I have a more urgent problem that we must look to as well!" Phillip smiled at his wife. "I have learned that there is a very pretty lake up in the mountains behind Flagstaff Hill, and I have arranged for some mules for tomorrow to take us all up there to have a luncheon at the lake! We can look for a suitable building site on the way, and we will spend tomorrow afternoon refreshing ourselves in some clear fresh water and renewing our energy for the decisions that will follow. Now, I must inform the cook to package some refreshments and send a message to arrange to have the animals ready for the morning." Phillip rose and disappeared below decks.

"James, you must help me!" Katherine implored him. "I have no intention of being abandoned here for months on end while you go exploring! Phillip will simply not listen to reason!"

"Reason! Katherine, before you go any further I must warn you that I agree whole heartedly with your husband in this. I will use my powers to suggest that we all go north to make this show for the Sultan, for I do not believe it will be very dangerous, but when we head south to take on whatever the Dutch and French have in store, no, I have no intention of taking Natalie and I will not argue to take you and the child you are carrying!"

"You men are so unreasonable! You will insist on dumping us here like bags of potatoes, and go off on your adventures! It is unfair. I was with you when we took the French ship in the Atlantic and when we captured the treasure ships last year!"

"Yes, and if I dare remind you Lady Katherine Hollis, you nearly got Phillip killed in the process! Can you not see Kate that for Phillip to be able to function well and make the decisions that will be required of him, he must be at peace about your welfare? If he has to weigh using this frigate as a weapon and risking your safety, he is lost! I will not take Natalie into danger if it can be helped. In the Atlantic, we had no choice for we were set upon. Here we have a choice, and you must accept it, as you said you would!"

Katherine smiled back at James and nodded, but under her breath she muttered, "Men" to Natalie who just chuckled.

At that moment James jumped to his feet and pulled Natalie up behind him. "I have forgotten, my dear, that we have invited several officers of the fort for dinner! We must be off at once for the army will never forgive such a slight. Katherine, give my regards to Phillip and have him send a message to let us know what time we shall be ready for the outing in the morning. Come Natalie, no time to linger. We must fly!"

There was a quiet knock on the door and before Phillip could respond, Katherine stuck her head through, smiling. "Master Huan has arrived, dearest. He is coming up this instant."

"Entertain him on the quarterdeck for three minutes, Kate, and I will be with you. I am just completing the orders for Patrick; he is to leave for Kedah at daybreak. Has James returned from Triton?"

"Not yet, Phillip, but Natalie is here so I expect him shortly! Andy and Angeline have gone ashore for the afternoon. I believe she said something about taking a ride up the hillside."

The elder spokesman of the Chinese community was seated between the two women enjoying a glass of cold lemon tea when Phillip made his way topside a few minutes later. "How good it is to see you once more, Honorable Koh Huan; you do me great honor in coming to our humble ship! I trust your travels went well?"

"Thank you Lord Hollis, yes! Our short journey was most efficiently concluded to mutual satisfaction. I believe it may have also been of some small benefit to you as well, but perhaps we may speak of that later. I understand that in our absence you made a short journey of your own, to the cool waters of the lake above Flagstaff Hill! I trust it was a refreshing and pleasant distraction from your duties here aboard the Onyx."

Both women blushed slightly for the trip up into the mountains had been refreshing indeed, and the two couples had separated for a time to allow them to disrobe and enjoy the clear waters of the lake. "It was indeed a lovely day, and it certainly proved beneficial in presenting a clear view of what a home on the upper reaches of Flagstaff Hill might afford. The view is certainly special and I believe that as the colony continues to grow, such an investment now might bring a very good return in future years. I have already spoken with Mr. Denning, and he has agreed that the colony will sell us a very nice slice of the hill, about two thirds of the way to the lake, and just beyond the governor's house, although slightly further to the south. As well, we have acquired a property on the coast, about half way between Chulia Street and the River. The property down here in the town will comprise two acres, while the hillside property will be seven acres. I believe we are prepared to proceed with plans to begin construction, if your offer of assistance is still open to us."

"Ah, you have moved with great haste! In my country, nothing of consequence could be done so quickly, as it would be seen as foolish and rash." Koh smiled at Phillip. "We will observe your customs and not mine, perhaps! Yes, I am delighted to be of any assistance you may require, and I have also rashly begun to prepare some drawing and pricing for various buildings. The land on the shore here, have you seen it?"

"Why yes, we walked it only yesterday. I would be delighted to show you if you would like to see it."

"That will not be necessary, Lord Hollis. Tell me, is it north or south of the large red building that even now is nearing completion?"

"It is to the north, Koh Huan; the land begins perhaps one hundred paces north of that building. Mr. Denning insisted that if we went further south we would have possible difficulty with the soil, as it gets lower and wetter."

"Ah yes, this was my concern. It seems that the good Mr. Denning is aware of your reputation and has chosen to treat you as you deserve, for he has been trying to dispose of the land to the south for some time! The land you have chosen will prove more than adequate, and two acres is a very good sized parcel. I believe it will probably prove to back onto my own humble property! Now then, what do you propose to build?"

The discussion went on for some time, with Koh Huan full of advice and ideas of how best to build while still keeping a goodly portion of the land clear for future development or possible sale. In the end, it was decided to build a combination warehouse, office, and residence. The residence would be located above the offices, which would be to the rear of the warehouse. Much more time was spent on ideas for the hill-top home, for while the dock side building would be purely functional, the retreat would be anything but. Phillip decided that it must have no fewer than six bedrooms, and at least three of those must be large doubles. Furthermore, servants' quarters would be required, as well as a separated kitchen, and various sitting rooms, dining rooms, and a library. As Koh Huan had told him at their last meeting that building on the hillside would be expensive, Phillip was prepared for a very high estimate for the construction. As they talked and more details were suggested by

Katherine and Natalie, Koh Huan began to move beads back and forth on a set of wires stretched between two wooden poles. The number he suggested to Phillip when he had completed his calculation had Phillip puzzled. "For which project is this, and what does it include?" he asked.

"Well, this would be for the completion of both structures, as well as clearing the land on the hillside. It does not include all the furnishings for the house, although, at this price I am sure we can supply at least the beds and a few other things. I have also allowed a small amount for creating a landing at the dockside property, although not a wharf suitable to tie up one of your frigates! The only thing I am as yet uncertain about will be the glass, Sir Phillip. Good glass for windows such as you have described will not be available locally, and there will be some cost to have it brought from India or even China."

"But Huan, even without the glass, for that amount of money I could barely keep one ship at sea for a year! How can you possibly undertake such a project for so little? We must have misunderstood what it is I wish to build."

"No, I do not believe so! Understand that there could be some adjustments, for I am still somewhat uncertain about this curved staircase, but I believe I have fairly represented what is required. We can begin work on your warehouse and office building in three days. I will visit with Mr. Denning tomorrow to get a detailed map for the hillside property. After I have had my sons walk the land, we can make a more accurate plan for the house there. I will arrange for teak timbers to be purchased and delivered to the warehouse property tomorrow."

Phillip made a small bow to Koh Huan in acknowledgement of an agreement. He was still in shock, for the total cost of the project was hardly more than one quarter of what he had feared.

CHAPTER EIGHTEEN
Success & Frustration

By mid-morning of the 12th of March, both Triton and Onyx weighed anchor and began to sail slowly to the north. The Emerald was already well to the north, and would await them in the channel off Kuah, along with the Sultan's troops, who were being shipped across the twenty miles that separated Langkawi from the mainland. Katherine was quietly ecstatic that Phillip had acquiesced to her and James' entreaties, and that she would be that much closer to both Phillip and the action.

The action, in the end, proved to be minimal. The Burmese spies had already warned their countrymen of the imminent arrival of Phillip's ships, and what Burmese soldiers were left on the island had moved well inland. Leaving Katherine with James and Natalie, Phillip and Patrick circumnavigated the islands and had one running engagement when they came upon a group of Burmese junks approaching from the north-west. They managed to sink one and damage another, but the bulk of the force turned back to the north and disappeared over the horizon in the gathering dusk. Two days later, Patrick had some excitement when he was set upon by six large proas as he investigated a river on the east side of the island, just south of the smaller Island of Dendang. Using his carronades to great effect, he sank the first two of the proas, while two more closed in from his rear. Just as things were getting interesting indeed, Onyx stuck her bows into the river and began a barrage from her forward guns. It was too much for the Burmese, who promptly reversed course and made for the safety of the small tributaries where they could not be followed. By the time Phillip and Patrick returned to the waiting Triton off Kuah, there was little more to be done, except to make a sweep around the east side one last time to keep any more Burmese from resupplying their troops.

The Sultan's army, in the meantime, emboldened with their new muskets, were making a concerted push inland to harass whatever Burmese were still entrenched on the Island of Langkawi. In only three weeks, the Sultan's chief general, also an uncle, declared that the Burmese were defeated and sufficiently cowed to pose no further immediate threat. The Onyx and Emerald were again on patrol off the north shore and Emerald managed to sink another junk that was leaving an inlet in late afternoon. The junk, full of retreating Burmese soldiers, settled in the shallows. In short order, a troop of the Sultan's army appeared on shore to round up the survivors. The great Burmese incursion was over!

With a mandatory stop at Kuala Kedah for celebrations with the beaming Sultan, which lasted for three days and resulted in beautiful gems for the two wives and gems of information for Phillip and James, they were on their way back to George Town. They had been gone less than the month they had estimated. Before leaving, the vizier took Phillip aside and renewed his offer that the two women would be most welcome to visit for whatever time might be required for the warships to make their southern patrol.

Coming into the harbour at George Town, the first thing Phillip noticed were the three masts of Celeste riding at anchor squarely in front of the future home of Hollis and Company Shipping. Ross had made excellent time and the partners were all eager to know how the voyage had gone. The sale of the teak in Calcutta had provided a slightly less desirable result than Mr. Newcombe had anticipated, for unfortunately the Portuguese had just imported several cargoes of teak into Goa, which had dampened the prices. Nevertheless, the venture had been profitable enough to pay for the real cargo of value, opium. Some bales of cotton were used to fill the hold, and Percy assured them that, while the cotton would not make them any real profit, it would serve its purpose of providing a manifest that the Chinese could accept. The opium, meanwhile, would provide enough credits with the Co Hong that they would hopefully return with a fortune in silk, porcelain, and jade. The East India Company had been quite generous with the opium, selling it at a sharp discount as a favour for the promised help Phillip was providing with the Dutch and the pirates. Percy Newcombe announced with obvious glee that they had acquired 100 chests! Each chest of opium weighed exactly 135 pounds, and could be worth up to 500 pounds sterling toward the purchase of silks and porcelain. With any luck at all, they would at least treble that by the time the cargo reached London. They would arrive at the wrong time to bring back tea, as it would not be in season, but that could not be helped, unless Phillip was prepared to let the ship sit in Canton until Christmas.

As they dropped anchor, Phillip was surprised to see that progress on the warehouse was already clearly visible from the anchorage. Huge teak logs were standing upright in the soil and many cross-members were already tied to them; a roof of sorts was evident from the ships and, along the back wall, there seemed to be a platform half way up the walls, which no doubt would be the residence over the offices.

Another surprise awaited them at the docks, where a much recovered Timmon Brunner waited, with another man beside him. The second fellow proved to be Juan Ortega, a seaman rescued by a passing merchantman in the islands that dotted the south portion of the Malacca Strait. The island was Carimon, and was the most northerly of what were known as the Sunda Islands. The seaman, a Spaniard, had been befriended by Brunner at George Town, and, between the two, they had traced out locations on a map that they were sure showed where the French were located. The Dutch, the Spaniard insisted, were still based well to the south in Batavia, their stronghold on the Island of Java. Brunner, however, had been on board a Dutch Ship when he was taken by the Burmese. He insisted that his ship had been re-supplied at a town called Tanjungpinang on the Island of Bintang, some sixty or seventy miles to the west of Carimon, and that it was at this port that he had seen both a fifty gun Dutch two decker and a French frigate.

This information matched what the Sultan had provided, which told of attacks coming from the south, across from the Island of Singapore. If the Dutch were indeed ensconced on Bintang, which had been a pirate stronghold for hundreds of years, and the French had a renegade frigate working from that locale, possibly also from Carimon, it would make the south end of the Malacca Strait a perfect hunting ground. It would also answer why English shipping had been the hardest hit.

A meeting with Koh Huan was also very encouraging. He had some information on pirate teams, using the large seagoing proas, essentially twin hulled galleys with lateen sails, and Malay junks working from Battam, which was half way between the islands of Carimon and Bintang. They were said to be a mix of Malay and Sumatran bandits working under the leadership of a vicious thug named Ibn Satna. In what information the Chinese had been able to gather, it seemed that there might be well over a thousand men involved in various groups under this bandit chief. Certainly, Koh assured them, they were also in league with the French, who had several ships in the region. While the galleys were light craft, and no match for a frigate, they were fast and manoeuvrable, and carried large crews. The junks were both larger and very weatherly craft with bamboo sails and mounting six pounders or even stubby iron cannons of larger bores. The real danger lay in the number that might attack at one time, overwhelming their opponents, as Phillip had already seen in the Burmese waters. Taking Phillip aside, Koh added one more bit of information.

"Sir Phillip, I believe it is safe to say that your enemies to the south are both aware of your presence here and are being kept abreast of your plans. I would caution you to keep your final plans very close to your heart and make sure they are not known at the fort. There is at least one officer there who is in regular contact with the French, a certain major whom I believe you and Captain Peters have met with on several occasions."

On the building front, Koh Huan had much news as well, for the hilltop retreat was coming along at a great pace! The land had been cleared and found to be stable, foundations had been laid, and walls were being erected. The greatest problem seemed to be the availability of glass for windows. While some glass was to be had, nothing of the size and amount that Phillip's plan called for. It would require a trip to India, and possibly further, to acquire the amount of glass that would be needed and no ship for the Indian subcontinent had departed in their absence. Should Phillip choose to send one of his ships, Huan suggested, they could also bring back furnishings and cloth for draperies and upholstery, tiles for fireplaces, and hardware difficult to find in George Town. Huan further suggested that the voyage could easily be made to be financially advantageous if spices were purchased for sale in India. Here, he assured them he could be humbly helpful in gathering a cargo. At first Phillip was prepared to dismiss the idea, and then as he gave the notion some thought, it occurred to him that the voyage would be a fine way to keep his women safe and occupied while he made his first foray into the south.

In the back of his mind, he was still concerned with the news from Koh Huan about the possible treachery of Major Harris and what, if anything, he could do about it. Andy Barg would be more than ready to act on his behalf, but any action against the major would certainly have huge consequences with the fort. He would need proof, and that would be hard to come by. Feeling stymied, he called a meeting with the partners, outlining the information he had received, but not its source.

"Are you confident in the source of your news?" Ross asked.

"Yes, and if I was at liberty to reveal his name, I believe you all would agree with me."

"I am more than ready to take your word for it, Phillip. I was only asking to frame our discussion in such a way that we could just carry on with the assumption that we are dealing with facts." Ross replied.

"No harm done, Ross." James smiled, "It was a good question, but what can we do about it? That is our real question. My guess is, unless we caught the major red handed, and perhaps even if we did, we would simply be rebuffed by the colonel and it would devolve into another army against navy tirade."

"If we cannot touch the man, can we use him?" Ross asked. "What if we casually feed him misleading information about our plans? Could that be to our benefit?"

"I don't suppose the Funchal solution could be employed, sir? No one need be the wiser and I am sure I could arrange things." Patrick kept his eyes on Phillip as he spoke, not knowing if any others in the room understood his meaning.

"No, the risk is unacceptable. I think we might have something in Ross's suggestion though. James, you have spent more time with the soldiers than any of us. What do you think?"

"I have been thinking about all the seemingly innocuous questions that dog has asked me when we have been together. As I am sure I can rely on him to keep asking, we must simply decide what we want to tell him."

The suggestions came swiftly and plentifully, and, soon enough James had a broad smile on his face. "I am going to enjoy misleading this arrogant traitor. He will have to hold himself back from just running off with his information!"

The next question, Phillip thought, was which of his ships he should send off to India with the wives? Celeste was loaded and bound for China. Onyx would never do, as she was the stoutest and most powerful, and besides he was not going to run off to India and send James and Patrick south alone. It would have to be the

Triton or the Emerald, and it would depend on what he might find in the south as to which of his consorts he wished to have along. Emerald could get into tighter places and shallower water, but she was also much weaker in a ship to ship action, and would require closer support. On the other hand, if he sent Patrick off with the two wives to shop in India, he would have both frigates to move against the French, and James was a known commodity in a scrap. It was a matter of giving up the shallower draft of Emerald for the increased fire power of Triton.

After a brief but heated discussion with his three partners, it was decided that Emerald would accept the duty of carrying the two women, their maids, and a hastily arranged cargo of spice and pepper to Madras, while Triton and Onyx made ready to begin their first foray into the southern waters, where they hoped to find the French, or baring that, Ibn Satna's pirates.

While Koh Huan organized the purchase of cargo for the Emerald, and James engaged Major Harris in a luncheon, Phillip and the two women took a day to visit the hillside construction site. From a distance, it appeared very like a huge anthill, with hundreds of two legged ants scurrying about, carrying loads that defied their small stature. The skeleton of the two story house was already standing and men were crawling over every conceivable surface, laying down planks and beams, hammering in wooden dowels, and erecting the framework that would make up the roof. Katherine and Natalie were delighted with the progress, especially when the foreman, one of Koh Huan's sons, invited them to climb up to examine the view from the second floor. Some of the trees had been cleared away from the front of the house, exposing a view of the lower hillside to the east, with the entire settlement and the channel to the mainland spread out before them. The new warehouse, under construction along the docks, was clearly visible nearly two miles away. Katherine, who was perched precariously on beams and planks, despite her now noticeable bump, observed that the installation of a telescope at the front windows would enable messages to be sent back and forth from the lower residence and offices.

The loading of the Emerald was well underway when, three days later Celeste, Triton, and Onyx weighed anchor. Phillip, over Katherine's heated objections, had insisted that Dr. Cluff would transfer over to the Emerald to be available should there be any complications with the pregnancy, now in its fifth month. With good weather and allowing for several weeks in Madras to procure everything on the increasingly long shopping list, it would be late June before the Emerald was likely to return. Phillip was not willing to chance any possible delay that could affect the birth of their child. James would still have Mr. Curtis, and Mr. Fowler, the surgeon on Emerald, would now shift to Onyx. With tearful goodbyes from the wives, the two frigates turned their bows to the south to begin the real task they had sailed for, accompanied by Celeste, for they would escort her through the Singapore Strait.

The three ships sailed along in close proximity for three days as they made their way through mostly calm seas and light winds, into the southern reaches of the Strait of Malacca. As they approached the island of Carimon, late on the 19th of April, the two frigate captains met in Phillip's cabin to discuss strategy. With them were Dick Forest, Ross Day, Pierre Doucette, and Timmon Brunner. With Brunner's map spread out, Timmon and Dick Forest explained the various channels and islands to the waiting officers. Carimon itself was quite simple; a kidney shaped island of about fifteen miles north to south and not above six miles at its widest point. Directly south of Carimon lay the Strait of Gelam, which separated it from the north Shore of Gelam Island, itself the northern most point of seven islands making up the Kundar Group. North to south, the Kundar Islands were only about twenty-five miles in length, but contained a myriad of narrow channels and gulfs where small coastal vessels might hide. It would be impossible to check all of them, and besides, most were much too narrow for the frigates to enter. For this first search, they would have to be satisfied with studying the coastline and looking for villages that might be used as bases for the pirates. The decision was reached that, while Triton escorted Celeste to the entrance to the South China Sea, Onyx would spend two days scouring the small island group. Should trouble arise, they would run and not fight independently against what could be overwhelming numbers of pirates in highly manoeuvrable oared galleys. Should villages with too many boats be discovered, they were to be noted on the charts to be dealt with at the merger of the expedition. By starting their search near the western edge of the Singapore Strait, and reaching south of it, they would be hundreds of miles from where James had casually told Major Harris they were planning to concentrate their efforts.

Early the following morning, Triton and Celeste parted company with Onyx, heading east down the Singapore Strait, while Onyx began her surveillance south along the eastern coast of Carimon. By mid-morning, as Phillip turned Onyx westward to peak into the Gelam Strait, he saw nothing but more empty seas, which was the story of the morning. In fact, if anything, there was too much nothing. Two small villages had been all but deserted, and even here, at Tanjung Balai, the main town on Carimon, there were less than a dozen boats pulled up on shore, and those were all small coastal fishing boats. With a dip of his pennant, Phillip turned back to the east and began to thread his way around the Island of Buru, on the northeast corner of the Kundar Group. Just to the south of Buru lay the islands of Belat and Madura, and in the small channel that separated them Andy Barg, perched in the maintop, swore he saw a group of large boats. They were well up the channel, however, and Phillip decided to round Madura and peak in from the southwest side. Madura was only about three miles wide, so rounding it did not take above half an hour, but as Onyx rounded her southwest corner, a group of large sea-going proas could be seen madly paddling to place themselves northeast of a small island in the channel between Madura and Balat, and effectively out of Onyx's range. The group was noted on Brunner's chart, and Onyx, with some frustrated seamen aboard, continued to the south.

Next morning found Onyx at anchor off the south east corner of Carimon as Triton ghosted in under courses alone. The two ships sailed south together to re-examine the river on Madura, but found nothing. Resigned, they turned east to thread their way through a group of small islands that would put them in the Durian Strait, where they would spend the night. The next morning, they continued their search further eastward, separating to cover as much coastline as possible and joining back together periodically to compare notes. In this fashion, they searched the Islands of Sugi and Combol, crossed the Combol Strait and covered the coastline of Bulan, all with little to show for their trouble. It was on the southwest corner of Battam, where a narrow channel separated the larger island from Setoko to the south, that they caught their first real hint that they were finally on the right track. In the narrow channel, only a mile wide at its widest and not much over a quarter mile wide between several of the islands that dotted its six mile length they saw signs of several large encampments where many boats had been beached. The east end of the channel was guarded by an island that Brunner called Awi. Past the island the channel opened up into a wider waterway that gave access to the Singapore Strait only fifteen miles to the north, while twenty miles to the east, across open water, lay Bintang and the reputed Dutch base at Tanjung Pinang. It was a perfect spot from which to attack either to the north along the east coast of Battam or to dodge to the northwest and come out between Battam and Bulan, where a myriad of islands made for easy escape routes.

Hopeful of tempting the Dutch to come out, Phillip decided to keep Onyx well offshore of Bintan and send James in with Triton, to cruise just off the town of Tanjung to look for shipping. Should the reputed Dutch two decker be in the harbour, perhaps she would come out to challenge the English presence. James sailed Triton to within a mile of the harbour, but luck was not with them, for the harbour was empty except for several fishing boats and two large galleys pulled well up on shore. As firing into a supposedly neutral harbour was not in the plans, James reluctantly turned back out to sea, utterly frustrated.

CHAPTER NINETEEN

Redemption

Just as James and the Triton began to close on Onyx, the lookout in the maintop sang out.

"Deck there, sail on the south horizon."

"What heading?" Terrance, who was officer of the watch called back.

"Sir, five points off the larboard bow. Second sail just off to the right."

Without a word, Bill Collins crossed the quarterdeck, grabbed a glass, and ran for the rat lines. Moments later he shouted down, "Sir, looks like a fair sized schooner in the lead with a lateen sailed galley in the rear. Both heading north, about five miles off our larboard beam."

With the Triton heading nearly due west, and Onyx still several miles to the northwest, the two sail would not be visible to Phillip for several more minutes. Terrance called for James but the captain, along with Timmon Brunner, who had transferred over to get a good look at the anchorage, was already climbing onto the quarterdeck. Brunner took one look and assured James that the two vessels were just rounding the west end of an island called Dompak, and were doubtless enroute for Tanjung.

James checked the wind, which was still out of the northeast, and decided to appear to be disinterested and turn to the northwest, but reduce sail. "Terrance, can you make out Onyx to the northwest?" he asked.

"Yes, sir, about three miles, heading nearly due south."

"Send a signal to Onyx. 'Enemy in sight 180 degrees true, northbound.' Prepare to change course, new course to be due east. Take her around through the wind. I don't want that schooner to think we are one bit interested in her." Whistles trilled and men rushed on deck to bring the frigate around. The rigging was already alive with men who were busily taking in sail.

"Smartly now, bring her around Mr. Collins. Once we are on our course have the men called to action."

"Let go the helm, new course 090, Pull and away! Watch those sheets, Mr. Vandegraffe! Fischer, get your men pulling with a will!"

Slowly at first, then with increasing momentum the Triton spun 'round through the wind and reversed course, heading back toward Bintan.

"Sir," Terrance called down from his perch in the rigging, "Onyx is altering course to the southwest. The two sail are still heading northwest, but the galley is edging to the north. Range just under four miles and still closing."

"Very good Terrance. Tell me when we get within three miles and then come down," James responded. "Bill, as soon as Terrance calls out I want you to alter course four points to starboard. I want to have us between that schooner and the shoreline. As soon as we make our new course, begin to pile on sail. We will need to run her down as quickly as possible before she turns and runs."

"Captain, the first sail is a sixteen gun brig, and she has just raised a pennant on her foremast. She is turning slightly more to the northwest. I think she has not yet noticed Onyx, for she is steering right for her! The galley is turning to the northeast; I believe her oars are out."

"Enough, Mr. Bernard, come on down. Mr. Collins, alter course!"

On Onyx, meanwhile Phillip was watching James' manoeuvres with interest. The men were already at their stations and, from their vantage point further to the west, Dick Forest could plot the triangle of ships with some precision. The two-masted brig was heading nearly toward Onyx on a tack that had taken her around the tip of Dompak Island. If she was not startled too soon, she should continue on that course until she could turn up through the wind to make a reach for Tanjung. The galley, on the other hand, had opted to use its oars to turn directly into the wind and make a straight run up the coast. When James reversed course, Phillip had guessed that he was positioning himself to intercept the galley and get directly upwind of it. That left the brig for Onyx. When James again changed course and began to turn downwind, Phillip was ready and issued orders for Onyx to alter course to 120 degrees. It would put him across the brig's bows, but keep him slightly upwind, giving him the weather gage, and would force the schooner to make a move.

"Pierre, courses and topsails, if you please. Keep her tight to this course, we don't want that brig getting upwind of us."

"Topsails and courses, sir. Helmsman, watch that compass and no drift now." Pierre was clearly enjoying the chance at action after the tiring disappointment of checking every bay and river mouth for the past four days.

"Deck there, sail is four points off the starboard bow," The lookout called from the maintop. "I make it two and one-half miles. She is still holding her course."

"She must believe we are French," Pierre marvelled. "Otherwise the captain would be incredibly bold to place himself virtually in the Onyx's lap."

"Think on it Pierre; there has been no English warship in these waters for over eighteen months. Between the French and the Dutch, they have owned this place for too long. That captain is seeing what he expects to see. I just hope he is confused for another ten minutes! After that, it will not matter, for he will be ours."

"Do you intend to fire on him?" Pierre asked.

"No, not unless he tries to run or fires first. I want to board him and inspect his papers, take a good look around, and see what he is. If he is a privateer, as I suspect, we will help him out by lightening his load for him."

"Sir?"

"We will push his cannon overboard and strip him of his powder, Pierre. If we pull his teeth and let him continue, the ones who sent him will surely hear of it."

"Ah, and so we hope to bring them out!" Pierre smiled broadly.

"Just so, my friend!"

At that moment, their conversation was interrupted by another call from the lookout. "Deck there, the brig is altering course. She is turning to the west."

"That captain still has his eyes on James! He is finally getting nervous by James coming down along the coast to meet him and that galley." Phillip smiled at Pierre. "What do you make of her range?"

"Inside two miles, and I believe she has finally seen her real danger, for she seems to be continuing her turn through west."

"Alter course; give me two points to starboard."

"Two points to starboard! Helmsman, let go."

"Andy, run out the bow chasers. When you have range, give me one shot across her bows."

James was now heading slightly west of south and closing with the galley, which was still downwind and now within one mile. The galley had two cannon in her bows, but they did not yet appear to be manned. He was about to issue an order to run out his guns, when the first of the galley's bow-chasers erupted in smoke. That got everyone's attention right promptly! Fortunately, the galley's crew were more intent on stealth than marksmanship, for the shot fell just off the larboard bow. It did, however, signal that her intentions were clear.

"Terrance, I do not want that galley closing with us! Who knows how many men are aboard her. Open fire with the larboard bow chaser and prepare to alter course four points to starboard. I intend giving her a full broadside from this range."

"Yes sir! Bill, larboard bow chaser! Mr. Vandegraffe, prepare to alter course four points to starboard immediately after the gun fires." Terrance tossed off the orders, checking if he had missed anything. The boats were in the water, and the deck had already been wetted and sanded down, to lessen the risk of a stray spark and to give the men extra grip in heaving the guns in and out. The men were all at their stations. "Shall we run out the main guns, sir?"

"Yes, Mr Bernard, run out. No point in pretending we are friends any longer." He had just issued the order when men could be seen preparing the first of the galley's guns for firing once more. As they did so, the galley altered course slightly to give the second of her bow chasers a more direct line on the frigate. Her second gun fired just as James' bow chaser barked out a greeting. None of the shots caused any damage, although the galley's shot did bounce and hit the hull of the frigate, but it had lost much of its energy and bounced off. Two shots from Triton bracketed the galley.

As Triton turned broadside to the galley, her main guns began to fire in order as they came to bear. The rolling broadside was deliberate and the fourth shot landed squarely amidships, sending up a cloud of dust and splinters. The galley seemed to lurch, as several of her oars on the starboard side were put out of action. As she righted, her two bow chasers fired again and this time one of them tore through the rigging, leaving a neat hole in the foretopsail, and sending men scrambling up the ratlines to make repairs.

The distance was closing and James could see a large group of men crowding into the bows of the galley, preparing to board the frigate.

"Mr. Vandegraffe, carronades loaded with grape and at the ready. Give her another broadside at three cables; then reload the twelve pounders with canister!"

The second broadside was much better, and several holes appeared in the galley's hull, while her huge lateen sail was riddled with holes and began to slew around as her rigging was shredded. The galley's two bow cannons went off again and one shot blurred past the corner of James' vision, as he felt the concussion of its passing. The other shot struck the foremast topsail yard, bringing down a hailstorm of splinters, and collapsing the sail.

With only two guns in her bow, the galley was not going to win a gunnery match against James' full broadsides, and her captain knew it. He was coming on as fast as his men could pull the oars, but there was still a quarter mile of open water to cross and very soon the frigate's carronades would be in accurate range. In the meantime, Triton's next broadside erupted, sending a hail of twelve pound balls blistering into the galley. One shot scored a direct hit, upsetting one of the cannons in her bow. Through his glass, James could see the mayhem as the overturned cannon crushed her gun crew and punched a hole into the group of men crowding the bow. Still she came on, and the momentary gap in the bow was quickly filled as more men crowded forward.

At three hundred yards, the carronades began to fire their deadly load of grapeshot, and moments later the main guns, in carefully sighted rolling fire, spewed out their fusillade of canister. The bow of the galley turned red, as dozens of men were hewn down like so many weeds by a scythe. The gunners were busily reloading as the galley began to come around to try to grapple the larger frigate.

"Depress the guns and wait for her now! As she comes alongside, every gun must find its mark down onto that deck. We have only one more chance to clear her!"

Tensely, the men waited until the final moment, and then the entire side of the frigate erupted in a hail of death. From the forward carronades to the last of the twelve pounders, the side of the frigate lit up in one great thundering, blinding crash. The deck of the galley seemed for a moment to disappear, and then the screaming and shrieks of wounded men replaced the mind numbing, deafening thunder of the guns. While James felt sorry for the men chained to the oars, he had no remorse for the crowd of cutthroats that were now vastly diminished.

"Prepare to repel boarders!" Terrance shouted down to the main deck, but the galley was drifting thirty yards off the larboard beam, unable to close with half her men down and all the starboard oars out of action.

"Reload the guns, Terrance, but do not fire. If they try to attack I will spare no one, but I would have them take this message back to Ibn Satna. This must be a clear lesson that they cannot ignore." Even as he spoke, the galley began to limp away, low in the water, and leaving a trail of bodies being thrown over the side, that soon aroused the interest of an ever increasing number of sharks.

The captain of the brig was not interested in copying his consort's boldness, and when the second of Philip's shots splashed just in front of his bow, he brailed up his sails and came around. While the sound of James's guns could still be clearly heard in the distance, Onyx drew alongside and backed her sails, keeping the brig covered with a row of twenty-four pound cannon that left the brig's captain no doubt of what his fate would be should he attempt anything foolish.

"Pierre, take a boat across and bring me her captain and all her papers. Let us find out whom we are dealing with." Phillip stood on his quarterdeck surveying the brig, now less than half a cable off his lee. Off to the southeast, he could see Triton, but the galley was hidden behind her. The gunfire had stopped and Phillip was anxious to reunite with his brother–in–law and assure himself that all was well, but securing the brig had to come first.

By the time Pierre's boat was alongside the brig, the lookout in the maintop called down that Triton was again underway and closing with Onyx. Ten minutes passed before Pierre was seen back on the deck of the brig along with several armed seamen and what Phillip assumed was the captain of the brig. His assumption proved correct, for a few minutes later the launch again hooked onto the chains and Pierre and his unhappy companion climbed back to the deck. Phillip had retired to his cabin to await his guest, and mull over his options. He had no real authority, apart from an unwritten instruction from the Admiralty to harass the French and Dutch if they were seen to be in league with the pirates. Officially, the peace of Amiens was still in effect, but if the French or Dutch were using privateers to assist and aid Ibn Satna, they were fair game.

Pierre knocked and entered, following a clearly uneasy officer, who by his appearance could only be a Dutchman.

"Captain, this is Henrick Von Leuven. He is the captain of "Zee Heks". I believe it means sea witch, sir. He claims he had no knowledge of the galley he was accompanying and that they only happened to be at the same place purely by accident. I have his papers, sir, but I am afraid I don't do very well with Dutch."

"That is of no consequence, Mr. Doucette, as we have an excellent translator aboard Triton and I believe she should be alongside in just a minute or two."

At this remark Captain Von Leuven's head jerked up sharply. "You haf no right to search mine documenten! I protest!"

"Protest all you like, sir. You were in company with a pirate galley that opened fire on my ships. In my eyes that makes you a pirate as well, unless your papers can convince me otherwise. As of this moment you are in my hands, and your brig is a lawful prize. Be silent now or I will declare you a pirate this minute and have you hanged from my yardarm!"

"This is outrageous! Our countries are not at war, you haf no authority here!"

"I am the owner and captain of a private ship. My ships were fired upon by a vessel that was clearly sailing in consort with your brig. I require no further authority, min Herr!"

A knock at the door announced the arrival of James Peters, smiling broadly. "Ah, Phillip, it seems you have done rather well. We dismasted that galley, destroyed half her oars, and reduced her crew by at least half, but we let her drift off. It did cost us considerable effort however, and you it seems, have found an intact brig without breaking a sweat."

"James, this is Captain Von Leuven, of the brig Zee Heks. At this moment, we are sorely in need of Mr. Brunner to translate some documents for us. Could you have him brought over?"

"No need, he came across with me and is presently on deck."

Pierre nodded to James and made for the door, reappearing moments later with Timmon Brunner in tow.

"Mr. Brunner, could you do me the favour of examining these documents and giving me a feel for what our friends in the Zee Heks were up to."

Immediately, Captain Von Leuven began a heated and vitriolic attack on poor Brunner, but after only a few seconds, Brunner began to answer in like terms and, shaking with rage, the captain fell silent.

Brunner took the papers and began to read. By the time he was half way through the second page, he looked up at the captain, at first incredulous, and then as he read more, with a look of pure venom.

"Captain Hollis, these papers are directions from Batavia. They come from the governor of the Dutch Colony. They are carefully worded, but the meaning is inescapable. Captain Von Leuven is charged with providing material support and aid as he is able to Ibn Satna, and other friends of the colony currently involved in safeguarding Dutch interests in the region. This other paper is from the French, and it instructs Captain Von Leuven to cooperate at all times with their ships in the region, and to inform them of any threats from British warships."

"Well, Captain Von Leuven, I believe that your own documents have condemned you. You are clearly in league with pirates, and have been giving them aid. I am taking your ship as a lawful prize, as you, through your confederates, fired upon my ships, threatening our welfare. You will be taken to George Town and handed over to the British authorities there to be dealt with as they see fit. Your brig will be restitution for the damage you have done to my ships, and the threat you posed in league with known pirates. Pierre, take him below and lock him up before I change my mind and hang him."

Everyone kept a studious and solemn visage until the now clearly frightened captain was ushered from the room. James was the first to crack. "Perfect! It could not be better, except we now need a way for this message to get south to Batavia."

"Oh, it will get there swiftly enough, I think. Those pirates that slunk away from your barrage will know exactly what happened. We have made our first inroads, but not the last. We have now shaken the hornet's nest, but we will still have to be prepared for what comes out! Right now, we need to get that crew on the brig below decks and secure; then we will sail back across to the east side of Kundar to see if we can trap those big proas we found."

"Who do we put in the brig, sir? She will need a crew to take her north."

"So she will, but I am loath to give up Pierre. What say we give her to Andy Barg and Mr. Vandegraffe? If we each give them a dozen hands they can sail her directly beck to George Town. I will write up orders for them, as well as a letter for the fort. I believe, upon reflection, that we should release the men on the brig, except for the captain and any other officers. They will only be a problem to care for and keep secure. What if we drop them right here at Tanjung? We could sail the brig into the harbour and have them put ashore. If nothing else, that will guarantee that the authorities get our message."

"It would surely make life easier for Andy and the governor at George Town! I will row over and send Vandegraffe across with a dozen hands. If we sail back across to that channel we came through, behind Awi Island, we could check on those sites again on our way back toward Kundar," James responded.

"What if the boats that were not there are up north in the Singapore channel? I believe that we shall send Andy in Zee Heks up ahead of us. I am willing to bet that not only would she not scare them off, she might actually draw them in! In any event, it would give us a look at the Rhio Strait, and we can go around the north side of Battam and then drop back down to Kundar in very little more time."

"This is why you are in charge, Phillip! Good plan, I think, and we can be at the south edge of the Singapore Channel by dark tonight if we get moving."

CHAPTER TWENTY
Emerald at the Crossroads

Katherine and Natalie were seated comfortably in the main cabin of the Emerald. Having left George Town on the morning of the eighteenth, they were now nearly half way to their destination, having passed just south of Little Andaman Island at first light. Natalie continued to question Katherine about her symptoms and when she had known for sure she was carrying Phillip's child.

"Natalie, this is becoming tiresome. Are you sure there is not something you want to tell me?" Katherine jibed more out of frustration than curiosity.

"Well, I just don't know!" an exasperated Natalie answered.

"What do you mean?" Now Katherine was really interested; her frustration with her sister-in-law evaporated.

"Well, I might be, but I am not sure. I mean, I do not feel sick at all; in fact, I feel fine, but..."

"But?" prompted Katherine.

"But it hasn't happened, and it should have happened weeks ago. I never miss. Well, at least not for a long time. I wish I would get sick or something, so I would be certain!"

Katherine held her sides and laughed. "Oh, you don't want to be sick, believe me. How many weeks ago, do you think?"

"I am not sure! With all that was going on, and going up to fight the Burmese, and then stopping to visit the Sultan, I just sort of lost track..."

"You mean to tell me that it should have come before we went north in the middle of March? That is six weeks ago. Natalie, you had best prepare yourself. I am betting you are on your way to motherhood."

The women paused, hearing a great commotion above them, with men being called on deck, and orders being screamed. As Katherine was about to rise to go and discover the issue, the door burst open and Wallis Foster stuck his shaggy head into the cabin.

"So sorry, Your Ladyship, but Captain Morrissey requests you are to remain in the cabin until further notice. We have sighted a sail on the horizon and it appears to be altering course to intercept us. Captain says he will come down presently to explain, ma'am." With that, Wallis was gone and the door secured.

"What do you make of her, sir?" Simon Elliot, off duty in his bunk, had scrambled up to the quarterdeck at the first call for all hands.

"A little early to tell, Mr. Elliot, but my first thought when I saw her was I had seen her before." The captain was looking off to the northwest, even as Emerald continued to alter course to the southwest. "Simon, where is Prentiss?"

"Beg pardon, sir, but I am right here." Prentiss spoke up from the wheel.

"Simon, put Marcello on the wheel. Prentiss, I want you to take a glass and get aloft. Tell me if I am dreaming or if that sail is who I suspect." Patrick kept his eyes on the northwest. How, he wondered, could that ship reappear after all this time and all these thousands of miles. As if he did not have enough to worry about, for the glass had been falling rapidly these past six hours, foretelling of a serious storm, and the sky to the south did not look inviting.

"Deck there, captain! I cannot be certain, but she sure looks like that Frenchie as was following us a'fore the Azores." Prentiss called down.

"What time, Mr. Foster?" asked Morrissey, still studying the horizon.

"Just about one bell of the first dog watch, sir. How far off do you make her?"

"I'd guess near three miles, but with this wind today it is hard to guess what she can do." Since early morning, the skies in the south had continued to darken and the winds, at first strong from the southeast, had been changing direction constantly. Now, they were nearly directly out of the south and, although they had been moderate for much of the afternoon, they were again strengthening.

"If the wind keeps up as it is, she will have quite a time to reach us. I would guess at least three or four hours, and by then it will be getting dark. We just might lose her again, sir." Elliot prompted.

"Oh yes, but I was counting on getting as far to the north as ever we could, Mr. Elliot. I do not have any wish to sail into that thickening mass of cloud down in the south. We are on the edge of typhoon season, much like hurricane season in the Caribbean, and I have been in one of those, and that was one too many!" Patrick now changed his attention to the south, where the black clouds seemed to be getting higher in the sky even as he spoke. "At any rate, it will be some time yet before we have to make a decision. I am going below to inform our two passengers of the situation. You have the deck, Mr. Elliot."

"You must do as seems best to you, Patrick. We will, of course, support you in any event. Which do you see as the greater danger? That French frigate, if indeed it is the Poseidon, has already met us once, although she did run after Phillip, and James nearly sank her consort. We know from the orders captured out of Tunder that her mission was to find us and sink us if possible. I imagine that after getting run off by two frigates, her captain will be anxious to redeem himself against a smaller brig. Still, a possible typhoon is no small matter, is it?"

"No, and I believe you have put it rather well, Katherine. The crux of the matter is that we know the Poseidon is a real and clear threat. We cannot be so sure of how bad the storm is, but, if Poseidon gets to us first, we will be in no shape to weather a storm, if we still float at all. If I surrender the ship, the French would probably take you off, and you might be safe, for you are not a threat to them, but I fear they will use both of you to force Phillip to surrender as well, and we know that they want him dead."

"I will not hear of that." Natalie spoke up with vehemence. "We chose to join in this expedition as full members, and we will not be used to blackmail Phillip or James. I will take a pistol to the first French officer who enters my cabin."

"Very well! I must say it is a commendable notion, Mrs. Peters. We will alter course as much as we can, to attempt to reach the relative safety of the storm front. I must warn you both however, this storm may be very bad, and I cannot promise you that we will survive it, either."

"If we are to go down, Patrick, I would rather it be to a force of nature than Napoleon's henchmen." Katherine stood and took Patrick's hand. "I believe you have made a good decision, and if we survive, I will certainly tell Phillip so."

Patrick hurried back on deck where Wallis and Simon were both standing and watching the French frigate. The Poseidon was certainly closer than she had been, and she was edging down as much as the strengthening south wind would allow her to do. "What do you make it, perhaps two and one-half?"

"Yes sir, but she is on a course she cannot hope to maintain if the wind keeps increasing as it has done this past half hour." Wallis Foster had his eye firmly to his glass and was concentrating on the Frenchman.

"Sir, if she comes round to parallel our course..." Simon Elliot was cut off by Patrick.

"If she does, we will alter our course and get as close to the wind as we can. It will send us directly toward that looming storm, but

I believe there is no help for it. We may have some chance in the edge of the storm to hide and ride it out, but gentlemen, we have little or no chance against a forty gun heavy frigate." Patrick looked determined and resolute, in spite of how he felt.

"Sir, I believe the frigate is altering course," Wallis was still calmly observing their pursuer. "She looks to be coming round through the wind, sir."

"No point in waiting, Wallis. Alter course two points to larboard. That will be about as close to the wind as we can hold. In all respects prepare the ship to reduce sail, but keep as much canvas aloft for the moment as she will bear. Get all the guns and boats doubly secured, batten down all hatches, prepare for storm rigging, and have the men secure manropes along the decks. We must not reduce sail until we absolutely have to, or that frigate will be upon us before we reach the edge of that storm bank, but we must be as ready as we can, so that in the final event we can secure for full weather status in just minutes." Patrick took up his glass to observe the French ship, now turning through the wind to take up a position on a nearly parallel course. She was still well over two miles off, and now that the courses were similar, she would be hard pressed to close very quickly. Looking to the south, Patrick quietly observed the swiftly growing, towering bank of angry looking cloud. Typhoon or not, this was not going to be fun, and with the Frenchman now firmly on his starboard quarter, he would have no choice but to head deeply enough into the storm that he would be unlikely to be able to claw his way back out, for the storm was moving north, and was now stretched from horizon to horizon ahead of him.

"Sir, if I may..." It was Simon Elliot, looking somewhat unsure of himself.

"What is it, Simon? I am more than prepared to listen to suggestions, especially if you could find a way to put that damned Frenchman south of us instead of north." Patrick tried to smile and sound calm, but it was not much of an act.

"Sorry sir, that is beyond me; I was just thinking sir; that storm down there has mostly been in front of us. That is, I believe the worst of that beast is still to the south west. If we could alter course once we are shielded by that rain and Poseidon can no longer see us, we might fare better heading back toward the Andaman Sea and the coast of Sumatra. I have been watching south sir, and that thing out there is still growing."

"I take your point, Mr. Elliot, but that frigate was heading east when she spotted us. If her captain has second thoughts about chasing us into a possible typhoon, my guess is he will turn back on his old course, and I do not relish the thought of coming out of the storm to find him ready to pounce." Patrick was not at all sure that he liked any of his options at the moment.

"Frenchman is still closing, sir." Wallis was taking turns looking through his glass and watching the men preparing the brig for the storm looming ahead. "Mr. Prentiss, please get forward and show those lubbers how to properly double lash a gun. I have seen better work on a Medway scow!"

"Sir, yes sir." Prentiss strode forward, already issuing orders and looking disgusted. "Porter, get those lines straightened and secure. Use the eye bolts for the first lash round, but use the stanchions securing to the bulwarks for the second. If you secure both ropes the same way and the eye bolt pulls free, you got nothin.' Whoever taught you how to secure a bloody gun then?"

"What do you make our distance to that storm front, Wallis?" Patrick was watching intently as the clouds continued to pile up ahead of them. Already, he could not make out the tops, for the bulging mass of the front of the storm hid them. At its base, the storm looked dark and ominous, while up higher, where the sun still shone full on the clouds, it looked a pale green.

"Well sir, if you can tell me her speed, I might hazard a guess, but I don't suppose it can be much above four miles now. There sure is a lot of water in those clouds! Last time I remember seeing clouds that green was in the South China Sea, and we got rain so hard you couldn't breathe. The deck was under six inches of water, just 'cause it couldn't run off fast enough!"

"Simon, get me Mr. Radley, and smartly! Wallis has just hit upon something that I now remember from the Caribbean." Patrick's eyes danced as he tried to visually inspect every possible point of the Emerald to be sure he had missed nothing.

"You call, sir?" Mr. Radley, the carpenter, looked up from below the break of the quarterdeck.

"Mr. Radley, we are heading into what I believe will be a prodigious storm. I expect we shall see rain in biblical amounts. What danger might we have if we drilled a series of extra drain holes all along the scuppers to allow the water to run off more quickly?"

"Well sir, we would weaken the plank some, I suppose, but why not rather just cut a few extra gaps as we have now? It would be much faster and do no more damage. I can have that done before we reach that bank, I believe."

"Make it so, Mr. Radley, and as quick as ever you can, for I do not believe we have much above half an hour." Patrick responded. Turning back to his two officers, he smiled grimly. "Now, is there anything we have forgotten?"

"Sir, that frigate is still near two miles off. I do not believe she will reach us before we reach this storm. We have to plan for reducing sail, sir. I would hate having men aloft when we reach that bank. Who knows how far ahead of the rain the wind will find us?" Wallis appeared more than a little nervous now that the choice had been made.

"I remember a storm we got caught by, some way west of St. Kitts. It seemed the clouds were still quite some way off, when we were struck by a gale that nearly knocked us on our beam ends, and that was in a seventy-four," Simon put in. "We were lucky to recover, for the full force of the storm followed and we were hard pressed."

"If we reduce sail now, that frigate will most certainly have us before we reach storm's edge, but I agree we must not take this thing lightly. Get all the top-men on deck, Wallis. We will send them up as soon as we have a chance of getting into cover."

In only a few moments, the top-men were gathered just aft of the foremast. Many of them were looking nervously to the south, where the sky was now nearly black in the setting sun.

"Men, we have a French frigate on our lee that has proven herself to be bothersome before. We also have yon storm over there, and it has the weather gage!" This produced some smiles and a few chuckles. "I am loathe to reduce sail until we must, for if we guess wrong, that Frenchman may reach us, but we must get her under storm canvas in the next few minutes and that is no mistake. I know it is a bad choice, but I want no one tossed overboard in the squall that will most certainly be running ahead of that storm." With a final look back over his shoulder at the French ship, now less than two miles off their starboard flank, he motioned the men aloft. "Take a care up there, and tie off if you can. Storm canvas only on the foremast and two reefs on the main, double preventers, but we will have to be ready to secure the main at a moment's notice."

Turning back to Wallis Foster on the quarterdeck, he smiled. "Well, Wallis, we are committed, for better or worse. Simon, have the bosun get lashings to the wheel and put three men on her. After that, we have done everything I can think of, except pray, and I am more than prepared to begin asking the Almighty for His help."

"Sir," Wallis spoke softly, "I believe our friends yonder are beginning to alter course. Yes, they are." More forcefully now, "Sir, they are turning through the wind and making to cross our stern. Yet, even with our reduced sail, they will be well over a mile off. Most likely out of range, if they even try to get a shot off. I believe, sir, that they are more worried about this storm than about sinking us."

"That may only prove them the wiser! They have left it until there is no way for us to turn back into the west now, for we could never hope to outrun these clouds, and I have no wish to run before this thing into the Bay of Bengal. It is only perhaps one hundred miles to Andaman Island and five hundred to the coast of Burma, where we would hardly be welcomed! While we still have the chance Mr. Foster, let us make our final move. As soon as Poseidon has passed our stern, give me a heading of 180 degrees and get the sea anchor ready. We will put her into the wind and trust to God the storm abates before we are out of sea. Prepare the top-men to brail up the mainsail. I think we will be in a squall in just a few more minutes." Patrick looked at his two officers once more, then back at the Poseidon. "Wallis, this is your watch. Once we are passed the squall line that will precede the full storm, we may be able to maneuver. If so, we will try to get back to a heading of 130 degrees and hope to run along the east edge of the storm, for, like Simon, I am convinced that the worst of it is still to the west."

"Oh look, Katherine, that French ship is sailing away on an opposite course! Perhaps Patrick was alarmed for nothing." Natalie was standing at the transom windows looking out as the French frigate, now on her new course heading east, passed directly astern of the Emerald, perhaps slightly over a mile off.

"Natalie, please do come away from the windows. It might not be safe, and anyway we should close the storm shutters before the weather worsens." Katherine was seated across the cabin, writing a letter to her husband.

"Oh, I do not think there can be much danger, Kate. They seem quite far off, and the seas are still quite calm." Natalie looked over her shoulder at Katherine.

"Sir, the Frenchman has opened his gun ports! He must be at extreme range, but if he carries twenty-fours like the Onyx, he might yet reach." Wallis exclaimed.

"Simon, go below and warn the ladies to vacate the main cabin! Take them to the gun room. Damn, I should have thought of that sooner!" Patrick now looked disgusted.

"Natalie, get down!" Katherine saw the flash of light as the side of the frigate erupted, but Natalie, looking back at Katherine, missed it entirely.

"What do you mean?" she asked, turning back toward the window, just as it dissolved into an awful sparkling cloud of flying death.

Katherine sat horrified and looked down to see Natalie's lower arm resting in her lap. Only then did she hear the scream, and realise that it was her own voice, and that she was covered in blood. Natalie was lying on the floor, a few paces from where she had been standing when the ball struck, taking out the transom window and sending wooden splinters and shards of glass hurtling around the cabin, like so many scythes. Just as Katherine began to rise, to get to her dear friend, the cabin door burst open and Simon fairly flew in. He took one look around and rushed to Natalie's side, screaming out for Dr. Cluff as he knelt beside the unconscious woman, and began wrapping a strip of Natalie's dress around the pumping stump of her arm.

Katherine stood, in a daze, and looking down, realised she held poor Natalie's arm in her hands. Suddenly, with a snap, time began to move forward again and, placing the arm on the table, she rushed forward to help Simon. Dr. Cluff appeared at the door, along with Patrick. Patrick took one look around the room and rushed to Katherine's side. He turned her around and grabbing her around the waist, he unceremoniously led her to the door.

"Katherine, please talk to me. Are you hurt? Are you in any pain?" He implored.

"I do not know, but Natalie is very bad. She was standing by the window when it just dissolved! I told her to get away, but I was too late. I must go to her!"

"Katherine, listen to me. Dr. Cluff and Simon are with her. I must first know that you are all right. You are covered in blood, Katherine! Are you hurt? Please help me; this is important." Just then, Dr. Cluff rolled Natalie over and Katherine saw the bloody pulp that had been the left side of Natalie's face; then she fainted.

Patrick gathered her up in his arms and rushed her forward to the passageway and down to the wardroom, where he found

Angeline and Anusha sipping tea with Natalie's maid Neepa. "Quickly, Angeline, please help me. You must undress the Countess at once and check her for injuries. I will be back as soon as I am able, but we have been hit, and I do not know if Lady Natalie still lives. Please stay here and see to Lady Katherine!" Without waiting for a response, Patrick lay Katherine's limp body on the table and backed from the room.

In the main cabin, things were not going well. For Dr. Cluff, the first order was to somehow staunch the bleeding. He tied off the severed arm and began to look for other major injuries. The worst of it seemed to be the mass of cuts that had turned the left side of Natalie's face into pulp. There was, at first glance, nothing left that looked remotely human. "Simon, help me get the poor thing to the table. We have no hope of moving her further. Thank God she is unconscious, for I do not know where to begin without causing her enormous pain."

"Whatever must be done, must be done quickly, for we are on the edge of a severe storm and in a very short time this vessel may be tossed like a cork!" Simon warned the doctor.

"Alright then, we must get her out of her clothes immediately, so that I may know the extent of her injuries. If it bothers you, please leave and send for her maid. Also, please call Phelps, and I will instruct him to fetch my instruments."

Carefully placing Natalie on the dining table, Simon ran for the door, and called for both Neepa and Phelps, then returned to the doctor's side. "Tell me what you require, Dr. Cluff, and I will do it; have no fear."

"Very good. First we must cut these clothes off and find out if there are more injuries, apart from her face and the arm, which I can deal with." As the doctor got to work, Neepa came in fearfully, and seeing her mistress still seemingly alive, she pushed Simon aside and sobbing as she worked, helped Dr. Cluff cut away Natalie's clothes and began to run her hands over every inch of Natalie's body, looking for more lacerations. There were many cuts all along the left side of Natalie's upper torso, where flying slivers of glass had penetrated her dress, but most of them did not seem significant.

Phelps was the next to arrive and Dr. Cluff called out a list of things he required, which sent the loblolly boy running back down the passageway.

As he left, Patrick stuck his head in the room, "What can we do to help you, Doctor Cluff? Does she yet live?" he asked fearfully.

"Yes, for the moment, but Mr. Morrissey, Simon tells me we are heading into a storm. I must have calm to have any hope of saving Mrs. Peters. There are just too many cuts and she has lost her arm, as well as part of her left breast and her face is destroyed. Is there any way we can turn about?"

"I will check, doctor, but I think not." Patrick shook his head.

"Then I cannot vouch for her life, captain," answered the doctor, clearly distraught.

Patrick ran for the deck and called to Wallis Foster. "Wallis, can we yet bring her around?"

"God only knows, sir. I think we only got hit by that one ball, which seemed to strike our stern, but the storm is getting perilously close. She will answer the helm, but we would have that gale on our stern perhaps in minutes. The good news is that the French frigate is continuing on her course, and we have nothing further to fear from her."

"Bring her around, and let us be quick at it, Wallis. That ball took out the transom windows and Mrs. Peters was standing just inside. She is gravely wounded and Dr. Cluff must have as calm a ship as we can give him if we are to have any hope of saving her." With the call, the men sprang for the rigging and, as soon as the men on deck had the sheets ready, Wallis called and the wheel went around as Emerald paid off to the wind and came about. Before the maneuver was complete, Patrick was already heading back down to the wardroom, where he had stationed a seaman at the door to keep everyone out while Angeline and Anusha were checking Katherine for injuries.

Knocking softly, he entered the wardroom, where Anusha had Katherine covered with a blanket, while she washed off blood that covered her face and arms. "She does not seem to be hurt, sir, and the baby still moves," Anusha announced quietly. "My mistress needs to be in a bed, where she can rest. If it suits, sir, I will place her in my bed for the time being."

"No, you may give her my cabin for now. You will have more room to care for her there, and I think she may not be able to return to the main cabin for some time. Please stay and watch over her for now. Thank you, Anusha."

In the main cabin, Phelps had returned with the doctor's equipment, including his bone saw, which he now handed to Dr. Cluff as he took firm hold of the remaining upper arm. Seeing Neepa begin to turn pale, Dr. Cluff asked the girl to go and fetch a bucket of clean water and as many clean cloths as she could find. As soon as the girl had left the room, the surgery began. The bone, sheared off jaggedly just above the elbow, had to be cut cleanly and a flap of skin left to cover the now gaping wound. With common seamen, the doctor would have made swift stitches and been done, but this was no common seaman, and time was required to make as neat a job as he could do under the circumstances.

The doctor was just finishing when Neepa returned. Using the cloths and water, he began to carefully examine the cuts to Natalie's face. They were not as extensive as he had at first feared, but there was no way to underestimate what the end result would look like, even if he had a clean, stable room to work in. The left side of her face was literally in ribbons, although some were several inches wide. As he worked at cleaning the site and slowly peeling the skin back and placing it where it seemed to belong, he was pleasantly surprised to find that Natalie's eye seemed to be intact, although whether it would function remained to be discovered. It also appeared that even part of her ear might be salvaged.

Looking up, he suddenly realised that the captain was standing in the doorway. "Sorry to bother you, Dr. Cluff, but I must get some men in here to get that transom window boarded up and closed before the storm hits us. They will not take very long, but I would appreciate it if you could cover Mrs. Peters, at least mostly, while I send them in."

"Of course, just give me one minute. Neepa, soak several of those clothes and we will drape them over Natalie's face to keep it moist and clean. Phelps, get me a sheet from the bed, and we will cover Mrs. Peters' body. We can at least try to save her some dignity."

Minutes later, Prentiss and Simon Elliot quietly entered the room and made their way to the now destroyed transom windows, where they closed the storm shutters and placed extra planks across to reinforce where the mullions had been reduced to flying debris only a few short minutes ago. Just as they were about to leave, the ship was wrenched about, as the first onslaught of the storm caught them.

Up on the quarterdeck, Patrick and Wallis stood side by side as the stern of the brig lifted to allow the first of the big rollers to pass harmlessly beneath her keel. The sudden wind gust preceding the storm had been strong and without warning, but it had done no damage, for they had been fully prepared. Now, it would be only a few minutes until the rain and waves would be upon them, but as long as they did not run out of room in Bengal Bay before the storm wore itself out, they might yet be all right.

As soon as the men left the cabin, Dr. Cluff went back to work, sewing up the worst of the cuts and lacerations on Natalie's body first, then with instructions to Neepa and Phelps about keeping her still at all cost, he prepared to rebuild her lacerated face by the light of three hastily arranged hanging lamps.

Katherine awoke to total darkness. Where was she? What had happened? Oh, Natalie! She had to get to Natalie. Feeling around, she discovered that she was in a hanging cot, but certainly not her own. Feeling around, she also discovered that she was not dressed. As she attempted to rise from the cot, which was moving most disconcertingly, the door of the little cabin opened and Angeline stepped in, holding a lighted candle in a storm glass.

"Lady Katherine, please I will assist you. You must not try to rise on your own. Think of the child."

"Angeline, what of Natalie? I must go to her! Please help me get to my feet and find me some clothes. I seem to have lost mine."

"I have clothing for you in this next room, my Lady. I believe that Dr. Cluff is still with Mistress Natalie, as is Neepa. It has been some time." Angeline held out her hand to help Katherine climb out of the bed, but, as she did, the brig took a lurch and Katherine landed on the deck with a thump. Climbing to her feet, Katherine allowed her maid to help her into clothes, and then entered the wardroom. Simon Elliot was seated at the table quietly talking with Anusha, and quickly rose as Katherine entered.

"Oh, please remain seated on my account, Mr. Elliot. I must be on my way to the cabin to check on Natalie."

"I only came from there a few minutes ago, ma'am. The doctor was very busy with Mrs. Peters and it looked he had quite a task yet. He has Neepa and Phelps with him ma'am and I don't know if it would be wise..."

"I have assisted Dr. Cluff before Mr. Elliot. Natalie is, apart from Phillip and Angeline, my best friend in the world, and I will go to help if I can. Thank you for your concern Simon. I do not mean to be curt, but I must go now." Leaving both Simon and Anusha behind, Katherine, with Angeline in tow, made her way along the passageway and up the steps to the main cabin, where she indeed found the doctor in total concentration, bent over the still lifeless body of Natalie Peters.

"Dr. Cluff, may we help in any way?" she asked as she entered the room.

"Ah, Katherine, you are whole then? I was concerned for you, my dear, but I had to take care of the worst of this before I dared start anything else. If it is not too great a strain for you, I should be most grateful should you be able to come and hold Natalie's head still.

Phelps, you can move down and take Mrs. Peters legs. Should she begin to come round, that will be the most demanding physically."

Katherine took a chair at Natalie's head and carefully placed her hands where they would not interfere with the doctor's work, but would still allow her to keep a good hold.

On deck, the rain was now coming down in sheets, and only a small storm sail on the foremast was propelling the Emerald before the storm. The temperature had dropped by twenty degrees in a matter of minutes, and the waves were still steadily increasing in size. Patrick and Wallis were together on the quarterdeck, quietly planning for the night's requirements. There would be no risk of landfall, for on their present course, they had a good seven hundred miles to run before nearing the northern extremity of the bay. Even with extreme winds and following seas, they could safely run for two or perhaps three days. Hopefully, the storm would abate long before that. For the present, the storm was not severe enough to be critical, but, if the winds continued to increase, the danger would be rogue waves, impossible to see at night, and the risk they posed of swamping the brig. Until the doctor was satisfied that Natalie was out of danger, they dared not try to come about and put the bow into the wind and ride it out. They would continue to run before the wind, and pray that morning would find them safe and whole.

As the wind increased and the waves grew, the work below in the main cabin became increasingly difficult and the stitching of Natalie's face became a race against time with Dr. Cluff repeatedly having to pause as the brig rose and fell on the swells. With Neepa continually mopping his brow so that he could see, Angeline holding a lantern at his side, and Katherine and Phelps holding Natalie as still as was humanly possible, slowly the muscle and skin was knit and stitched together to approximate a face. After hours of painstaking work, Dr. Cluff leaned back at last, "It is all we can do for now. I will give her another dose of laudanum to take her through the night. Phelps, we will carry Mrs. Peters to the bedchamber. Lady

Katherine, perhaps it would be better we moved your hammock to this room to give you both more space."

"No, I will stay with Natalie. I will not have her wake alone in her condition," Katherine responded. "Dr. Cluff, I learned only today that Natalie is with child. Do you have any hope that she may keep the baby with this trauma?"

"Only time will tell, Lady Katherine, but as soon as these waves calm somewhat, I would like very much to examine you as well. You have had a severe shock and while you were thankfully not hurt, we ought to make sure everything is as it should be. I will also be in, every few hours, to check on Natalie. Should she awake, you must call me immediately, for she will be in great pain, and I am concerned that she may not have the will to recover."

"What do you mean?"

"In severe injury, such as this, the will is the greatest factor in determining the outcome. I have seen men with lesser injury than this succumb because they did not have the will to go on, while others, for whom I held out little hope at all, recover because they had a reason to recover. If indeed, Natalie is carrying James' child, it may be the single greatest advantage we have, for if she can be convinced that the child is a gift she can give James in spite of what has transpired, she may rally. I do not wish to give you false hope, My Lady. She has lost a great deal of blood and there has been great trauma with the loss of her arm, but the greatest trauma will be when Natalie realises that her appearance has been altered so horribly. I have witnessed women who have given up on life with far lesser injury. If Natalie sinks into despair, she will succumb to her injury and let go of her life."

Natalie's head was swathed in bandages, her entire left side covered from the top of her head to her shoulder. Her upper left arm was strapped to her side, both to support the stump and to brace her chest, where her left breast had been extensively repaired. Katherine was in anguish at how Natalie might react when she awoke. Dr. Cluff had done a masterful job of repairing what he could, but nothing anyone could do would ever make the left side of Natalie's face lovely again.

CHAPTER TWENTY-ONE
Patience Rewarded

Morning, at the mouth of the Rhio Channel, and the Island of Singapore was invisible twelve miles across the strait. The cruise north the previous evening had been largely without incident, and they had anchored in a quiet bay to spend the night. Now, as three sets of sail were hoisted to begin another day of searching by James and Phillip, and the beginning of the trip north for Andy, they had slowly sailed out of the bay and into the Singapore Strait proper. Not a sail was in sight as Andy led the way and began to maneuver Zee Heks into the centre of the channel. The hoped-for reunion of Zee Heks and the pirate proas and junks had not occurred, but there were still at least twenty miles to cross the face of Battam, and another forty miles to the south entry to the Strait of Malacca. The two frigates were still hanging back to allow the brig to appear to be alone.

Rounding the north east corner of Battam, Andy noticed that the north coast turned back to the south, creating a peninsula with a large bay just around to the west. It was three miles wide at its mouth and showed considerable depth. He gave orders to alter course and turned the brig into the centre of the bay. It was at least five miles deep, and was constricted to about a mile wide at its midpoint. Just as Andy was about to give orders to go about and resume course, he saw movement along the eastern edge of the bay, just south of the constricted bottleneck. Grabbing a glass he watched for a moment and just when he was certain that he had imagined it, the bright yellow nose of a large sea going proa edged around the headland. It was perhaps two miles off, and Andy's heart began to beat faster, for, as he watched, another appeared behind the first.

With orders racing, the brig turned her bow into the west, so that she was lying across the mouth of the bay, and then backed her sails to keep her stationary. After only a few minutes that seemed like an eternity to Andy, the lookout called down that Onyx had raised a black pennant to her foremast, the sign that Philip understood Andy's action. The yards were swung 'round and slowly the brig began to enter the bay, keeping to the centre. One by one, more of the big brightly painted proas began to appear around the promontory that marked the narrow point in the bay. Their sails were furled on their yards, for they were relying on their oars alone. Andy crept in until he was perhaps a mile from the narrowest spot, then he turned broadside to the proas and clewed up his sails. Looking back, he now saw the two frigates beginning to slide into the bay along the east side, staying hidden from the long double hulled galleys. It also robbed them of much of the east wind, and their progress would be slow.

Looking south, the progress of the first of the big galleys was anything but slow. They were now well within one-half mile, and their oars were flashing in the morning sunlight. He could not let them get close enough to board the brig, for with his small crew he had virtually no defence. "Mr. Vandegraffe, have the men man the larboard guns at once. We will fire one broadside, then retreat to allow the two frigates to maneuver and carry the fight. Those proas carry four times the manpower we have, and we would not last ten minutes."

"Sir, at last count there are seven galleys approaching. At even sixty men per galley, that is more than a match for the manpower of even the two frigates," Vandegraffe responded. "Should we perhaps just retreat, now that we have found them?"

"No, I say we concentrate all our fire on the very first of the galleys. If we sink her, or at least weaken her ability to join in the fight, we will have taken a goodly bite out of their forces. Prepare to run out!"

"Larboard guns! Run out. All fire to be on that first galley. Have a good eye, and be quick about it. After you fire, get the sails drawing. Helmsman, new course eight points to starboard heading due north."

One by one the six gun captains raised their hands as their guns were loaded and ready to fire. It left no one to man the sheets, for with only two dozen men aboard, they were all at the guns, with the exception of Andy and the helmsman, for even Vandegraffe had run forward to assist.

"Fire!" One gun belched; then, after a brief pause, the other five guns spat out their six pound spherical messengers. Four of the shots missed the oncoming galley entirely, but the other two made up for it. The first shot struck the mast twenty feet above the deck shearing it off with a snap, and dropping it, rigging and all, over the larboard side of the approaching boat. This slewed the galley around just as the five gun volley of the brig arrived, and allowed one of the shots to punch soundly through the galley's starboard hull.

Before the pirates had time to register their surprise, the brig was already lowering her sails and beginning to get underway. Turning the brig and getting enough wind in her sails to get any speed on her was, however, not a quick process and Andy was watching the second galley rapidly closing the gap, with dozens of shouting and gesturing savages congregating near her bow. This was going to be a very close run thing, if they were not to be boarded and hacked to bits.

When the nearest galley was within four hundred yards Andy heard and felt the first of Onyx's bow chasers nearly simultaneously. A ball whizzed past the rear of the Zee Heks and landed in the water between him and the first galley. The Zee Heks was just getting underway, and the galley suddenly turned. Her captain had seen enough. With two frigates under all plain sail entering the fray, he turned and began to retreat back into the pack that had been following him. In the general confusion that followed, the galleys became entangled for just a few minutes, but it was all that Triton and Onyx needed to turn broadside at a half mile range and unleash their cannon into the pack of galleys now turning and trying to make for the narrow neck of the bay. One of the galleys was overturned as it fought with its comrades for space in which to come about, while a second was sunk by two direct hits from Onyx's twenty-four pound guns. With the first one that Zee Heks had damaged, that put three of the galleys out of commission and left only four more visible as they paddled south around the headland.

Phillip was already issuing orders to come about and follow the remaining galleys into the bay. Even at the bottleneck, there was at least a mile of room in which to turn, and it appeared that the bay opened significantly beyond it. He did not wish to see the pirates escape, especially if, as he suspected, there might be more in the lower bay. As Onyx picked up speed and began to traverse the outer bay, working her way south into the neck, Triton followed close behind, while Zee Heks remained in the outer bay.

As Onyx cleared the neck of the bay, Phillip got a good look at the inner bay. It was nearly round, perhaps two miles across, with a small divot at the bottom, where a stream flowed in, and another small bay on the east side, about half way down, that the proas were now madly rowing for. Signalling to James to follow, Phillip altered course to glide along the eastern side of the bay, with his guns run out and loaded. As Onyx cleared the mouth of the gap in the eastern shore, it was met with a salvo of cannon fire. Three shots hammered the planking on the larboard side while two more sang through the rigging. Two men on the forecastle went down in the hail of splinters, and another was struck savagely by a falling block from the foremast rigging. As more of the bay opened up before him, Phillip was startled to see a twelve gun sloop and a large junk being towed into place by the proas, to allow them to get their guns aligned on the bay opening. Clearly, there were many more of the galleys crowded in the back of the bay and into a small river that flowed into it from the east.

Before they had another chance to fire, Phillip called out, "Fire as you bear, Pierre!"

The boats were not over two cables off when the side of Onyx erupted in sheets of flame and billowing smoke. With the wind in their faces, the smoke rolled back over the gunners, but they were prepared. With kerchiefs over their noses, the men worked with a will and as the last guns fired from the stern, those in the bow were being pulled back to their places. First to fire were the carronades, loaded with grapeshot, and then again came the great twenty-four pound balls, hammering the side of the small brig into sawdust. Three of her guns were dismounted in the first broadside, and as Onyx drifted slowly past to concentrate on the junk, there were streams of red running out of what was left of her scuppers. Just then, the junk opened fire with three cannons mounted on her side. They were old bonze beasts, but they were large, probably thirty-two pound fort cannons, and maybe larger. Two of the guns hammered shells into the side of Onyx, one of them punching a hole twixt wind and water that would have the carpenter busy for some hours, but the third gun exploded when the pirates touched her off. There was a huge flash of fire as the barrel blew itself apart, hurtling bronze, wood, bone and blood into the air and across her deck. In a moment, the great bamboo sail caught fire, and then, what must have been extra powder on deck, went up with a savage whoosh and the whole junk seemed to sag into the water.

It made no difference to Pierre, who called on the men to give her one last broadside, as Onyx was nearly past. As the guns thundered their terrible melody one last time, the twelve-pounders on the deck of Triton could be heard pummelling what was left of the sloop again. This time there was no response from the pirates, for the proas were now all at the shore with men running into the jungle to hide.

"Bring her 'round, Mr. Doucette. We will make one more pass. I want you to concentrate on those galleys. Round shot and take your time to place it well! I want those galleys gutted." Phillip was striding back and forth across his deck, raising his glass to watch as the pirates vanished into the jungles.

"Sir, the pirates have left the slaves chained in the galleys." Dick Forest muttered beside Phillip. "If we sink them, those poor devils will all drown."

"Yes, Mr. Forest, I know, but if we attempted to rescue them, they would like as not turn on us in an instant." Yet it went against everything Phillip believed in. "Mr. Doucette, hold your fire. Dick, call Brunner up here."

The Dutchman came on the run. "Sir, you called for me?"

"Mr. Brunner, you know something first hand of these galleys, and while I hate to remind you, I require your advice."

"Sir. What do you wish?"

"The pirates seem to have run off into the jungle leaving many of the slaves in those galleys chained to their seats. I have no wish to harm them if it can be avoided, but I also do not wish to leave these boats afloat. Do you believe that we can safely approach and free the men at the oars before we sink the boats?"

"May I, sir?" Brunner asked, pointing at the glass in Phillip's hand.

"Of course, here you are." Phillip handed the Dutchman the telescope.

Brunner scanned the boats as Onyx once again passed the open mouth of the small bay. The junk, now a floating hulk, was burning freely, while the small brig was lying low in the water, her main mast sheared off twelve feet above her deck. Several small boats were in the water taking men off the brig, but none dared get too close to the junk, lest she explode.

"Sir, them men look to be Iban's offa Sarawak, or Dayak's outta the islands east of Makassar. They is mostly head hunters. You free them and you had better do so from a distance. They not going to thank you, just slit your throat." Brunner shook his head for emphasis, as he returned the glass to Phillip.

Phillip looked once around the deck, pursed his lips, and gave the order. "Sink them all, Pierre." Then he turned on his heel and left the deck for his cabin.

"You heard the captain! Deliberate fire, and fore to aft. I want those proas resting on sand inside of ten minutes. Mr. Harris, back the main sail; we will hold our position." Pierre had no issue with sinking the proas, galley slaves or no, for he knew that they either had to deal with them now or face them later. "Mr. Harris, please call down and check on the carpenter. I want to know how much water we are taking in."

One by one the great guns deliberately took aim and soon the line of proas on shore began to resemble scattered driftwood. One well-placed shot from the number three gun cleanly cut one of the boats in half, but there was no cheering on the deck of the Onyx for the men at their guns could see the rowers struggling in the water, still chained to bits of seats and hull, even as they settled into the sandy bottom.

As Triton ranged alongside, her guns, too, began to pound out a cadence of death, although she first sent one last broadside into the sloop, which seemed to crack whatever had still held her together, for, with a lurch it seemed her keel gave way and she folded up and sank beneath the surface of the bay, only her foremast sticking crookedly out of the water. After one last salvo form Onyx, it was time to come around and return to the mouth of the bay, where Andy waited in Zee Heks.

The trip south had gone from frustration and disappointment to a critical success. They had captured a Dutch brig, sunk a sloop and burned a junk to the waterline. They had destroyed a large fleet of galleys, even though the pirates had escaped. The Dutch in Java and their French masters would have to take notice. The Singapore Strait was no longer uncontested.

In this last skirmish, Phillip had lost two men on Onyx, while another's life hung in the balance and two more were laid up with wounds that would, God willing, heal with a little time. On Triton and Zee Heks, there were only a few minor injuries. It was, all things considered, a startlingly good outcome. As English ships turned north to leave the bay on Battam behind them, a hurried conference confirmed the decision that they would all head back to George Town to plan the next phase of the mission. Onyx would require some hours yet to repair the shot hole in her larboard bow, but she could limp along as repairs were completed, and they were in no great rush after the morning's triumph.

Mid-morning found the trio in the heart of the strait heading north toward the Island of Singapore. At the south east corner of the island, Onyx turned west to continue down the Strait, while Triton and Zee Heks turned north to follow the Jahore Strait that separated Singapore from the mainland of Jahore. Both Dick Forest and Timmon Brunner assured Phillip that the channel was both navigable and worth inspecting. It would be a half day's work to navigate the roughly forty miles around the island, taking soundings, but it would give them valuable information on any likely pirate strongholds and also provide plenty of time for Onyx to undertake her needed repairs. They agreed to meet at the south west entrance to the channel. Should they not arrive before dark, the Onyx would take up a position at the west mouth and, weather permitting, would keep a lamp lit at the maintop.

James and Andy turned north to enter the channel, easily wide enough to have the two ships abreast with comfortable room in the two mile wide opening. As they turned west, however, the strait began to narrow and soon enough they were reduced to threading their way single file through the many turns and around islands in the stream. The winds were light from the northeast and progress was slow and deliberate. Twice, coming around a bend in the strait, they found groups of fishermen in the bays along the north shore. These were clearly simple fishermen, and around the next bend they came upon their village with children playing on the sand and women hiding behind huts. This was no pirate camp, only a poor fishing village, and the two warships passed by peacefully.

They came upon two major rivers entering the strait from the mainland to the north, but neither of them held any sign of large landings, only more fishing villages, and these quite small. Still, with the light winds and innumerable stops to check inlets and rivers, it was getting on to near dark before the two ships made the turn southwest to rejoin Onyx still some eight miles ahead. As James peered ahead into the gathering gloom, he wondered if, indeed, they should anchor in the channel and await morning before attempting to navigate the last miles. As they slowly continued to drift down, he was about to call over to Zee Heks to recommend to Andy that they anchor when the lookout at the foremast head called out.

"Deck there, light dead ahead."

"Mr. Fischer, get a man in the bows with a lead. We will proceed at bare steerage. Take two reefs in the mainsail. Set a lantern on the sternpost to guide Andy. We will creep along as best we can." James paced the quarterdeck anxiously.

"Sir, we could put a boat in the water and have the men swing a lead out ahead of us." Fischer proffered. "It would give us more time to alter course if we must."

James looked over at him speculatively, and then nodded, "Make it so. Relieve the men every half hour if need be, although I doubt we are much over three miles from that light, which I assume is Phillip."

Soon the launch was rowing out ahead of the Triton and calls were coming back announcing depths on the lead line. The channel was already widening and there was plenty of water under the wooden hulls. Still, safe was better than sorry and it was well past full dark when Triton and her consort anchored alongside Onyx.

For Phillip, it had been a peaceful day in light drizzle as they had navigated around the south side of Singapore Island. By shortly after noon, the repairs to the hull had been completed and the remainder of the day had been uneventful, with the singular exception of seaman Harry Prentiss having a broken tooth extracted on the main deck, which had caused quite a commotion. Finally, the bosun had been obliged to warn the men to get back to their duties. For men accustomed to the violence of battle, where a man might lose an arm in a moment, the practise of a pre-planned and drawn out painful event was a great novelty, and more than a few shillings changed hands on whether poor Prentiss would cry out or faint dead away. In the event, he proved a stoic and did neither, thanking the surgeon through a wad filled mouth after the surgery, and collecting on several bets made through his mess mates. The officers turned a blind eye to the illegal wagering as it was good for morale.

In a late night meeting in Philip's dining room, all the officers agreed that Singapore Island would make a great base to compliment Prince of Wales Island further north. It was larger, it was located at the bottom of the Strait of Malacca, and it guarded the entrance to the South China Sea. It would keep the Dutch bottled up in Batavia, and would make an excellent crossroads for goods from India, China, and the New South Wales colony. Dick Forest, especially, waxed enthusiastic and vowed to send a message to Stamford Raffles, the young man they had met in Madras, who had great ideas about expanding British influence in the region.

CHAPTER TWENTY-TWO
Recovery and Reality

The sky was ash grey and the waves were still ominously large, but the rain, which had come down in sheets, nearly flooding the Emerald, had abated to a steady downpour. The winds had also moderated and Patrick no longer feared for the ship's safety. It was now just a matter of riding out the tail end of the storm that had proven to be much less than the full typhoon he had feared. Still, they had needed men at the pumps all night, but, at last report, the water in the hold was down to two feet, and was now receding apace. They had managed to run before the storm for most of the night, and were now well north of their planned route, but still safely in the heart of the Bay of Bengal and were now again making headway into the west. If the storm continued to weaken, they would be able to resume their course for Madras by mid-day. Apart from that one ball from the French frigate, they had been very fortunate. How he would ever face James, though, he could not imagine, for Natalie's injuries would ever be a reminder of his failure to protect the two women placed in his charge.

Katherine had hardly slept all night. Fitfully dozing, she would rise every half hour to check on Natalie, who spent much of the night moaning and tossing in her cot. By two AM, Natalie's fever had become alarming and she had sent for Dr. Cluff. They had taken turns, with Neepa, Anusha, and Angeline, bathing her with cool water, but still the fever raged through the night, as the sweat poured from her shaking frame. In the early hours of the morning, things began to improve and now she seemed to be resting more comfortably, but Natalie had not yet regained consciousness. At some point in the night, Katherine could no longer remember a clear sequence of events, Natalie had clawed at her missing arm, opening the wound which Dr. Cluff had been obliged to re-stitch.

Anusha was watching Natalie now, and Katherine sat in the cabin, dozing over a weak cup of tea. The horror of the previous evening's events still seemed unreal. How could just that one ball, one shot out of an entire broadside, have caused so much pain and anguish? Yet, she knew in her heart that the seamen on board a warship had to face that prospect every time they went into battle, and why, she wondered, should she or Natalie be exempt. James would be devastated, and she knew that Patrick blamed himself for not moving the two women to a safer place earlier, but there were so many variables it was useless to second guess every possible outcome of what might have been.

She heard a louder moan coming from the bed chamber and quickly rose and crossed the room. As she did, she heard Natalie call out, "Mother, mother, oh James, where are you!"

"I believe she is waking, ma'am." Anusha was standing at Natalie's side with a wet cloth in her hand.

Kate crossed to the bed, "Natalie, can you hear me?" She asked quietly.

"Um... Kate. Kate wha' 'appened? Where am I?" Natalie mumbled as she tried in vain to move, for they had tied her down for her own safety.

"Natalie, please lie still. You are badly hurt, my dear. You must stay still and rest. Lie back now, and I will tell you everything." Katherine had no idea how she was going to tell Natalie what had transpired, but she had to find a way to calm her friend.

Her words seemed to penetrate Natalie's fevered brain, for she settled back in the bed and relaxed somewhat.

"Natalie, last evening you were standing at the window in the cabin. The French fired on Emerald and a shot hit the window casing. The window blew in and you were badly hurt. Your head is bandaged because the flying glass cut you. Natalie, your arm, your left arm was also hit."

"Kate, am I blind? I cannot see."

"No, dearest, your face is covered with bandages, but you are not going to be blind. Only your left side was hit." Katherine fought back tears as she tried to reassure her friend and find a way to tell her how bad things were.

"Kate, my arm is gone! I remember Dr. Cluff cutting my arm. Oh, God it hurts so! Kate help me, I do not want to die." Natalie began to sob into her bandages.

"Dearest, you will surely not die, but you are badly hurt. Yes, I am afraid that your arm, your left arm, was lost. I am so sorry, Natalie. I will call the doctor and get you something for the pain." Katherine nodded to Neepa to go for Dr. Cluff, who came at once.

"I can give her some laudanum, but we must be cautious if she is still carrying the child you spoke of, for I fear it may do harm. I have some of the leaves I first purchased in Cape Town for Terrence. I acquired more when we were in Madras, for they seemed to have a very salubrious effect, but I do not know how Natalie could chew and swallow them in her condition." Dr. Cluff was looking down at Natalie but speaking to Katherine as though Natalie were still unconscious.

"Give me leaves; do not hurt my baby!" Natalie whimpered from her bed.

"Very well my dear. I will fetch you some of the leaves. Please try to rest. I will fix your bandage soon, so you can see." Dr. Cluff motioned for Katherine to follow him from the room.

"Katherine, with the trauma of losing the arm, and the pain she is enduring from all the cuts, I doubt she will keep the child. Yet, I am loath to tell her, for she needs every hope she can grasp right now."

The following days were a nightmare of constant pain for Natalie, and a ceaseless struggle for Katherine to try to keep her friend calm and encouraged. It was three days before they could clear enough of the bandages so that Natalie could use her right eye, but they kept her away from any mirrors. The swelling and discolouration of the left side of Natalie's face made it impossible to tell if the eye would be saved, for it was swollen shut. The good news, with the change of bandages was that her nose was fine, only swollen, for the cuts were all further to the side of her face and into her hair, much of which the doctor had been forced to cut away to stitch her scalp. The best news though, was that there did not seem to be any infection, with the exception of some slight redness around the stump of Natalie's arm, and that, the doctor was not overly concerned about.

The storm had dwindled away in the day after the attack, and by the 24th of April, the first day that Natalie could see again, they were only two days out of Madras. It had been decided to continue the voyage, for Dr. Cluff wanted a port with facilities and medicines, and a calm place for the women to rest and recuperate.

By the afternoon, two days later, when they made landfall, Natalie was beginning to walk about the cabin with either Katherine or Neepa steadying her. Since she first awoke, she had cried in pain several times, but seemed determined not to allow her injury to fill her with self-pity. There was, as yet, no sign that she had lost the baby, and Dr. Cluff was becoming cautiously optimistic, although he kept telling Katherine that it was yet early. The swelling and discoloration of her face were beginning to improve slightly as well, and the left eye was beginning to open somewhat, though the doctor kept it bandaged.

It was their first night in the teeming port and Natalie lay awake in her cot, covered in sweat, both from the heat and the pain that was her constant companion. With her right hand she gently caressed her belly, hoping against hope that the child had survived her ordeal. Natalie had heard Dr. Cluff tell Kate that he doubted she would keep the child, but she was determined. As another phantom shock of pain had her reaching for her nonexistent left wrist she grimaced and bit her lip to keep from crying out. She just had to hold on and keep this baby, for, she thought, it might be her only chance. How would James ever bring himself to wish to make love to her again with her missing arm, her scarred left breast, and disfigured face? If she could at least save the child, she would have something to give him. Then, if he could not love her, she would set him free, and release herself from the pain. Natalie groaned softly and gritted her teeth as another wave of pain nearly overcame her. No, she would not give in, not yet, not until she knew about the baby.

Next day, Katherine went ashore with Patrick to meet with Allan Newcombe, the son of her father's business partner. He proved most helpful in finding suitable merchants, both to purchase their spice and pepper for a very nice profit, and to provide the list of merchandise they required for the completion of the house. While all this was underway, Natalie continued to improve, and by the second week of their stay in Madras, she was accompanying Katherine on short trips into the city. Her left eye had opened and she had some sight from it, but she was having trouble focusing. Dr. Cluff found an eye doctor in the city and brought him to Emerald. He told Natalie that she would never have full use of the eye again, but promised to create a set of spectacles that would give her some relief.

Natalie had taken to wearing a turban like device with a veil to cover her partially shaved head and the left side of her face. Katherine told her it gave her an aura of mystery, and Natalie even smiled. Each day seemed to get better, and Natalie was even learning to make use of the stump of her left arm in a limited fashion by the time they had Emerald reloaded and were preparing to depart. They had been in Madras for three weeks, and the time had done everyone a world of good. The transom windows had been replaced and the new glass not only brightened the cabin, it removed another painful reminder of the attack. Mr. Burke and his good friend Mr. Raffles had come by twice to visit, and Mr. Raffles announced that he would be coming out to George Town in the near future to take over for the Company and looked forward to seeing the new house on Flagstaff Hill.

The return trip to George Town was uneventful, except that, for Natalie, every lurch of the ship was another adventure in learning to balance without her left hand. It was a sunny morning on the twenty-fourth of May when Emerald rounded the north point of Prince of Wales Island and anchored in the bay. The last two days Natalie had grown more and more silent, and finally Katherine broached the subject they had avoided, how to break the news to James. It was decided that, if the Triton was in port, Katherine would go over and explain to James while Natalie waited.

Both the frigates were lying at anchor as they wafted into the bay, and, before they had any chance to put their plans into effect, there was a boat in the water coming from Onyx with James and Phillip plainly aboard. Natalie fairly ran to hide in the cabin, while Katherine waited on deck. All the seamen and even the officers kept well back, allowing Kate to speak privately with her husband and brother-in-law.

James blanched with the news, afraid at first that Natalie had been killed. When Katherine held his hands and told him she was alive, but what to expect, he fairly flew down to the cabin where his fearful wife awaited him. Phillip and Katherine waited on deck as Patrick came over, somewhat reticently, to speak with his partner. It took some time before James and Natalie came up on deck, both visibly shaken, but with James's arm protectively around his wife, and a thin smile on his lips. They remained only a short time and then departed for the privacy of Triton's cabin.

Phillip, Katherine, and Patrick adjourned to the cabin of the Emerald where, taking turns, Kate and Patrick filled Phillip in on all the details of the attack, the storm, and Natalie's injuries and recovery to date. At the mention of Poseidon, Phillip stood up and began to pace the cabin angrily.

"This is entirely my fault! I should have sunk that bastard when I had the chance! I chose to let him go and now it has cost Natalie dearly. I swear, I will hunt him down and I will sink him if it is the last thing I do." Phillip was simply livid. Katherine had never seen him so angry, not even when she had shot the French officer off Cape Verde.

"It is also my fault, Phillip," Patrick rejoined. "I should have moved the women out of the main cabin when we saw the Frenchman turning across our stern. I thought he was out of range, but that is no excuse. I feel I have failed all of you."

"We can all sit here and take turns blaming ourselves or each other, and it will make no difference. Natalie's life is forever altered, and that cannot be undone. What we must do now is provide unconditional support to her and James, and then plan for what comes next." Katherine looked at both men meaningfully. "I agree, though. Poseidon must be made to pay for this. Before we can undertake that mission however, we have a hold full of material for the house that I am sure Koh Huan will be eager to see. I suggest, Patrick, that you make arrangements to begin unloading tomorrow. Now, husband, we will return to Onyx."

The following days were filled with trips to the house on Flagstaff Hill, which was nearing completion, checking furnishings coming out of Emerald's hold, meeting with Koh Huan, and exploring the recently completed warehouse and office building. For the first two days, James and Natalie had been conspicuously absent. Then a message arrived from Triton inviting the Hollis's to dinner. It was a very private event, with just the four of them. Natalie wore her turban during dinner and James sat at her side, helping her cut her meat and obviously trying to make things as easy as he could.

Finally, Natalie laid down her fork and somewhat hesitantly looked around the table. "I am sorry, but this simply will not do. I refuse to spend the rest of my life denying what has happened or hiding behind it. James, dearest, I know you are trying very hard to be helpful and to make things as easy for me as you can. Thank you, but you must stop. You will all have to let me struggle, because, if I do not, I will remain as I am, an invalid, and that cannot be. Katherine already knows, as is only fitting, but I have an announcement to make. James, I am carrying your child. I did not want to tell you before I knew how you would feel about me, for I did not want to tie you to me if you found my appearance unbearable. You have set my mind at ease that you still wish to remain as my husband, and now you deserve to know that you will be a father soon. I will be a mother, and I need to learn how to function so that I can take care of our child. Now I wish to quit hiding." With that rather earth shattering announcement, Natalie rose and removed the turban, and then leaned over and kissed her husband.

James flew from his chair and wrapped his arms around his wife. "Oh, dearest, how could you ever doubt how I would feel about you? I did not marry you for your appearance and fashion; I married the fine woman who resides beneath all that, and she is still there." Looking over at a startled Phillip, James smiled "I think that a toast is in order. I propose we all drink to motherhood!"

Everyone laughed and then wept with joy and relief. Phillip went over and embraced his sister for a long moment, whispering in her ear, then shook James' hand warmly.

"I would like to make one more toast," Natalie said through her tears. "I would like to propose a toast to my best friend, and the person who literally carried me through these dark days. I would most assuredly not be here without her unwavering love and support. To Kate, God bless her!"

CHAPTER TWENTY-THREE
The Hunt is Sounded

It was only four days later that Esmeralda, a six hundred ton China trader, entered the anchorage at George Town. After calling on the fort, her captain, Richard Howe, paid a call on Phillip at his newly furnished office at the company warehouse.

"Sir Phillip, an honour, I assure you. I was informed at the fort of your recent success against those damnable pirates that haunt the Singapore Channel. You are to be commended, Sir Phillip, yes indeed, and I shall certainly carry the news to Madras and thence back to England in due course." Captain Howe, certainly well into his fifties, appeared to be nearly as broad as he was tall, yet did not look flabby, nor did he carry himself as one well past his prime. Rather, he looked like a solid ox of a man, although a diminutive ox, his height being barely above five feet. His hair had clearly once been a shimmering gold, but was now mixed with abundant streaks of grey, but there was no less gold in his demeanour, for his smile was quick and genuine and there was still a merry twinkle in his eye.

"Thank you, Captain Howe. That is most generous. I say, I served with a lieutenant Andrew Howe in Agamemnon for a short while in '96. Would that be any relation at all?"

"My word, yes! Andrew is my eldest son, and last word was he had been made master and commander of a sloop sailing out of Barbados. It was certainly kind of you to remember him, My Lord."

"He was a good friend and able shipmate. I am pleased to hear that he got his foot up. Do send my greetings." Phillip smiled, remembering the younger Howe as a fiendish prankster and tireless womanizer in those youthful days stationed in Gibraltar. "Did you encounter any trouble on the trip out? Any sign of a French frigate?"

"No trouble ourselves, clear sail all the way from Cape Town. Came direct you see. Only reason we came by here was we got warning about some trouble for British shipping getting too near Batavia. But sir, now as you mention it, we spoke with a schooner sailing out of New South Wales. We met just north of Simeulue, on the west side of Sumatra, and he said he had been chased by a heavy frigate for three hours before he lost him in the dusk. Might be the one you are asking after."

"Yes, and if that schooner was running up the west side of Java, it would put the French in a good position to reach down to Batavia or cross up to Pondicherry for supplies. Thank you, Captain Howe; now may I offer you a chilled lemon tonic?"

"Simeulue is the northernmost of a string of islands that run northwest to southeast all along the west coast of Sumatra. There are perhaps eight major islands and hundreds of small ones. There is a settlement on the southeast side of Simeulue called Singabang, and another called Ganungsitoli further south on Nias, but that is about it. In all, I would guess, about seven hundred miles from one end to the other." Dick Forest pointed to the chart spread on the table as he spoke. Seated around him in the Hollis & Company shipping office were Phillip, James, Patrick, Pierre, Andy, Terrance, Wallis Foster and Simon Elliot, for this was a war council of the first order. Word that their prey, for that surely was what Poseidon now was, might be within reach, had everyone eagerly listening to the old sailing master's every word.

"Dick, how far is it to Simeulue?" asked James, looking intently at the map.

"I would make it just fewer than six hundred nautical miles, if we keep fairly tight to the north shore going round Aceh. There is a good channel between Kutaraja and a small group of islands just off the north point of Sumatra." Dick responded.

"So, Poseidon may be out there, but we are still looking for a slender needle in a relatively large hay stack. Can we narrow things down a bit?" Terrance Bernard looked sceptically at the chart. "Did Captain Howe know about where the French frigate appeared?"

"I do not believe so," Phillip responded. "He was just relating what he heard from another captain, so even if he had some idea, it would be second hand. I think it will depend on whether Poseidon is working with the forces out of Batavia, or if she is based out of Pondicherry."

"The fact that we ran into her between Pondicherry and Sumatra could indeed indicate the northern base, but, then again, she might have been just coming on station," Patrick put in.

"But if she is only just arrived now, where was she all these months?" Pierre asked critically. "We left her in the Atlantic nearly a year ago, and if her mission was not revoked, where was she? I would wager she slowly followed us out and has been keeping out of sight. That captain left his brothers to their fate in the North Atlantic by turning and running from a fight where he could have made a difference. I will admit, his consort acted foolishly and put him in a bad place, but the fact is, he ran."

"What are you driving at, Pierre?" Phillip asked.

"Look, Poseidon got a chance to redeem herself at Patrick's expense. She was clearly the larger and much more powerful ship; she was well placed to run down on Emerald and finish her. It would have provided redemption of sorts for her failure in the North Atlantic. Why did she fire one long range volley and retire again?" Pierre put his hands face up before him and shrugged.

"Perhaps her captain is unsure of his men or he is unqualified to captain a ship. Perhaps he is just shy," responded Wallis with a shake of his head.

"No, I do not believe that is the answer," Andy Barg spoke out for the first time. "Think about what Pierre just gave us. If Poseidon ran in the Atlantic, because the captain of Tunder proved an inept fool, and placed himself where we had a clear two on one advantage, then one might question his loyalty to his brothers in Tunder, but not his wisdom in not placing himself in the identical position. Tactically, it was not the wrong choice, for had he continued, he would have faced the combined broadsides of two virtually unharmed frigates to his one, for by the time he came up, the matter was already decided for Tunder. Yet, in the Bay of Bengal, he had massive superiority, a forty gun heavy frigate against a brig. All he had to do was keep at his maximum range and damage Emerald enough that the oncoming storm would finish the job. Yet, he took one very long ranged broadside, almost guaranteed to do little damage, if any, and then he again sailed away. Why?"

"Are you suggesting that, in spite of what we know this captain's orders are, he is trying not to engage us?" Patrick asked incredulously. "That makes no sense!"

"None of his actions make any sense," Andy responded. "I am only trying to find something common to his actions that might explain them, that's all."

"Hold on just a moment!" Phillip intervened between what was beginning to look like a brewing argument. "Let us examine Andy and Pierre's premise for a minute. It might put several events in a different perspective. Back off Funchal, the Poseidon stayed well back, in retrospect too far, content, it seemed, to track us, yet keep clear of us. When Tunder appeared, we assumed that we were fortunate to have her well before us, and increased sail to give ourselves room to deal with one frigate before the second could close with us. Why would the captain of Tunder, unless, as we assumed, he was a total fool, place himself in such a difficult situation? He expected Poseidon to be there and to engage us quickly; it is the only reasonable answer to his otherwise inexplicable actions. If Poseidon had been closer, or had come up in great haste when Tunder showed herself, we would have had to divide our forces and things might have gone very differently. Poseidon held back, and ultimately declined action, leaving her consort to her fate. We assumed her captain was simply afraid after the thorough trouncing we gave Tunder, but what if he had different motives all along?"

"But why?" James joined into the seemingly unanswerable question. "What is their plan, to anger us, as they have done with the attack on Emerald, that nearly killed Natalie? To what purpose, to draw us into pitched battle against both the French and that supposed Dutch fifty gun two decker that none of us have even seen?"

"What if the captain of Poseidon never meant to even hit Emerald? What if it was a fluke shot? All the rest of that entire broadside fell well short or wide of Emerald's stern, correct?" Andy was looking at Patrick.

"Well yes, that is true, but..."

"But we have all seen it before, a gunner accidentally places an extra load of powder into the barrel, an elevation error goes unnoticed, a perfect ball flies further than anyone would expect!" Andy shrugged his shoulders. "What if that one perfect ball that struck the transom windows was never meant to be? What if that captain fired what he believed to be a useless salvo, perhaps to fool his men, perhaps to appease his officers, before he retired, using the oncoming storm as an excuse?"

"I agree that if that were so, it would explain everything very neatly. But the huge question that looms is why? What is this about?" Phillip looked at Andy and Pierre for answers to their scenario.

"You are forgetting that storm." Patrick was clearly angry now. "That was no little squall; it looked like it might be a full blown typhoon, and we were right on its edge. That Frenchman had reason to turn and run."

"Yet, he was in a much larger ship; he was upwind, and he had ample opportunity to take a run at you and still continue east around the worst of the storm." Pierre stepped back into the conversation, "Your report is clear that the storm was mostly to your west, and that you had discussions with your officers about turning back to the east to get around the heart of the storm, which was precisely where the French frigate was headed. You also stated that you believed the French frigate was well out of range when he fired that ill–fated broadside."

"Are you two trying to tell us that my dear wife was maimed and nearly killed because of an accident?" James was ashen and shaking. "What would you have me tell Natalie? 'Oh dear, it is all right, it was only a fluke accident that unfortunately you must endure for the rest of your life'!"

"James, what we are trying to do is to make sense of our situation and prepare accordingly. It does not change what happened, but it may affect what will happen. Let us at least examine this argument." Phillip took James' arm and looked him in the eye. "Listen brother, I want revenge for what happened as much as you do, for I was the one who let Poseidon run in the Atlantic, but if there is more to this, we need to know what it is."

James looked as if he was about to argue, then nodded his head and sat back.

Simon Elliot now took the floor, "If I may sir, there is something else that bothers me, has been these last few minutes. Captain, you said Captain Howe told you that he spoke with a schooner that had been chased by a heavy frigate for three hours before losing him in the dusk, is that not so?"

"Yes, more or less exactly what he said," Phillip responded.

"How does that strike you?" Simon asked the group.

There were voices from all around the table, but most were expressing the same sentiment. Not a likely scenario, unless the winds had been light and variable. In any steady wind, the frigate should have had a huge advantage.

"I am ready to go out on a limb right now and make a prediction," Pierre spoke over the hubbub of proposed answers to Simon's question. "For whatever reason, the captain of Poseidon is intent on avoiding any conflict with us or any British shipping."

Now James sat forward and pursed his lips, "If you are right, and I am not saying that you are, how do we make contact? If, if, I say, this captain is trying to avoid fighting us, how do we discover it without endangering our ships and men?"

"Or, if indeed this captain is trying to send us a message, how do we approach without getting him killed by his own men?" Wallis asked, with a shrug of his shoulders.

"Let us remember that this is still all supposition," Phillip proffered. "There could well be other explanations for what has happened, although, short of this captain being totally inept, I cannot muster one at the moment. In any event, it seems likely that our quarry is somewhere to the west of Sumatra, and that is where I propose to go. The question is, who all goes and how soon do we leave? What are your thoughts?"

Patrick spoke first, "We have been back from Madras for ten days, and Emerald has been unloaded and is fit to leave on 48 hours' notice. We just require water, food, and rounding up the last of the men from shore leave."

"As for Triton and Onyx, we have been sitting idle for near a month. It would not take long to have everyone on board and as for supplies, we can leave as soon as the water butts are filled," Pierre noted, "I imagine we sail without our clerks, but we will manage just fine."

"Certainly Katherine and Natalie will remain here." Phillip looked at James, "Do you wish to remain with Natalie for a time? I can put Pierre in charge of Triton for this voyage and not one soul in this room or elsewhere would blame you, James."

"No, I will command my ship, and Natalie would not have it any other way. I would ask, however, that we postpone sailing for two or three days. It will give us time to settle Katherine and Natalie into the house on Flagstaff Hill, which is nearly ready for them. I will feel better if they are up there and away from the town. I would also like to leave a few men to guard the residence and the warehouse while we are gone."

"I agree!" Phillip looked around at the gathered leaders of his little fleet. "Today is June first; I propose we set sail on the fourth. I further propose to divide our forces. James, you will take Patrick and Emerald with you and retrace our last voyage south through the Strait of Malacca, past Kundar, and all the way to the southern tip of Sumatra. I want you to cross through the Sunda Strait and meet Onyx as she comes down the west coast of Sumatra. I will go 'round the north tip of Aceh and seek out our quarry along the west shore islands. Pierre, you, Terrance and Patrick are in charge of readying the ships. James and I will be occupied in getting Katherine and Natalie settled. Andy, you will come with us. Any questions?"

"Why divide our forces?" James knew others in the group were wondering but perhaps not prepared to speak out.

"Because, if we find Poseidon on the west side of Sumatra, I believe we have a better chance of solving this question if we do not arrive with an overwhelmingly superior force. Also, I would like to see if our spring offensive against Ibn Satna has left a lingering effect, and by crossing the Sunda Strait, you may discover if the Dutch are actively patrolling it."

As the men filed out of the office, Andy Barg remained gazing quizzically at Phillip.

"What is it, Andy? Is something bothering you?"

"By your leave sir, I am wondering what the real reason is that you are sending James and Patrick out on a wild goose chase. You know full well we could check all those bays on the way back from circling Sumatra. Why is it you want Poseidon to yourself?"

"Sometimes, Andy, you ask impertinent questions."

"Yes sir, I am aware of that. So let me tell you what I think, sir. I think you are determined to capture that frigate yourself. I think you are convinced that Natalie's unfortunate injury is your fault and you need to redeem yourself. I think, sir, that you do not want to share that capture with James or anyone else, no matter what James or Patrick might feel about their need to get even."

"If you are through thinking Andy, you can get back to work. For now, I will tell you what I think. I think I don't answer to you, or anyone else."

Andy smiled sadly and walked out, leaving Phillip alone with his doubts and his regrets.

CHAPTER TWENTY-FOUR
China

The Celeste had been at anchor in the river for nearly three weeks while Mr Newcombe continued to stay mostly ashore negotiating with the Chinese. Not one bale or crate had been moved and Ross was becoming ever more concerned. Time was running out to get away before the monsoon set in. They had no immediate danger of running low on supplies and water was available every few days, but Percy had made it clear that they could not leave the river without the Chinese government's good will. They were effectively hostages to the negotiations and those did not seem to be going anywhere. Ross had only ventured ashore on two occasions when Percy had shown him the area where the barbarians were allowed to roam. After purchasing a few items to take home, he had been satisfied to remain on the ship while Percy continued the endless wrangling with the merchants. There were thirteen members of the Co Hong, the official merchant group that was authorized to deal with Europeans. They were strictly controlled by the government in Peking, and only they could purchase Ross's cargo and sell him the goods he wished to purchase.

Fortunately, that strict control did not apply to the casual Chinese hawkers in their sampans who came by regularly with offers of hot food. Ross had become a devout addict to Chinese cooking and now had a regular daily relationship with a little old couple who made the most marvelous dishes, cooking them right on their boat, for almost nothing. His officers teased him on occasion that he must be having a secret affair with the little old woman, who looked like she might be nearly one hundred, but he just smiled. Secretly, he wondered how he might kidnap the two and have them cook for him all the way home. He had already convinced Mr Newcombe to help him in the purchase of several large jugs of 'jiangyou,' the rich brown salty sauce that seemed to be a constant in the cuisine. Several attempts to interest Mr. Edmondson, his cook, in the joys of Chinese food had fallen flat and he wondered in desperate moments if he might trade him for a Chinaman!

"Sir, I believe Mr. Newcombe is approaching." It was Bill Hotchkins down on the main deck.

"Very well, Mr. Hotchkins. I am going to my cabin. Have Mr Newcombe come aft when he is aboard."

"Yes, sir."

It did not take long for the sampan to deposit Percy at the side of Celeste. He smiled and waved at Bill Hotchkins as he reached the deck, then proceeded aft to the main cabin.

"Ross, good news. I just came from a meeting with Doh Han and we are finally where we need to be. All this delay, I discovered this morning was an internal power play between several of the Co Hong and the Hoppo, who is the representative of the government. We are officially here as a Company ship, of course, but we are irregular, and the government is trying for an even bigger slice of the pie. Not so different from our politicians, I suppose. At any rate, they have come to an accommodation, and it is one we can live with. I have disposed of all our cargo and arranged, for a very good bargain, to get us reloaded in the next several days and out of China before the government changes its mind. The port is officially closed until the trading season starts in October. No one comes up river at this time of the year, because the southwest monsoon will trap them here until January, when the winds reverse. The other factor, of course, is that there is no tea for sale now. It is seasonal and will not be available until November or so at the earliest. Still, we have made an accommodation, as I said. All the unloading and reloading must, however, be done at night, as we are not officially here at all. The Factor here is not overly pleased with us, but with your letters from the King and the Company, he will do as he is bidden."

"So, now that we have sat here idle these weeks, it is not likely that we will beat the monsoon back to George Town. Had we been able to make a fast turnaround, it might have just been possible. As it was, we were fortunate in our winds coming north, for the northwest monsoon was weak and ended early. I would not count on that happening again. It is nearly June, and even if the monsoons are late, I doubt they will be late enough. How soon do you suppose we can plan to depart?"

"I believe that will depend mostly on us now. That is why I came back. Can we, in all respects, be ready to unload the cargo that we can reach first tonight? I need to return to shore very shortly, but I must know what we can do, for there is great concern about the 100 cases of opium we carry. It is never allowed to come in directly and must be offloaded on Linton Island, from where it is smuggled into the country. The Chinese merchants are anxious to have it and would like to see it ashore. I explained that we must first unload the rest of the cargo to reach it, for I fear that it is only the opium that makes our presence bearable."

"I can have the men prepare, in all respects, to unload tonight, but I must say, Mr. Newcombe, that the idea does not entice me greatly. It is an invitation to disaster. What sort of lighters will they employ?"

"I believe that this, also, may be somewhat unusual, for typically, they employ large sampans and barges, but in our instance they will bring two junks alongside. We are well out into the river now, but we will need to move further down into the mouth this afternoon. I believe the goods will not go ashore here at all, but may be taken north to Shanghai."

"That will be helpful, for the larger junks will ride higher and can load much more quickly."

"I must return to shore now. I will be back before dark to give you instructions for loading, but we will have to mix the loads, and the Hongs want the first of the opium on this first junk. I believe they need to make a point of getting it out of Canton."

The size of the first junk startled Ross when it slowly drifted down the river to come alongside of Celeste near the end of the second dog watch. It was much larger than any he had seen on the river in their weeks of waiting, and might well take nearly half their total cargo. The loading got underway almost as soon as the junk was cabled to the Celeste, for the hatches were open and the men standing at the capstan. Once the initial difficulty of communication had been overcome by a system of sign language and flags, the unloading proceeded throughout the night. By the end of the middle watch, the junk was ready to pull away, and Ross's crew was ready to sleep where they fell, no matter that a light rain was falling. In the next two nights, all the cargo was off-loaded and the first of the crates of goods for England were aboard.

"Captain, can we continue loading into this morning?" asked a breathless Percy Newcombe as he trotted across the deck from the entry port.

"If the goods are here, we will certainly load. Is there some problem?" Ross asked

"I believe we may be able to depart tomorrow! The only question is if we can we get the ship loaded that quickly. I know it is usually a matter of several days at least, and we have not made much of a beginning last night. Are the men able to continue?"

"Yes, I will vouch for the men, but what has prompted this sudden urgency?"

"Captain, there is some unrest ashore just now, and the Factor believes they may use this ship as a convenient target of their anger. Should that happen, I do not know how the government might respond, but we cannot be seen to be firing on Chinese citizens, no matter if we are threatened. My contact Doh Han, at the Hong is even now having our cargo brought down. To facilitate our departure, a large barge is being readied right at the moment. It seems much of our cargo is already aboard. The Chinese will be coming out within the hour. Oh, by the way, the Hong was pleased with our cargo, and we have been given more credits than I supposed. I have taken the liberty of making a very special purchase on your partner's behalf. There will be three large crates coming up separately this morning on a large sampan. We will want them stowed carefully, for they contain a quite lovely collection of jade that Doh Han assures me is from the time of Emperor Yuan of the Western Han Dynasty! Ross, these carvings date back to the time of Christ. I have paid a pretty penny for them, but I think Phillip will be very excited, for he asked me specifically to look for some fine jade pieces for him."

"Knowing Phillip, he will be ecstatic! Well, Percy, I suppose I should give the men the good news. They will be quite prepared to work hard this morning if it means we can depart. No word, I suppose of hiring a Chinese cook?" Ross was determined to extend his new found gastronomic love affair.

"Perhaps, but it would be difficult. You must understand, Ross, that we would have no way to communicate with such a fellow. You would have to smuggle him out of China, and we would not have access to many of the vegetables that make up so much of the cooking."

"I will teach the man English myself! As to the vegetables, I am sure we can load sufficient here, and surely they exist beyond China!"

"I will see what may be done. I suppose that means I should be prepared for what will grace our table all the way back to George Town?" Percy smiled good naturedly.

At that very moment, half way round the world, two men were sitting down to a late dinner at White's. It had been a long and trying day for Sir John Jervis, who had spent much of the afternoon in Parliament assuring nervous members that Britain would survive another war with Napoleon.

"I thought it rather clever, Sir John, when you told the House that you could not guarantee Napoleon would not reach England, only that he would not reach it by sea!" Lord Bromley smiled at his friend.

"They must believe that to be true, or they will lose heart before we even begin what I believe will be a long and difficult war." Lord St. Vincent grimly smiled at the banker who was one of a small cadre that made up an unofficial and semi-secret closet cabinet that included the Prince of Wales. "This is going to tax all of us before we are done, and should we not succeed, you had better brush up on your French!"

"Have you any word on our mutual friend down in Penang?"

"None since they arrived in Madras, but that is to be expected. I believe you were already informed about the situation Phillip found in the Atlantic?"

"Yes, someone very high in the Regime has taken a distinct dislike to our colleague. I suppose having one's fortune severely diminished would have that effect. I only hope he manages to contain the problem in Java and return. Of course, they will have no idea that war is again underway. I suppose though, that after the attack he suffered while we were ostensibly at peace, he will not be too complacent on his return trip."

"Complacency is not in his nature. Why else do you suppose we chose him? That, and his total disregard for authority and convention. I should certainly like to have him back now, along with those frigates of his! What I would not give for another captain like him. Lord Cochrane is in the same mold, and, of course, Horatio, but they have had to take greater command, and that limits their ability to dash about causing havoc. I would love for another renegade to stir up the people's lust, even if we would have a devil of a time controlling him. Hard to threaten a man with all the wealth he has, and the connections, including the Prince, who thinks him another Nelson."

"Yes, well having a small fortune handed to you might have that effect," Bromley smiled at Sir John, who had also benefitted hugely from Phillip's earlier raid on Napoleon's treasure ships, "and with this renewal of hostilities, Phillip is likely to become even wealthier. His estate manager, Sam Cobb, just informed the bank that they have recently purchased another three square miles of farm land to grow more wheat, and they are opening another copper mine in partnership with the Duke. That man Cobb has a mind like a steel trap. I should love to have him at the bank, I can tell you."

"Perhaps I should conscript him into the Admiralty. God knows we have enough dead wood there to build a first rate!"

CHAPTER TWENTY-FIVE
The Dead Man's Gambit

The next several days were a virtual whirlwind of activity. All of Katherine and Natalie's things were removed to the house on Flagstaff Hill, as were Angeline, Neepa and Anusha's. A staff was hired to run the house, with Koh Huan's help, and as the last of the furnishings were carried up to the house from the warehouse below, the two clerks traded in their order books for tea on their new veranda. The house was a great success, and Phillip was delighted to see Natalie wandering around the new gardens smiling and chatting with James, who was valiantly making an effort to appear diligently interested. Katherine, now just two months from Dr. Cluff's expected due date, was satisfied to sit with Phillip and enjoy the view from their second floor balcony. The promised telescope had been installed, and Katherine experimented at length with focusing on the warehouse, the fort, and of course the Onyx.

It was their first night in the new house, when, at three a.m. Phillip and Katherine awoke with a start to screaming and howling noises coming from very nearby. Katherine pulled up the covers around her as Phillip struggled to light a lamp beside the bed. As flickering light filled the room, they were astonished to find two small grey monkeys standing on the foot board of their bed and loudly shrieking at them. Katherine had left the windows open to allow the cool night breeze into the room and the monkeys had entered along with the night zephyrs. Just as Phillip was slowly creeping from the bed, preparatory to an attempt to coerce the simian visitors to vacate the bedroom, the door burst open and a much disheveled James Peters stumbled in, poker in hand, to rescue his friends from some obviously vicious attack. The combination of Phillip's light and James' sudden arrival sent the two dusky visitors into new shrieks and mad capers around the room, followed by two half-dressed officers waving arms and a fireplace poker. Round the room they went, time and again, the little monkeys easily eluding the two officers by climbing over furniture and leaping across the bed, much to Katherine's dismay. By the time the last of the unwelcomed night callers had been herded out the window and the latch secured, some half hour later, Katherine was herself howling with glee and unbridled scorn for her husband and friend. Rolling in the bed and holding her large stomach for support, with tears streaming down her face, she contemplated the two men, both puffing and near exhaustion, as they held onto each other for mutual support. This was the picture Natalie beheld as she cautiously peered around the corner of the door, her eyes wide in disbelief. Needless to say, the night was over! Natalie crawled up into the bed with Katherine to hear the tale retold with hilarious embellishments, while the two husbands were dispatched to the kitchens to find tea and biscuits. The night would ever after be remembered as 'the Night of the Great Monkey Invasion.'

It was the very next morning that the embarrassed husbands took their leave and boarded ship to begin their next hunt. With the winds out of the north, all three ships sailed together until they were clear of the south coast of Prince of Wales Island. Then with a waved farewell, the Triton and Emerald continued southbound while Onyx turned to the west, to make its way past the town of Kutaraja on the north end of Sumatra. On a long beam reach, it would be slow going, but Phillip knew he had the shorter journey in the long run, and as the winds were likely to change to the northwest in the coming days, he was happy to be able to make his westing under mostly clear skies and moderate seas.

It was the afternoon of the sixth of June when Onyx made her way into the Indian Ocean and began the long eleven hundred mile run to the south southeast that would take them to the Island of Krakatau, where they were to meet James and Patrick. Having left Dr. Cluff behind to care for Katherine and Natalie, Phillip had obtained the services of Mr. McCormack, a surgeon stationed at the George Town hospital. He was proving to be an amiable addition to the crew, and, as Onyx turned to plow along the west coast of Sumatra, he was busily teaching Pierre to play a game he called dominoes. Both laughter and muttered imprecations were heard coming from the wardroom whenever Pierre was off duty. The winds stayed out of the north for another precious day and with all sails set, Onyx made good over two hundred miles in twenty-four hours of glorious sailing. As evening of the seventh of June approached, so did Simeulue Island and the first reported location of where the French frigate had been seen. The town of Sinabang lay well to the south on the eastern coast of the island and Phillip was determined to see it in full daylight. With the whole island only being eighty miles long, Phillip decided to lay up for the night and proceed the next morning.

Morning found the wind shifted to the west and Onyx had to keep well offshore to avoid being becalmed. Nevertheless, the glass showed no sign of any large ship in the shallow harbour as they passed Sinabang, and Phillip, checking charts hourly with Dick Forest, decided to proceed southeast through a channel between smaller islands rather than try to go about and investigate the west shore of Simeulue. It was sixty miles to the islands, which again proved to be empty. Next day Onyx pushed on to the south, where the next large island, Nias, awaited. The largest town in all the islands along the west coast of Sumatra was Gunungsitoli and it was located on the west coast of Nias. This would be the best bet for finding the frigate if she was at anchor. Gunungsitoli had good water and a decent sheltered harbour according to the information obtained from Timmon Brunner and Juan Ortega. Brunner was with Phillip on Onyx, while Juan had sailed with Patrick on Emerald.

It was just before noon when Onyx cleared the north approach to the harbour, but again her arrival was met with disappointment. Empty! Phillip was contemplating whether to continue south around Nias when Dick Forest and Brunner came up on deck with a tattered chart in hand.

"Captain, I believe that Mr. Brunner may have a rather good suggestion. Across the channel to Sumatra, perhaps ninety miles to the east northeast lies a very sheltered and deep bay, with a large island perhaps ten miles out, guarding its mouth. Well, inside the bay is a large village that on this chart is listed as Sibolo. Mr. Brunner believes it is the same anchorage that the Dutch call Sibolga, and says it is well known as a secure anchorage in any weather. It is not more than a half day's sail from our location, and I believe that, if the Dutch know of it, certainly the French will as well."

"We have nothing better to go on, Mr. Forest," Phillip grimaced. "Very well, chart us a course for this bay and let us hope our hunting improves."

"Yes, sir. Mr. Horner, give us zero seven zero degrees." The bosun's whistle sounded and the top men jumped for the rat-lines as others ran for their stations to begin to turn the big frigate nearly downwind. "Sir, I would suggest we might well make this island called Musala by dark and then lay up until dawn to check that bay and the town."

"Very well, but let us aim for the south shore of the island, for I believe the wind is again beginning to shift into the north. That will probably also bring a fresh bout of rain, so have the men prepare to gather water again." The rains had come with almost predictable frequency every afternoon by three bells. They usually lasted for two or three hours and then it cleared again toward evening, but Phillip was adamant that the water casks be filled regularly, more to keep the water fresh than from any fear of running low, for there was ample opportunity to find water in the many islands they sailed through.

It was, indeed, evening when Onyx sailed into a broad bay near the centre of the south shore of Musala Island. As the sun was setting, the lookout on the foremast called out that he spotted movement on shore. Andy Barg, who had the watch, instantly climbed into the rigging with a glass and proclaimed the activity to be a small herd of wild pigs rooting along the shoreline. It being too late in the day to investigate further, a delegation consisting of Andy, Dick Forest, Paul Marsden, and the cook were soon at Phillip's door, begging for permission to take a boat ashore at first light. Paul and the cook promised fresh pork for the ship's coppers, while Dick Forest and Andy were anxious to climb the ridge behind the shoreline. According to Dick's chart, the ridge might be a spine that tied the two halves of the island together, and if it was, they would be able to see across into a large bay on the north side.

"I will grant you two hours ashore, and no more. We must be on our way by mid-morning if we are to investigate this Sibolga village in good time." Phillip well knew that if Paul and Dick got ashore he would have a devil of a time getting them back in two hours, but it was worth trying.

First light saw the launch half way to shore, with enough volunteers aboard to have it skimming along. On the beach, Paul and the cook, along with a dozen men armed with muskets, began to follow the tracks into the dense jungle. Meanwhile, Dick Forest and Andy, with two companions, began the difficult climb to the ridge, only perhaps a quarter of a mile away, but, Dick estimated, four to five hundred feet above them. The climb was brutal; vines wrapping around their arms and torsos slowed them down, gullies and ravines had to be crossed, and a constant lookout for snakes was mandated when Andy nearly stepped on what the men were sure was an asp. They were half way up when they heard a gunshot and then, shortly after, two more. Clearly Paul had found his pigs. By the time they neared what they believed was the summit of the ridge, their two hours were nearly gone. Climbing over the last rocky slope, they were crestfallen to discover another ridge above them, perhaps thirty feet higher. Dick despaired and resignedly suggested that they turn back. Andy took one look up, and told Dick to hold on for five minutes. Off he went, clambering among the rocks and bushes. In only a few short minutes, the remaining trio spotted him nearing the ridge above. Suddenly, he stopped and seemed to be very keenly interested in something outside of their viewing range. Turning, he waved and beckoned them to join him. A few tense moments later, Dick peered over the jungle to the north and down into a large square bay, perhaps three miles across, with a hooked promontory on the northwest corner. Lying at anchor inside that promontory was a large three masted ship. Taking out his glass from the leather case strapped to his back, he made sure of Andy's find. No doubt at all. This was the elusive frigate; it had to be Poseidon!

Turning, Dick could see Onyx at anchor below him. Phillip had warned them that if they were late he would fire a gun to bring them back, and they were surely going to be late. That gun might well be heard by the French.

"Andy, how do we keep the captain from firing that gun?" Dick asked in hushed tones, as though the French, more than two miles distant, might hear him.

Digging in his small backpack Andy retrieved a small piece of mirror. With a smile he turned to the sun and began to twist the mirror in his hands. "Watch with your glass; you should be able to see if they notice," he instructed the sailing master.

"Nothing, no wait, yes, I believe there is some action on deck. I believe Pierre is waving back, and now the captain is on the quarterdeck as well. Yes, I am sure they have seen us signal, but to what end? They will not know what we have seen. Finding us up on this ridge may only prompt the gun!"

"I think not. The captain will know I would not signal without reason. I believe he will wait for a time. Now, if it suits you, I will start down ahead, for I can make better time alone. You and the men will follow as quickly as you can your way." With that, Andy was off, leaving a somewhat disconcerted but very excited Dick Forest in his wake.

Paul Marsden and his team were waiting somewhat impatiently at the launch as Andy Barg stepped from the jungle and waved. "Paul, Dick is just behind me by a few minutes and we bring news. That French frigate is just across the headland in a bay on the north side of the island. We must get to Onyx and notify the captain."

"Well, Mr. Barg, we have been waiting on you this last hour. Three hogs are in the boat ready to transport and we have been wondering if you were really worth waiting for, but perhaps with this news you may just have redeemed yourself."

At that moment there was a sound of crashing branches behind Andy and a very scraped and bruised Dick Forest tumbled onto the beach, out of breath and clearly exhausted, followed by his two scraped, bleeding, and totally disheveled companions. With some assistance Dick was hoisted into the launch and unceremoniously dropped atop three very dead wild pigs.

"What distance around the island Mr. Forest?" Phillip asked after hearing the news.

"I would put the distance to the west side at about six miles, perhaps four miles to clear the north corner and then another four miles to get to the edge of the bay she is sitting in. In all, I would estimate no more than fifteen miles, but the wind is still out of the northeast, and that will make the last four miles a problem unless we head further north and then come about, but that could possibly result in the risk of being seen.'

"If your sketch of the island is any good, we should be able to round far enough to the north to enable us to come about through the wind and sail down to this sheltered cove to the southeast. Mr. Doucette, all hands; prepare to get underway. Set a course due west.

Mr. Marsden, when you have finished with your hogs, sir, you may prepare to load powder for the guns."

It took two hours to clear the northwest corner of the bay and Onyx was cleared for action with her starboard guns run out and fully manned, only to find the bay empty. Phillip was disheartened at coming so close and losing the frigate again.

Just then, the lookout stationed at the break of the foremast called out. "Deck there, sail on the east horizon."

"Andy, get up with a glass, and tell me what you see!" The mood on deck changed from frustration to hope in one brief moment.

"Captain, she is east bound, heading for the mainland," Andy called down minutes later. "I make her near five miles off."

"Mr Doucette, alter course two points to larboard, as close to the wind as she will come. Poseidon must be clear of the east end of the island now, so very soon we will see what our friend may do, for he will be caught against the shore if he does not alter course." Phillip was pacing the quarterdeck in anticipation once more. "Give me the name of that lookout, Mr Doucette. He should have seen Poseidon in the east much sooner. Just because we were looking for her in the bay is no excuse not to have been scanning that horizon!"

"I make it fifteen miles to the entrance to Sibolga Bay, Sir." Dick was again studying his chart.

"Mr. Doucette, you may house the guns." Phillip turned and left the deck.

Back in his cabin Phillip pondered his next move. If Poseidon continued into the bay at Sibolga, he would effectively have her trapped. The imponderable question was what the captain of Poseidon really wanted. He could understand the decision in the Atlantic to turn away from two frigates after Tunder had been severely mauled, but he still thought it cowardly. Poseidon could have come up quicker and forced Phillip to divide his force, but had not. Not attacking and sinking Emerald in the Bay of Bengal, however, just made no sense at all, and letting that schooner escape north of Simeulue was either just bad luck, poor seamanship, or deliberate. The problem was, there were easily explainable reasons for all of Poseidon's actions, and none of them had to point to deliberate decisions to avoid any contact with the British ships. Yet, the question haunted him, for if there was an opportunity to avoid this upcoming confrontation turning into a blood bath, he would take it. Still, he had to be prepared to open fire and destroy the French frigate or risk being destroyed in turn. That was, after all, what he was sent out here to do. Damned poor alternatives, and for the hundredth time, he wondered why he had allowed Sir John to drag him into this situation.

A knock at the cabin door distracted him from his musings. "Enter," he called, and Pierre stuck his head into the cabin.

"Captain, it appears the ship ahead is turning slightly to the northeast, and that can only mean she is heading into Sibolga. Surely she has seen us by now, for we are slowly gaining on her, so we must conclude she has allies in the bay, for Brunner assures me that, while there is a fort of sorts on an island in the mouth of the bay, the Dutch were driven out when we took Padang in '95. He asserts that it is unoccupied."

"Pierre, what if he is purposely going into the bay to be bottled up?" Phillip asked, still mulling over his options and the French captain's motives. "I have been trying to make sense of this man's actions since we spoke with Captain Howe in George Town, but I have gotten no closer to understanding him at all."

"Surely," Pierre responded, "he cannot expect us to simply sail away as he has repeatedly done. If he wished to avoid us, why not sail south and hope to keep us at a distance while he makes for Batavia? No, he is putting himself in a position where we can lock him into this bay and he either has to have friends in the bay for reinforcements, which give him an advantage, or he is prepared to wait us out. If he wanted to engage us, he has the weather gage now. He can simply turn up wind and we are at his mercy."

"Pierre, let us assume that, for whatever reason, this captain is unwilling to engage us. What are his options once inside the bay at

Sibolga? He can run has ship aground and abandon her, perhaps burning her to the water line, he can surrender her to us intact, or he has to be prepared to sit in the bay and wait us out, assuming we do not follow him in. Hell's bells, Pierre, none of this is sensible."

"Begging your pardon, Phillip," Pierre smiled at his cousin and long-time friend. "Perhaps your greatest problem is that you are placing yourself in this captain's place, and that is also illogical. You are expecting him to do what you might do, but he never has! Phillip, this man has an agenda, and he will follow it through. I believe we can only wait and see, and, as you indicated earlier, be prepared."

"My Pierre, you are such a formidable help!" Phillip laughed at last and shook his head. "You may, however be correct in at least one thing. This fellow's logic escapes me. It is not something that I would normally engage in before a potential battle, but I believe we ought to have a glass to help muddy our thinking even more, for a clear head has been of no use at all."

As the two friends sat with their brandy, there came another knock at the door, and without leave, Andy Barg stepped in. "Mr. Forest has the watch for the moment, sir. The French frigate has just cleared the entrance to the bay at Sibogo."

"I believe it is Sibolga, Andy, but I could be mistaken. What is her present course?"

"It appears she is trying to make for the northern portion of the bay, sir. She will be north of the town and that is the narrowest side of the bay. The fool will be totally closed in for there is no other outlet and we have seen no sign of any masts apart from a few fishing boats at the town site. We are nearing the mouth of the bay sir; do you wish us to proceed?"

"We will come up on deck at once, Andy."

The frigate was now only perhaps two miles ahead, almost directly before the village, and was beginning to come about. To the east of Onyx, at just over a mile, lay Poncan Ketek Island, the site of the old Dutch fort, occupied until the British had chased the Dutch out of Sumatra in '95. The old fort was now abandoned, as the British had a small garrison further south in Padang, making Poncan Island redundant. Still, if someone had taken over the fort it would be a formidable challenge to get into the bay.

"Mr. Forest, any sign of life at that fort on the island?" If Poseidon had allies on the island, it would place Onyx in a very uncomfortable position between the two.

"Nothing at all sir, and there is no sign of any guns. I believe Brunner was correct, the island appears to be abandoned." Dick was peering through his glass as they got ever closer.

"Captain, the frigate has gone about and is heading northwest into the arm of the bay." Pierre was standing at the larboard rail, concentrating on the movement of the frigate ahead. "I think he means to take her up into the northern bay, sir."

"Well, he has locked himself in sure enough now, sir. There is only one way out of that bay and we are in the middle of it." Andy Barg stood beside Phillip, shaking his head.

"Dick, how far back does this bay go?" Phillip was watching the frigate through his glass, and could now just see her transom with the name Poseidon clearly legible.

"I believe it goes up about three miles to the north and then opens up behind yon headland. My chart shows a bay beyond that of about two miles across, but the mouth is barely half a mile wide. I have no details of depth, sir."

"There is a long narrow island about half way to the north end of the bay. I do not believe he can reach the western side, so he is going to have to come about again." Pierre's attention was fixed on every move the Frenchman made and his comments were more to himself than the rest of the quarterdeck.

Just as Phillip raised his glass to concentrate on the Poseidon once more, a cry went up from the foremast lookout, "Deck there, she is reefing her sails."

"I believe that he means to anchor off that island Mr. Doucette." Phillip looked over at Pierre, "To what purpose, I cannot imagine."

"Sir, I now expect he will turn into the wind. He is going to show us his stern and then, I believe, he will drop anchor with the island to his larboard beam." Pierre was shaking his head.

"Why the devil would he do that?" Dick Forest asked.

"Dick, have you ever seen a dog react to a larger or more aggressive one? What does he do?" Pierre smiled at Dick.

"I don't know. He lays down with his belly up, I suppose." Dick answered perplexed.

"Yes, it is called a submissive posture," Andy Barg put in. "In animal parlance, it means 'you do not need to attack, I give up'!"

"Pierre, do we still have that French signal book we took off of Tunder?" Phillip was looking across the diminishing distance to the Poseidon. "Andy, reduce sail, prepare to come about. We will give her three cables and position ourselves across her stern. Pierre, I want to send that captain a message. I would like to invite him to come across to Onyx, invite, not command, and we will guarantee his safety." Phillip looked around at the faces on the quarterdeck. Some looked puzzled, others grim. "Oh, and one more thing; I do not want the guns run out. Keep the men at the ready, but keep them down below decks and out of sight. Have someone inform Carter that I will be expecting guests. He is to get out the good glasses and a decent bottle of wine."

As soon as Onyx drifted into position behind the French warship, the flags were raised on the main mast. Soon now, he would find the answers to so many questions. Phillip watched from his quarterdeck, wondering what reply he would receive to his invitation. What would he do if the French captain did not respond? After Poseidon opened fire on Emerald, she was fair game and he needed no further provocation to turn her into a floating pyre. But could he do it? He had been full of righteous indignation when Emerald had returned with Natalie crippled by Poseidon's broadside, but, after all the speculation about this ship and her actions, he just was not sure.

His turmoil was suspended when Andy shouted that Poseidon was lowering a boat. All eyes were on the French frigate, and particularly on her starboard beam, where her launch was being lowered into the bay. Pierre stood at the rail, glass in hand, gazing intently at the men gathered at the Poseidon's rail. Suddenly, he visibly started, steadied himself again, and then turned on his heel and made for the captain.

"Sir, I know that man getting into their launch. In fact, I am nearly as close to him as I am to you. That is Armand Le Croix; Phillip, I named my son after him! He was with me in the Royal Navy. We were like brothers. I was told he had been purged, guillotined. What is he doing here?"

"I do not know, Pierre, but we will find out soon enough. I think, for the moment you should go below and await us in my cabin. I do not want any surprises here on deck. Not for him or for us. I will bring him down as soon as he comes aboard."

Pierre, with one last look over his shoulder, left the quarterdeck, and Phillip renewed his observation of the approaching boat with greater interest. It took only a few minutes for the launch to cross the interval between the two frigates, and then a seemingly endless time before a head appeared at the break of the bulwarks, followed by a body in full uniform of a French officer. A receiving party, led by Andy Barg was waiting, with Phillip standing just further off to accept the French Captain when announced.

"Captaine Armand Ferrier at your service, Lieutenant," the man spoke with a heavy accent, but seemingly without malice.

"Captain, may I introduce our captain, Sir Phillip Hollis." Andy stepped aside to allow Phillip to move forward and extend his hand. It was a risk, Phillip knew, because, if it was refused, it would be a rebuff that would colour the rest of the visit. Fortunately, the French captain extended his hand as well, and using his still adequate French, Phillip invited the captain to join him in his cabin.

"My second lieutenant is in the launch as well. May he come aboard?" Captain Ferrier asked.

"Of course! Andy please show the lieutenant around for a few minutes. If you will join me Captain Ferrier?" Phillip turned and led the way across the deck. When they were out of range of the officers gathered at the rail, Phillip leaned in and asked pleasantly, "Did I catch that name right? You did say Ferrier, did you not?"

"Why yes, captain. That is correct."

"Oh, I thought so, but then I thought I might have been in error. You see captain, I thought it might have been Le Croix."

The man beside him stiffened instantly and seemed to turn somewhat pale. "I do not know that name; I am sorry."

They arrived at the door to Phillip's cabin just then. "Forgive me, please do come in, captain." Opening the door, Phillip stepped aside to allow the French officer to precede him into the cabin, where Pierre Doucette waited, standing beside Phillip's desk.

"Mon Dieu! Pierre!"

"Good day Armand. It has been a very long time since we were last together. I had heard that you were no longer among the living. Yet, you look quite alive to me."

"How do you come to be here, Pierre? On a British frigate, in the south seas?" Armand was clearly struggling to catch his equilibrium.

"I might ask you the same question. You, the most loyal officer I ever knew, in the republican navy, captaining a frigate charged with murder and mayhem. I have seen your orders, Armand. We got them off of Tunder when we captured her."

"Yes, I know, and you also know that I refused to obey those orders." Armand was clearly feeling very threatened and unsure of himself.

"Gentlemen, may I suggest we sit and sort this out from the beginning. I believe Carter has some refreshments for us. Perhaps we can begin to find our way if we relax just slightly. Captain Le Croix, or do you still prefer Ferrier?"

"Armand Le Croix has been dead for six years, Sir Phillip. It is difficult to resurrect him on such sudden notice, and I would be very loath for any of my crew to hear that name, but yes, you are correct of course, I am Armand Le Croix."

"Does Celeste know?" Pierre asked quietly.

"No. It was better that she did not. When the time came, there was not so much left of our marriage anyway. She joined her family in Paris. They were all on the barricades, devoted revolutionaries, and she fit right in. I could tell no one, Pierre, not even you. I was dead and this other fellow, Ferrier, just happened to be a perfect fit. I killed him with a hammer, Pierre, right in the alley where I found him. He was a deserter from the navy; the right size and the right age. I became him and found a ship. With all the killing going on, with all the decent officers gone or dead, it did not take long to work my way up."

"Excuse me, sir, but could I interest you in a glass?" Phillip was feeling for an avenue to enter the conversation.

"Of course. Forgive me, Captain Hollis. What would you like to know? I suppose that you must have many questions."

"There are several, but I am most curious about one thing; you placed yourself and your ship in a position where we could have destroyed you with ease. Why? It is incomprehensible to me."

"I was sure it would be, and that is exactly why I did it! I was fairly certain it was you, Sir Phillip, and I knew of your reputation. You are a good commander, and you are respected in the French navy, but I knew of you from Pierre, and from what I heard from some colleagues. You have a reputation for trying to avoid bloodshed. I counted on giving you every opportunity to do so."

"Tell me Captain Le Croix; where does that leave us now? I have ample reason to sink your ship, both because I have intercepted your orders, and because you have fired on my ship, the Emerald, nearly killing my sister, and costing her an arm and part of her face."

The captain blanched, "I most humbly apologise, Sir Phillip. I regret extremely that I was the cause of such grief to you and your sister. It was certainly not my intention. I fired on Emerald, yes, but only because I believed I was out of range. I had to make a show, for my first lieutenant was beginning to openly question my loyalty, and there are others on Poseidon who are utterly devoted to the cause of the revolution, or to that mad Corsican. Most of my men believe that we have simply been unlucky. They were angry, but also relieved when we deserted Tunder, for I made certain that we would be too far back to be able to intervene in time to affect the outcome. I knew she was waiting out there, and I was supposed to be much closer, but none of my officers were privy to my orders. When you had already captured her, and we would have faced two ships against one, and my men with very little practise on the great guns for lack of powder, well, I convinced them that I was more concerned for their lives than about ending yours. Then, when we came across the brig alone in the Bay of Bengal, I had to act, or at least seem to. Fortunately, the storm was coming, and I used it as an excuse to leave the area before we could grapple with the Emerald. I fired the parting salvo to placate my men, for they were beginning to talk about taking over the ship. I am so very sorry for your sister! I did not know."

"Armand, what are you doing out here?" Pierre asked his old friend.

"Well, I had to follow you, because my orders were to sink you or not to come back to France! We knew that you were heading for these waters to intervene against us and the Dutch, or what is left of them. I needed a way to surrender the Poseidon without getting half the men killed or getting myself killed by my own men. The men know I am the only true seaman among the officers, half of which are political appointees with no real sea experience at all. The problem is that the others are more than ready to kill me, or strip me of my command and take over."

"The officer who accompanied you, where does he fit in?" asked Phillip. "Is he with you or against you?"

"Rousseau, yes, I brought him because he is the most vehement opponent I have. He is the Revolutionary Council's appointment to our crew. I was afraid to leave him behind, for he might have taken the ship," Le Croix responded. "I must explain myself, Sir Phillip. I only joined the revolutionary navy to seek revenge for those of my brothers who were slaughtered or forced out of the true French Navy. I have been waiting for a day when I could strike a blow against this wretched revolution. You provided the chance, for we were holed up in Toulon for most of the last war. When you stole Clorinde and went after those French merchant ships, you really angered someone very high in the regime, yes."

At the mention of the merchantmen, Phillip cast Pierre a quick glance full of meaning.

"We were sent out to hunt you down, three frigates and two brigs, and I was chosen to captain the Poseidon only at the last moment. I knew then, that this was my only chance to make a difference. Now, we must come to a plan, very quickly, to take the Poseidon. I believe that because I have failed in every attempt to take a British ship, the revolutionary officers will soon take over. There are three of them, and possibly half the men will follow them blindly because of their political connections."

"Armand, where are the other ships?" asked Pierre, pondering the options they might have.

"Well, you took the Tunder, and we left Sirene in the Atlantic. I believe she and the two brigs that accompanied her will long ago be back in Le Havre. They took our dispatches off Grand Canary, but declined to join us going into the Indian Ocean, mostly because of my encouragement that they take the news of Tunder's capture to France."

"What will be the key to take your ship? Do we need to take all the officers?" Phillip was looking for a way to avoid firing on Armand's ship. "Can we get men aboard in the night?"

"Captain, what if we keep Rousseau here on the Onyx as a sign of good faith, and I accompany Armand back to Poseidon? I could take my throwing knives in my sleeve, and when we are back in the main cabin, we invite the First Lieutenant into the cabin to discuss their options. I think that we must capture him before we make any move. Your people know that we have two frigates and a brig out here, is that not so?"

Le Croix nodded.

"Yes, but they do not know where our other two ships are, and I will make a very convincing argument that even now they are coming up from the south and will be here, possibly in a matter of hours. That will leave you hopelessly outnumbered. With your two most senior officers out of the picture, can you convince the others to follow your orders?"

"I see your plan, Pierre, but I am not certain. Still, it is going to be a throw of the dice, yes? I must ask a question. Sir Phillip, what will you do with my men? As I said earlier, perhaps half of them will take orders from me because they are seamen first; many are not even French, and have no politics, but the others, about one hundred or so, will be difficult. Without leadership, I do not think they would mutiny and take the ship, but we must account for them."

The conversation continued for some time as details of the takeover were finalized. An hour later, with Rousseau confined to Pierre's cabin off the wardroom with a guard at the door, the Poseidon's boat was on its way back. On Onyx in the meantime, men were quietly going about from gun to gun on the starboard side facing the Poseidon, and loading the twenty-four pounders with grapeshot, but leaving the gun doors closed.

Climbing onto the deck of Poseidon, Armand and Pierre were met by the first lieutenant and the sailing master. "Where is Rousseau, Captain Ferrier? What is this cochon doing on our deck?"

"We will speak in my cabin, citizen Moreau, not on deck. Mr. Filbert, you have the watch until further notice." Armand nodded to the sailing master and turned on his heel, leading Pierre along as quickly as possible. It was imperative to reach the seclusion of the cabin before things got out of hand. As they went aft, Armand noticed a master's mate near the door and called him over. "Jean, come with me." When the seaman approached, Armand nodded to him and, in a low tone that would not be heard by the lieutenant he added, "Jean, no one comes in or goes out of my cabin until I give the order; is that clear?"

CHAPTER TWENTY-SIX
The Prize

The rain had finally stopped and James looked across the channel to where Emerald was keeping pace, one half mile to leeward. They had made good time down the Malacca Strait, with the winds staying favourably out of the northwest, and had reached the Island of Singapore in three days. The next three days had been spent in a fruitless search for any sign of the pirates they had encountered on their last voyage. The bays were all uniformly empty, and one channel after another had proved a fruitless search. Even the bay sheltering the town of Tanjung was devoid of anything larger than a coastal fishing boat. It was as if the pirates had vanished into thin air.

They were now well to the south, some two hundred miles from their furthest reach on the previous mission, and were about to enter the Banka Channel between what the charts called Bangka Island and Sumatra. The channel, shaped like a number 7, looked to be about 100 miles long and varied between 10 to 20 miles wide. Bangka Island, 120 miles long, and shaped like a sea horse, might provide a rich hunting ground, for it lay half way between Batavia in the south and the Singapore Channel in the north. At the western tip of the island, beneath the sea horse's mouth, lay the town of Muntok, which held an important tin mine that the Dutch had been monopolizing for years.

As they rounded the tip of the island James could see smoke curling up at the town site and called to Mr Vandegraffe, standing aft of the binnacle. "Call all hands on deck. Man the guns; two reefs in the fore course." The Emerald followed Triton's lead and shortened sail, while closing the gap between them. As they rounded the point, opening the view into the harbour of Muntok, they spied a large merchantman, just sheeting her sails as she glided south to leave the harbour. Riding low in the water, she was clearly fully loaded. The only cargo any ship would load in Muntok was tin, and a fully loaded merchantman with a hold full of tin would be a very fine prize indeed. As soon as they were seen, the action aboard the merchantman seemed to become more frantic.

"Deck there, a mast three points off the larboard bow." The voice from the foretop was clearly excited.

As the merchantman cleared the harbour entrance, Bill Collins, standing at the lee rail, could see the twin masts of a brig of war lurking behind her. His glass instantly came up. "Captain, there is a brig just behind that merchantman. Looks like she is coming around to clear her stern, sir."

"Prepare to run out the larboard guns. Get the swivels set in the bows,." James called out. "Message to Emerald, 'close with merchantman'. Bill, we will intercept that brig. Hold fire until I give you the word." Striding forward to the break in the quarterdeck, James looked down at the row of gunners waiting at their guns. "Gentlemen, deliberate fire at the word. Make every shot count; I do not want that brig out there getting anywhere near this ship!"

The response was a resounding cheer, as the gun captains instantly prodded their fellows and began sighting down their barrels.

Turning James addressed Terrance, who had just come up on deck. "You have the helm; send Collins to the guns."

As the distance to the harbour continued to close, it was clear that the merchantman had no chance of getting out and clear before being intercepted by James' force. The brig, which might have been able to run, continued around the stern of the merchantman and ranged up alongside, interposing herself on Patrick's course.

"Now, just let her open her gun ports, and we will have them both!" James was pacing the quarterdeck in anticipation. "Terrance, what do you think of that merchantman?"

"Sir, I would guess she must be near a thousand tons," Ross answered, knowing exactly what James was thinking. Any excuse and they could take her and claim her as a prize. If the Dutch were smart, they would continue to run, guns housed, hoping the British ships would hold back. If they did, and James attacked, there could be protests and legal challenges that could make the entire prize worthless or worse.

"Deck there, brig is opening her gun ports, sir!" The call from the foretop was echoed by Ross at the rail with his glass firmly trained on the Dutch brig. The range to the brig was now down well within a mile, and the brig would have them in range in a matter of minutes. "Deck there, the merchant ship has opened her gun ports. Looks to be at least fifteen cannon to a side, sir."

"Sir, do we fire or wait for her to decide the issue?" Ross asked, looking at James.

"We give her two more cables. If she continues to place herself in our path, we will take her in any way we can. Prepare to alter course three points to starboard. Repeat message to Emerald, 'Close with merchantman.'"

The distance continued to close as the ponderous merchantman slowly maintained her turn to the southwest, while the brig continued to sail west, blocking James and Patrick's path. With Patrick off James' starboard bow, Emerald had a better angle on the merchantman, was slightly ahead of the brig, and just might have enough of an angle to get ahead of her. While James watched, the brig began to turn slightly to larboard, and in that instant, her starboard side was covered in smoke, as she fired on the Emerald. From behind her, James saw three puffs of smoke as the big merchantman fired her last three cannon on her starboard side.

"Come about, three points to starboard; fire as you bear!" James barked out the order even as Emerald, some quarter mile to starboard began to execute the very same move. James, examining her through his glass, could not see much damage, apart from two holes in her main sail and some rigging. There were already men in the ratlines as she turned. Looking back at the Dutch brig, James saw she was continuing her turn, as though to run alongside the fleeing merchantman. "Too late for you, min Herr. You are mine now!" The bow of Triton was already coming around, and moments later the first of her guns began the answer to the brig. Emerald, which had begun her turn just slightly later, began her fire as the last of Triton's guns finished her first salvo.

"Hit her again. I want her dead in the water." James no longer needed his glass, for they were close enough now to see the shots land. The brig had been holed several times and her sails were shredded, yet her masts stood, and as James watched she again fired her starboard guns at Emerald. This time she aimed lower, and James could see puffs of dust where Emerald's hull was hit, but it would not alter the outcome, for, just then, Triton and Emerald both opened fire again. This time there would be no reprieve for the Dutch brig. Her bowsprit exploded in a cloud, taking first her foremast and then the main, as her forestays were sheared and her standing rigging collapsed. As the last of Triton's guns fired, the brig was already low in the water, and she was going nowhere. Being barely a mile from harbour, James was not worried about her men finding refuge, and he continued on past the stricken brig, even as her boats were filling with men abandoning the now derelict escort.

Two shots from Emerald's bow chasers were enough to convince the captain of the merchantman to back her sails, and close her gun ports. While Emerald had taken several hits from the Dutchman, she was not seriously damaged, and Patrick was determined to take the merchantman before James came up with him. With Wallis Foster taking charge of repairs, Patrick had a boat in the water as soon as the merchantman hove to. She was the Texel, sailing out of Batavia, and bound for Holland. Carrying thirty-two guns, she would have been a much more formidable foe than the brig, but her crew of seventy-four men were not nearly enough to man all the guns and sail the ship. It was likely that east-bound out of Texel, Holland, her name-sake harbour, she had probably carried several hundred more crew, but they had most likely been left behind in Batavia. She was an eleven hundred ton VOC company ship, and there would have been hell to pay, except that she and her consort had been so conveniently taunted into firing.

The captain reluctantly agreed to sign an affidavit that he had, indeed, been sailing in consort with the "Drakensburg", a Dutch brig of war, and that he had opened fire on the Emerald. In a hasty conference with James, it was decided to take the captured crew ashore under a flag of truce and leave them in Muntok. Boats were lowered from Texel, and ferried the men ashore under a white flag, while Triton drifted back into the bay to cover them with her guns.

Once the boats were safely back aboard the Texel, a conference was called aboard the Triton between Patrick, Wallis, James, and Terrance. "Wait until Phillip finds out about this." Patrick was clearly excited by the prospect of the captured Dutch ship.

"Yes, I hope we are not starting another war!" Wallis warned. "We have very little reason to have intercepted and captured a VOC China trader, and the Admiralty is sure to hear about this from the Dutch Government!"

"I think we are within our rights. After all, the Drakensburg fired on us first, clearly an act of aggression, which was followed by Texel before we fired. All we did was defend ourselves," James intervened. "In those circumstances, the Texel should be a lawful prize. There is no doubt we will have to submit a report to the Admiralty, however, so I want a written report from each of you as to exactly what happened, in order."

"The question is what do we do with her?" Ross looked directly at James. "I do not suppose we wish to sail her down past Batavia to inform the Dutch. That would be like waving a flag at a bull."

"No, we need to take her back to George Town, and, I believe, she should have an escort. We did not find any of Ibn Satna's people on the way down, but that does not mean they are not still lurking about. I would suggest, Patrick, that you take Emerald back with Texel. I will continue with our planned voyage around the southern tip of Sumatra to meet with Phillip."

"Yes, I see your point. Can you spare me some hands to help us crew her? I can take twenty or thirty men off Emerald, but this is a large ship, we will need at least fifty men to safely get her back."

"Terrance, detail forty hands to help with Texel. Include Mr Vandegraffe; he will make a good watch commander. I will keep Terrance with me, but I will send Bob Conrad across as well. He will make a good bosun. Whom do you propose to make her captain?"

"I believe I will take her myself and leave Wallis in charge of Emerald. If he has Simon to aid him, it will be a very good experience for him." Patrick smiled at James. "Besides, I want the chance to see what this great ship can do if handled well. She appears to be well built and I want to examine her from bow to stern on the way back. Perhaps we sell the tin in George Town or Madras?"

"I suggest we wait until we have conferred with Phillip! How much damage do you have on Emerald from that broadside you took?" James was trying to remember to fill in all the blanks that Phillip would surely ask him about.

"She does not seem too badly damaged, James. We have a few sails that will require patching, and we have three holes in the hull, but, fortunately, all are above the waterline. The men are already busy repairing the rigging. Was there anything else, Wallis?"

"Sir, one of the boats was holed, and we have four men in the orlop, but none are very badly injured, except Finn, who will surely lose some time, for he broke his foot when a twenty-four pound carronade ball fell from his grasp!"

Everyone laughed at the poor man's clumsy misfortune.

"All-in-all, lucky I would say. Well, I do not believe we wish to remain here in front of Muntok for any longer than is necessary."

James looked around at the others. "We will send over the men right away, but I suggest you take Emerald and Texel around back to the north of the island. If you require time, anchor there for the rest of the day, but keep out of sight if you can, Patrick. I will continue south down the channel to find Phillip at the west end of the Sunda Strait. If all goes well, we will meet again in George Town in a few weeks."

Terrance smiled at Patrick, "Take good care of Texel; she has to be worth a fortune. I would not be surprised if that cargo is worth a hundred thousand or more."

"Really, Mr Bernard, why do you think I am taking charge of her myself?" Patrick laughed as the men prepared to return to their charges.

At that moment, a knock at the cabin door momentarily held everyone in their tracks. "Enter," James replied.

"Excuse me sir, gentlemen," Simon Elliot nodded to all present as he stepped into the cabin. "I thought you might like to know, sir, that the hold of the Texel contains much more than just tin."

"What do you mean, Simon?" asked Patrick.

"Sir, we just did a bit of exploring, Marcello and I, and the upper hold is filled with bales of silk, sir. I believe that is not all, for the silk seems to be wrapped around chinese plates and bowls of all sorts. It will take quite some time to take a close inventory, unless we wish to await Mr. Brunner, sir, for he could read the Dutch manifests. There is something else, sir. The forward hold is crammed with chests of tea! There must be eighty at least, perhaps more. She must be on her way back from Canton, although she would have left late."

Patrick took a long look at James and smiled. "Gentlemen, I believe that before we depart, we really should have a toast to our new merchantman!"

James grinned back at Patrick. "Mr Elliot, please remain and join us. If you are correct sir, we have just captured the richest prize in the eastern ocean!"

It was two hours later that James and the Triton finally parted company with Texel and Emerald. As he sailed away to the south, James could not help but wonder what this new event would mean for their lives. It was not that he really needed the money, but to take this sort of prize, notwithstanding the vast wealth they had captured in the Atlantic barely a year ago, was really a once in a lifetime dream!

Meanwhile, five hundred miles to the northwest, Moreau followed Captain Le Croix into the cabin, clearly furious with the situation. He stomped past Pierre and accosted the captain, "This time you have gone too far. I am taking over this ship in the name of the Revolutionary Government of France. You may consider yourself under arrest."

Pierre quickly stepped up behind the officer and placed a knife at his throat. "I would rethink that if I were you. Right now you have ten seconds to decide whether you wish to be a dead cochon. Think quickly, or I will be delighted to end your miserable life right here and now."

Moreau blanched, and then began to turn, but Pierre grabbed the back of his shirt collar and jerked him downward, still keeping the knife at his throat. "Sit down and keep very still, for I am looking for an excuse to end your life."

"You will never get away with this! I will have your head in a basket, Ferrier!"

"Oh, by the way, my name is not Ferrier; I think I am tired of hearing that name. My name is Captain Armand Le Croix, of the Royal French Navy. I am taking this ship, and surrendering her to the Earl of Brixton. That frigate out there has two more ships coming up at this very minute, and we will join them. You, unfortunately, along with some of your rabid friends, will not be remaining on this ship. You will be set ashore on this island, where I am sure you can begin your own revolution. Who knows, Moreau, in the time it takes your friends to build their first guillotine you may be condemned to be its first victim. Loyalty was never a strong suit among your kind."

"I suggest, Armand that we tie this one up and make sure he is quiet until we have things under control. Is there someone on board you trust completely?"

"Yes, Daniel Filbert, our sailing master, will be with me, and certainly Jean Picard the master's mate, among others. I will fetch a cord from the chart room and some rags for Moreau's mouth."

In a matter of minutes Lieutenant Moreau was trussed up and lying on the chart room floor, while Jean Picard was sent to fetch M. Filbert. There was a thin sheen of sweat on Armand's face, but he smiled cautiously at Pierre as they waited. "If they will not join us, you had better be ready to jump out of the windows, for I will not leave this ship alive."

"Then, my friend, it is incumbent upon us to convince them," Pierre smiled back.

A knock at the door, and the sailing master poked his head through. "You asked for me, captain?"

"Yes, come in, Daniel, you too, Jean. Please close the door." Armand tried to appear casual but he was sure he fooled no one.

"My sailing master, Daniel Filbert, and chief mate, Jean Picard. Gentlemen, this is Pierre Doucette, formerly of the Royal French Navy, and now serving with his cousin, Captain Sir Phillip Hollis, whose frigate is in the bay behind us. Sir Phillip also has two other warships, even now approaching from the south. That frigate, along with Lord Hollis's other ships, are his private property, not British Navy vessels. Our government has sent us on this mission specifically to kill Sir Phillip, in spite of the fact that our two countries are no longer at war. I have refused to obey these orders, for I believe they are altogether illegal, immoral, and unjustified. It is my intention, gentlemen, to turn this ship over to Sir Phillip Hollis and to join him. You also ought to know, Daniel and Jean, that my name is not Ferrier, it is Le Croix."

"Armand Le Croix? You are That Armand Le Croix?" Daniel Filbert asked incredulously.

"I am, yes. I am now asking you to join me. I want your help and support. Together, we can save this ship and her men, at least those who will join us. The revolution claimed too many good men from our navy, simply because they would not join in the drivel that men like Moreau spouted. I am tired of the brutality and the dishonesty. I need to know where each of you stands."

"Moreau, he was in here with you." Picard looked around cautiously, "What happened to him? Did you kill him, captain?"

Pierre answered, "No, he is alive and resting in the chart room. If you decide you cannot join us, you may join him there. You will not be harmed; I promise you."

"Captain, I cannot speak for Jean, but I believe you know my sympathies already. Tell me, what will become of us after we take this ship? Will we be free men, or prisoners?"

"We will be free and will remain, for the most part, on the Poseidon. We will join Onyx and sail south to rendezvous with Phillip's other ships. Those men whom we cannot trust will be set ashore here."

"I am with you, captain. I am sure more than half the crew will be as well, but there are some we must account for and quickly, for they will turn Poseidon into a pyre before they give her up. I suggest, sir, that perhaps I should go below and have a quick chat with Pinneau. He will need to secure the magazine, yes? He will be with us, for he has no love for Bonaparte and he hates Moreau."

"I think that is a good idea, captain. If it suits, I will go below and find Marcel Tetreault. He will join you for certain. I think we can gather enough men quietly to stand with you so that the others will have to make a decision quickly."

"I wish to avoid violence, but we must take absolute control, and quickly, for if we do not, the Onyx has orders to open fire and sink us." Armand responded. "Pierre and I will wait for you to return here for no more than fifteen minutes. After that, I will wave a signal flag out that rear window. It will signal the Onyx to open fire."

"Have no fear, captain; we will return," responded Jean. "Oh, I almost forgot; where is Rousseau? He is the only real danger, now that Moreau is accounted for."

"He is awaiting our decision from the cable tier of the Onyx," Pierre replied.

"A most delightful spot for him, too!" smiled the sailing master as he rose to begin the reverse mutiny.

As the two men departed, Armand looked over at Pierre. "Now we find out if they were telling the truth. Either we have begun to take the ship, or we have committed suicide. There are pistols in the desk; I suggest we load them and bar the door until we know the answer."

The next fifteen minutes seemed to last several hours to Pierre. Everything on Poseidon seemed to continue as normal, but the tension of waiting for the return of the two men was almost unbearable. Both officers remained seated at the rear transom, each with two pistols at the ready. If they were deceived, Pierre would cover the door while Armand opened the window and pushed out the red flag he held in his arm. It would signal Phillip to open fire, for they would be dead moments later.

A quiet knock startled Pierre so badly he felt his heart in his mouth. He rose and crossed to the door. "Who?" he asked quietly.

"It is I, Filbert. I have friends with me. They are with us."

"The door is open, come on in." Pierre responded, stepping back and cocking both pistols.

The door opened slowly and Daniel poked his head through. He spotted Pierre behind the door with two pistols at the ready. "We will come in slowly; have no fear, we are all of one mind and with you." He looked back at the men with him. "Keep your hands out where they may be seen, yes? This is no time for a misunderstanding."

Five men followed the sailing master into the cabin. All were armed with cutlasses and some also carried pistols. "Captain, is this true, what Daniel has told us? You are taking the ship?"

"Yes, Maurice, it is true. We are finished with the revolutionary council and I will not serve that Corsican atheist, Bonaparte." Le Croix looked hard at each of the men. "Are you with me?"

"We are here to stand with you, sir. I do not know much of politics, nor do I wish to, but you have been a good captain, and I will not serve that swine, Moreau, or Rousseau, either. What do you want of us?"

"Stefan, you go below and find Jean Picard. We need to know what has happened with Pinneau. Jean was to have him secure the magazine."

A knock at the door, and Jean stuck his head through. "No need, captain, I am here. Pinneau is with us, and has Therrien with him in the magazine. I have four men on the afterdeck waiting for us to arrive. Three more are on the gun deck with pistols hidden beneath their jackets in case there is trouble."

"It is time." Captain Le Croix stood and walked to the door. "We will assemble on the afterdeck and call all the men to muster on the gun deck."

The takeover was almost completed without casualties. At the last moment, two men tried to rush the quarterdeck, but were held back by men below the break with drawn pistols. As they halted, several others who decided to join them, pushed forward. One of the men grabbed a belaying pin and another, a pike from a rack at the main mast. As they surged forward, a shot rang out and one man dropped to the deck clutching his shoulder. Everyone stopped where they were, looking up to the raised afterdeck where ten men stood in a row, pistols and muskets at the ready.

Jean Picard stepped to the rail, "None of you is required to join us, should your loyalty be only to the revolution and Napoleon. You will be taken ashore with supplies. Those who wish to join the captain in taking this ship, and will join with those who no longer believe in the terror and its aftermath, step to the starboard side of the ship. Those who wish to leave, go to the larboard side."

It turned out to be slightly better than Le Croix had forecast, and only ninety-four of the two hundred and sixty-seven men aboard took their places at the larboard bulwark. There was some name calling and jeering on both sides, but no further violence broke out. The men who wished to leave were then allowed below in small parties under guard, to gather their belongings and were given a launch to ferry them over to the island. When the last boat load was ready to cast off, Moreau was brought up from the cabin and Rousseau was rowed over from Onyx. At the last minute Marcel Tetreault came running up with the French flag he had hauled down from the mizzen, and threw it into the boat. "Here, Moreau, now you can identify your base here on the island, and see how much help you will get from these people you scorned!"

On Onyx, Phillip let out a huge sigh of relief when the first boat left the side of Poseidon for the island's shore. They had heard the single gunshot and were anxiously waiting to see which way things would go. If not for Pierre on the French frigate, he might have been prepared to open the gun ports and destroy the Frenchman no matter what. Now, with Pierre waving from the stern of the Poseidon he was relieved and realized he needed to breathe deeply.

All in all, it took several hours for the whole scenario to play itself out. By the time the Poseidon was ready to weigh anchor and slowly turn out to starboard, it was late afternoon, but Phillip did not wish to remain in the bay any longer with nearly one hundred very angry Frenchmen stewing on the island. The two frigates returned to the very bay where Phillip had started from that momentous morning, and anchored for the night. Phillip and Dick Forest were rowed across to the Poseidon to meet with Pierre and Armand Le Croix.

"Captain, I must ask you, how well can you trust these men of yours that have remained with you?" Phillip asked after pleasantries were completed.

"It has only been a few hours, you understand, so it is early to make judgments, but I believe they are with me, at least for now."

"Pierre, do we leave them intact or take half to Onyx and bring some of our crew over here?" Phillip asked again.

"I believe we need to keep them together. For one thing, if we separate them they will feel that they are not trusted. More importantly though, if they stay together, we can have the men we know are trustworthy moving among them, and we will find out more than you can over there on Onyx where most of your men have no French and will not catch a problem in the making."

"I take it you wish to remain here?"

"Yes, if it suits you, sir. Armand is short two officers and I can give him relief, but more importantly, I can have the time to bring Armand into our plan and get a sense of what shape Poseidon is in."

"Sir Phillip, if I may, I agree totally with Pierre." Armand, still somewhat hesitantly, voiced his opinion. "We have known each other for so long, and will work well together. Also, keeping the men all here will allow us to build a unity and purpose that has been lacking for the entire voyage. About half my men are not French. They are Lombards, or Spaniards, and have no loyalty to any one, except a bit to me, for I defended them against that tyrant Moreau. Give us our orders, I beg you, and let us build some trust on Poseidon."

"Very well," Phillip smiled back at Le Croix. "For the next few days we will continue south along this coast, for we must rendezvous with our other frigate and brig, and they will be awaiting us at Krakatau Island, just west of the Java Strait. I want you to stay in my lee, just in case there are any problems, so that we can respond if we must."

"Of course; that is most wise, Sir Phillip. Again I wish to thank you for having enough faith to allow us to succeed in bringing you the Poseidon. It would have been simpler for you, and safer too, I think, to have simply destroyed her. I would have been satisfied if that was your choice, for it would have still denied her to the Corsican."

"Armand, please just call me Phillip. I do not use my title on board. I, too, am relieved that everything went as well as it did."

CHAPTER TWENTY-SEVEN
The Cost

It would be at least five days of steady sailing to make Krakatau and that would give ample time to discover what sort of problems might arise on Poseidon. For the first two days everything went well, including the weather, for the summer monsoon seemed to be late, and the winds, out of the west only brought occasional showers, not the daily deluge to be expected once the monsoon really set in.

The third day south bound, Pierre was at the helm with Marcel Tetreault when Denis Plouffe came to the break, and looking up, requested permission to approach them on the quarterdeck. Pierre nodded and the seaman leaped up the steps in two jumps.

Coming up close to the two men, and appearing concerned, Denis spoke softly, "We have a problem, I think. Therrien overheard some men talking last night. I think there were three or four, but I do not know for sure. One of them was Sebastian Dotard. I was surprised when he stayed with us! They are unhappy and Therrien believes they will try to incite some of the crew to kill Captain Le Croix."

"Very well, I will deal with this now. Marcel, get word to Jean Picard. I want him and at least one other outside the door to the captain's cabin. No one enters or leaves except by my leave, including the captain. We must keep him safe, even from himself. Once you have Picard in place, get down to M. Pinneau and fetch us four pistols. Plouffe, you will remain here with me until Marcel returns. When he is back, you will take Therrien and bring me this Dotard."

It was a tense few minutes while Pierre waited for Marcel Tetreault to return to the quarterdeck. To pass the time, he spoke deliberately with Plouffe and learned that the man was from just outside Barfleur, not twenty miles from where Pierre himself had been raised. At once the two seemed closer and comparisons were soon underway of strict parents, loving grandparents, and of being sent to sea to reduce the number of mouths to feed. Marcel's hurried arrival put an end to the reminiscences and brought back the urgency of the moment.

"All right, get me this Dotard, but be careful. I do not wish to inflame the entire ship if it can be avoided."

Moments later, there was a commotion on the forward gangway as the sailor Dotard was embraced by two seamen, each with a pistol in his ribs, and encouraged to move aft. As the threesome approached the quarterdeck, Pierre noticed two more men following surreptitiously behind them.

"Marcel, who are those two men behind Therrien?" Pierre asked quietly.

"Porfier and Gagne!, I should have known. They are in Dotard's mess and all three are good for nothings."

"Watch them closely. I do not wish for this to escalate, but if we must, we will bring them all up here and deal with this now. I need to know. Are you prepared to take my orders no matter what they are?"

"Whatever you say, sir; I will do it. I will cut all three of them and throw them overboard before they try to kill the captain or take this ship. Have no fear; we are committed to you and the captain, Monsieur Doucette."

"Thank you, Marcel. Now, let us finish this once and for all." Pierre nodded to the men now standing just below the break in the deck. "Come up gentlemen, please. Perhaps Denis, you might invite those two men who have been following you as well."

Plouffe turned then, and seeing Porfier and Gagne behind him, he turned his pistol on the two and waved them forward. At first they hesitated, but, looking up, they could see the gun in Marcel Tetreault's hand as well as two pistols stuck in Pierre's waist. At first hesitantly, and then with increasing bravado, they joined their friend in climbing to the quarterdeck.

"You are Sebastian Dotard, is that so?" Pierre asked the first of the three.

"I am Dotard, yes. What is that to you?" came the answer, with a sneer.

With no warning at all Therrien's pistol smacked across Dotard's face, breaking out a tooth. "You keep a civil tongue in your mouth Dotard or I will enjoy to cut it out, yes?"

Dotard wiped his hand across his face and grimaced. "I am Sebastian Dotard, sir."

"I understand you have had second thoughts about your loyalty to Captain Le Croix and this ship. Perhaps you would like to change your mind?" Pierre studied the surly seaman, waiting for that moment when all would be clear.

"I have said nothing." Dotard glared at Therrien.

"You said you would kill our captain." Pierre looked hard at the face of Dotard. "Well, you will not have that chance, but I will give you something. You may try to kill me instead." Pierre took out the two pistols from his waist and turned one to give it to Dotard. "Here, take this. Shoot me if you dare, but, I warn you now, I will kill you if you do."

Dotard hesitated and Pierre reached out and forced the gun into the now visibly frightened seaman's hand. Then Pierre turned his back and walked five paces to the rear rail, where he turned and faced the shaking Dotard. "You want vengeance for the revolution; well, you may take it on me, for I also was a Royalist Officer! Now, no more whispers in the dark; you may bring your hatred and anger into the light of day. Raise that pistol and fire if you wish vengeance, for if you do not, you will be thrown off this ship and left to your own resources."

The struggle was clear on Dotard's face as he stood shaking with shame and anger. The gun, which had been held halfway up was slowly lowered to his side as he fumed. Then, with a grunt, he brought the gun up quickly and fired, but he was too late, for Pierre's bullet was already lodged in his chest and the shot went wild as Dotard crumpled to the deck.

"Take these two others below and put them in chains until the captain decides what to do with them. Throw that mess overboard!" Pierre turned and went below to report to Le Croix.

James was sailing down the east coast of Sumatra, having left Patrick and the Texel three days before. The Triton was making good time as she plowed south for the winds were, so far, still mostly from the west. As she approached the south tip, however, she would need to turn west, or at least southwest, and if the winds continued to stiffen into the awaited monsoon, that was going to be difficult. James knew he could continue south until he was off the tip of Java, when he would have to turn west to make the passage through the Sunda Strait, separating Java and Sumatra. The strait was narrowest at the eastern end, where it was only fifteen miles wide, but would open to some sixty miles by the time he reached Krakatau, where he hoped to meet up with Phillip.

The morning of June 16th dawned to a light drizzle, with winds moderately gusting from the southwest. It was going to be a difficult day of tacking across the wind to get into the strait and keep off the shore of Java. The men would earn their pay today, James thought, as he climbed to the quarterdeck.

The rain came in sheets at times and then slowed down to a misty drizzle under low cloud that promised little relief. The bosun, Bill Collins, stood beside James just to starboard of the binnacle waiting for the lookouts to call out a sighting. They had left the last of the Sumatran shore behind them just over an hour ago, and soon the coast of Java should come into view, if the clouds would lift just a bit.

"Should be in the center of the Sunda Strait now, sir." Bill cautiously informed the captain.

"Yes, and there should be a bloody great island dead ahead of us. We have to find that island to know which way we go about," James fretted. "I am hopeful we can reach the east side of it, and then, when we have the island behind us, we turn into the west and make our westing before we turn back into the southeast to get down far enough to come back up on Krakatau."

"Deck there, land off the starboard bow, breakers at a half-mile sir." The voice came from Tommy Fischer in the foremast.

"Two points to larboard, Mr. Collins." James was smiling at last. The island was exactly where he wanted it.

They cleared the island in the next half hour and once it was clearly well behind them, they made the turn through the wind to take it close hauled on the larboard bows. This course would take them well to the north of Krakatau, but in thirty miles, they would be able to turn back to the south and get into the group of islands that held Krakatau, and hopefully, Phillip.

It was just after noon when they spotted one of the islands that James was sure was just north of Krakatau on his chart. "Prepare to come round, Terrance," James told his trusted right hand, "I believe we have reached the islands. We have been fortunate indeed. If we can just duck down this channel we should come out right on target! Let's hope for no surprises now."

As the Triton came round through the wind, there came a call from the main top. "Deck there, sail on the starboard quarter!"

James cast a concerned look at Terrance, "It could be Phillip. We did not set a firm date, but he might well have gotten here ahead of us."

"Josiah, take a glass and tell me what you see," Terrance called out.

"Sir, she is a two decker, heading due west, under two miles and closing. She is coming around to the northwest," came the call from Turner in the rigging.

"All men to stations! Man the guns; give me two points to larboard, Terrance." James strode to the starboard bulwarks, looking forward into the rain and spray. No, this would not be Phillip! It could only be that oft discussed Dutch warship. Like the Leopard, the Dutch ship was no longer fit for the line of battle, but she was still a fifty gun fourth rate, with 18 and 24 pound cannons and much more than a match for the thirty-two twelve pounders that Triton carried.

"She has the weather gage, sir. We have little room to maneuver, unless we turn and run to the north." Terrance was standing beside James waiting for orders.

"With the wind behind her, we will have a devil of a time to get clear. Perhaps we can get around and get behind that last island."

The deck was a flurry of activity as men ran across the gun deck to take up their stations. "Terrance, rig the nets and get relieving ropes on the yards. Bill, take the helm. Prepare to come around, new heading to be 340 degrees."

As Triton slowly began to swing to her new heading, the sight of flames shooting from the side of the other ship told James all he needed to know. He would not get away this time. "Down, everyone, down!"

Round shot tore through the rigging, taking one man off the yards and sending the main topsail down in a thundering mass of rigging and spars. Men were trapped under the fallen debris. Others struggled to cut away the rigging and heave at the yards still hanging over the starboard beam.

"What is your heading Mr Collins?"

"Just through 040, sir."

"Hold her there. Run out the starboard guns. Fire as she bears!" James called to Tommy Fischer on the gun deck. The two-decker was clawing her way into range not a mile off the Triton's starboard quarter. The rearmost guns began to fire, but the angle was poor and the range was long for the twelve pounders, and the first broadside did little damage.

"Bill, as soon as those lines are clear, bring her 'round to 320 degrees."

Again, the Triton began to turn toward the northwest, but again, the other ship veered to the east and opened fire with both decks of her great guns. The sail on the mizzen was shredded, and James could hear the shots hitting the hull beneath his feet. He was not sure how much of this Triton could take, but he was hopelessly outgunned and the two-decker had the range to pound his ship into sawdust if he could not get some sails drawing and pull away. Normally a frigate could easily outsail a fourth rate, but with his upper main mast gone, and the mizzen a flapping mess, he had no illusions.

"Land on the larboard beam," came the cry from aloft.

"That has to be our first island. If we can get around it, perhaps we can buy some time," Terrance encouraged.

"If she hits us again, we may not have enough left aloft to make anything!" James responded. "Perhaps we should turn and fight. We cannot win, but we may be able to damage her enough to get away."

"She has to be that Dutch 50 gun ship we were warned of. If she is, she is very close to home, and can afford to take much more damage than we," Terrance muttered.

"What is her range?" James called up to the rigging, where Josiah Turner was still clinging to the rat lines.

"Well inside a mile, sir, and she is turning to run up parallel with us. Her guns are coming back out!"

Just as Josiah spoke the side of the Dutch ship lit up again, and the sound of her thunderous broadside followed. The foremast shook and the foretop collapsed, the mast buckling just above the fore course. The front of the frigate was wreathed in fallen lines and canvas. Two forward guns were out of action, covered in collapsed rigging and spars.

"Sir, Potts reports six feet in the bilge. We are taking in water; some of those shots must have holed her at the waterline," Terrance reported to James.

"Fire! Get those guns firing at all cost! We must hold her off," James shouted back. "Terrance, take the gun deck!"

Ten of Triton's sixteen starboard guns were still firing, but the frigate was barely making any way at all. Only her main course was still drawing, and she was hampered by the upper foremast still dragging alongside. The fifty gun Dutch ship was closing for the kill. Half the men on Triton's gun deck were down or occupied with clearing wreckage when the big Dutchman opened fire again. James looked up and saw Josiah Turner blown right off his perch, cut neatly in half by an eighteen pound ball. Again lines fell and now, looking down, he saw that only six guns were still in action. The deck was awash in blood, not enough men were left to even man the other guns, if they could be put back into action. Everywhere he looked James saw men he knew and loved bleeding or already dead. There was no point in trying to fight on and only lose more lives. Perhaps it would be better to raise a white flag and surrender.

So, James thought, this was what it was like to lose your ship. No, he would not give up! They still had steerage, and he would try to get to the north side of the island and get clear. Off on his beam, the Dutchman was closing in, now just three cables off, and he doubted Triton could take two more broadsides. If only he had ten more minutes, he might make the corner! He was not going to get it and deep inside he already knew it.

His last six guns barked out their response one more time, this time hitting home at the close range, but it was not enough, and right after his salvo, the Dutchman opened up again. This time he was no longer worried about James' rigging and everything was aimed at the hull. The number eight gun disappeared in a mist of red flying splinters of what had been the rail. James felt the Triton shudder as twenty four and eighteen pound round shot hammered her hull. One ball whined just behind him, and James turned to see that the wheel, and the two men standing at her, were gone. Down on the gun deck there he saw bedlam. Two more guns had been overturned, parts of bodies lay in a grim mass, and blood ran red across the deck. This was madness in its senseless carnage. Terrance Bernard was trying to help another man back up, but it was no use, for the deck was a shambles, and Terrance was hurt as well, holding his side as he tried vainly to get back to his feet.

"Deck there, sail off the larboard bow! French frigate closing on our bows sir, coming right round the headland."

Well, that was their death-knell then. Trapped between two ships, both much heavier than Triton, and his ship a floating wreck as it was. It was time to lower the flag and save some lives.

"Frenchman is opening her gun ports, sir."

"Get everyone down. There is no need to lose more lives." James looked around for someone to take his orders. Freddie Howell was still standing on the quarterdeck. "Fred, get a bit of white cloth on the mizzen. Anything you can run up. We will try to save some of the lads, if we can."

"Sir, French frigate just opened fire! She is firing on the Dutchman, sir! There is another frigate behind her; it is the Onyx sir! Sir Phillip is here!"

Phillip had heard the gunfire nearly one-half an hour earlier as they approached the islands just to the north of Krakatau in the early afternoon. Signals had been sent across to Poseidon, half a mile to his leeward, and with a more direct approach to the channel. Both ships had altered course and prepared for battle. As Poseidon had come around the north edge of the island, with Onyx directly behind her, the battle was well underway and Phillip could see that Triton was already severely wounded, probably crippled. The Dutch captain had been so thoroughly concentrated on the destruction of Triton he had not noticed the two frigates coming into range through the low cloud and rain. It reminded Phillip of the lesson he had taught the men only a year ago; you are never so vulnerable as when you believe you are already the victor. Now would come a very different sort of contest, for Poseidon, like Onyx, carried twenty-four pound cannon and the two heavy forty gun frigates were more than a match for one old fifty gun two-decker. He just hoped it was in time to save James and his crew.

Poseidon opened fire first, with a rippling broadside that shook the Dutchman as the shots hammered into his bows. Before the big two decker could even swing around, Onyx poked her bows past Triton and the Dutchman knew he was in trouble. Phillip's constant insistence on practice, practice, practice now paid off in spades. As Poseidon continued onward to the east to stay ahead of the Dutch warship, Phillip turned Onyx to the south, coming alongside her and opening fire with everything he had. With Poseidon shelling the Dutchman across her bows, and Onyx throwing more than five hundred sixty pounds on each broadside, the Dutch ship was now the one in jeopardy. With her gunners already tired from the repeated shelling of the Triton, Onyx was firing three broadsides to each one the Dutchman could mount. After the second broadside from Poseidon, the big two-Decker's foremast collapsed over her larboard quarter, throwing her front guns out of action completely. Phillip's twenty-four pound cannons were concentrating on her hull and battering her gun ports into one long scarlet gash across her side. After the third broadside, with the Dutchman falling off the Onyx's rear quarter, Phillip brought the Onyx around to the east, crossing under the Dutch ship's stern. She was the Batavia, Phillip noticed just before his guns battered her name out of existence. Shooting directly through her weak stern, Phillip was sending twenty-four pound shot scything down the length of her two gun decks, clearing men and causing total bedlam as guns exploded and overturned. Looking round her stern, he saw that Pierre and Armand had ranged the Poseidon along her starboard quarter and were also continuing to pummel the now seriously listing ship. The Batavia had not fired a great gun for several minutes, and it was doubtful that she ever would again.

"Andy, take her round through the wind. The Dutchman has no fight left in him; it is time to see to James and Triton. We will leave this to Poseidon to finish up. Pierre and Armand will know what to do."

On Triton, meanwhile, James was down on the gun deck, holding Terrance Bernard in his arms as the feisty officer lay gasping for breath. "Hold on dear friend! We have been through too much for me to lose you now! The doctor is on his way."

"No, James, not his time, I think. I got lucky once, you remember." Terrance paused, clenching his teeth against the pain, "Please give my fondest regards to Natalie, James. Take good care of her; she is a fine woman! I have a sister in Canterbury, Marjorie; please see she gets my things. I have left her my prize money already. Think of me sometimes my friend, and know I went happy to be here with you and Phillip." With that he was gone, a great gash in his side from a flying splinter that could never have been healed. James rose and stumbled forward, seeing to the men as best he could, those that were left. Still stunned from the barrage Triton had taken, he tried to remember how many men had been on board. He had given Patrick forty, he thought, that left him with just under two hundred, but he was no longer sure. Everything was a fog; Terrance was gone, as were Josiah Turner, Freddie Howell, and so many more.

Bill Collins came up from the bows, a bloody rag wrapped around his head and one arm hanging limp at his side, "Sir, we will not swim much longer and the boats are mostly shot through. What would you have us do, sir?"

"Speak up Bill, I can barely hear you. Gather the men aft. See to the injured first, and check with the surgeon down on the orlop."

"Sir, they are no longer in the orlop; it is flooded. I sent them to your cabin, sir."

"Very well, get everyone up on deck. Prepare to abandon ship. Throw anything that will float over the side for the men to cling to." James felt the weight of the world on his shoulders, but he had to carry on and give direction.

"Sir," another voice cut into his muddled thoughts. "Sir, the Onyx is coming alongside sir!" James looked around and there was Tom Fischer pulling on his hand.

Somehow, he was not hearing well, James thought, and reached his hand up to his ear, only to have it come away bloody. So, he thought, I must have been hit, but he felt nothing, and that too was strange. He was having trouble staying focused.

"Tom, please help Mr. Collins get the men on deck. We must prepare to abandon the Triton. Get a message to Onyx, 'require assistance.'"

James looked out over what was left of the gun deck bulwark, and there was Onyx, coming alongside like some mythic knight in a storybook, riding to the rescue just in time. But it would not be in time for Terrance and so many more. What was it Terrance had told him? 'Take care of Natalie.' Yes, he must carry on and take care of his dear wife. Someone rudely grabbed him from behind. He turned to protest, only to see Phillip wrapping his arms around him.

"Phillip, how on earth did you get here? Do you know that Terrance is dead?" He asked incredulously. "I am so sorry, and I have lost your ship."

"James, you have been injured. Please come with me. We have Onyx alongside and are taking everyone off. The Triton is finished. We must go now."

"Oh, yes I suppose so; just let me go below to get my papers. I must not leave them or the Admiralty will be furious; I will face court martial for this!"

"James, never fear! I have sent someone for your papers. We must go now or we will have to swim, for Triton cannot last many minutes more."

There were only ninety-two men left alive on the Triton, and of those, forty-seven were wounded including her captain. Just over one hundred had perished in her unequal battle with the Dutch ship that had taken just thirty-seven minutes. Poseidon had taken the Dutchman's surrender, allowed her men to take to their boats, and then had sunk the Batavia. She would rest on the bottom not a quarter mile from Triton, for she went down not ten minutes after the last man was taken off. She, too, carried one hundred men to their rest, still scattered on her decks and within her hull.

Triton's men were divided between the two ships and, after firing a last salute to their fallen comrades, the two frigates headed east and north, back to George Town. It was a sad trip back up the Sumatran coast for Onyx and Poseidon. James' hearing returned after two days, and his muddled state also improved. The surgeon could find no wounds and determined that the shell that had taken the wheel beside him had probably caused the damage. It was strange but it was the only conclusion that made sense.

As James recovered, he told Phillip about the Texel and how he had sent Emerald home to safeguard her passage. It put Phillip's fears to rest, for he had wondered if both ships had been lost.

CHAPTER TWENTY-EIGHT
Reunions

It was ten days later, on the twenty-sixth of June, that Onyx and Poseidon put into the harbour on Prince of Wales Island. The crew, tired, and somewhat disheartened, were happy to hear the anchors drop. Phillip led James ashore and the two men hired a donkey cart to take them up the hill where Katherine and Natalie waited. James, while physically recovered, was in a melancholy state that Phillip had been unable to relieve. James blamed himself for the loss of Triton and all those men who had grown dear to him. Especially, the death of Terrance Bernard plagued him fiercely. Phillip hoped that the site of Natalie and the gardens would provide some respite.

In the following days, James' melancholy slowly improved with the help of Katherine and Natalie's endless encouragement. A memorial service was held in the little church in George Town for all the men lost on the voyage, and that seemed to help bring closure for James and all the crew. The very next day, Captain Armand Le Croix, accompanied by Pierre, made a pilgrimage up the hill to the great house to meet Natalie and apologize.

Natalie had already been apprised of the entire story of Armand's history and the role he had played in trying to safe-guard the Hollis ships, while not losing control of Poseidon.

"Madam Peters, I humbly come to beg your forgiveness. When I see what hurt I have inflicted upon you, I am indeed filled with remorse. It was never my intention to ever strike your brig, only to keep my men from taking the Poseidon and turning her loose against all your ships."

The difficulty of reining in her emotions was clear to see on Natalie's face. "I understand Captain Le Croix, and you are forgiven. I hold no malice against you. It was an unfortunate accident, and while the consequences to me were significant, it may have also allowed many other lives to be spared, for by leaving the Emerald as you did, you caused our officers to question their assumptions about Poseidon. Those questions, I believe, allowed you and my brother to come together, forestalling a certain engagement that might have seen many killed, and for that we must all be thankful. Also, your actions were certainly critical in saving my husband's life, for which I thank you. As long as the tyranny of men like Talleyrand and Bonaparte goes unchecked, I am afraid many more will suffer much worse than I have. That we are united in our effort to prevent that is enough for me."

"I also would like to welcome you, Captain Le Croix, to our little family." James reached out his hand to Armand, "We did not meet on our return voyage, but I want to assure you it was not due to any animosity, rather to my own difficulties after losing my ship, and my first officer and very good friend Terrance Bernard."

"Ah yes, Captain Peters, I am aware of your loss also, and you have my sympathy. It was our very great pleasure to be able to come to your aid, I am only so sorry we could not have arrived sooner to have saved Triton and more of your men."

"You did save half my men, and destroyed that Dutch man of war as well. I am sorry that I was not able to cheer you in that accomplishment, but I heartily give you my good wishes now."
In the harbour things were busy indeed as both the Onyx and Poseidon were checked over from stem to stern. A good beach was found only ten miles south of the townsite where both ships could be hauled down and have their hulls checked and missing copper replaced. This kept the men busy and helped greatly to integrate

Armand's crew into the Hollis family. The two frigates were barely back, anchored off the warehouse when a great cry went up one afternoon at the end of the first week of July. Sails were sighted creeping up the Strait of Malacca, and proved to be none other than Ross Day with the Celeste.

The Celeste had had a rough time of it for the past three weeks, trying to work westward against a stubborn southwest monsoon. The trip south from Canton had gone well enough, for the late start to the monsoon had allowed them to reach Kuching, on Sarawak, in good order. The last five hundred miles, nearly straight west had been a futile battle of tacking against a steady southwest wind and sheets of rain each afternoon. Eventually, they had inched their way, and once they could turn north into the Malacca Strait, things had improved.

Now everyone was in port. Onyx and Poseidon, the two heavy frigates; Emerald, glistening again in her repainted and re-worked state; the two big merchantmen, Celeste and Texel, both loaded with cargoes too rich to imagine; and the little Zee Heks, which Phillip really did not know what to do with. She had been sitting at anchor since they brought her in, and Phillip knew he had no need of her. Ross came up with the idea of giving her to the George Town colony, as a good stout vessel to make periodic runs to Madras. She would be a decent packet ship and could defend herself if required.

Phillip tossed the idea around with James for a few days and was surprised when James advised against taking any action with the brig for the time being. He would not elaborate on his thoughts, only insisting that he might have an option worth considering in a few more days.

The cargo in Texel had been thoroughly catalogued by the time Phillip and James got in, and it was special indeed. The only concern was for the many crates of tea in her forward hold. Tea, if transported quickly, was worth a fortune in Europe, but it was a time sensitive commodity, and should have been westward bound earlier. The reason, they discovered was that Texel had only left

China in late March, well behind the usual rush in January. Still, the cases were well sealed, and might still fetch a solid price if they could leave by early autumn. The rest of the cargo was spectacular. A hundred tons of tin lay beneath crates of silk and Chinese porcelain. The lists of figurines and bowls, platters and fancy dishes, had everyone smiling.

With the monsoon now well established, there was no reason to hurry in preparing to return to England. The winds would not likely change until early fall, and Phillip was certainly not prepared to leave until Katherine delivered their child. Natalie was not due until November and James was quite satisfied to remain in the house on Flagstaff Hill with his wife.

One sunny morning, when Phillip and Katherine were breakfasting on the east terrace under a thatched awning, the topic of Angeline came up, as Phillip noticed young Simon Elliot walking up the hill.

"Yes, dear, Angeline seems quite taken with him, and Andy has made it clear that he has no intention of settling down. I understand that Simon approached Andy to ask his permission to spend time with Angeline."

"Well, the girl certainly deserves the attention. I only hope she is not disappointed. Naval officers generally do not make good husbands."

"Oh, and why did you not tell me that before we were married?"

"With us, it is different. I have much more freedom than the average officer, and besides, you agreed that we did not want a traditional hide-bound marriage."

"Oh, did I? I did not agree that I wanted a bad husband. I suspect Simon might be just as good a prospect as any other man, and he does seem to care for Angeline. I am beginning to believe you have one set of expectations for yourself and another for everyone else, Phillip Hollis. You would think you were Angeline's father, as protective as you get."

Phillip was now clearly over his head and was delighted when James arrived to join them and distract his wife from her discerning judgment of his protective attitude toward Angeline.

James sat down to join them. "Lovely view from up here, isn't it?" he commented.

"Oh yes, I never tire of it at all. In fact, while you were gone, Natalie and I spent most mornings out here, even in the rain. It has such a delightful prospect," Katherine agreed.

"Yes, I fear we would miss it, should we go back." James answered.

"What do you mean exactly?" Phillip asked with some concern.

"I mean Phillip that we have decided to stay. Please, before you begin to argue, hear me out. Natalie is comfortable here. She knows she has a place and her limitations, that is, her injury, are not the cause of any great notice. She fears that she would be the object of curiosity and scorn back among her old friends in London. She does not want that, nor do I. We have discussed this at some length, and I have a proposal to make, Phillip."

"Go ahead. What exactly do you have in mind?"

"You were speaking of getting rid of the Zee Heks, Phillip. What if, instead, you left her with me here? In fact, I have been thinking; why not leave both brigs out here? We could begin what I believe could be a very nice business of taking cargo between the Spice Islands and Madras and even the colony at New South Wales. With two weatherly brigs, we could make fast runs and both of them could protect themselves better than most sloops running out here. We could take some of the guns out of Emerald to give her greater ability to carry goods. I think that Simon Elliot might be willing to stay as well, for he has been spending quite a lot of time around, mostly visiting with Angeline!"

"James, are you serious about this? It may get very lonely out here after we are all gone. I do not imagine we would get back very often. Will Natalie manage?"

"You know, dear, I think she just might," Katherine put in. "I have heard her talking about her garden, and the fact that the few

English women here treat her with respect and kindness. She and Angeline have also become quite close, and if Angeline stays with Simon, it may not be such a bad thing."

"Well, I suppose we would have to talk to Patrick, although he is so thrilled with Texel that I doubt if he would mind giving up Emerald one bit. There is something to having a fully functioning base out here. I dare say you might wish to rename the Zee Heks!"

"Oh yes, I believe I already gave you a name I would choose once before. If it is up to me, no offense, Katherine, but I will call her the Natalie! I believe we could sail her to India and back on a regular basis, bringing supplies out to Padang and taking spices back to Madras or even Calcutta. The Emerald could make similar trips either to New South Wales, or trading into the Islands to the east. With the warehouse in town, we could purchase goods when the prices are best and ship our own goods, making a good profit. Every few years, we could make a trip back home with a load of spice or pepper, and I am sure one of the merchantmen will be out periodically."

"Well, you know James, I have been thinking that should Sir John be correct, and war breaks out with France again in the near future, we might well be forced to give up the frigates, at least one, for I shall have to replace Triton, which after all was only leased to us. Should that occur, and I believe it will, we will only have Celeste and Texel to carry on with our Hollis & Company plans in the west. We may stop off in India on the way home and sell off the tin that Texel is carrying. If we do, I believe I may place another ship on order there. I understand we can have one built for a fraction of the cost at home, and of teak rather than oak, which will last much longer in these waters. We would have to leave someone behind to see to her construction and bring her out."

"Whom, do you think?"

"I wonder if Dick might just like that task. We have leave from John Company for this expedition only, and that because we were here to eradicate their problem with the French assisted piracy.

I have no doubt they will take a dim view of our activities going forward and we will no doubt be barred from the lucrative tea trade. Nevertheless, we can perhaps make inroads into other areas. We can certainly carry on trade from England to the West Indies and you may do very well stationed here trading with the locals and occasionally darting into Madras. You might even make some inroads into dealing with the Sumatrans at Muntok, if you can keep the Dutch at bay. They have mountains of tin, and you could sell that in Madras or Calcutta, perhaps even in New South Wales..."
The talk went on for most of the morning.

It was on the seventh of August that little Edmond Phillip Desmond Hollis came into the world with an ear piercing cry. His father, Phillip,was proud as any Sultan and while the women folk cared for Katherine and little Edmond, celebrations were held at the Company office with all officers in attendance. The child was showered with more gifts than Katherine and Phillip could possibly know what to do with, including a thousand year old jade horse from Ross that outweighed the infant by twenty pounds, while Uncle James had built a fancy, leather covered rocking horse with glass eyes from India. A jewel encrusted dagger was received from the Sultan of Kedah, Koh Huan sent over a beautifully carved teak model of Onyx. Katherine was all smiles, and with Natalie and Angeline hovering about, and Anusha and Neepa barely putting the child down, she was allowed to rest and recuperate at her leisure.

Exactly one month later, with the summer monsoon waning, a flotilla of Hollis ships weighed anchor and began the long voyage back to England. Emerald and the renamed Natalie stayed behind, as did James and Simon Elliot, along with Natalie, and not surprisingly Angeline, who announced that she was going to stay with Simon and build a life for herself. She and Katherine had a difficult and teary farewell, but Katherine was happy for her, and Anusha was travelling back to England with Katherine, unwilling to give up her little Edmond. Enough men had volunteered to remain behind to form a nucleus crew for both the brigs that would easily be augmented with Chinese and Malay seamen, and James and Simon were already busy planning the first trip, which Simon would make to New South Wales.

Dick Forest, indeed, had been delighted with the prospect of spending the better part of a year in Calcutta, having a new nine hundred ton merchant ship built. Once completed, she would be sailed to George Town, loaded with spices and pepper, and sailed to England. Torey Speaks offered to remain with Dick and help oversee the construction and find a crew to sail what would become the Sapphire. All the tin in the hold of Texel, now renamed the Topaz, was sold in Calcutta; traded to the East India Company Factor, to make room for textiles and spices. Dick had further been delighted to find the young Stamford Raffles in Calcutta, and the two were thick as thieves going over Dick's notes on the prospects of Singapore Island as a future base for British Interests in the Far East.

CHAPTER TWENTY-NINE
Homeward bound

The three Hollis ships plus the Poseidon then began their long journey back from Calcutta on the first day of October. With the two large merchantmen, it would be a slower trip back, for they would be lucky indeed to average five knots over the twelve thousand nautical miles they would have to travel to reach home once more. When the convoy dropped anchor under Table Mountain in Cape Town they were greeted with the news that England and France were again at war, and had been since May. There were two Royal Navy frigates in the harbour. The captain of one was none other than Allan Blake, Phillip's old friend, whom he had last seen commanding a supply ship in Polgwidden Cove in March of 1802, when Phillip was preparing to leave on his voyage to relieve Napoleon Bonaparte of a fortune in gold and gems.

"How did you get here, my friend?" Phillip asked as Blake was rowed over to the Onyx.

"Well, it may have been partly your fault, My Lord Brixton. You see, when hostilities began in May, I was in the right place at the right time so to speak, for someone had put a word in the First Lord's ear that my talents were being wasted, for I was not any good at commanding a supply ship!"

"Ha, and now you have had to give up a comfortable great cabin for the meager room in a frigate! I am surprised you even rowed over."

"Yes, it is a great sacrifice. Seriously, Phillip I do not know how to thank you. To be given another chance at a fighting ship, well, I never dreamed it was possible."

"As I understand it, we will need all the good captains we can find. How are things going at home?"

"Well enough for the moment, but Bonaparte is stretching his muscles across the continent. It will be a long and drawn out affair unless our allies begin to do much better than they have."

"We must drink a toast to your good fortune. Come into the cabin, if you do not mind the domestic nature of the place. I am afraid that Katherine and little Edmond have claimed a large portion!"

"A child? Phillip, I did hear of your marriage, but good gracious you are sailing with your family? I would have brought a suitable gift had I known."

"You are a gift enough! Come and meet Katherine."

They spent a pleasant week in Cape Town and then resumed the voyage home, arriving at the mouth of the Medway in cold blustery weather on the sixth of February, 1804. The trip had been mostly uneventful, which Katherine was sure they were due after all the issues they had faced on the outward journey.

Coaching up to London, Phillip and Katherine's first stop was at the house on Grosvenor Square, where there were tears and hugs and a grandmother's first sight of her grandson. There was also serious discussion of Natalie's condition, and the decision to remain in the Orient, as well as curiosity about the birth of her child, which should now be four months old. The Chapley family had already coached down to London to join in the reunion, and while the women were busy coddling the young heir, Phillip provided Walter with the details of their voyage and remarkable profits.

The next day, Phillip sent a note to the Admiralty, announcing his return. It was answered almost within the hour, with a carefully worded summons. As Phillip strode into the Admiralty, he was immediately whisked up the stairs and directly into Sir John's habitual place of choice at the great boardroom table.

"Phillip, I thank God you have returned. We have much to discuss, but first, tell me, do I get Triton back? I am so in need of frigates!"

"Sir John, I am most sorry to tell you, but Triton lies at the bottom of the Sunda Strait, right alongside a Dutch fifty gun two decker named Batavia. I am afraid I owe you the Ruby, sir as we agreed. I do have something else to offer you though if you are in need of frigates."

"We are indeed, and I am all ears."

"I have brought back Onyx as well as her twin. The French forty gun heavy frigate, Poseidon, has surrendered to us, including her crew and captain, who volunteered to give us his ship. Now, as things stand, he did not actually offer the ship to England, but to me, but I think we can come to some agreement on terms to transfer her to you, and perhaps Ruby as well. The captain, Armand Le Croix, was a Royalist officer, and has no interest in returning to a France under Napoleon. I can probably give him a position on one of my ships, and such of his crew as wish to serve."

"Oh Phillip, something tells me this will be another costly venture! What is it you require? Perhaps a Dukedom! Is being just an Earl becoming tiresome already?" Sir John laughed and then sighed. "Phillip, you know that was in jest. You have been so much more than generous, both to myself and to your country, and yet, I am so much more than desperate! What can we offer you?"

"I would like to be allowed to trade freely with India and China! I want an exclusion from the East India Company's monopoly on tea and opium. In exchange, I will offer you a forty gun heavy frigate, as well as the Ruby, for a very reasonable price, and if you wish, I will also offer to reinstate my commission and serve for as long as my health, or your needs, dictate. I will, however want some time ashore first, and periodically during the conflict. I must see to the needs of my wife and son, as well as the estate."

"Phillip, congratulations, you have a child! But you know that I have no power over the Company, at least not directly; still, I will see what can be accomplished. I believe that some arrangement may be possible, for a limited number of ships, and for a prescribed time. The Company likes to think that it is a pseudo nation state but it can be bargained with. I should think that if you had success in your recent voyage it should also give them some reason to be generous."

"Three ships, and for as long as I live; that is the bargain. In return you get the brig and a forty gun frigate for five thousand pounds, and if you wish, my services."

"Five thousand pounds, really Phillip we will be delighted to give you at least five times that amount for the frigate. It would cost the Government over twenty to build a heavy forty gun frigate, and it would take a good deal of time we do not have. To have one delivered to our door, so to speak, well, you could name your price! I will send you word in forty-eight hours. Where, pray tell, is the frigate now?" Sir John looked determined to have that ship.

"She is in the Medway, being unloaded of my goods from China and India, along with my two merchantmen, the Topaz and Celeste. The Emerald and Natalie brigs have remained at our base in George Town, along with James Peters and my sister Natalie."

"Phillip, I am sorry to hear that your good friend and partner, Mr. Peters has not returned with you. In your absence, he has been awarded a knighthood by the King for conspicuous service to the Crown. I should have greatly enjoyed seeing your sister's face at the prospect of the ceremony! You must get them the news on your next ship. Now, I really must remain here for at least another three hours as the board is meeting, but I am convinced that there is a story here that I must have. Can you meet me at the club at the start of the first dog watch? I will send a note for Bromley at least to join us."

So it was that Phillip found himself surrounded by several old friends, including Lord Hawkesbury, Lord Bromley, and Lord St Vincent, as he recounted the tale of his voyage to the east. There were many questions and more than a few raised eyebrows at the events surrounding the raid on the pirates and the capture of both Dutch and French ships during a supposed peace. Now that the peace was over, it hardly mattered, and at any rate, whether he knew it or not, the sinking of the Batavia had occurred after the war had resumed. After the tale was done, there were smiles all around, exclamations of good will, and a toast to Sir Phillip's good fortune. Then it appeared that the others also had news for Phillip.

Sir John's news was that the Company would grant Phillip's request with some conditions that could be worked out over time. Furthermore, the Government would be delighted to purchase the heavy frigate at a knocked down price of twelve thousand pounds, with a note of thanks from the Prime Minister. "I have one concern only, Phillip, and that is your offer to rejoin the Service. It is not that you are not qualified. Heavens, we all know about that. It is rather whether after this time of freedom, and with your other responsibilities, including sitting in the House, you would really wish to put yourself back under the rule of senior captains and admirals. While I can give you a certain amount of freedom, at least for a time, you are aware that blatant favouritism will be bad for the service. This is a difficult situation, for I personally would love nothing better than to give you Poseidon and send you out on Admiralty orders into the Med to wreak havoc! Your old friend has also asked for you, you know, and he would be greatly pleased should I send you out under his flag. Yet, I believe, Phillip, that we must take time to consider your position at some greater length. Perhaps we can meet in a few days and consider the pros and cons.

"I have some news for you as well, Phillip," Lord Bromley remarked, "We have made the investment we spoke of before you departed. It carried an instant premium of over 13%, for the bankers forced Napoleon to discount the payment! He thought he would get one hundred million francs for the sale of the territory, but he ended up with just over sixty. Furthermore, the interest to the Americans is fixed at 6% going forward with a maturity of twenty years with a first redemption after only nine years. You will do very well with this investment, I think. We have also taken the liberty of disposing of another lot of gems, both yours and Sir John's, this to the Swedish Crown for a very fine premium indeed. On another front, with the resumption of hostilities the price of copper has soared, and your investment with the Duke has brought more than a considerable return already. I believe that Mr. Cobb has enlarged your holdings by some hundred thousand pounds."

"Yes, well, even after the division to the men and to my partners, I will realise at least another two hundred thousand or more in the holds of both Celeste and Topaz, so that will not pose any problem. Furthermore, with the two brigs now trading between Madras, George Town, and New South Wales, we have an excellent opportunity to enlarge our interests in the Far East. I am having another nine hundred ton merchantman constructed in Calcutta, even as we speak. Perhaps you are correct Sir John, and I have become too accustomed to having things the way I wish them to be; yet I am loath to remain ashore while others risk their lives for the good of king and country. I have excellent partners in Hollis Shipping, and they will manage quite well without me for a time. I also understand that, should I be stationed within reasonable range, I could have a jobbing captain take my ship for a time should I be required in Parliament. Perhaps we could arrange things so that, if required, I might be allowed another leave such as the one I have taken these past two years. I must say, I would enjoy helping to take the fight to Bonaparte."

"I believe that could serve, Phillip," put in Lord Hawkesbury. "However, it might not allow us a great deal of latitude should some other matter arise with any degree of urgency. I know that I am poaching on Sir John's estate here, and I do so advisedly, but you have proven an even more adept agent for the government than your dear father, God rest his soul. The government, and the Crown, are not oblivious to the service you have provided, and could certainly continue to provide, and in this capacity you would still be very much continuing to take the fight to our enemies. Both your excellent work in befriending the Sultan of Kedah, nipping at the heels of the Burmese, and, of course, ridding the Singapore Channel of pirates, if even temporarily, are to our great benefit. As to the Burmese issue, we have received a report overland from India that seems to indicate that the Siamese King, Rama, has taken particular note of your adventure. I believe that while he covets Kedah, he will not interfere with our holdings or our interests further to the south. You have a way of making an impact that through our regular channels we seem to be frustrated to emulate! Enough said, but in that regard, Phillip, I might say that there could be an opportunity in the near future, should you have any interest in a cruise to the western coast of South America… How many guns did you say your new Topaz carries?" Phillip looked around the table at the expectant faces, wondering what on earth he was going to tell Katherine this time…

CPSIA information can be obtained at www.ICGtesting.com
Printed in the USA
LVOW12s1412281114

415907LV00002B/12/P